O^{The}pen Door

The Open Door

Latifa al-Zayyat

Translated by
Marilyn Booth

The American University in Cairo Press
Cairo • New York

English translation copyright © 2000 by
The American University in Cairo Press
113 Sharia Kasr el Aini, Cairo, Egypt
420 Fifth Avenue, New York, NY 10018-2729
http://www.aucpress.com

First paperback edition 2002

Copyright © 1960 by the Estate of Latifa al-Zayyat
First published in Arabic in 1960 as *al-Bab al-maftuh*
Protected under the Berne Convention

Dar el Kutub No. 16708/01
ISBN 977 424 698 5

Printed in Egypt

To my teacher, Rashad Rushdi

L. Z.

Translator's
Acknowledgments

I want to thank Ferial Ghazoul for urging me to embark on this translation; Neil Hewison, Pauline Wickham, and Aleya Serour at the AUC Press for their forbearance, professionalism, fine work, and good humor; Mandy McClure for her fine editing; Joel Beinin for filling in a few historical details; and Sahar Tawfiq and Sharif Elmusa for some felicitous phrasing.

Translator's Introduction

When Gamal 'Abd al-Nasser nationalized the Suez Canal for Egypt on July 26, 1956, the Arab world heralded him as a hero, and globally he became a celebrated symbol of resistance to the European imperialist march that had for so long forcibly shaped the lives of so many. The moment marked a period of consolidation and triumph for 'Abd al-Nasser's regime, and it ended a decade of turbulent political activity in an Egypt that was trying to free itself of both British oversight and the political system of the past. As much as it was a decade of struggle, of disillusionment and hardship, it was also a decade of youth activism and of popular optimism about the future of a newly independent country. And it is the decade that Latifa al-Zayyat chronicles in her classic, first novel, *The Open Door*. Published in 1960, the novel appeared as that earlier optimism was wearing off, after a period in which 'Abd al-Nasser's regime had imprisoned many of its opponents and had strictly curtailed freedom of expression and the right to organize. Significant and crucial strides made in land reform were, if not wholly offset by, at least tempered by, a sense of drift and uncertainty. Yet the memory of recent triumphs was still fresh, and a young generation grappling with its collective identity welcomed what was a bold and innovative literary work. Like Egyptian men, Egyptian women had been writing and publishing fiction since before the turn of the twentieth century. But to confront issues of personal freedom and sexuality in the context of received social expectations and the constraints of political inertia, economic travail, and class—and to do so as a woman writing about female experience—was new and shocking, no less so than the bold step of describing the physicality of male and female adolescent and post-adolescent sexual awakening, as al-Zayyat does in this novel. A later generation of writing women remembers reading—or hearing about—*The Open Door* as a formative experience. Remarked novelist Hala Badri in a reminiscence (al-Bahrawi, ed., 1996) offered to a conference on al-Zayyat held shortly before her death in 1996:

> In my childhood, the name 'Latifa al-Zayyat' echoed around me as one of the icons of national liberation. The great writer remained in my imagination merely a name, until the film version of *The Open Door* came out. Our home witnessed many conversations about the boldness of its themes. The adults re-read the novel . . . and began to discuss it. What arrested them was not the point that choosing the way one lives privately is inseparable from public commitment, but rather the courageous conclusions that emerge through the dialogues. For conversations between the heroine and her female cousin hint that a woman's body becomes parched when her relationship with a man is unsatisfying. This might appear obvious to us now, but at that time it was startling and provocative. The women around me were quietly thankful to this woman who had been able to express an experience that they could not articulate out loud though it was common among them. Thus, *The Open Door* did not simply broach a single signification; it sparked heated debate in many homes, among them mine—just an ordinary home in Cairo.

Al-Zayyat's novel was one of a few novels by Arab women that appeared around the same time, landmark works such as the Lebanese writer Layla al-Ba'albaki's novel *I Live*, that heralded the present explosion of feminist writing in the Arab world and the entry of female Arab writers into the modern literary canon. Because this entry remains unfamiliar to most outside the Arab world, it is worth tracing that history at the risk of repeating what close observers know.

Referring to a body of literature and other creative arts that is recognized as emblematic of the dominant ideology, values, and organization of social forces in a given society, a canon is thus inseparable from—indeed, it is often central to—struggles over political power and economic and social processes and structures. Thus, a canon is also a vision of 'the way things ought to be' that constructs an image of the society's past as perfect, as an ideal. A canon cannot be a fixed entity but rather is a process, a site of struggle over the power to name what is central to cultural and political definition. The canon of Arabic literature in the twentieth century, like that of any literature, is always subject to pressure and always in re-formation (as is the way Arabic literature is inserted into 'world literature' by Euro/American publishers and critics). As a shifting body of texts, a canon can be usefully examined by looking at its margins (which are also unstable). Literary marginality is of course bound up in social and political marginalization. Women writers have had to fight their marginality—their marginalization—but they have also used marginality as a privileged position, one that widens their gaze and the modes of expression available to them. Ironically, as marginalization along both gender and class lines has come increasingly to shape texts by contemporary women fiction writers, those writers have themselves become more accepted as part of the 'mainstream' canon.

In her autobiographical meditation, *Hamlat taftish: awraq shakhsiya* (Operation Search: Personal Papers, 1992), the Egyptian fiction writer, political activist, and literary scholar Latifa al-Zayyat (1923–96) presents her childhood in the Delta cities of Dimyat (Damietta) and Mansura as an entry point into a dynamic of withdrawal versus engagement that she sees as marking her adult life. The rooftops of her childhood homes take on complex symbolic meaning: mysterious because they are initially unattainable, they become sites of desire, refuges, places of imagined freedom from the constraints of a socialized existence. In al-Zayyat's first home, the stairs leading to the roof are inhabited by a snake that will not succumb to the snake-charmers the family engages; the snake also serves as a socializing force, scaring the children away from the freedom of the roof. In her second home, though, the rooftop becomes attainable, if furtively, and the little room perched on top is a place available for childhood meditation. In this context, the author constructs a remarkable image: her seven-year-old self, sitting crouched on the floor against the wall in that little rooftop room. The object of her contemplation is a young poet, in his late twenties, who sits at a desk, lost in thought, oblivious to her presence, for when his meditation is disrupted, he is startled to find her there.

Young Latifa al-Zayyat, future writer of a landmark work of fiction, gazes from the margins of the room to the man, the poet, at its center. Sitting above her, he is the sign of centrality, of 'high' literature, the scion of a longstanding tradition of poetic composition. The author refers to him as al-Sha'ir al-Hamshari: this is Muhammad 'Abd al-Mu'ti al-Hamshari (1908–38). As a romantic poet in the thirties, this poet was also representative of ways in which social notions of the literary were being turned inside out, for the poetic art he practiced constituted a sharp break with the neoclassical poetry that had long held sway. But from the vantage point of young Latifa, he was the marker of literariness and of a kind of absolute value. True to the history of European romanticism, and like several other Arab romantic poets of the time, al-Hamshari would die young, as the adolescent al-Zayyat finds out, several years later, from her older brother.

Al-Zayyat situates this childhood incident in the rooftop room as a time of innocence, presaging her awakening realization of the presence of tragedy, unfairness, and evil in the world in which she lives—a shadow embodied in the poet's early death. But she also situates it as a trope of connectedness and relation: her seven-year-old self contemplates the self-absorbed poet, in total silence, as a way of contemplating herself, a way of searching for a sense of completion, a groping for identity and meaning through loving connection with others. This image offers an entry point into al-Zayyat's writing, and indeed into a history of women's writing in modern Egypt. For the author gestures to the process of forming a female identity when she sketches the silent, admiring seven-year-old in her rooftop refuge, a little girl whom the reader knows will become a leader in the student movement of the 1940s, a committed lifelong activist in cultural–political struggle, a noted professor, and an innovative writer of fiction, autobiography, and criticism. This image, the little girl on the margins gazing at the man poet who holds his words inside, not making them available to her, is juxtaposed with that of the author's mother as storyteller. Al-Zayyat recalls being simultaneously frightened and fascinated as her mother related to her the real-life tale of Rayya and Sakina, a pair of female serial killers in 1920s Alexandria whose story generated an outpouring of popular narratives at the time. Al-Zayyat stresses that it was the narrative itself, the *realness* of it, that attracted her, not its moral. Her mother's narration is further contrasted with the products of mass culture, as al-Zayyat recalls seeing the movie version of Rayya and Sakina years later—and remaining unmoved.

While al-Zayyat makes no reference in any of this to her own writing career, she situates her own writing and a history of women writing through the implicit contrast between the poet on the rooftop and the storytelling mother to whom a frightened little girl comes for comfort in the night, between the romantic poet in quiet isolation and the popular narrative centering on female anti-heroes—between, finally, different languages and worlds. The image echoes against an autobiographical image of childhood evoked by the poet 'A'isha Taymur (1840–1902) in the preface to a fictional tale (al-Taimuriyya, 1990) written nearly forty years before al-Zayyat was born:

> Says the one with the broken wing, Aisha Ismat daughter of Ismail Pasha Taimur: Ever since my cradle cushion was rolled up, and my foot roved the carpet of the world, ever since I became aware of where enticements and reason dwelt for me, and I grew conscious of the inviolable space around my father and grandfather—ever since that time, my fledgling aim was to nurse eagerly on tales of the nations of old. I aged while still young trying to get to the root of the words of those who have gone before. I used to be infatuated with the evening chatter of the elderly women, wanting to listen to the choicest stories. . . .
>
> When my mental faculties were prepared for learning, and my powers of understanding had reached a state of receptivity, there came to me the mistress of compassion and probity, the treasurehouse of knowledge and wonders that amaze—my mother, may God protect her with His grace and forgiveness. Bearing the instruments of embroidery and weaving, she began to work seriously on my education, striving to instill in me cleverness and comprehension. But I was incapable of learning, and I had no desire or readiness to become refined in the occupations of women. I used to flee from her as the prey escapes the net, rushing headlong into the assemblages of writers, with no sense of embarrassment.

Little 'A'isha tries to find a secluded spot in which to write, where the screeching of the pen (her favorite sound) will not draw a rebuke. If Taymur and al-Zayyat were generations apart, both had to struggle to make space, psychic and social, for their writing; and for both, the oral narratives of women family members were an early inspiration, and an image contrasting with that of the isolated writer in a tower (or in a rooftop room). The woman as storyteller, bringing together a community and shaping its history against an official, written history, would become a consistent motif in writings by women in Egypt. The first short-story collection by a woman to be published in Egypt was Suhayr al-Qalamawi's (b. 1911) collection *Ahadith jaddati* (My Grandmother's Tales, Cairo, 1935). Al-Qalamawi bases the whole structure and narrative rhythm of this collection on the same traditional female social role that al-Zayyat portrays her mother as enacting and that Taymur constructs: that of preserver and renewer of community history through oral narrative, a trope that saturates the contemporary scene. As a grandmother reminisces about the good old days to her granddaughter, in the gentle generational conflict that emerges al-Qalamawi offers a social critique and an oblique vision of wartime from the perspective of those who stayed home. This was in line with most of the fiction appearing in Egypt in the 1930s, comprising critical realist depictions of middle-class Egyptian society and, through middle-class eyes, peasant society. Since the turn of the century, fiction had gradually become established as a respectable literary practice, indeed an indispensable one for a society in the throes of resistance to a colonial presence and reorientation toward an independent future. Fiction's fortunes were enhanced by a lively non-official press, which welcomed short stories and serialized novels along with poetry and nonfiction. Aspiring fiction writers got practice by translating and adapting European works of fiction, often loosely, for the press and for publishing houses. Most of these writers were men, and as fiction writing developed in sophistication and acceptance through the first half of the century, it was the names of men that occupied central positions in an evolving canon of fictional writing: Muhammad and Mahmud Taymur, Tahir Lashin, Yahya Haqqi, Yusuf Idris, Naguib Mahfouz, and others. But women had started to write and publish fiction around the same time. Mostly ignored by critics, they published in the growing number of women's magazines that began to appear in the 1890s, and also in some mainstream magazines like *al-Hilal*. Labiba Hashim (1880–1947), a Lebanese immigrant to Egypt, published 'story-essays' in the early women's press, including her own magazine, *Fatat al-sharq* (1906). These are quasi-fictional presentations of characters and situations interwoven with expository prose; the narrative 'proves' the point of the essay. Hashim published arabizations of European works and tried her hand at writing fully formed short stories, as well as producing polemics on women's education and emancipation. Another immigrant from the Lebanon, Zaynab Fawwaz (c.1850–1914), published a play and an historical novel around the turn of the century while contributing essays and poetry to the press. In attempting this variety of literary practices, Hashim and Fawwaz were writers of their time.

While finding and creating outlets in the press, Hashim and other women published books. Between 1900 and 1925, thirty-one Arab women authors published at least sixty-two volumes in Arabic in Egypt. Of course, this is a tiny number compared to the publishing output of men, and most of these authors, with the exception of another Lebanese immigrant, Mayy Ziyada (1886–1941), never achieved canonical status. As time went on, women tended to concentrate on short-story writing while men turned to the novel, as Hilary Kilpatrick (1985) has noted. Perhaps this was partly because short-story writing could more easily be fitted in with women's other duties—a factor that women writing today in Egypt have indicated as significant to their own careers. But this concentration on the short story may have also had an impact on the status of these women as writers, or perhaps it is the other way around: for the novel was seen as the more worthy genre, both in terms of the literary skill it required and in terms of the comprehensive social vision it could offer.

So when al-Qalamawi published *My Grandmother's Tales*, at least two generations of publishing women had preceded her. But, again with the exception of the essayist and prose poet Mayy Ziyada, the visibility of the women who had published had been very restricted, limited by the relative marginality of the outlets in which they published; by the inability, dictated by social practice, to maintain any kind of public intellectual presence; and by a general lack of critical attention. By the 1930s, as notions about women's status in society were slowly shifting—in tandem and sometimes in tension with nationalist ideologies and programs—women could participate more visibly in cultural production. Al-Qalamawi's work came at a time when textual and social visibility, fought for by early feminists and pro-feminist nationalists, was becoming more possible. She used this new space, paradoxically, to articulate the private world of upper- and middle-class women at the turn of the century. This strategy offered a social critique that differed from that of contemporary men writers. It was a critique founded in what some critics have seen as characteristic of women's writing, a 'dailiness' that captures the everyday, supposedly trivial but in fact fundamental events that shape us. This characteristic, and an emotionalism that is seen to accompany it, have often been used to dismiss writing by women and to deny it a place in the canon, on the basis that this writing deals with what is 'unimportant.' Al-Qalamawi's book in fact had the benefit of an introduction by the noted litterateur Taha Husayn (1889–1973), who was her professor as she worked toward the first MA to be earned by a woman in an Egyptian university. Even as Husayn praises the work, the nature of his praise has the effect of relegating the work to a certain sphere. He delights in what he calls the work's "sweet ingenuousness," which begins, he says, "with the first sentence." 'Feminine' and 'naive' are equated.

Feminist critics the world over have been reevaluating and valorizing these very characteristics—triviality, simplicity, primacy of emotion, dailiness—as Miriam Cooke (1988) has done with regard to Lebanese women writers of the Lebanese civil war period. Al-Qalamawi's short stories, never accepted by critics as a central work of Arabic literature, in fact constituted a new and important, experimental, addition to the literature of realist social critique in Egypt.

Two decades later, as more and more women and men were publishing fiction, Latifa al-Zayyat began work on *The Open Door*. It was a moment when writers who had become part of the canon of modern Arabic literature, like Naguib Mahfouz and Yusuf Idris, were bringing what is usually labeled an Arabic realist tradition of social critique to its height, to a point where in the case of Mahfouz, for example, this approach had been so fully explored that he would feel the need to turn in new directions. Sakina Fu'ad, Asma' Halim, Sophie Abdullah, and others were working within this fold to explore the constraints and possibilities specific to women's lives in Egypt at mid-century. Al-Zayyat's novel, which on the surface of it seems to participate fully and unequivocally in a realist approach to social critique, pointed to some of the ways in which the Arabic novel would develop away from that approach. *The Open Door* did so by privileging and interweaving two kinds of marginality, one social and one literary: the first, putting a female perspective at the center, within a context of family and community; the second, using everyday rather than literary diction. Many other Egyptian writers had been experimenting with the use of an Egyptian colloquial Arabic in writing dialogue; for some time, the vernacular's status as a literary language had been an issue among the intelligentsia. Yet al-Zayyat's use of it may have contributed to the fact that *The Open Door* was denied recognition as a major achievement in Arabic literature in a formal and graphic sense noted below.

Born in 1923 in the Delta town of Dimyat, Latifa al-Zayyat was a generation older than her protagonist, Layla. Layla witnesses and participates in the 1946 demonstrations as a middle-school student; her creator was one of the university student leaders at that time, active in the National Committee of Workers and Students, elected its secretary. Al-Zayyat earned her doctorate in 1957 and went on to become a revered and inspiring professor of English literary criticism at 'Ayn Shams University in Cairo. She also served as Director of the Arts Academy in the early 1970s. She was president of the Committee to

Defend National Culture, which she helped to found in 1979 with other intellectuals concerned about the impact of the Camp David accords on Egyptian society and culture. She was active in many cultural organizations and women's organizations, and wrote magazine columns on gender issues for the popular magazine *Hawwa'*. She published many books and articles on literary criticism; although she was silent as a fiction writer for many years after *The Open Door* appeared, she resumed her activity in that sphere and published a short-story collection in 1986, *al-Shaykhukha wa-qisas ukhra: majmu'a qisasiya* (Old Age and Other Stories: A Short Story Collection), followed by two novels and a play (*al-Rajul alladhi 'arafa tuhmatahu: riwaya qasira* [The Man Aware of his Accusation: A Novella], published in the journal *Adab wa-naqd* in 1991 and as a book in 1995; *Sahib al-bayt: riwaya* [Owner of the House: A Novel], 1994; *Bay' wa-shira': masrahiya* [Purchase and Sale: A Play], 1994). She published her acclaimed, innovative autobiographical work in 1992. She was awarded the State Prize for Literature in 1996.

In her life and commitment, al-Zayyat was at the center of her country's struggle. And to appreciate this novel's intertwining of the public and the personal, one must have an understanding of the political events that surround and infuse it. The novel opens with the dramatic and violently-met mass demonstrations of February 21, 1946.

Egypt was still reeling economically from World War II, in which German and British (and British colonial) soldiers had marched and fought on Egyptian soil; British and Australian soldiers investigating Cairo's pleasures had not endeared themselves to the populace. There was strong resentment of Britain's continued hold over Egypt; having announced a nominal independence in 1923, after some forty years of occupation, London retained for itself the right to dictate financial organization, to station troops and control Egypt's military, and to control the Suez Canal. Negotiations for a true independence had resulted in the 1936 Anglo-Egyptian Treaty, hardly an improvement. Power was deadlocked among the Palace, where the scion of the Turkish dynasty founded early in the nineteenth century by Muhammad Ali held sway; the British Ambassador; and the Egyptian Parliament, where the two major parties locked horns. The Wafd (or Delegation), formed after World War I to demand self-determination from the Great Powers, had evolved into a popular mass party, yet had generated as much cynicism as had the Liberal Constitutionalists, the bastion of a landholding elite, for popular perception was quick to notice indications that holding onto power seemed more important to many of its leaders than did the country's needs—a perception that emerges in this novel through conversations among the residents of no. 3 Ya'qub Street. During the war, Great Britain's local representatives had not hesitated to make it clear where true power lay; thus, the fiery students at Cairo University—and elsewhere—held few illusions. Student activism was nothing new for Egypt's young intelligentsia, as Ahmed Abdalla shows in his history of student activism in Egypt. As the 1930s wore on, both rightist organizations and leftist groupings, including communists, drew support from students, and communist student leaders—female and male—were important in the demonstrations of the 1940s. (Cairo Faculty of Medicine, where Layla's brother Mahmud and her cousin 'Isam are enrolled, was one of the centers of activism.) As the novel sketches, this was a generation for which new ideas about social organization and personal freedom were inseparable from political demands—even if, as al-Zayyat trenchantly shows, the young often had difficulty squaring theory and practice. And such ideas, and the activism, trickled down from the universities to Cairo's secondary schools; Khedive Isma'il School, a site in the novel, was known as a center of student activism (Abdalla, 55), and the authorities worried about pre-university students on the rampage. These young and enthusiastic forces swelled the numbers of popular demonstrations into the impressive thousands. Early in 1946 public anger seemed on the upswing, and in the second week of February thousands of students held a meeting at which they called for abrogation of the 1936 Treaty and a stop to continued negotiations. They called for a general strike, and the date set was February 21. On that day—as Chapter One describes—when four armored British cars rolled past the British Qasr al-Nil barracks and plowed into the Isma'iliya (now Liberation) Square demonstrations in downtown Cairo, the throngs answered by bodily attacking the armored cars and setting them on fire.

Isma'il Sidqi, remembered as the repressive prime minister of the 1930s (1930–33), had been summoned back into power just before this mass show of public protest; it is his measures that the patriarch at no. 3 Ya'qub Street in the old, middle-class neighborhood of Sayyida Zaynab (named for one of Cairo's major shrines, to the Prophet Muhammad's granddaughter) fears. Sidqi Pasha resumed negotiations with the British, as he had leaders of popular protest arrested and proved himself—once again—no friend to industrial workers and their attempts to organize. This unpopular prime minister represented for many the reactionary stranglehold of the old aristocracy; it seems no accident that al-Zayyat names her young, upper-class male anti-hero 'Sidqi.'

Sidqi's negotiations, like those of past decades, failed; one major reason was Britain's reluctance to let go of a strategic presence in Egypt. Though British troops withdrew from Cairo and the Delta, they remained in the Canal Zone, and hence that region took on symbolic as well as practical importance in the resistance to neo-colonialism. In 1951, after Sidqi's successor did abrogate the 1936 treaty, volunteer commandos and British troops skirmished in the Zone. In Cairo—as we see in the novel—the university becomes a recruiting ground and a training camp where, according to Abdalla, 10,000 students were trained in military maneuvers, and student battalions began to leave for the Canal Zone in November. There, they joined others—industrial workers, the union of Suez Canal workers, military officers, peasants—and al-Zayyat's portrayal of this resistance as badly provisioned and lacking support from the government is historically accurate. Yet the resistance incurred British response. In January, 1952, the

British attacked an Egyptian police barracks at Isma'iliya (on the Canal), believing that Egyptian police were taking part in the resistance there. Cairo erupted as the news came that fifty Egyptians had died. As policemen and firemen looked on in passive solidarity, crowds set fire to institutions and neighborhoods affiliated with the British presence in what became known as the Cairo Fire and Black Saturday (January 26, 1952). The fire also consumed commercial establishments—like Cicurel, the exclusive department store where Layla's cousin Gamila shops for her trousseau—associated with Europeans or those perceived as Europeanized locals (les Grands Magasins Cicurel et Oreco was owned by a prominent Cairo family of Jewish Egyptians, and twice rebuilt by the Egyptian government). This event and the ensuing declaration of martial law and harsh repression of all popular resistance stripped the monarchy of any remaining moral authority, and may have hastened the July Revolution of that year, in which the Free Officers assumed power. King Faruq was made to abdicate and to sail from Alexandria three days after the coup, as the populace—and al-Zayyat's fictional personae—celebrated.

But the end of the *ancien régime* did not mean the end of the British presence. More negotiations resulted in a 1954 agreement stipulating the withdrawal within twenty months of British forces from their base at the Suez Canal, and indeed they were gone in April of 1956. But then a new drama began. Maneuvering between the imperative of acquiring massive aid for arms and for development on the one hand, and the imperative of maintaining independence from Western financial and political institutions on the other, 'Abd al-Nasser was deciding whether to accept the conditions for a British- and US-financed project to build the Aswan High Dam when the US pulled out. In "a dramatic act of defiance," as William Cleveland puts it, 'Abd al-Nasser announced the nationalization of the Suez Canal, explaining that its revenues would go to projects that Western governments were unwilling to finance. Non-aligned governments and populations applauded the move as a signal of independence from the Great Powers, who were not at all pleased by 'Abd al-Nasser's move. As negotiations were mounted to find a way out, a secret agreement among Britain, France, and Israel, who all had their own reasons to oppose 'Abd al-Nasser, resulted in an Israeli strike into Sinai on October 29, 1956, followed by a wave of British bombing two days later, and then by British and French paratroop landings in Port Said (November 5) and an advance on Suez City—events that bring *The Open Door* to a close. The next day, a United Nations ceasefire marked the end of that advance, as US troops moved in and the British and French—and eventually the Israelis—withdrew. Although this was not a military victory for Egypt, it was a political victory for 'Abd al-Nasser and a defining moment for the nation.

The Open Door chronicles the political and sexual coming-to-awareness of a middle-class girl in the Egyptian provinces. Al-Zayyat has called it an attempt to capture her own vision of the world as she was growing into adulthood. The main character, Layla, is ten years younger than al-Zayyat would have been as the political events that mark the story unfold. Layla's growth is paralleled by that of the broad-based nationalist resistance to continued British control over the reins of government through the thirties and forties, despite Egypt's nominal 1923 independence. As Hiba Sharif has noted in an essay on this novel, every advance or retreat in the political realm is matched by one in Layla's personal realm and vice versa—one realm does not precede the other (though, as Hilary Kilpatrick (1992) has noted astutely, some key political events of the time—the war of 1948—are ignored, perhaps because they do not fit into the scheme of Layla's own development). Through the structure of her novel, al-Zayyat suggests an intimate and inseparable relation between personal liberation and the political freedom of self-determination. Sketching the lives of middle-class girls in intimate detail, some of which might sound foreign to an Egyptian teenager now (banana sandwiches and forbidden dancing at school; the old kerosene burners that preceded *butagaz*), she draws on historical references to fill out that struggle. It seems no accident that Layla's college-student cousin 'Isam finds her reading Salama Musa (1887–1958) and arguing for his polemics. Not only does this suggest Layla's precocious intelligence, which her parents would rather ignore, but Musa as cultural symbol signals both a national/ist identity transcending Coptic and Muslim identities and a sympathy for leftist allegiances. Musa was a Copt and a Fabian socialist for whom national allegiance and the issue of independence became paramount. Like many of his contemporaries in the 1920s–30s, he believed in the possibility of adapting Western institutions while retaining local cultural and political autonomy. He was an outspoken proponent of women's rights and a firm supporter of Egypt's early feminist movement. He authored a celebrated autobiography and was an influential magazine editor. Layla's choice of reading matter tells us where her sympathies lie.

But it is another aspect of the novel that I want to emphasize here. In a recent autobiographical essay, al-Zayyat herself says she thinks the novel was a new presence on the literary scene in its emphasis on the construction of dramatic moments, at a time when most novels contained a large amount of external description of scenes, characters, and events. Very much a work of its time in interrogating an ideology of middle-class life, *The Open Door* diverged in its method of interrogation. The novel is striking for its long passages of dialogue largely unmediated by description. And much of the dialogue seemingly does not contribute to the onward march of the narrative—just one example being an exchange among Layla, her cousin, and her aunt about which cloth to use for an engagement dress and which for the wedding dress. In fact, though, such immediate dramatic moments subtly echo and call to mind the dramas of public life, as they also speak to the importance in consciousness formation of little moments. The novel is woven through the daily conversations of its characters, the 'small' as well as the 'large' events of mundane existence. Characters have distinctive voices, even in some cases distinctive colloquial idioms, as they would in real life. More often than not, these conversations take place among women without any men around, or with one man, always a family member, present. Like al-Qalamawi's *My Grandmother's Tales*, they successfully place the focus on women's worlds, and on female perspectives. Many men and fewer women had already given fictional treatment to the question of women's status in society, of women's education, marriage practices, and so forth, criticizing received practices and calling for change. But they did so from what might be called an externalized point of view, even when a female character was central to the action.

But as I have noted, there is a further aspect to the primacy of dialogue in *The Open Door*. Al-Zayyat unabashedly uses a colloquial register—in this case, the spoken Arabic of the urbanized middle classes—in her dialogue. She was not alone in this; the use of colloquial Arabic in fiction, drama, and poetry had been a hot issue among writers since the turn of the century, although the context and direction of the debate differed for each genre. In fiction, some writers had supported the use of the colloquial on the basis that a colloquial register best suited the requirements of a literature of realistic depiction. For others, using the colloquial expressed a political stance, a signal of the author's populist alignment. But there was fierce opposition to the use of colloquial Arabic in literary expression; many writers saw it as a debased or corrupted tongue, to which they contrasted a supposedly 'pure' classical idiom. Political and religious considerations were important: use of the colloquial was variously seen as destructive of an ideal of Arab unity; as culturally divisive; as insulting to the language of the Qur'an. Naguib Mahfouz, for example, has steadfastly opposed its use, although even he lets colloquial usages creep in now and then.

When al-Zayyat was writing *The Open Door* in the late 1950s, the first wave of experimentation with colloquial dialogue, in the 1920s and 1930s, had subsided somewhat. And in well-known novels and short stories of that period, for instance Ibrahim 'Abd al-Qadir al-

Mazini's (1890–1949) *Ibrahim al-katib* and short stories by the Taymur brothers, use of the colloquial is guarded and uneven. As early as Muhammad Haykal's *Zaynab* (1913; often heralded as the first true Arabic novel although it was preceded by several decades of novel writing in Arabic), when peasant or proletarian characters speak or are spoken to, the speech may be couched in a colloquial register. But the educated characters tend to speak in a register of formal speech among or within themselves, especially when articulating what the author sees as a profound thought or a timeless truth.

In the 1950s, al-Zayyat had before her the example of the socialist writer 'Abd al-Rahman al-Sharqawi (1920–87), author of the much-acclaimed novel *al-Ard* (The Land, first published serially in 1953), which attempted a representation of peasant resistance to authoritarian regimes of the pre-1952 period. Al-Sharqawi's use of the colloquial, more sustained than that of previous writers, revolved around his portrayal of peasant society. As Hilary Kilpatrick (1992) has said, "the feel for the violent, aggressive way of speaking characteristic of the peasants is perhaps the single most important factor contributing to the illusion of realism in [*The Land*]."

Al-Zayyat—like al-Sharqawi, a member of the leftist intelligentsia of this period—employs the colloquial differently, grounding in it a portrayal not of peasants or proletarians—those 'others'—but of a petit bourgeois intelligentsia and the remnants of a Turkish aristocracy, her own social group. Furthermore, she uses colloquial not only in the dialogue but also for internal monologue and indirect free discourse, thus going further than even al-Sharqawi. And this dominance of the colloquial enhances al-Zayyat's portrayal of the mundane, of the everyday as a political arena, more specifically of the interrelationships between the gendering of expectations and behavior on the one hand, and the politics of national liberation on the other. It seems to me that this deployment of language can be seen as a feminist act, as basic to al-Zayyat's production of what is unquestionably a feminist text in its assumptions, its authorial stance, as well as in its subject matter. In its very structure and language, the novel questions the culture's consignment to the margins of, first, female experience and articulation; second, the mundane as literary subject; and third, the language that is the medium of everyday experience. And her colloquial is lively, precise, *female*: characters emerge in their choice of expression. Layla's mother betrays her allegiance to received behavior patterns through her choice of expressions and proverbs, which her children mimic satirically, and which contrast utterly with the dry, self-satisfied stiltedness of Dr. Ramzi. Gamila and her mother betray their aspirations as they hover between the French loanwords that label coveted things and their own social and linguistic antecedents; that wealth is not matched by social finesse in Gamila's fiancé is hilariously evident in his language. Al-Zayyat draws close to colloquial poets of the time and earlier as she beautifully and precisely catches not only the phrases but the pronunciation of different social groups. And, to my knowledge, no writer in Arabic before or since has captured middle-class adolescent girlhood so precisely through its own rhythms as al-Zayyat does here, dramatizing the story's conflicts in the three-way conversations among 'Adila, Layla, and Sanaa. The power of the vernacular in al-Zayyat's hands is a strength of the work that the translator can only imperfectly convey. And part of this power has to do with the naming practices of everyday life and language. When al-Zayyat refers to Layla's mother and aunt as Umm Layla and Umm Gamila ('Mother of Layla,' 'Mother of Gamila') rather than as Saniya and Samira, is she deploying description to remind us of how Layla is enmeshed in family, a closely woven net of relationships that she must navigate as she struggles to name her own experience? At the time, in this conservative middle-class environment as well as among working-class and peasant families, parents were often named after their children, and known to acquaintances as 'Father of . . . ' or 'Mother of . . . .' Furthermore, in a society where the expected label would be to call these women after their sons (thus,

Umm Mahmud and Umm 'Isam), is al-Zayyat deliberately replacing this practice with a female genealogy?

The Open Door was nominated for a state prize, a nomination upheld by a unanimous vote of the state-appointed committee, according to al-Zayyat. But the writer and literary arbiter 'Abbas al-'Aqqad (1889–1964), in his capacity as a permanent member of the Higher Council on the Arts and Letters, threatened to resign unless the prize were rescinded. And the prize was withdrawn, on the basis that al-Zayyat had been "immoderate in [her] use of the colloquial." Perhaps this was an indication of how new al-Zayyat's use of language in *The Open Door* was on the Egyptian literary scene, a novelty she herself has commented on.

Since the days of *The Open Door*, the literary scene has shifted, and opened up. The past thirty years have been a period of great experimentation in every genre, of large strides in critical work, of an enormous expansion in governmental and non-governmental literary publishing, of the founding of important literary journals. Of course, within that period there have been times of relative literary quiescence, such as the time just after the 1967 war, a time of deep political–personal crisis for the intelligentsia that left many writers silent for years. Writers have also had to contend with a great deal of formal and informal censorship, to this day. Repression and political crisis have not stopped them, of course. The self-examination sparked by 1967, for example, helped to fertilize a tremendous creative ferment in the 1970s, in poetry, fiction, and drama alike. In fiction, writers had by and large left the fold of social realism in favor of a literary expression that focused more on inner formulations of identity and the fragmentary, self-contradictory subjectivity of characters, expressed through a more impressionistic and fragmented kind of narrative. Some experimented with forms, images, and themes drawn from 'the heritage'—medieval Islamic, pharaonic, Coptic, folkloric. Some tried their hands at new kinds of historical fiction, crafting styles that echoed and subverted those of the chroniclers of medieval Arab societies. Some took on the voice of the traditional storyteller or ballad singer. In fact, the prominent novelist and critic Edwar al-Kharrat has linked modernist and postmodernist Arabic literature to "a whole legacy of Arab culture," challenging the prevailing academic tendency of past decades (among both Arab and Euro/American academics) to define and periodicize the history of modern Arabic fiction according to categories of Euro/American experience.

Searching for their own literary voices, women and men writers of the 1970s and 1980s shaped the language in new ways. For one thing, no longer was the division between linguistic registers—'classical' or 'modern standard' Arabic versus the colloquial—conceived as impermeable. The notion of what might be considered canonical opened up. Among other things, this meant a reevaluation of many works by women that had been previously dismissed or ignored—similar to the reevaluation by feminist critics that has gone on in the realms of European and North American literatures. In particular, contemporary women writers began to regard themselves consciously as part of an historically continuing tradition of women writers. Women writers in Egypt, along with many men writers, are concerned with deconstructing rather than abandoning the dominant tradition. Women writers have certainly demonstrated an active, probing, subversive relationship to that tradition, questioning the privileging of any one position as the position of truth by, for example, rewriting established works from a differently gendered perspective.

If al-Zayyat's articulation of marginality, in both *The Open Door* and *Operation Search*, is not primarily one of class (marginalization through class position, as well as gender, is represented by a secondary character, Sayyida, the servant who is exploited sexually by Layla's first love), the double marginalization of class and gender, with its multiplier effects, is there. Al-Zayyat produced for her time a counterhegemonic discourse, one that tries to make possible a new way of seeing things, a new way of acting, by taking the margins of social existence and articulation as centers. Thus, we return to the image of the seven-year-old girl, crouched on the floor, silent, gazing at the man poet, the representative of all that is literary. But the seven-year-old next to the wall would find a voice; she would question the center, literarily and politically; she would mount her own search campaign in further novels, an autobiographical text, and in drama. The seven-year-old on the roof would participate in opening out the horizons of Arabic literary practice.

As Hala Badri suggested in the comment quoted above, what was startling and bold when *The Open Door*—novel and movie—emerged may be obvious now, for the transformations in girls' and women's lives that al-Zayyat and others struggled to institute then have become part of contemporary history. And the intensely melodramatic quality of the text may temper its power for readers of the new millennium. Yet we should not dismiss this novel. It was an historically important event; it remains a timely literary work. For in an environment of increasing conservatism, in a global situation where women's rights to choose their own futures become touchstones for issues of all sorts, those transformations begin to look tenuous, and the social and political struggles that al-Zayyat and other independent-minded, courageous writers have made part of their fictional worlds are indeed not entirely a thing of the past.

I am indebted to the following sources, which also offer further background to the interested reader:

Ahmed Abdalla, *The Student Movement and National Politics in Egypt 1923–1973* (London: Al Saqi Books, 1985).

Sayyid al-Bahrawi, ed., *Latifa al-Zayyat: al-adab wa'l-watan* (Cairo: Nur: Dar al-Mar'a al-Arabiya, Markaz al-Buhuth al-Arabiya, 1996).

Joel Beinin and Zachary Lockman, *Workers on the Nile: Nationalism, Communism, Islam, and the Egyptian Working Class, 1882–1954* (Princeton: Princeton UP, 1987).

Jacques Berque, *Egypt: Imperialism and Revolution*, trans. Jean Stewart (New York and Washington: Praeger, 1972).

Marilyn Booth, "Introduction," in Marilyn Booth, ed. and trans., *My Grandmother's Cactus: Stories by Egyptian Women* (London: Quartet Books, 1991).

———, "Latifa al-Zayyat," *Encyclopedia of Arabic Literature*, ed. J. S. Meisami and Paul Starkey (London and New York: Routledge, 1998), 2: 825.

William L. Cleveland, *A History of the Modern Middle East* (Boulder, San Francisco, and Oxford: Westview Press, 1994).

Miriam Cooke, *War's Other Voices: Women Writers on the Lebanese Civil War* (Cambridge: Cambridge University Press, 1988).

Albert Hourani, *A History of the Arab Peoples* (Cambridge: Belknap, 1991).

Hilary Kilpatrick, "Women and Literature in the Arab World: The Arab East," in Mineke Schipper, ed., *Unheard Words: Women and Literature in Africa, the Arab World, Asia, the Caribbean and Latin America*, trans. by Barbara P. Fasting (London: Allison and Busby, 1985).

———, "The Egyptian Novel from *Zaynab* to 1980," in M. M. Badawi, ed., *Modern Arabic Literature* [Cambridge History of Arabic Literature vol. 4] (Cambridge: Cambridge University Press, 1992).

Hiba Sharif, "al-Bab al-maftuh," *Hagar: Kitab al-Mar'a* 1 (1993): 134–43.

Aisha Ismat al-Taimuriyya, "Introduction to the Results of Circumstances in Words and Deeds," trans. Marilyn Booth, in Margot Badran and Miriam Cooke, eds., *Opening the Gates: A Century of Arab Feminist Writing* (Bloomington and Indianapolis: Indiana University Press, 1990).

Latifa al-Zayyat, *Hamlat taftish: awraq shakhsiya* (Cairo: Kitab al-Hilal, 1992).

The Open Door

Chapter One

February 21, 1946. Seven o'clock in the evening: the tranquil sky bore a pleasant coolness, and there was a clean purity to the air as if the heavens had poured down rain and washed the earth. Yet Cairo was not its normal, brightly lit self; its main streets were not choked with the usual crowds streaming through the cinema houses, shops, and cafes, or congregating at bus and tramway stops. The cinema houses were on strike, and so were other businesses, and no buses or trams were running. Police cars and vans slunk along streets packed with rifle-bearing soldiers. The few civilians in sight walked slowly in the streets or stood at intersections, knots of two, three, or four engaged in conversation. One could hear all sorts of dialects and levels of education in their speech, but every exchange turned upon the same subject, that morning's events in Ismailiya Square.

"That clash was no coincidence, no sir! They meant to provoke people. A demonstration of forty thousand folks, a big show of protest against the English, that's what people came out for—and what happens? Those English bring out five armored cars to plow into it!"

"Don't forget we Egyptians are brave—a country of tough guys. The tank crushed the lad and right away the students raised his shirt high to show everyone; there was blood all over it. Then the crowd just went mad. They attacked the English tanks and pulled 'em apart, and then they started throwing their bodies right on the guns—why, you'd have thought they were made of sugar for all the people swarming around them."

"Now, personally, I consider this demonstration a new stage in our national struggle. First: this was a direct clash with the English. Second: the army refused to break up the demonstration. Not only that—our army vehicles were moving through the city plastered with nationalist slogans!"

"Then there's the way the workers joined the students. And everybody—all the Egyptian people."

"I'm telling you, this is a nation of toughies—even the women came out of their houses. There were women all over the place in Bab al-Sha'riya."

"Let's get to the point—and that's the weapons. The bullets were coming thick and fast from the army posts. The people were unarmed. If only they had had guns!"

"Fine, but did you see all of those bricks, raining down on the English? Brother, I couldn't believe it! Where'd folks come up with so many bricks?"

"Yes, and how about when they set fire to those barricades the English were trying to hide themselves behind?"

"Those boys were ripping off their gallabiyas, soaking them in gas, and setting fire to them. They were totally in flames, might eat up a guy's whole body, but what did they care? They would just crawl along, bullets pouring down like rain, paying no attention, no sir, went on moving, right to the attack . . . ."

"This wasn't simply an anti-English thing today. No, people were attacking the English *and* the king, and agents of imperialism in general. And I say this is a new stage of national consciousness, that's my own personal view of the situation."

"Well, me—even if I live to be a hundred I won't ever forget that scene in Sulayman Pasha Street. No, sir."

"Badges, badges of blood! The blood of those who died, those who were wounded, all for Egypt's sake. Twenty-three dead, and 122 injured."

———

For those talking excitedly on the street the battle had ended. Final gains and losses had been tallied. But the battle had not yet ended, nor had any sums been figured, for the family of Muhammad Effendi Sulayman, civil servant in the Ministry of Finance and resident of No.3 Ya'qub Street in the neighborhood of Sayyida Zaynab.

In the apartment's large entrance hall, which served the family as an everyday living room, sat Sulayman Effendi himself. Ensconced in a cushioned wooden armchair facing the front door, he was repeating verses from the Qur'an in an undertone, stopping from time to time to listen hard whenever footsteps sounded on the stairs. As they came closer he would train his gray eyes on the door, his face set severely. But invariably the footsteps continued on, right past the door, up the stairs to the floors above. At that, his shoulders would slump and his sallow complexion would go even paler, giving more prominence to the patches of reddened skin on his face. Eventually he would resume his murmured repetition of verses from the Holy Book.

In the formal sitting room that adjoined the front hall, Sulayman Effendi's wife stood at the window. She was not a tall woman, but her full figure and light skin were attractive. At the moment the upper half of that compact body hung so far out of the window that she seemed almost to dangle. All her fiber was telescoped into her small, hazel eyes, flitting right and left, staring into the distance as if they could almost of their own accord pierce the dimness of the evening street.

In front of the round table that graced the center of the sitting room stood eleven-year-old Layla, a robust girl with skin darker than her mother's. She was fiddling with a wooden cigarette box, her motions mechanical, her bright eyes gazing into the distance, at nothing in particular. With a final, sharp tap to the lid of the cigarette box, she marched into the living room, passing her seated father as she headed straight for the front door. She reached for the sliding bolt. Her father's lips trembled, his face going even whiter as he raised eyes so faded they might have been gazing from a corpse rather than from Sulayman Effendi. He stared at his daughter.

"Where're you going?" he asked in low, edgy tones.

"To look for Mahmud." At her words and the hint of defiance in her voice, his dreary eyes flashed. He closed them. "Get back inside." He reinforced his words with a fling of his hand, as if sensing the weary incapacity his broken voice conveyed.

Layla went over to him. Pausing by his chair, she searched for words that would not come. She put out her hand, meaning to lay it gently on his shoulder, but halfway there it hung motionless in mid-air and then dropped heavily to her side. Tears curtaining her eyes, she scurried to her mother in the next room and seized her arm.

"Mama . . . Mama!"

At her touch and her whisper the figure at the window gave a little jump, as if grazed by an electric current, and whirled round, a startled fear contouring her face.

"What is it?"

"Don't be afraid, Mama. Don't worry, I know Mahmud is fine. He'll come now, he must, he'll come. This morning . . . " But her tears choked off the rest of her sentence.

Her father fidgeted in his chair. That morning—just that morning—he had urged his son, "Don't go out, Mahmud." Already at the front door, the lad had paused.

"Nothing to worry about, Papa. It's to be a peaceful demonstration."

"So the demonstration can't go on without you?"

Mahmud had laughed. "Sure, Papa—but look, if everyone said that, then it really wouldn't go on."

"You're still a child. When you start at the university, then you can do what you like."

"I'm not so little. I'm in my fourth year of high school, and I am exactly seventeen years old."

Now, hours later, Mahmud's father bit his lower lip until it stung. If only he had given the boy a good thrashing and then had locked him in—if he had just thrown him into a room and taken the key from the lock—then at least he would know his son's whereabouts. But if he were to inform the police at this point, no doubt they would arrest him, and if they arrested him . . . . It was Sidqi. Sidqi Pasha, who buried people alive. But what could he do? The boy might be hurt, wounded. He might be . . . . "Spite the Devil," he muttered to himself.

The clock on the wall above him began to sound the hour. Hardly breathing, Mahmud's mother listened and counted: seven chimes. She faltered for a moment, hung back, then rushed into the front room and planted herself before her husband, fixing him with frightened eyes that swung sharply from side to side.

"The boy is gone! He's gone for good! Gone!" She struck one palm against the other in a gesture of futility, seemingly unaware of the noise she was creating. Her normally soft, slightly limp features abruptly acquired an unfamiliar hardness. "If you won't go out—" The words died on her lips as her flustered husband struggled to his feet. On the stairs the sound of footsteps grew louder, the footfalls of more than one person, heavy and slow, steps that dragged. Layla ran to the door, her father close behind, and burst onto the landing with a shout.

"Mahmud!"

Still inside, her mother reeled and would have fallen had her fingertips not clutched the edge of the chair just in time. But when Mahmud came in, leaning on Isam's shoulder, she collapsed onto the floor in a faint.

The next morning Layla asked to see her brother before leaving for school. Her mother, eyes red and swollen, gave her a peculiar look as if she held a secret she was unwilling to share. Mahmud was still sleeping, she told her daughter in a whisper. Layla was uneasy, wondering what her mother's expression and manner of speaking meant.

"What's happened, Mama?"

As her mother leaned over, her swollen eyes took on a hard glint, the resistant fear of one who senses that she is the target of a well-aimed pistol. She spoke in the same whispered tone. "A bullet. A bullet went into his thigh."

"I already know that, Mama."

Her father broke in, lather covering his face. "Really, now—you like to make everything sound so terrible. I told you the doctor said it was a simple wound, no more than a scratch."

His wife waved his words away and began to count the day's household chores on her fingers, that strange, secretive look still masking her eyes. Layla gave her shoulders a dismissive shake and stood by the front door to await her cousin Gamila, her mother's sister's daughter who lived on the seventh floor. The moment she spied Gamila's hand through the door's glass panel, reaching across to ring the doorbell, Layla flung the door open. She closed it behind her slowly and very, very carefully.

It was not until they were on their way down the stairs that Gamila spoke. "What's wrong, Layla?"

"Nothing."

"No, I don't believe you. On the Prophet's honor, is there really nothing wrong?"

They came out into the street and turned in the direction of their school. "Yesterday was quite a day!" said Layla.

"Why? Did something happen?"

"Isam didn't say anything?" Layla struck her palm against her chest to dramatize her words.

"Say anything about what?" Gamila asked uncomfortably.

Layla rolled her eyes as she whispered. "About what happened to Mahmud, my brother Mahmud."

Gamila stopped, her discomfort and anxiety getting the better of her. "What? What's wrong with Mahmud?"

Layla's eyes hardened and froze as if she had just espied a gun barrel trained at her skull. She leaned close to Gamila, her words coming out in a measured, loud whisper.

"A bullet . . . a bullet in his thigh."

Gamila's schoolbag fell from her hand. Layla gave her a stare and walked on. Gamila ran to catch up, her breath coming in short gasps. "A bullet! Where on earth did this bullet come from, anyway?"

Layla's head jerked upward. "The English got him. They hit him because he is a nationalist. Because he is a hero."

"They hit him? Where?"

"Gamila, you never know what's going on! In the demonstration, of course, the one yesterday in Ismailiya Square."

"And what did the doctor say? Mightn't it be just a scratch?"

They were in front of the school. Layla did mean to tell her cousin what the doctor had said and what her father had echoed so firmly, but she saw the look of alarm in Gamila's eyes and noticed the awed respect, too. She couldn't help herself as they went inside. "What can he say? It was a bullet, after all."

A bullet. Mahmud a nationalist. A demonstration. The news caught fire through the school, and Layla found herself—a mere first-year student at the secondary school—the center of attention and admiration. It went on all day long. Older girls swarmed around her and teachers stopped her in the corridors to ask questions. The intensity of their interest intoxicated her, and she let her imagination go. His name? Mahmud Sulayman. His age? Seventeen. Layla, why didn't he go to the hospital? How could he go to the hospital, they would have arrested him there! So what did he do, then? Well, after he'd been wounded he just went on pelting the English back, the blood was absolutely pouring out but he didn't stop, his friend kept repeating "enough, stop" but it was no use. His buddy stayed right behind him all the way home, yes, dragged him home to the Astra Building, and they brought in a doctor, a relative, so that no one would find out, and he stayed in hiding as long as it was light, because if he had gone out in broad daylight wounded like that—well what a disaster it could have been!

By the end of the school day Mahmud had become a legend throughout the school building. It was he who had set fire to the jeeps, and to the barricades behind which the English were hiding. It was he . . . and then it was he . . . Layla was sorry to see the school day end.

At the school entrance Inayat stopped her, tugging at her black leather belt to tighten it further around her small waist as the ringlets jostled each other across her forehead. Layla blushed. There was not a girl in her class who did not long for Inayat's attention. Moving the tip of her high-heeled shoe around in the sand, Inayat said, "Your brother Mahmud—what does he look like, Layla?"

A look of bewilderment crossed Layla's face.

"I mean, is he dark, light? Tall, short?"

"He's not dark and he's not light, he isn't tall, but he isn't short, either."

Inayat laughed and tilted her head pertly so that it almost met her shoulder. "Lovely!" Layla blushed harder but she managed to raise her eyes to the other girl provokingly, with a grin. "*Zayy al-qamar*, he's as gorgeous as a full moon." She could prove the truth of her words, she realized. She took off the pendant that hung on a chain around her neck and showed Inayat Mahmud's portrait in the little cameo. Inayat studied the tiny photograph carefully, and pursed her lips and said grudgingly, "Not bad. Pretty good-looking, in fact."

Layla took back the necklace and hung it around her neck, staring at the ground. Then she raised her head sharply. "I'll tell Mahmud that—I'll say, 'Inayat says you're good-looking.'"

"So how would Mahmud know who I am, anyway?"

"All the students at Khedive Ismail know you, in fact they say you're the reigning beauty queen of the Saniya School."

Inayat laughed agreeably and pinched Layla's cheek. "Careful, Layla—watch out I don't get mad at you."

Layla stamped her foot on the ground. "I'll say it. I will. I'll tell him."

She took off running in the direction of home. The moment she arrived, she burst into Mahmud's room, calling his name.

—

But she stopped, suddenly aware of tension in the air. Mahmud was lying on his side, facing the wall, his eyes wide and unmoving as if he had not budged since yesterday. Isam, her aunt's son, sat on the edge of the bed rubbing his chin, and her mother stood next to him, a glass of lemonade in her hand.

"Come on, son. Sit up and wet your lips."

There was no sign that Mahmud had heard a word. His mother stepped over to a nearby table and set down the lemonade. She bent over the bed and reached out to feel his forehead.

"What's wrong, my boy? Tell me—I want to know that you're all right. What's the matter—where does it hurt? What are you feeling?"

Mahmud's face clouded and he spoke without turning to them. "Nothing."

"What do you mean, nothing?" His mother turned to Isam. "How do you like this state of affairs, Isam? From the minute he got home he's been like this, he won't say a word, just lies here moping in this black mood of his."

Suddenly Mahmud rolled over on the bed and sat up. He faced his mother. "Why all this fuss?" His voice was abnormally loud, the words seeming to force themselves with difficulty from his throat. "Why? I told you, it's a scratch. Child's play, just child's play." Repeating the phrase, his voice faded and he fell back onto the bed, his energy spent. His mother looked hard at him for a moment. His face had no color and his eyes were a glassy green, with the pale stare of feverishness. Drops of sweat stood out on his forehead. His mother opened her mouth to speak then pressed her lips together tightly and turned to leave the room. As she reached the door, Mahmud's faint voice came. "Mama . . . "

She stepped back into the room, but did not come all the way over to his bed. Mahmud sat up and beckoned her nearer. He leaned over to her as if he had a secret to tell. "You know—you know when you slaughter a hen and the blood runs out"—his voice was a whisper— "and the hen goes on moving, just for a moment, and then falls down, boom, and that's it?" His eyes grew dark and his face went gloomy. He brought his fist down hard on the bedside table as he spoke in a voice that managed to be both a whisper and a wail.

"People died, lots of people—and that's exactly how they died."

"You'll feel better if you nap awhile longer, Mahmud," said his mother, stretching out her hands to his shoulders, trying to help him to lie back. He pushed one hand away slowly, his eyes searching out Isam's gaze. "Why? Why, Isam?"

Isam shrugged lightly and said calmly, "Why what?"

Mahmud gave his head a vigorous shake as if trying to come out of a nightmare. He slumped back against the headboard. "Nothing." His mother left the room. Layla took her place next to the bedside table and stood there looking anxiously at Mahmud in the silence.

"You mean, you don't want to talk about it!" exclaimed Isam.

"What's the point? If I told you about it, you wouldn't understand anyway. You're a guy who is all reason, all sense and balance. A guy who doesn't react to things, who never weakens."

"Quit it, you! Enough nonsense, on your papa's good name!"

Mahmud smiled thinly and a hint of color crept into his face. "Look, Isam, do you know what I feel like? I feel as if someone hit me hard, really gave me a beating. And I couldn't hit back. I couldn't even yell anything."

Layla's lips trembled and her face showed a wave of convulsions as if in response to a stabbing internal pain.

"One day soon," said Isam, "when the weapons are in our hands, they won't be able . . . "

Wailing "Mahmud!" and pouncing on her brother, Layla interrupted. She shook him by the shoulders. "Mahmud! Mahmud, you're the one who hit the English; it wasn't them who struck you. You, it was *you*, Mahmud." Her brother was silent, and so she twisted to face Isam, her hands still clamped firmly on Mahmud's stooped shoulders.

"Isam," she wheedled, "it was Mahmud, Mahmud who hit the English. Wasn't it, Isam?"

"Could there be any doubt?" responded Isam with a reassuring smile.

But Layla was not mollified. She turned back to Mahmud. "You, Mahmud, you. You." The wail was more subdued now. Try as he might, Mahmud could not avoid the blend of hope and flat despair in those eyes that confronted him squarely. She buried her face in his shoulder and he stared into the distance. "Yes, Layla. It was us—we struck the English."

Still sheltered on his shoulder, Layla began to laugh, laugh after laugh interspersed with sobbing. She raised her head, a smile on her face and tears glinting in her eyes. "I knew it, I just knew it. And besides, that's what I told them at school."

"What exactly did you tell them?" asked Mahmud.

"Everything, and the teachers were really delighted to hear what you did, they think you're wonderful, and—" Mahmud put his hand over her mouth. Layla pushed it away, her laughter now a teasing voice. "Even Inayat, she says you're handsome!" At that, Mahmud tried to conceal his smile.

"Inayat! Inayat who?" asked Isam. Her arms still around her brother, Layla turned to him. "You mean you don't know who Inayat is? She's the beauty queen of the Saniya School!"

"Oh, her! You son of a gun!" exclaimed Isam. "Inayat! She's a knock-out."

Mahmud could not stop laughing. Satisfied that she had accomplished her mission, Layla sprang off the bed and hurried toward the door, but Mahmud stopped her.

"Layla."

"Yes?"

"First of all, you're a liar."

"Liar! What d'you mean, liar?"

"I mean . . . well . . . how would Inayat know, anyway? How could she have possibly seen me, to be able to say I'm a handsome hunk or an ugly ogre?"

Isam peered from brother to sister, a sly grin curving his lips. Pointing to the cameo hanging on her chest, Layla said, "She saw this picture of you."

Now a glint of inquisitive attention snared Mahmud's eyes. "Show me—which picture is it?" She took off the necklace and laid it in his open hands. He studied his own likeness with interest. Isam's grin widened, and he struck Mahmud on the thigh. "Mahmud—"

Mahmud turned to him, his left hand clutching the cameo. "What, Isam?"

"So what do you have to say now about that beating you got?" Mahmud kicked Isam and let the necklace drop to the floor. His sister knelt hastily to retrieve it; as her head bobbed up, level with Mahmud's, she paused in mid-movement, her eyes flashing as if an extraordinary thought had just popped into her head. "Me, too! When I get bigger I'll show those Englishmen! I'll carry a gun, I really will, and I'll shoot them all. When I grow up."

"Could there be any doubt?" laughed Isam, as Layla rose to her full height quickly and wheeled around to go out, with the measured bounce of the demonstrators, waving her right hand up and down, intoning, "Weapons, weapons, we want weapons. Weapons, wea–" She stopped dead, her arm dropped to her side and the words stalled on her lips. Her father was entering the room.

———

In a few days' time life regained its normal course. Preoccupied with daily demands, people acted as if the events of that day had been erased from their memories. Mahmud returned to school, and Layla no longer heard questions about him or the demonstration. At first she felt resentful, but gradually her own concerns took over.

One morning she woke up early as usual so that she could collar the newspaper before her father and brother were even up. Perched on the armchair in the front room, facing the apartment's front door, she waited, her eyes shifting between the threshold and the clock until the newspaper appeared under the door. She had finished reading it and the clock said half past six, but still no one else in the family had emerged. She got to her feet, stretched contentedly, and tossed the paper onto the chair. But halfway to the door to her room she retraced her steps. She refolded the paper and ran her fingers along the crease, biting her lower lip, vexed at what she had to do out of fear of her father's scathing remarks. She hurried to her room, struggled into her school pinafore, and searched frantically for stockings and shoes, under the bed, beneath the wardrobe. She tugged a comb through her short black hair as she poked her feet into her shoes, grabbed one book from the table, retrieved another from beneath her pillow, threw them into her leather book bag, then scampered toward the dining room as if someone were in close pursuit. Careening into Mahmud did not stop her, but she did slow down when she saw her father standing before the basin, shaving. She worked her mouth into a polite smile.

"Good morning, Papa."

Her father muttered something unintelligible as he tilted his head back to shave his neck. She disappeared into the dining room and immediately demanded food in a loud voice. Her mother glared at her.

"The *ful*-beans for breakfast haven't arrived yet." But her mother's cold look did nothing to dampen her enthusiasm.

"Anything's fine!"

"Why are you in such a rush? It's not even quite seven and the first bell isn't until eight thirty."

"But that errand."

"Ten minutes."

"I just want to eat, okay?" She yanked a chair away from the table, sat down, and rolled a bit of cheese in half of a bread round. She spread a thin layer of jam on top and gnawed industriously at her sandwich, swallowing it in lumps so that she could be off for school, off to slam her school bag on the grass and join her classmates. Then the bell would ring and after a prolonged search for her bag she would head for arithmetic class.

———

She settled into her seat, rested her arm on the desktop, and propped her chin on it, her eyes glued to the teacher's hand as it moved across the blackboard. She must understand every word, she must, and every sum. She must. Miss Nawal said she had gotten better at arithmetic but she absolutely had to do even better—and better. Best in the class, so that Miss Nawal would show some fondness for her. Miss Nawal had to like her, she simply must.

This was the only *must* in eleven-year-old Layla's life. She must triumph, she must win over this slender teacher who pulled back her hair and wore it massed behind her head, who preferred mannish clothing, who could focus her small round eyes so intensely on you that it was as if she was going inside your head and ferreting out your thoughts; this teacher whose delicate lips would disappear whenever she tried to hold back a smile. Layla had begun the school year with a careful, polite smile always on her own lips. She sat primly through arithmetic class, her arms folded, ignoring the whispers of Adila, her deskmate. And even when Adila swung her legs to kick Layla under the desk, Layla restrained herself, only biting her lower lip. All of that, and she might as well not even have been in the room for all that Miss Nawal cared! When class was over, Layla waited until the last pupil had laid her workbook on the teacher's table, and only then she placed hers on the pile, straightening the whole stack, and starting to pick it up so that she could carry it to the teachers' room behind Miss Nawal. But Miss Nawal pressed her lips together and took the workbooks from her after thanking her. This peculiar teacher who refused to let a pupil carry her workbooks for her baffled Layla, but she did not give up. She knew a strategy that always worked. You could give the teacher an enchanting rose, and then when you went into the teachers' room with whatever excuse you drummed up, you'd find the teacher there, the flower before her in a glass, and immediately you would know that some sort of bond had formed between the two of you. Hadn't the teacher kept the flower, after all? And preserved it carefully? Your rose, in front of her, in the glass. But Miss Nawal did not do what she was supposed to do. She did not preserve the flower in a glass. In fact, she did not even take the rose from the classroom. Nafisa took it—snub-nosed, kinky-haired Nafisa. At first it had all gone according to plan, but then things had gone awry. Walking into the classroom before the start of class, Layla had given the rose to the teacher. Miss Nawal had inhaled its scent and then had laid it carefully on top of her attendance book before turning to write the day's arithmetic problems on the blackboard. But before she had finished writing out the first one, she turned abruptly to face the class.

"Whoever is first to solve this problem gets the rose." So Nafisa got it as Layla looked on, her face stricken. She would snub Miss Nawal, she decided. And she did, until something transpired at home that caused her to revoke her decision. Her mother had asked her to bring her the alarm clock so that she could wind it. As Layla rushed over to her mother, the clock slipped out of her hand and the glass over its face broke. It shattered into pieces, just as the green vase with the hand-painted white roses had shattered, just as the doll that said "mama" and had eyes that opened and shut had broken—just like everything in the house, in fact. Everything her fingers picked up. Her mother let out a scream, and went on screaming, as if something really horrid had happened, like a fire breaking out in the building. She bore down on Layla, face red with anger, and slapped both of her palms hard. Wiping the sweat from her forehead, she wailed, "What am I going to do with you? But what can I do with such rotten luck? God made you a real problem-child—may He take you and give us some peace!"

Her father, appearing in the doorway to his room, brought the matter to a close in his unruffled way, his voice firm but empty of anger. "I told you before that this one's no ordinary girl. She's a *fitiwwa*, a real bull in a china shop." He turned, went back into his room, and shut the door behind him.

———

Layla stood before the oval mirror in her room. She stuck out her tongue, then ran it round her lips. Girl! Girl . . . *girl* . . . "A nice girl," the Headmistress had said in the courtyard, pinching her on the cheek. The headmistress was fond of her, and so was Miss Zaynab, and Miss Zahiya, and Miss Ratiba, all of the teachers, in fact. All except . . . . Layla sucked her tongue in and clamped her mouth shut. All except Miss Nawal. Because they had to like her. They had to—everyone in the school had to like her. Miss Nawal had to like her. She had to. Layla closed her eyes and turned her back to the mirror. She could see Nafisa in her mind's eye, holding a red rose to her snub nose. Suddenly she hurried to her book bag and took out her arithmetic workbook, her fat exercise book, and a pencil. She had an idea. She sprawled across the floor and opened the workbook to its first page.

Thus began a fierce attempt to conquer those numbers. Stark, bold numbers, skipping along before her eyes, figures coming together or splitting apart, adding, subtracting without any obvious logic, multiplying, dividing, suddenly confronting her with an answer that stared her wickedly in the face. Use your brain, Miss Nawal had said. But in arithmetic her brain refused to budge. In Arabic composition her mind worked just fine; one word brought another, and one sentence yielded the next, and her hand flew to keep up with her mind: a flitting bird, streaking through the sky far above the flock, diving to its nest with anxious love for its tiny baby birdies, encircling them with its wings to keep them warm. Or: here she was, a little child lost and wandering among unfamiliar people who stared at her but didn't see the tears in her eyes. Or she was Madame Curie, or she was a hero smashing the prison bars to save the folk from the colonizers. She was all of them, and others, too, if she wished. Or at the very least she could feel herself identifying and sympathizing with all of them. But in arithmetic, where was she? With a grocer, selling sugar and buying oil. With a faucet, dripping X number of times per minute. With a basin, filling slowly to the brim with all of those uncountable drops. She was with numbers that danced before your eyes without any beauty or sense. But, sense or nonsense, she absolutely had to understand every word and every letter.

She began to get the better of the numbers. She grasped one strand from here, and wound in another from there; she twisted them together and held them delightedly in her fist. She began to make progress. Miss Nawal encouraged her at every step, until ahead of her remained only Nafisa. That girl could still solve the problems quicker than she could, and the grades in her workbook remained higher than the marks in Layla's. Layla put all her energy into this mission: trying to outdo Nafisa.

———

Nafisa was standing up to respond to a question from Miss Nawal. She got to her feet unhurriedly, spoke carefully, and answered precisely what was asked of her, no more and no less. Layla wondered if it was possible to surpass Nafisa, who was so very strong in arithmetic. All through elementary school she had done better than Layla, always staying several levels ahead. Now, could Layla possibly pass her in first-year secondary school arithmetic, when it was so difficult? And she was so weak—weak at arithmetic, weak in everything.

Without warning, Miss Nawal directed a question at Layla, who stammered an answer. She sat down again and tried to focus all of her attention on the arithmetic problems. Silence came over the class, as Miss Nawal walked up and down the rows, reading the solutions from above the pupils' heads. When she stopped at Layla's desk, Layla bent her head lower, the pencil motionless in her hand as if she were thinking hard. Miss Nawal read, pressed her lips together, and bent over Layla.

"You're doing well indeed, my dear."

Layla's eyes met Miss Nawal's. She felt a lump stuck in her throat and swallowed the saliva in her mouth with difficulty. Miss Nawal put out her hand and ruffled Layla's hair, as if she were combing it from the nape to the crown, and then walked on.

Layla reached her hands up to pat her hair into place, but they hung in midair and she felt her eyes tear over as she realized that, yes, she could outdo Nafisa, and ten more as good as Nafisa, as long as Miss Nawal stood by her.

———

School was over for the day. Layla stood under the sycamore tree in the schoolyard. Gamila sat facing her on a wooden bench, and settled next to her on the grass was Sanaa. In the middle stood Adila, doing an imitation of their English teacher. Sucking in her cheeks and holding her body rigid, her arms stiffly to her sides, Adila marched, raising one leg and then the other in exaggerated regimental fashion. Her voice came out hollow as if she were a wooden doll. Gamila was laughing so hard that she had to cover her face with her hands. Sanaa doubled over, supporting her shaking middle with one hand. Layla's cheeks puffed up into little balls and her eyes narrowed to slits; the howls spun from her mouth in waves that came faster and faster until one swept over the next and she could hardly breathe. She turned her back on her school-mates, leaning against the sycamore trunk, trying to regain her breath. She took out her handkerchief to dry her tears. Her hand stopped in midair, her eyes still streaming, as she suddenly became aware that Adila had not completed her sentence and the laughter had stopped abruptly. What had happened? She whirled round to face her class-mates. Sanaa had lowered her eyes to the ground and was yanking out clumps of grass, barely getting one fistful out before fiercely seizing another, as if she had been assigned the task. Gamila seemed to be star-ing at a distant horizon.

"What is that bit of red on your pinafore, Layla?" came Adila's voice. Layla's head whipped around and she pulled the back of the pinafore forward anxiously. "Ink, must be ink. What else could it be?"

Gamila shook her head slowly, her eyes resting somberly on her cousin. At her mournful look, a sense of dread seemed to fill Layla's body. She didn't know where the sensation came from, and uncom-fortably she started forward, meaning to throw her arms around Gamila. But she stopped dead when she caught sight of Adila's mock-ing, superior gaze.

"Congratulations, Madame Layla," said Adila with a smile of scorn. "You've grown up now."

Gamila gently drew Layla away. In the school bathroom she cut away the red spot with a razor. When Layla's mother saw the pinafore she exclaimed, "My dear! Why didn't you wash the spot out instead of cut-ting your pinafore?" But this time she did not treat Layla roughly at all.

———

Layla shifted her body warily in her bed, stretching slowly as if she were made of fragile glass that might shatter at a touch. She lay on her back, her eyes staring into the darkness. How strange this all was! She had only sensed the curious heaviness in her body when she had seen that look in Gamila's eyes. And it was the same expression she'd caught in her mother's gaze. What had happened, of course, had happened long before Adila's discovery of it, maybe even while she had sat in class that morning, but still, she had not felt the slightest bit sick or tired this morning. To the contrary, she'd felt light in mind and body, she had been ready to run and laugh and bury her face in the blooms of the garden. She'd felt strong, and smart, and as if she could get ahead of Nafisa in arithmetic. But now, Layla realized suddenly, her eyes still wide open in the darkened room, it all seemed totally insignificant. Everything did—Miss Nawal, Nafisa, arithmetic. It seemed as if all of those events had happened to her a long time ago. She closed her eyes and tried to summon the image of Miss Nawal bending over her desk. She concentrated so hard on that image that she felt sweat breaking out on her forehead. Yet the picture remained faint, fleeting, out of focus; and it was quickly erased by the scene at the sycamore tree, and Gamila, giving her a look that reflected a sorrowful, loving sympathy.

"But why, Gamila, why?" Layla found herself saying out loud. "I *want* to get older. Yes, I do." Her eyes open again, she stared into the blackness.

To grow older. To become like her mother. No! To become like . . . like the history supervisor who helped their teachers, the woman with the broad, pale forehead, who held her head so erect, with her long, carefully coiffed black hair, and her gait as measured and dignified as that of any queen.

Layla heard the front door open. The light on in the front hall seeped into her bedroom, and to the bed where she lay; and then it disappeared as her father headed for his room, which shared a wall with hers. When she had arrived home from school that afternoon, he had already gone out. At the table her mother told her that he had been invited to dine out.

Now her father would learn of it. He would certainly find out, for her mother would tell him. What would he say, she wondered? He would be happy, of course, and he would show it, as he had when Mahmud's chin had first sprouted a beard.

On that day, she recalled, her father had stopped Mahmud and had drawn him over to the window where the light was stronger. He had stared at his son, and the look in his eyes had made Layla wonder whether he still had his feet on the ground! He seemed to be soaring somewhere above, Mahmud in tow. His face had reddened; he had laughed and laughed, for no reason at all.

The laughs died away . . . the stillness grew to encompass everything, and Layla's eyes stared into the darkness, as if in wait. Now she could hear her mother's voice, lowered; she stiffened as she made out her own name, and heard it come up again and again in the conversation. Then silence hung thickly over the room once again, an absolute stillness, a massed darkness.

A sobbing wail sliced through the silence and Layla jumped out of bed as if stung. But immediately she recognized her father's tones in that wail. She stood transfixed in the middle of the room. She heard pleading invocations to God cut into the sobbing—"Lord, give me strength! She's just a helpless girl. Oh God!"—interrupted from time to time by her mother's voice, calm and low.

"That's enough, *ya sidi!* The girl can hear us."

"Protect us, Lord, protect us! Shield us from harm." The voice grew fainter until, with a final choked sob, it was silent. Layla felt a desolate emptiness expand to fill her chest, and a tremor that began on her lips moved to her hands and legs. Sweat trickled from the nape of her neck all the way down her back. Moving about in the darkness, groping for the door, she struck against something and wanted to scream, to call out to her mother. "Don't be afraid, dear," her mother had said that afternoon; now, the scream faded on her lips. Her legs felt heavy; she dragged herself back to the bed and lay down on her back. "Don't be afraid, dear, don't worry. You've grown up." And Layla tugged at the coverlet, yanking it over her body, over her face, pulling it up to the very top of her head.

———

On that remarkable evening Layla had not been able to fathom why Gamila had given her that melancholy gaze, or why her father had wept. It was only with the passage of years that she came to understand—and then she understood very well, indeed. She grew to the realization that to reach womanhood was to enter a prison where the confines of one's life were clearly and decisively fixed. At its door stood her father, her brother, and her mother. Prison life, she discovered, is painful for both the warden and the woman he imprisons. The warden cannot sleep at night, fearful that the prisoner will fly, anxious lest that prisoner escape the confines. Those prison limits are marked by trenches, deeply dredged by ordinary folk, by all of them; by people who heed the limits and have made themselves sentries. Yet the prisoner feels in her bones that she is strong, that she has powers within her, ones she has never before sensed; she knows the abrupt and shocking strength of a body developing, growing. She finds herself held by powers that sweep all before them, that impel her toward freedom. She sees forces in her body that those border trenches work to enclose and contain; and she knows powers in her mind that the confines themselves work to impound. For they are insensible limits that neither hear, nor see, nor perceive. Layla's father had outlined those confines as the family sat around the table, eating lunch. His voice showed no uncertainty or hesitation.

"Layla, you must realize that you have grown up. From now on you are absolutely not to go out by yourself. No visits. Straight home from school."

Turning his eyes on Mahmud, he added, "I don't want to see any novels or girlie magazines around here. Understand?"

Mahmud dropped his head and twisted his lower lip. His father's voice grew less harsh. "If there's something you want to read, you can read it outside the house. Don't try to bring it here and hide it. I don't want anything poisoning the girl's mind." His eyes met Mahmud's, a man-to-man gaze, and son gave father a knowing smile.

"And, Mahmud, I don't see any reason why your friends need to visit you at home. Aren't the cafe and the club enough, pal?"

Mahmud's smile broadened. "Yes, Papa, they are. But what about Isam? He studies with me."

Her mother's eyes traveled upward from her plate, clouded with worry. "Isam—now really, is he a stranger? He's your cousin, my sister's son! Layla's not going to cover herself up in front of her cousin."

Their father wiped his mouth with his napkin. "Isam, well, never mind that. Isam is one of us."

Layla said nothing. No one expected any words from her. Now it was her mother's turn—her mother's turn to play a never-ending role. And she performed it so assiduously that now, whenever Layla heard steps, she would automatically throw a glance behind her, in expectation of her mother's harsh words of blame for whatever it was she had most recently done, whatever error she had supposedly committed or problem she had caused. The worst of it was that she never knew what it might turn out to be. Something "improper," something "inappropriate," something that did not befit the daughter of respectable folk. A sudden laugh, straight from the heart, was "improper." Why? Too loud. Any statement that Layla thought frank and sincere was labeled "out of bounds." Out of what bounds? The bounds of polite conduct. "There's something, dear, called the fundamentals—the rules, the right way to behave."

And then there was the matter of sitting. "Goodness, Layla! Either you sprawl across the chair like a know-it-all or you swing one leg across the other—what will people say? I can already hear them grumbling—'She wasn't brought up right.'"

"People, people. I'm sick of people. I don't want to see anyone."

"Stop it! People must see you, of course. Otherwise, they'd say, 'Why's she hidden away? Is her arm crippled, or what? Or is she lame?'"

If she refrained from going into the living room to greet guests, her mother accused her of being "a recluse—you don't like anyone." But if, on the other hand, she did go in to greet them, her mother scolded her for not conversing animatedly. Yet if she spoke up, her mother said she was interfering in adults' business. If she stayed, sitting in silent politeness, her mother waved her out of the room! But whenever she tried to make a hasty retreat, her mother would say, "Why were you in such a rush?"

"Mama, I don't know what to do! You've completely confused me now. Everything I do turns out to be wrong, wrong, wrong!"

"Whoever lives by the fundamentals can't possibly go wrong."

"So what are these fundamentals?"

"The fundamentals are when one . . . " And so her mother would set new limits, add new restrictions. They were like water dripping rhythmically onto a sleeping person, the regularity of them stealing the sleep from her eyes, drop by drop, hour after hour, day by day, year after year.

And year after year, Layla grew.

Chapter Two

At seventeen Layla had filled out into a bronze-skinned, moderately tall young woman. Her face was pleasantly round, her features fine and regular under a wide brow. Her eyes were a rich hazel, deep and tapered with an intense sparkle, narrowing to shimmering slits when her rosy cheeks lifted in a smile. She could break into confident laughter that absorbed her entire face, transforming her lips, eyes, and even her nose. When a conversation sparked her interest she would tilt her head, immersed as the words tumbled from her ears straight into her heart; and if someone said something that aroused her enthusiasm or compassion her eyes would glisten with sudden tears. Her face radiated movement, liveliness, and a luminous glow.

And that glowing face shone in utter contrast to her body. For she walked as if bound in heavy chains, dragging her body behind her, shoulders hunched and head pitched forward as if determined to get where she was going with the utmost haste before she could possibly attract the glances of others. If she sat down she found it almost impossible to settle in any position. She never knew where to put her hands; they seemed bodies apart, foreign to her. Her movements spoke of heaviness and fear, especially at home; at school she moved more freely. For school was part of the world she loved with its echoing chorus of varied sounds: the bell; ringing laughter, and sometimes suppressed chuckles; steps sounding through the corridor hurrying to class; eyes that spoke in smiles, and loud mirth in the classroom. Then there were the whispered conspiracies drummed up against the teacher; the loyalty that bound the girls together and neither threat nor punishment would fracture; the notes passed around when speech was out of the question; the midday break and the clusters of friends drawn to each other. That world included, too, murmured jokes that elicited blushing cheeks first, and only then peals of laughter; stories told in undertones in remote crannies of the school grounds, leaving listeners with their mouths stupidly agape; the rhythm of spoons against plates in the cafeteria; the endless banana sandwiches and insult sessions, and the times they had locked themselves into a classroom at break time to dance. Political discussions, disagreements over the merits of Umm Kulthum's singing as opposed to the crooning of Abd al-Wahhab, friendships that flowered and faded just as suddenly, the break-ups and tears and peace-making. Layla was capable of drawing the entire class's attention with her practiced naughtiness, angering the teacher, then making amends, making impromptu speeches on nationalist occasions and distinguishing herself in school literary clubs. The Arabic teacher acknowledged her superiority; she could be school champion at ping pong. She was an energetic Girl Scout, a team player at basketball and leader of a gang of girls wallowing in mutual adoration. But at the end of the school day, after the last pupil had departed, the school silent and empty, she would go into her classroom, gather her books, and leave for home with dragging steps.

———

No sooner was she home than her mother started nagging, her voice and manner rough. There was always some little thing. Either it was something that should have been done and had been neglected, or it was something that should never have happened but had. Then her father's taciturn, expressionless demeanor would appear, to impose his deathly stillness on everyone in the apartment. Her mother's walk would become a hushed tiptoe as she turned this way and that, peering everywhere with anxious eyes to reassure herself that all was properly prepared; then the main, midday meal would begin. Sitting at table, her father would find something with which to rebuke her mother, quietly, of course, his voice hardly above a whisper. Naturally, her mother was vigilant not to commit any act that might draw censure. But there were her siblings; and of course she had to bear full responsibility for *their* conduct. Her brother had said such-and-such, and it shouldn't have been said; he had done this or that when he should have known better. Her mother never responded, but her tightly pressed lips would grow white.

Lunch was a far happier affair when Mahmud was not tied up at the College of Medicine; when, instead, he would come home at the end of a long morning and pull a chair up to the table, letting them enjoy his amiable, bright face, as his restless, green eyes roved around the room. With a pretence at seriousness in his voice, his delicate, pale lips would launch into the day's events. "Well, today . . . ," and he would go on to tell them everything—what transpired at the college, the exchange he had overheard in the tram, the latest book he had read, the newest joke going around. He imitated people, offered commentaries, exaggerated, and asserted as evidence opinions that were odd indeed, views that set him apart from others. The atmosphere at the midday meal would shift completely, as if his entrance had brought a fresh breeze from outside into the Sulayman home. His mother's taut, worried features relaxed, her face now that of a sweet child as she laughed in that gentle, quick, understated way she had. But the sight really worth seeing was their father's face. Eyes trained on Mahmud, never lifting off his face, as if the young medical student was a miracle moving across the face of the earth, the father would sit motionless, listening raptly, the mask falling gradually from his face; that dour mien, normally empty of expression, would take on a bearing of affectionate concern. And at the point when Mahmud's dramatic narrative displayed his own superiority or courage or cleverness or humor, the father's gaze would lightly layer with tears.

Then Mahmud would start on his mocking criticisms of the social conditions and niceties that reigned his society. He was merciless; of those many traditions ringed in haloes of sanctity, there was not a single practice that his devastating attacks skirted. Layla's eyes glowed, her mother's lips trembled, and the father's face always darkened, suspecting a danger he could not define. But Mahmud would slip adroitly out of the dilemma he had created, mixing just enough humor into his sarcastic flings to keep his father busy with the hopeless attempt to suppress his laughter, uncertain of whether his son was serious or merely pulling his leg.

Conversation flew every which way, but mostly it settled back into politics, especially when Isam joined them for lunch. And more often than not he did, for he and Mahmud were inseparable, always together at the College of Medicine, always together when they studied. Whenever talk turned to politics Layla craned forward over the table, leveling her eyes at Mahmud, her ears trained on whatever Isam and her father said but her gaze never leaving her brother. Now and then the muscles in her face twitched as if she had a response at the ready, a stinging riposte; her mouth would move, silently forming letters, but then her face would ease into a smile as Mahmud answered, for invariably he said exactly what she had wanted to express.

"Gamila, do you know what Papa says?" she commented one day to her cousin. "He says that Mahmud and I think with our hearts, not with our minds."

"He's kidding you, silly."

"Well, I know, but anyway, it's the truth."

When Mahmud straightened his spine, it signalled that serious discussion was about to begin. As he spoke, he looked hard at Isam, as if his friend and cousin were responsible for everything the government did.

"So can you tell me what this Wafdist government of yours has done now? 'The Wafd,' we insisted, over and over. 'Only the Wafd can save the country.' So then, what has the Wafd actually done?"

"It's a question of time," Isam protested. "The world wasn't created in a single day, you know."

"Don't drive me up the wall, Isam. You know perfectly well that the negotiations won't lead to anything. The whole country knows it, too. And it isn't as if everyone has just woken up to the fact—we've all known it for years."

Wiping his mouth, their father would join the conversation. "In any case, the Wafd is the best of the lot."

Mahmud leaned forward, the words storming from his mouth as if he were picking a quarrel. "The Wafd is the lousiest of the lot, because the people trusted the Wafd, and then it went and betrayed their trust."

Their father would hurry off to the bathroom without answering, for he must do his ablutions swiftly so that he would not be late for the afternoon prayer.

"It isn't a question of zeal or energy, Master Mahmud," Isam would say serenely to Mahmud. "You say, Can you tell me what the government is doing? Yes, sure I can—it's resisting the King! It's fighting the English!"

Mahmud leaned back in his chair. "Right, it's fighting them both. It *would* be, if it were truly the popular government that it claims to be."

"So, fight them with what?"

"With us, with the people. With the army. The army is itching to get involved! Our army is all peasants, Egyptians, like me and you!"

Then Layla would feel a prickling in her scalp, which would deepen and seem to run through her from head to toe. It was the same tremor that overwhelmed her whenever she listened to the radio and heard about one of Egypt's past glories, and whenever she read a luminous chapter in her country's history, and also whenever she learned of an injustice that had befallen Egypt's people. It was the involuntary shiver of one whose dearest possession generates equal measures of pride and protective fear.

"The people?" Isam would say. "The Egyptian people fight the British Empire? Brother, use that head of yours." And Mahmud would lose the self-control he had been trying hard to maintain. He'd fling out whatever came into his mind first, with no trace of embarrassment, cursing the grandfathers of the British Empire, and the grandfathers of the grandfathers, and the King, and the government; he would hurl invective at the very idea of rationality and at those who use their heads, and he would end with a grand accusation directed at Isam for treachery and betrayal, for appeasing the colonialists. Things would get so bad that even his mother would speak up. "Mahmud, honey, don't get so worked up! Why are you letting it get your goat? Who do you think you are—a prince or a minister?" At that, Mahmud would laugh, and so would Isam, and lunch would be over. Layla would go into her room, shut the door, and take a deep breath.

———

Here in her room she found her own world, too, the realm into which she could withdraw whenever she wanted; her world, in which she stood alone, at a distance from everyone else in the house, even Mahmud. In that world she could live, with her dreams and her joys, her bruises and her longings for things she could not even define, desires that now and again she could feel cavorting through every speck of her being, dancing until she began to sense her body as an airy lightness. Scurrying to the window, yanking it wide open, she'd be certain that in this state of exuberant joy she could fly. Surely she could soar with those birds circling far above! But at other moments those indistinct longings planted themselves stolidly in the territory above her heart, accumulating layer upon layer to press heavily on her chest.

She fancied them layers of mourning for something gone and something to come; but what? Layer upon layer, so many that they threatened to smother her, and she would run to her wardrobe, bury her open mouth in a heap of clothes, and scream with all the strength she had inside her. It seemed to her that her whole being was screaming, and when she stepped back from the wardrobe she was shaking all over. She threw herself across her bed and started to sob. All she wanted was to be left alone in her room, as far away as she could be from others. That was why she was constantly conciliating everyone around her. She wanted no voice invading her hidden world. If she were to show the slightest rebelliousness or excitability, her mother would scold her by the hour. Her father would yank her from bed to deliver a lesson in morals. No, she wanted no silly business from outside to distract her from this marvelous private world.

Studying did not take up much of her time. She moved effortlessly from one grade to the next, and her family expected no more than that. So her time at home was mostly apportioned to her own reading and to daydreams, although now and again her mother pulled her roughly out into a reality that appeared barren and dull. It was so empty of poetry!

She had to receive her mother's visitors, for instance, and to engage them appealingly in conversation. By now she had ample training. She had learned how to smile politely; when and how to let a laugh emerge; when to sit down and when to leave the room. She knew how to assume the manner of an interested listener no matter how trivial the subject, when to nod her head, when to let her admiration or her astonishment show.

She detested it. All of it, with all of her heart. She considered it a baneful curb on her freedom and a mortal danger to her human sympathies. So sometimes she did make mistakes, as happened the evening Samia Hanim visited.

———

Layla's mother came into her room. "Hurry now, up you get! Put on your clothes so you can come in and say hello to Samia Hanim."

This Samia Hanim was one of her mother's relatives, from the well-off branch of the family. Layla hung her head.

"I don't want to come in and see anyone."

"Why not?"

"Just because."

"Because why?"

Layla tossed her head. "I don't want to see her. I don't like her. I haven't liked her since the day of the sherbet."

She closed her eyes. She could envision Samia Hanim in her parlor, jumping up from the lacquered wood *fauteil* with its Aubusson upholstery as if disaster had just hit. She could see her mother's hand out, suspended in the air, while the *sufragi* who served them, suddenly realizing his blunder, stepped swiftly back from her mother with his full tray of sherbets, swinging around to offer them to Zaynab Hanim first, the guest of importance. Layla shook her head hard, her eyes still shut. What an ordeal! But the worst of it was that her mother had not even been angry.

"Everyone has their own slot in this world of ours," she had said. "If everyone knew their place, then no one would suffer."

Layla had smeared her hand across her tears. "And this Zaynab Hanim," she asked sarcastically. "What makes her better than you? Because she's rich?"

"Yes, because she's rich," her mother had said simply.

Now, Layla opened her eyes to find her mother still standing over her. Without a word she got up to put on her clothes. And without a word she sat listening as the guest chattered to her mother. Conversation turned to a famous singer, a neighbor of Samia Hanim's. Guess how much he owns? How much money, how many buildings? And then they moved to his voice. When that topic appeared to have been exhausted—for it was utterly clear that Layla's mother understood nothing in the realm of love songs—Samia Hanim turned to Layla. "His voice just slays me, it's unbelievable, don't you think so, Layla?"

"But he sounds like he's crying when he sings," said Layla. "Like he's some woman."

It was not long before Samia Hanim rose to her feet, agitated. She was accustomed to listeners who hung wide-eyed on every word she uttered. She tossed her fur across her shoulders as she took her annoyed leave.

"Your daughter is terribly spirited, Saniya Hanim." She spit out the consonants and drew the word "spirited" out. Her mother closed the apartment door behind the guest and turned to Layla, her face severe.

"How could you say those ridiculous things to Samia Hanim?"

"I just said what came to mind, and that's that!"

"What came to mind? If everyone said whatever was on their mind the world would have gone up in flames long ago."

"Or whatever they feel—that's what they should say."

"Whatever they feel! That's for your own private self, not for saying in front of people."

"So people should just lie, you mean."

"That's not lying—that's being courteous. One has to make people feel good. Flatter them."

"Even when you don't like them?"

"Even when you don't like them."

Tears flooded Layla's eyes and her voice came out choked. "So people should just lie? They should just tell lies?"

Her mother's face grew gentler, and she put her hand softly on Layla's shoulder. "I worry about you, Layla, and I feel sorry for you, too. You have no idea what the world is like. The world demands as much, and anyone who doesn't go along with it—well, they're the ones who suffer for it."

Layla's eyelids dropped. Her mother withdrew her hand gently from her daughter's shoulder. She went into her room, closed the door behind her, and went immediately to her window. She pressed longingly against the window frame. If only she could get out of this house! The anger welled up inside her body and lay motionless, its vastness caught in her throat, drying out her mouth and tongue. It was an anger that began undefined but soon came to concentrate on the figure of her mother, the sort of ire she used to feel as a child when her mother would hurl her down on her back, pin her to the floor, and open her mouth forcibly to pour in the castor oil. This time it was not her mouth that her mother had opened by force, but rather her eyes. Yes. Her mother had opened her eyes—but onto what?

Onto the world, onto life. "You have no idea what the world is like," her mother had said. She might as well have said, "You will have to learn how to lie and dissimulate, my dear." Of course, those were not the words she had used, but she might as well have. And why not? It was all so simple. Very basic, very clear; and her mother had not batted an eyelid as she spoke. "Because the world demands it. Because life demands it."

What sort of life was this? A life that didn't deserve to be lived, she thought. It was a foolish, trivial sort of life controlled by ridiculous, silly men and women like Samia Hanim and her sister, Dawlat Hanim. Now, *she* was another one. Dawlat Hanim. Layla felt a chill ooze through her body. She closed the window, pressed her forehead to the pane, and decided not to dwell on the subject of Dawlat Hanim. To keep herself from thinking, she began to dream.

Mmm. But where would she meet him? At a dance party, that was it. She would be wearing a white dress just like the one Audrey Hepburn had worn in *Sabrina*, and when he saw her . . . , What a bunch of nonsense. She didn't even know how to dance. Even if she did, it was absolutely clear that she would live and die without going to a single dance party. Fine. Let's change the scenario. At the university? Never. Her father had raised objections even to the thought of Layla starting secondary school, and if it hadn't been for Mahmud she would not have been able to go on with her studies. Let alone the university! During a visit, perhaps? Ugh, not so great, not very romantic at all, she thought. But there was no alternative, no other opportunity she would have. So it must happen during a visit. But where would her mother be at the time? She would be in the parlor with the lady of the house while she, Layla, would wander out into the garden. But she didn't know anyone who had a garden except Samia Hanim and her sisters. No! She could not imagine such a scene unfolding with Sidqi, son of Samia Hanim. But why not? He was elegant. Dark. Tall. He looked a lot like Gregory Peck, in fact. But she did not like his voice, not at all. Or the way he looked at people. There was an artificially arrogant timbre to his voice. And his gaze practically shouted: "Look at me! I'm humble, I'm sweet, I'm democratic by nature." When he had driven them home after their last visit to Samia Hanim, she had sat beside him stiffly, her eyes staring straight ahead, not daring to look his way. When her mother had thanked him, he had said in his pretentious voice while eyeing Layla with a look of amusement on his face, "Any trouble you cause me is a pleasure, *tante*."

She had wanted so much to slap him! No, indeed, the man she imagined, the man who would fall in love with her, the man she would love in turn, would be nothing at all like Sidqi. Nor would he be like her father; in fact, he would not be like any man she had ever met. He would be . . . she didn't know what he would be like, but she knew very well that he would be unlike all the others. And what would he look like? Dark, tall, attractive, strong features, with big, black eyes, like . . . well, for example, like Sidqi, but only in looks. Only that.

Sidqi . . . Sidqi. Hmm. Now, just suppose Sidqi were to fall in love with her. Yes, they would walk into the garden. The light of the moon would shimmer through the tree branches, throwing golden patches onto the garden path; the fragrance of narcissus would encase them. In an unsteady voice from which the usual arrogance had vanished he would say, "Layla . . . ," as he gazed into her eyes. He would sound flustered; his voice would wobble. "Layla, there's something I want to tell you but I don't know where to start." She would simply laugh and run ahead of him, and when he had almost caught up she would whirl her head round and flash him a look out of the corner of her eye.

"What is it you want to say, Sidqi Bey?"

"Please, Layla," he would beg. "Please, stop this Bey business."

She would shrug lightly and bend over the basin of carnations. She would pick one—a red one—and bring it to her nose. Then she would scatter its petals, one by one, tossing them into the air.

"Please, be serious. I love you, I love you, Layla." Then he would take her into his arms and try to kiss her. It would be at this moment that she would shove him away and slap him, hard. The echo of her hand would sound through the whole garden as he put his hand to his cheek.

"I'm sorry," he would murmur. "Layla, I'm sorry, but I just can't control myself."

Her laugh would be full of scorn. "So you think because I'm poor I'm an easy pick-up. You think people with no money have no honor, don't you, Mister Sidqi."

No, no. She couldn't say that. First, none of this happened in real life, it was just Yusuf Wahbi in the movies. Second, maybe she was capable of sounding that eloquent in her room, but she'd never be like that when other people were around. She was a coward, after all, with people. So let's cut that part and go back to the slap and the apology.

"I'm sorry," he would murmur. "Layla, I'm sorry, but I just can't control myself."

He would take her hand, pleading for forgiveness, but his hand would go on, to her arm, up her arm, to her shoulder, and then to her chest, her waist . . . his hand would appraise her, just exactly as Dawlat Hanim's hand had done.

Dawlat Hanim. There she was again.

Layla moved away from the window and paced the room, face hidden behind her hands. It had measured her, that palm, from top to bottom, exactly as if she were a water buffalo up for sale. That woman! Though she had endured tribulations that would shatter a stone, nothing seemed to have made a difference. She was the same as ever—not only her elongated frame and formidable personality, but also her stunning ability to take over everyone within her reach, and then to mold their lives according to her own designs. Not a thing had changed—except her clothes, of course, for now she wore black.

As a child, whenever Layla moved into Dawlat Hanim's circle of vision, the woman would drag her into the strongest available patch of light and study her features closely. With a slap to Layla's thigh, she'd exclaim, "Still a pretty one, you little wretch!" The rest of her words were always meant for the adults clustered around her. "See, Layla's got something attractive about her face, and whenever I see her I have to make sure that it's still there."

She had never gotten angry with the woman, not in those days. Nor had she gotten upset when Dawlat Hanim had said to her, on a day long ago, "Goodness, Layla! Your hair is a scandal, my dear. A little girl like you with such long hair?" The tears had pooled in Layla's eyes when she saw the locks of soft black hair on the floor. But laughter overcame her tears when, the haircut done, Dawlat Hanim said to her, "That's better, now your face shows, you're very pretty now, you little wretch."

No, she had not even gotten angry then. After all, she had loved Dawlat Hanim. When she had come into their sitting room on that day, she had flung herself onto the woman's chest. She had not seen Dawlat Hanim since it had happened.

Sitting on the bed now, Layla found her legs jittering uncontrollably. If only she had not gone into the sitting room that day! But she had wanted to; that time, her mother had not forced her. She had rushed forward of her own accord, wholeheartedly. Layla let the events unfold in her mind's eye, one scene after another, examining each stage as if she took pleasure in self-inflicted pain. Although a whole week had passed since the encounter, it was alive in her imagination down to the tiniest detail.

"Well, my goodness, now, Layla! You've become a real bride—how lovely you are!" Dawlat Hanim had exclaimed. Layla had felt genuinely happy, and had asked for news of Dawlat Hanim's daughter. "How's Sanaa, and—" On the point of uttering Safaa's name—she was so used to coupling it with Sanaa's—she suddenly realized what she had been about to say.

"*Wallahi*, actually Sanaa is in Alexandria with her husband. Just this morning she called me! She was saying—" Dawlat Hanim turned to Layla's mother suddenly. "And by the way, Saniya, what on earth did you do to that groom I fetched for your sister's girl, Gamila? The fellow asked for me yesterday, called me on the telephone . . . ."

Her mother bowed her head. "What can we do? Seems luck isn't on our side, Dawlat Hanim."

"Luck isn't on your side—what do you mean? The fellow's right there, he's ready and willing—so the rejection must have come from your side."

Her mother's tone was contrite. "Truthfully, I don't know what to say, Dawlat Hanim. Samira, my sister, really tried with the girl, tried and tried, but it was no use. A hundred times we must have said to her, 'Honey, the only thing that can shame a man is his pocket.'"

"Enough nonsense. Tomorrow he'll find one far better!" Dawlat Hanim shifted her glance, and her eyes fell on Layla. "Tell you what, Saniya—take him for Layla."

She saw a look of astonishment on her mother's face, replaced quickly by an apologetic smile. "The girl's still little—too young to start thinking about marriage, Dawlat Hanim. She's only seventeen."

"Too young! No one's ever too young. Stand up, Layla."

Sitting on her bed, remembering, Layla swiped her hand in an arc across her face. "Enough," she moaned, her voice audible though she was speaking only to herself. But the scene had imprinted itself on her gaze and refused to vanish; that voice rang in her ears.

She had been standing in the middle of the room, Dawlat Hanim facing her, probing her with a shrewd eye. Pulling her closer, Dawlat Hanim ran her right hand slowly from top to toe, and then from bottom to top, stopping as it crept up to her waist and then again on her chest.

Layla covered her eyes, still sitting on the bed, and whispered, "*Ya Rabb*, Oh God." Although she tried to block it out, Dawlat Hanim's voice echoed in her ears. "The girl has to have a proper dress, one that reveals her shape, and she needs a corset to lift her breasts and keep her middle in. As she is now, she's a disaster." She had faced Layla's mother sternly, and Layla recalled the exact words she had said. "Shame on you! This girl's on the brink of marriage now. And like any girl—if she doesn't dress right, she won't bring any sort of price in the market."

Layla jumped up from the bed. A slave, nothing but a *jariya*! A *jariya* in the slave market! Dressing and adorning herself to raise her price. But why was she so angry? Why so worked up? Wasn't this the truth, after all? But how *could* it be? Yet, it was the truth. This was the way life was; such were the conditions of a girl's life in the society in which she, herself, lived. She would have to accept this situation or die . . . . Die?

Layla sank into the cushions of the Asyuti armchair, hugging her legs to her chest. This was life. Whenever a girl was born, they smiled in resignation. When she began to grow up, they imprisoned her, and trained her in the art—yes, the art of—life! They taught her to smile, to yield to others, to wear perfume, to exude sympathy. And to lie—to wear a corset that would pull in her middle and lift her chest so her price would go up in the market and she could marry. Marry whom? Any old person; after all, "the only thing that can shame a man is his pocket." So she'd put on that white veil, and she would move to the husband's residence, "because that's the way the world works." And everything was just so easy and straightforward and understood by all. But . . . but she would have to be very careful indeed. She must not have feelings or emotions; she must not use her mind, or fall in love. Or else—or else they would kill her, as they had killed Safaa.

Layla shivered and shrunk further into the chair, remembering that when she had voiced this thought, in this very room, her mother had looked at her oddly, as if she were a complete stranger to this home, her mouth dropping open in surprise, before she hurried out of the room without saying a word in response. Layla was nothing less than delighted, though, by what had happened after Dawlat Hanim had left; she was utterly satisfied with every word she had said, and every gesture she had made.

———

It had been one of those very rare occasions when she had dared say precisely what needed to be said. She'd been sprawled across her bed, too drained to cry, without even a thought in her head. Coming in, her mother had said a few words that had seemed to ring in her ears so echoingly that she could not even understand them. Then her mother had grabbed her roughly by the shoulder and given her a violent shake. "What's the matter? Have you gone to sleep?"

She raised her face to meet her mother's. "What's the matter with *you*? Why is your face so yellowish?" Layla dropped her face back into the pillow. Her mother spoke more gently.

"Don't pay any attention to what Dawlat said. You know it is far too early for this talk of marriage."

A layer of tears veiled Layla's eyes. She kept her face in the pillow; her voice was barely audible. "What does she want from me?"

"Who?"

"That woman."

"Why would she want anything from you?"

She sprang up on the bed and faced her mother. "Does she want to kill me like she killed her own daughter?"

"Hold that tongue of yours if you want to keep it!"

She spoke quietly, deliberately, as if merely repeating a widely known fact. "Didn't she kill her daughter?"

"You really don't have any feelings—a poor wretched woman like that, to say such things about her!"

But her mother's words had no visible effect. "Well, isn't it true that she committed suicide?"

"Where did you hear that?"

"I just know. I know why she killed herself, too, Mama—d'you want me to tell you why? Did Dawlat Hanim make her swallow the poison?" Layla lay back on her bed slowly with a sad smile. "She was the one who poisoned her life, and closed the doors of mercy in her face. Safaa had nothing else—no alternative but poison."

Her mouth wide open, Layla's mother stared at her soundlessly, strangely, as if this were the first time she'd ever seen her daughter's face, and hurried from the room.

———

Layla stretched her legs out and leant back into the chair. For three days, her mother had not said a word to her. Three whole days! She knew perfectly well why her mother had been so angry. In the first place it was because she had known about Safaa's suicide, for at the time her mother had simply told her that Safaa "had died." And then she had made it worse by adding, "D'you want me to tell you why she killed herself?"

Her mother was always vigilant about keeping such matters from Layla. But she would hear a word here, a phrase there; she'd gather the stray ends of conversation and weave them together thoughtfully in her mind, which was precisely how she got to know Safaa's story. First, she heard that Safaa had killed herself by swallowing an entire bottle of sleeping pills, which she had been taking to help her sleep in the shadow of a husband whose pocket was the only thing that did not shame him. What Layla did not know then was that Safaa had died on the very night that she had gone in desperation to her mother. Dawlat

Hanim had gone by the rules—by those same "fundamentals" that Layla's mother was so fond of invoking—and had refused to shelter her daughter. She had slammed the door in Safaa's face. So Safaa had returned to her husband's home and killed herself. Layla had learned that later, and still later she learned of the love story, and of Dawlat Hanim's angry reaction; of the request for divorce and the husband's refusal. She learned all of that after a time—a time long enough to have turned that lovely young woman to dust.

And it had not changed Dawlat Hanim in the slightest, even if she was the mother of that lovely young woman. She had gone through the sort of experience that would shred your insides, yet here she was, same as ever. She had grieved over her daughter's death, of course, as any mother would; but had Dawlat Hanim doubted for even a moment the wisdom of her own actions? No, pondered Layla, she had not felt the slightest uncertainty, and neither had anyone else. She walked with head held high, with a firm gait, and she imposed this respectability of hers on others. Lord, what kind of strength was this? What sort of invulnerability did it impose? What sort of self-confidence did it require? And where did people find such abilities—where? Furthermore, why didn't anyone else see this woman's ways through Layla's eyes? Why had their respect for Dawlat Hanim *grown* after her daughter's death? What was the secret? What could the secret of such respect be?

At her wit's end, Layla struck her palms together soundlessly and got up to pace the room. Was it possible that she was wrong? Had she misjudged this woman? Had she been wrong this time, too? Whoever knows the fundamentals cannot go wrong. That's what her mother always said. Cannot go wrong, and cannot—Layla stopped dead in the middle of the room, her eyes widening, her voice coming out in a whisper. "Cannot go wrong, and cannot weaken, and will not lose any confidence in her self." She pressed her lips tightly together, her eyes flashing as if she had suddenly stumbled upon a truth for which she had searched long and hard. And it was such a simple business, the matter that had required all this thinking. So simple! Her mother had known it without having to search far and wide. Whoever knows the fundamentals cannot go wrong. Exactly like . . . like in the game of rummy. If one knew the basic rules of the game, and then stuck to them, and played assuredly, confident through it all that she was doing what was right and proper, she'd never make a mistake. Ever. It wasn't important whether one won or lost, but it was very important to play according to those fundamental rules.

So Dawlat Hanim, playing the game, had killed her daughter. But she had been right to do so for she had followed the basic rules of the game. And that was why people respected her. Layla toppled heavily onto the bed. Their consciences! What about their consciences? Didn't they have any? No, it seemed not. What was important was the appearance of things. What people saw was what counted.

And Mama . . . One day she'd asked her mother, "Mama, couldn't you have just gotten me two dresses instead of three, and then bought me two undershirts? All of my underwear is falling apart." But what was it her mother had said in response? "People don't see your underwear. What's important is a good appearance."

And then *Mahmud* had said—

———

Layla's door flew open and in rushed Mahmud, still in his outdoor clothes. "You're just sitting here, when the whole city's boiling over?!" Layla, well aware of her brother's tendency to exaggerate, just smiled and gave her legs a little shake. "Boiling over with what?"

"The government's gone and cancelled the treaty, the '36 Treaty."

As she jumped to her feet she could feel the blood rushing hotly into her face. "You're joking!"

"Turn on the radio and you'll hear it for yourself!"

She shot into the front room, intent on switching on the radio, but as she passed her brother she stopped with a sudden impulse to fling her arms around him and give him a kiss. But she turned aside as an abrupt shyness came over her, and merely gave him an embarrassed smile.

She could not get to sleep that night. Her whole body pulsed with excitement as she lay on her back, wide awake, as if awaiting something that she was sure would happen.

Chapter Three

The next morning Layla was late getting to school. The bell was already ringing as she arrived. Passing through the main entrance, her demeanor stiffened, as if she were in wary anticipation of some particular event. As she glanced round, though, her features relaxed and she took off at a run. The bell was still ringing, but the pupils had not yet formed themselves into the usual line. Girls were scattered in small knots across the courtyard, and she began to flit from one group to another in some confusion, without knowing why she did so. The words that flew into her ears tumbled directly into her heart; a shiver that began in her feet ran all the way up her body, until it came to concentrate in her head, leaving a prickly feeling down to the ends of her hair.

"Bring down the girls who've gone up to the classrooms! No, no work today, none of the girls will work." "Aliya, go see about the first-year girls, reassure them if they're scared." "Scared? They're all fired up!" "Yes, they're even bolder and braver than the older girls." "We're every bit as ready as the boys are." "Girls, girls—girls have just as many feelings about it all!" "We have to show what we feel!"

The bell rang and rang, supervisors and teachers clapped their hands, but the girls remained scattered in their little groups. Layla found her own friends.

"Come on over here, *Sitt* Layla!" called out Adila. "Come see your cousin, she doesn't want to go!"

Layla looked astonished. "Go? Go where?"

"The demonstration, of course."

"You're all going out there, to join a demonstration?"

"Of course we're going. The whole city's jumping with excitement, all the schools will join in, why shouldn't we show how we feel, too?"

Discussion stopped suddenly as the headmistress appeared in the courtyard, but the bell went on ringing, its shrill urgency outdoing all. The small groups fell together into a single, huge, human mass, each knot of girls bolstering the next, and the shouting rose.

"Down with imperialism! We want weapons—weapons!"

The headmistress approached the microphone. Woman's job was motherhood, she said. Woman's place was in the home, she said. Weapons and fighting were for men.

A stifling silence fell heavily over them, but just for a moment. A dark figure, her short curls bouncing, her shoulders wide and firm, broke the ranks. Her black eyes shone as she crossed the yard and mounted the four steps that divided the students from the headmistress. She stood in front of the woman. Her voice shook as it came through the microphone.

"Our esteemed headmistress says that woman belongs in the home and man belongs in the struggle. I want to say that when the English were killing Egyptians in 1919 they didn't distinguish between women and men. And when the English stole the Egyptians' freedom they didn't distinguish between men and women. And when they plundered the livelihood of so many Egyptians, they didn't stop to think whether *that* belonged to men or to women."

Yells went up from the crowd, and students skittered about, hugging each other. As the voices rose they became one: "Down with the English! Weapons, weapons—we want weapons!

The headmistress stepped back.

"She's great!" Layla said to her friend Sanaa.

"Yeah, that's true toughness. Could you do something like that?"

Layla laughed as she closed her eyes and tried to imagine herself in such a situation. "I wish." Then, a moment later: "What's her name?"

"Samia Zaki. She's in her prep year, science division."

By unspoken agreement Samia was now the leader, and the pupils followed her to the school's main gate. Samia pounded on it and the girls followed her example, but it remained tightly shut. The rhythmic slogans stopped as the would-be demonstrators broke up into groups, gesturing, shouting to each other. But all grew quiet as they heard a muffled commotion in the distance. They listened as it rose gradually into a deafening shout. One girl took the steps at a run.

"It's the boys—the students from Khedive Ismail School."

The girls gathered again into one mass and the shouts rose again in unison, slogans batted back and forth from the boys outside to the girls inside and back again. "No more imperialism!" "Down with the agents of imperialism!" "Weapons, weapons—we want weapons!" "We'll die so Egypt lives forever!" The girls hammered harder and harder on the gate and one of the boys climbed up the school wall. "Get away from the gate," he called. The girls drew back and the gate began to give way under a succession of blows from outside.

"Hurry up, Sanaa," said Adila. Sanaa followed her without even a glance back as the little group parted into two, Layla staying with Gamila, who declared, "I'm not leaving this place." Layla shrugged as she walked forward toward the gate. "Fine, stay. Me, I'm going."

"Layla, you'll have to take responsibility for whatever happens, you know," warned her cousin. "Suppose your family sees you—your father, or Mahmud?"

Layla's lips went pale. "My family, my family! Am I the only one

49

with family?" There was irritation in her voice, but she paused uncertainly, wavering between her solidly planted cousin and the mass of classmates pushing forward.

"Come back," urged Gamila. "Come back, it's better to stay here, this is going to be a mess." But just as she spoke a knot of girls pushed forward into Layla's path as she was trying to step back. She tried to push her way against the human mass that was surging ahead, but the crowd swept her forward with it and the distance between her and Gamila grew. And Layla found herself in the street.

The boys stepped back to clear a space for the girls, who pushed forward to take the lead in the procession. The boys fell in behind them. On either side of Khayrat Street passersby stopped and gathered, the owners of the little shops along the street emerged to watch, and so did the children who peopled the side streets. Faces filled the windows above the street, and balconies were crammed with watching figures. Layla walked on, staring round, fear vying with embarrassment to assail her. She was afraid someone she knew would catch sight of her; she felt an embarrassed shyness about her full body and was sure that every pair of eyes on the street was focusing on her. The rhythmic yells surged like waves and abated, the first wave chased by a second, the pair coming together into one swell. Applause, the watching women's trilling *zagharid*, all of those hands waving, hundreds of eyes sparkling, bodies everywhere, rising and falling in mad leaps. Mouths open wide to shout, drops of sweat glinting on a broad forehead, feet pounding, flags and banners fluttering, tears streaming down, and always the pushing, the pushing, on and on.

Blood pulsed into Layla's head and she felt a surge of energy. She felt alive, at once strong and weightless, as if she were one of those birds circling above. She pushed through the lines and found herself scrambling onto classmates' shoulders, heard herself calling out with a voice that was not her own. It seemed a voice that summoned her whole being, that united the old Layla with her future self and with the collective being of these thousands of people—faces, faces as far as she could see. Then that new voice was lost, caught up in thousands of others, and she slipped down from her perch.

A pair of eyes was drawing her, staring in mute insistence, in an unyielding appeal that enveloped her, to stifle the wells of strength in her body and spirit. She kept moving forward but she felt the eyes follow her with unabated pressure, as if they were aimed at the back of her neck. Layla saw herself at home, at the dinner table, her father's face darker than usual, twisted in anger, his hand out threateningly, her mother's paled lips. A fierce shudder ran through her body and at once her legs felt as though they would collapse. She whipped around. She saw her father. Yes, he was standing there, in that spot where she thought she had seen him, on the pavement at Lazoghli Square, next to the café. Even from here she could see his teeth as he chewed furiously on his lower lip.

Behind her the crowd pushed forward without mercy, pushing her further from her father, his face very dark indeed, and away from the image of her mother, her lips even paler now. Her father vanished from sight and she saw only the crowd of thousands, and herself melting into the whole. Everything around her was propelling her forward, everything, everyone, surrounding her, embracing her, protecting her. She began all of a sudden to shout again, in that voice that belonged to someone else, a voice that joined her whole self to them all.

———

Layla's father was still chewing on his lip as he opened the door. He opened it silently, impassively. He was equally cool as he closed it. Only then did he bring out the slipper concealed behind his back. He tried to throw her to the floor but her mother slipped between them. He pushed his wife away and she stood motionless to one side, her lips quivering. He yanked off Layla's shoes and against her feet sounded the slap of the hard slipper. As it hit against her legs and then her back, Layla could hear that slap mingling with the sound of a woman's laugh on the stairs outside, the screaming of a newborn, and her mother's choked sobbing. She heard her father's voice, shouting at her mother—"shut up!"—and again, the crack of the slippers, one blow after another, a momentary silence between each, a pause, suppressed breathing, then the slap ringing out again. Then there was the rustle of her book bag as she dragged it across the tiles, the squeak of teeth on leather as she clenched the bag in her mouth, her father's steps receding, the sharp sound of his door slamming, her mother's steps coming near, the sensation of her hands punctured by the iciness of the floor tiles as she crawled on hands and feet to her room.

Inside, she braced herself and got to her feet in time to close the door in her mother's face. She turned the key in the lock. She dragged her feet across to the chair that faced the bed and collapsed onto it. She seemed unable to breathe; she put her hand to her neck. She stood up slowly and practically ran across the room, whispering, "Where can I go? I can't possibly stay here." As if blinded, she knocked into her bed, the wardrobe, the chair. Her mother was knocking on the door, tapping, tapping, lightly.

"Open up, Layla." Her voice was a loud whisper. Layla stood still in the middle of the room and covered her face in her hands. "Where can I go? I could close a hundred doors but they still wouldn't go away. They won't leave me alone, they're always there, even right now with the door shut tight. Always there, my father, my mother, always there, bearing down on me, pressing down on my chest to squeeze my lungs to nothing. There isn't a single moment when I can forget, when I can dream, no, not a second when I can just think about anything I want, in any way I want, never a moment just for me, for me. It's always me and them, every single minute, me and them and the truth, the sad, sad truth, me and them, pressing down on me, on my body, on my body stretched out in the living room."

She paced the room. "What can I do? God, what will I do? " And paced. "Kill myself? Then what?" She pictured herself lying on the bed, eyes closed in death, her body rigid, her father pressed against the bed and crying hard, as hard as, well, as . . . a child. And all those people he feared so much were pointing at him and saying, "That's him—the one who killed his daughter." Then her mother's face would grow dark, threatening, and she'd scream at him. "You—you, you killed my daughter."

No. Her mother's face would never darken. She'd never scream at Layla's father. All her life, she would go on walking on tiptoe, her tears streaming down, voiceless, soundless. Layla fell weakly onto the foot of her bed and buried her face in her hands. Why live? Why? She wasn't a human being, she was just a mat, a mat rolled out in the front room, in front of the door, the sort on which people wiped their feet. No one loved her; there was not even anyone there to treat her like a human being. Her mother rapped harder on the door.

"Open up, my dear. Eat a bite, won't you, or at least have something to wet your throat a little? A drink of water, honey—"

Long ago, at the table. Layla, a child. Her father speaking.

"Layla isn't really our daughter. We found her at the entrance to the mosque. Look, Mahmud, even our skin—you and I are light, and so is Mama, but Layla—only Layla has such dark skin." She had stared at her mother, who had laughed.

"We found her in a little bundle, poor miserable thing," her mother had chuckled. "Let's raise her, we said, and get our reward in heaven."

Layla found herself drawing her hand back and hiding it behind herself exactly as she had done when a child. Her mother resumed knocking, lightly, and whispering. "Open, open up, my dear. Layla, come on, you're being silly, its silly to be so stubborn. You're acting like—" Layla swung her legs back and forth, back and forth, and muttered to herself, "Like a dog, an insect, like a mama bear. Papa said when he was in bed sick and I was hugging him, he said, just like a mama bear that hugs her cub so tight he dies."

"Why? Why did you hug him so hard? Why weren't you gentle like he wanted?" Everything she did, she did with her whole heart, she pitched right in, heart and soul, and she always thought that was right, but lo and behold, every time it turned out to be wrong. Everything she did—mistake upon mistake, and now, no one was left to love her. Well, what about at school? If Adila had seen her lying full length on the living room floor, she would have just shrugged her shoulders and said, "That was the wrong thing to do, you know. It was *your* mistake. You didn't speak up when they got on your case, because you're weak. What it all comes down to in the end is that you're just a feeble person."

Layla spoke out loud, her voice wispy, weepy. "What can I do, Adila? What can I possibly do?" Fine. It was true. She was weak, she was feeble, just like her mother. And just like her mother she would remain weak all her life. Her lips would just keep going paler and paler, and her tears would pour out endlessly, without a sound, without a voice.

Her mother's voice came from the other side of the door. "Dear, now, really, must we be so loud that they can hear us all the way to the end of the street? Open up, come on, dear, you'll die of hunger."

"Open the door, Layla," said Mahmud. "Papa's gone out."

Now she noticed that the room had grown dark. She had not turned on the light. The knocking on the door grew louder but still she did not answer. Mahmud sounded exasperated now. "Layla, do we have to break down the door?"

She sat for a moment longer and then got up hesitantly, walked to the door, turned the key, and sat down again, her back to the door. She heard footsteps behind her. The light went on, hurting her eyes, and she raised both hands to shade them.

"Get up, come on now, no more stubborn foolishness," said her mother. "Get up, my dear." Layla lowered her hands and looked wordlessly at her mother, whose eyes held a stunned expression that was now rapidly changing into a look of unqualified disapproval.

"Well, did anyone tell you to do the horrid thing you did? You've scandalized us; you've disgraced us all over the neighborhood. Now, isn't Gamila a girl just like you? Why did *you* have to go and do what you did?"

Mahmud came in, a glass of water in his hand, and brought it over to Layla, who took it without raising her eyes. Her insides churned as the water went down. She doubled over, and her mother reached from behind, bringing her arms around her daughter. Mahmud stood facing the window, his back to Layla. When their mother left the room, he swung round slowly and spoke, flustered, as if he found it difficult to bring up the subject.

"Layla, I'm sorry about what happened. I promise it won't happen again, ever."

Now Layla's tears came streaming, and her lower lip twisted. A wretched look came into her eyes. She shook her head as she spoke. "What's the use? What's the point, Mahmud? I've been killed, that's it, and it's all over. After what happened today, everything has changed, I'm not a person any more, just a mat. A doormat for shoes." Layla covered her face and broke into a wail that shook her whole body. Mahmud came close enough to lay his palm on her shoulder.

"Stop now, Layla, that's enough, c'mon, for my sake. Stop exaggerating."

"It's the truth."

Mahmud didn't speak for a moment, and then only hesitantly. "You know, Layla, the important thing is for you to understand that you were wrong. If you realize that, then you won't be in as much pain as you are right now."

Layla pushed Mahmud's hand away violently and jumped up, her lips trembling.

"You too? You too, Mahmud? You're saying I was wrong?" Her voice ebbed to nothing as she went on, over and over. "You too, Mahmud! You too!"

"Calm down a little, let's talk about this sensibly."

"Sensibly! Where's that sense you're talking about?" I don't understand anything at all, nothing at all. So I'm wrong ... wrong why? I haven't robbed anyone. I haven't killed anyone. I went out in a demonstration with a thousand other girls. All I did was to show what I felt."

Layla paused, as if she were pondering something. She spoke again in a fainter voice, as if addressing only herself. "Wrong. Yes, indeed, I was wrong. I showed what I felt as if I were a real human being. I forgot. I forgot that I'm not a person, I'm only a girl. A woman. Yes, I forgot." She laughed, though it sounded more like a wail, and looked squarely at Mahmud. "Isn't that what you wanted to say, Mahmud?"

"I didn't say anything so stupid, and you know it. You know I respect women. I believe that women are exactly like men." Layla finished his words for him as she flourished her hands in the theatrical posturing of a public speaker. "She has all the rights and bears all the responsibilities." Then she turned to Mahmud with a watery smile. "On paper, right? Right, Mahmud? On paper?"

"Paper—what paper?"

"They're such lovely words, when you see them written down. But when we get serious, when your sister shows what she feels, when she expresses herself like a human being, then all of a sudden she's wrong! Isn't that so? She's wrong, and the mistake becomes bigger than she is—it controls her from head to foot, her whole existence, everything she is."

Mahmud's voice was loud and sharp. "This isn't any way to have a sensible discussion! Calm down a little, and I'll explain it all to you, so you'll understand."

Layla shook her head. "I don't understand anything, Mahmud, I don't get it at all." The strain of anger in her voice had become a tone of despair. "What's right? What's wrong? I don't know whom to believe. Or whom not to believe. Or what to believe, or what not to believe. What should I believe? Who's right?"

Mahmud said nothing.

"So tell me, Mahmud. What should I do?"

She looked at him pleadingly, as if her life depended on how her brother would answer her question. Mahmud's panicky bewilderment showed in his face; how desperately he wanted to make it easier for her with his words! Any words; if only he could lie to her as he had done when she was little, thrusting her little head into his chest. But she was no longer little, he saw; she had grown more, grown older, than he had supposed. He wanted to tell her that it was not her problem, not hers alone anyway; it was his, he wanted to assure her; it was their whole generation's dilemma. But it seemed idiotic to spout grand philosophies when he could see a human being suffering in front of him.

His mother came into the room just then, carrying a platter of food. So Mahmud just mopped his face, and the question remained unanswered, suspended between them in the emptiness. Their mother put the platter down on a small wood table next to the chair.

"Sit down, dear, have a bite to eat. You poor little thing, *wallahi*, a bundle of misery! And now you've brought all sorts of trouble down on your head."

Layla's eyes did not leave Mahmud even to acknowledge her mother's presence. Her insistent wait for her brother's response made him uncomfortable, and when he did finally speak his voice was edgy. "Didn't you hear what she said? Obey her, Layla, sit down and eat."

Layla's eyes flickered shut and then opened to gaze at him again. "Leave the room first, both of you." The mother glanced at her son, waiting to see what he would decide. He beckoned her toward the door and followed her out. As he busied himself with closing the door behind him he deliberately met Layla's stare. Yes, his sister understood. She knew well that he, too, was confused, as bewildered as she was. And every bit as miserable and wretched. He knew what was wrong, what was right, she understood that—but he knew it on paper. Yes, on paper. She stared at the food and then looked away. She turned off the light and felt her way back to the chair.

Layla heard a light tap on her door. It continued, lightly but determinedly, even when she did not respond. Then the door opened and vivid light invaded the room. Isam stood at the door, an abashed smile on his face.

"May I come in?"

She was silent. Isam's smile faded, and he began rubbing his chin furiously.

"Isam, please leave me alone right now. Please."

Isam's face brightened immediately and he stepped into the room. He perched cautiously on the edge of the bed, facing Layla, and leaned forward, clasping his hands around his knees.

"Leave you alone! How can I do that, *ya sitti*, my dear lady—aren't you my little sister?"

Layla began punching the chair, in rhythmic, staccato raps. His sister! His *little sister*! That sentence simply no longer had any power to move her, although she had not forgotten that at one time, as she reached out desperately to be rescued, that expression had saved her. When Mahmud had leapt up in their building's courtyard one day, shouting "Layla isn't my sister! Layla isn't ours!" Isam had quickly faced him down. "Okay, then, she's my sister, she's my little sister." And that was that—end of discussion. I'm Isam's sister, Isam's little sister. From that day on he'd teased her with this title.

Isam sat motionless, his eyes still fixed on Layla. She became aware of her hand striking the chair and withdrew it, slipping her arm down tightly against her body. She slumped back against the chair and rested her head. Isam got to his feet and half sat on the armrest of Layla's chair. He leaned down toward her and put his hand gently to her cheek, stroking it from bottom to top, and pushing back a lock of hair that had fallen across her forehead. Layla held her breath until Isam's hand had completed its circuit. Her heart, beating violently, seemed to plunge all the way to her toes.

"What is this? You don't want to talk to me, *ya sitti*?"

Despite addressing her as an adult, his voice was light, diminutive, a voice to address a little girl—a silly, negligible little girl. Layla felt her head get hot, and she bounded up from the chair as if bitten, turned her back on Isam, and strode to the window. Behind her, Isam laid his hands on her shoulders. She whipped round roughly to face him. "Listen, Isam, I'm not a child—" As angry as her voice was, she left her sentence incomplete as she saw Isam's face convulse as if he were in severe pain. Beads of sweat shone on his forehead, and his breath blew hot onto her face. She felt his body touching hers, and stepped back as far as she could, until she was plastered against the window frame. Isam's features relaxed, his eyes softened, and they glowed in a way that pierced her body, a glow that came to rest somewhere unfathomable inside of her.

Her mother's footsteps broke the moment of stillness between them, a moment when his eyes were on hers and that light coursed deep within her. Isam gave his head a shake, as if he were trying to awaken from a dream. His face reddened and he yanked out his hand-kerchief to wipe his forehead dry. He began rubbing his hand across his chin nervously. As her mother opened the door halfway, Isam turned, without another look at Layla. Still on the other side of the door, her mother stepped back to make way for him. Isam closed the door gently, carefully. Layla heard whispers in the living room, and then she could hear footsteps moving further from her bedroom door. She went over to her mirror and leant her cheek against it. But the pure coldness of the glass did not extinguish whatever it was that flamed like sparks inside her chest. In fact, it seemed to fuel that warmth even more. She ran to the window, flung it wide open, and hung over the windowsill, dipping her head and arms into the air.

How long had the moment lasted? An instant? A whole life? Whatever it was, she had lived it before, every detail of it. When had that been, though? Before her birth, or after it? In reality, or through a dream? As a curtain of haze glided slowly off the moon, Layla felt the light douse her, drifting downward like flowerpetals from her hair and hands. A tremulous gust of cold seemed to lay her body bare to the moonlight. She straightened up, closed the window, and went back to her chair. The sight of the food, forgotten, made her hungry, and she swallowed her dinner ravenously. She shoved her head into a night-gown, turned off the light, and climbed into bed. She slept immediately, and deeply, waking at first dawn.

———

As she came out of her slumber Isam's name was on her tongue. Her eyes stayed closed around his image, as he stood facing her, his eyes focused with a thrilling brilliance on hers. Though lying in bed, she almost felt as if she were living that moment again, and it seemed as though an intense, concentrated beam of light had pierced her body to settle inside. She sighed, stretched, and opened her eyes. She called back to her mind Isam's features, yesterday, in her room, as he gazed at her. She tried to remember what he had looked like a year ago, one month ago, even the week before, but it eluded her. In fact she felt as though she had never set eyes on him before yesterday, when there he was, standing opposite her, looking at her, only yesterday, with his clean-shaven face, in his smart suit, the tones of the very darkest-roast coffee, with his sky-blue necktie and white shirt. Layla slipped her hands under her head, still on the pillow, and smiled. It was all so laugh-able: Isam, who was always there, who had been around her since child-hood, under the same roof—but only yesterday had she *seen* him. And this was another funny thing. How could it be that only yesterday she had seen him? After all, she'd seen him thousands of times, ever since those childhood days when he had played with her. He was the one who had taught her how to count from one to ten, how to write her name in Arabic and English. He was the one who had shielded her from Mahmud when he acted the bossy big brother. As an adolescent, too, she had seen him every day, but even then she had not really *seen* him! Why, when he had come to her yesterday he might as well have been an entirely new being. Or maybe it was just that she had always seen him with eyes other than yesterday's—the heart's eye, the eye . . . well, the eye of love. Layla shot upright in bed, hugged her thighs to her chest and held them there with her arms. Yes, that was it! Love. It really was. "Isam loves me," she whispered, "and I love Isam." She listened intently to the words, to each word in turn; as if they held some magic ingredient, they filled her with a tingling happiness. She repeated the sentence over and over as if it were the refrain to a song, listening to its rhythm in her soul with each repetition, nodding her head to its beat, elated with her discovery.

She felt like she would burst. She tried to shout, to sing, or dance, or skip. She leapt from the bed right into the middle of her room, raced to the window, and jerked the shutters wide open. The yellowness of dawn was already shredding the drear of night. Head upraised, chest open, she breathed in the light, as if she were sucking each ray deep into her body before facing the next.

Suddenly, standing at the window, she saw that a new stage of her life had begun. The world of her dreams had ended and could never return; her father had shattered that world. Now, before her, the world of reality lay open to her gaze. It was not their world, their grievous and restrictive world, a world that tied one down, but rather a world of freedom in which she could love, and love without fear or anxiety, censure or regret. It was her world, hers and his. It would be their world, one that the outer existence of others could neither penetrate nor control nor condemn as wrong. Her world was one in which she could show her feelings and express herself, like a bird flying unconstrained, in the full confidence that she was loved and desired, and yet was respectable too, and that everything she did was reasonable and acceptable.

Layla turned her back to the window and leaned her elbows against the sash, closing her eyes. She began walking the room, bending and swaying as if in a dance; then she stopped and opened her eyes. In the distance the mirror reflected back to her the image of a rosy-cheeked young woman whose eyes gave off a light that was reflected in her lips and cheeks. Yet she suspected that the sun beaming out of the mirror was deceiving her; she ran to the glass and pressed herself against it.

And Layla made a discovery. For the first time in her life it dawned on her that she was attractive, pretty, even. She found herself laughing out loud, all by herself, like a madwoman at the mirror, she thought. She stepped back a bit and tilted her head to one side, resting her temples in her palms. Gradually the waves of laughter rippling through her body stilled.

Chapter Four

Four days passed before Isam made an appearance. Layla waited for him from noon on the first day into the late afternoon, and on into the evening, and then into the second day, and the day following that. But still Isam did not appear.

At first she made all sorts of excuses for him. Perhaps he was ill. Or he had had an argument with Mahmud. But she knew that he was neither sick nor at odds with her brother, and that sooner or later she would have to confront the fact she had been trying to avoid. She understood that Isam was avoiding her—no one else, just her—and when she finally admitted as much to herself, she was overpowered by an excruciating fear. She felt abandoned; she imagined herself alone, in a darkly frightening, forlorn desert. In this remote place she could see no reassuring wall against which to lean; at a moment when she was weak and felt unable to stand on her own feet she espied no one in that empty space on whom she might rely. She felt the ground giving way beneath her, yet she could not even give a glance behind her, for all ties between her and what was back there—all the ties that had linked her to her dreams—were sundered. And staring about her she saw only sullen desert. Yet to stare straight ahead was no help either, for before her lay only an opaque darkness.

Had she been completely wrong? *Hadn't* Isam looked at her that way? And if he hadn't, then why was he staying away? Why avoid her? Had she tried to force Isam to feel a certain way about her? Had she imposed herself on him? But she hadn't said a word! Not a single word! God, what had she done? What had she done, that now she felt so humiliated, so paralyzed by her own puniness? How could she have done something that so disoriented her?

If only she could understand! If she knew the lay of the land her pain might be easier to bear. But try as she might, she could not understand why Isam had invaded her life in this way—and then why he had gone silently on by. She could always go upstairs to her aunt's apartment, of course, where she would certainly see Isam, and she could demand an explanation. But that was not a possibility she could contemplate, even if nothing were to change for a thousand years! She would not try to force someone else's hand; she would never impose herself, never. This feeling of ignominy was bad enough, this sensation of shame that she had had no part in forming. *He* had come to her; and then *he* had gone away.

All around Layla, the world followed its everyday course. She awoke in the morning, and went to bed at night; she went to school, ate, spoke to people, studied. It would astonish her to find herself laughing now and then, and growing enthusiastic from time to time about something or other. The newspapers had begun to argue the necessity of organizing armed struggle in the Suez Canal Zone. Those who wanted to fight could even volunteer now. Mahmud was anxious and nervous, hopping about like a chickpea in a hot skillet, as he suffered the agonies of trying to come to a decision. In every person's heart coiled a desire to be there at the Canal, face to face with the enemy in a battle of life and death. Layla was no exception. But every time this longing captured her heart she found an obscure pleasure in scorning herself. After all—and first of all—she was a girl, and a girl was not really a person. Even if she had been a man she would not be able to go, for she was weak, and the honor of struggling for the sake of Egypt was not the destiny of the weak!

But as she thought about this a confusing idea slyly invaded her thoughts. In the demonstration she had not been weak. In fact, she had felt very strong. She had been nimble and quick, and the crowd had protected and supported her. Even her father had not been able to frighten her then, amidst all those demonstrating people. So . . . ? Yet this thought gave way to others, and she reverted to self-mockery. Her strength—if it really had been strength of any sort—had not come from within her but rather from beyond. And anyway, she chided herself, she couldn't spend the rest of her life marching in a demonstration.

————

The afternoon was drawing to a close as Layla sat with her mother in the living room. Gamila had decided to accept the bridegroom, her mother told her. The engagement ceremony would be held soon.

"But Gamila was with me all day long in school and she didn't say a thing?!"

"Maybe she was afraid she'd hurt you."

Layla stared at her mother. "Hurt me?"

"I mean, because you're the same age, and now she'll be married before you are." Layla wanted to object to her mother's words, but she could not muster strength even for that. She sat silently as her mother recounted the story from start to finish. But as she listened, Layla began to take more than a polite interest, interrupting her mother to ask about details she found hard to accept, or perhaps to understand. The groom was the contractor who had supervised the construction of Dawlat Hanim's home in the new residential area of Doqqi. He'd asked her to please find him a bride, "daughter of a good family," of course, and light-skinned. Dawlat Hanim had thought of Gamila. She had shown him a photo and he had proposed, offering to pay as an advance on the dowry the sum of 300 Egyptian pounds to cover the cost of furnishing four rooms for their future home. Layla's aunt had thought the groom was a real catch; a girl would not be offered such a man more than once, she declared. But her financial circumstances would not allow her to shoulder the expense of a marriage for Gamila, for she and Gamila and Isam lived entirely on the pension that her late husband had left. The costs of Isam's medical school education "have just about broken me," she wailed, and "prices have climbed like wildfire." But she had not been frank about any of this at the start; after all, "one has one's self-respect, you know." Instead, said Layla's mother, Umm Gamila had explained that the girl was still young. But she had not said anything that would cut off the lines of communication with the groom, and she had Dawlat Hanim's abilities as an intermediary to count on. In fact, she'd tried deliberately and carefully to make sure that the tie grew stronger, too strong to cut. But Dawlat Hanim's patience had worn thin and Umm Gamila was forced to tell her the truth, admitting it tearfully. And the matchmaker took it upon herself to arrange everything. She took Gamila to Cicurel, the department store downtown where all the best people went. She bought her a dress of pink lace. From Cicurel they went on to the coiffeur, where Dawlat supervised Gamila's new hairdo and makeup. From there they went to Dawlat Hanim's home, where the bridegroom was waiting.

That was the turning point. When the groom saw Gamila before him, face to face, flesh and blood—"it's just not the same as a picture to see her in the flesh"—he fell for her, and he fell hard—"he fell in up to his ears," as Umm Layla put it so gleefully.

What was beyond dispute, though, was that Gamila did not fall in up to her ears, at least not at first. She told Layla that the groom was an old man, and he was vulgar, and he had a potbelly. But gradually things changed. The groom took Gamila and her mother home in his Ford, and on the way he showed them his villa out on the new and flashy Pyramids Road. He would empty the villa of its tenants, he said, so that the bride could move in. Gamila's head began to spin.

But Gamila's mother had not solved her problem. How was she to furnish four rooms with only three hundred pounds? Not to mention the garments that Gamila would have to have, and the nightgowns, and then the underclothes, and the rest. But she did not ponder the problem for very long. The next day Dawlat Hanim visited her to say that "the fellow is crazy about Gamila, he can't sleep through the night!" And that from his respect and desire to honor Gamila he proposed to furnish the house completely out of his own pocket, and to supply the kitchen with all it needed, too, including a Frigidaire and a gas stove. Moreover, he would still pay the dowry he had proposed, that three hundred pounds.

Well, said Umm Layla, the world was not vast enough to contain her sister's delight. She began "filling the girl's ear all the time; it doesn't hurt, you know, to let her hear it." Layla leaned her head back against the chair, imagining her aunt "chewing Gamila's ear off," as her mother put it. She could see in her mind's eye the image of her aunt: her full body, that glowing dark skin, her carefully coiffed hair, the delicate and kindly features. She envisioned her aunt, bending over Gamila, kissing her, giving her a hug, teasing her as if she were still a little girl, and at the same time imprisoning her in her bewitching kisses, smothering her with loving concern. Layla smiled lightly. She knew her aunt's ways. She knew them very well. Her aunt and her mother resembled each other only in their looks; in every other way, they could not have been more different. Aunt Samira was cleverer in the art of life; she always knew exactly what she wanted, and she got it, too, through her gentle persuasiveness, her kisses, and her affection. Perhaps Layla's mother knew what she wanted, at least some of the time, but she did not always get it. Her strategies were the reverse of her sister's: she mounted open attacks; she said exactly what she wanted; she reproached, and denounced, and lashed out. Aunt Samira, on the other hand, never said precisely what it was that she hoped for. She might hint, or make her desires known in a roundabout manner, now and then dropping a word to the wise, hemming and hawing and hedging. When she met resistance she would make a provisional retreat, just a step back, in order to regroup and advance once again. If Gamila said, "No, Mama, I don't like him, I don't want to marry him," she responded simply. "Fine, then forget about it, honey. All I want is to be sure that you are happy." A while later she would fling an offhand comment in Gamila's direction, about so-and-so, that girl who'd married for love but then had failed in her marriage, because after all, material security was the foundation of every successful union. Another time, she would say to her daughter, "Gigi, I just want you to have the finest automobile in town, the best dresses; you're so pretty, you're *gamila*, Gigi, and what a loss if such beauty goes to waste, my dear."

"Clever indeed," pronounced Layla's mother, pulling Layla from her reverie.

"Who?"

"My sister Samira, your aunt, she's so smart! She knows how to keep that girl under her wing. And the girl as well—*her* mind went to pieces when she heard this talk about the solitaire ring."

"What solitaire?"

"The groom—may your future hold the like—is going to get her a solitaire, and—" A rap sounded against the front door. Layla got up to open it. Sayyida, her aunt's maid, raised her sturdy face to Layla, her full lips opening in a smile.

"The young mistress says, 'Please come up for a bit.'" She gave Layla a folded piece of paper, which Layla opened. "Sanaa and Adila are here," she read. "I wish you would come up. And if you don't, I'll come down to get you. Kisses and hugs."

"Wait a minute," she said to Sayyida as the girl was closing the door. She grabbed a piece of paper and a pen and began to write, her face suddenly gloomy.

"Why don't you want to go up?" her mother asked.

"Headache."

"You know what they're going to say—it's jealousy! Do you want that?"

Layla chewed on her lip and bit back a flood of curses rushing through her head.

"Me? Me, jealous?!"

"Then go up and congratulate your aunt and the girl."

Torn, Layla stood in the middle of the room. She did not want to see Isam. Yet she could not cut herself off completely from her aunt, especially since if she did it would be explained in such a ridiculous manner, following on Gamila's engagement. Anyway, no doubt he was still out somewhere with Mahmud. If she did see him, if he was there, she would simply treat him in an ordinary fashion, just as if nothing at all had happened between them.

She opened the door and called out to Sayyida. "Okay, Sayyida, tell her I'll be there in a minute." Sayyida walked off slowly, moving her hips extravagantly from side to side.

Layla stood before her wardrobe. Without consciously choosing it, she stretched out her hand toward her prettiest dress, the one as red as the inside of a ripe watermelon. Aunt Samira had declared that it set off the loveliness of her skin beautifully. No, she wouldn't wear that one; she would not pretty herself up at all for him. She would make no effort whatsoever to get him back. She took her hand away from the dress and picked out a rose-colored blouse and plain black skirt. She ran a comb hurriedly through her short hair and climbed the stairs to her aunt's apartment. She rang the bell.

Dressed to go out, Isam opened the door. In that striped navy blue suit of which he was so proud, he stood motionless, blocking the doorway as if he did not want her to come in. Layla forgot completely how determined she had been to treat him in an ordinary way. The moment she saw him her face fell into a frown and she averted her eyes as he finally stepped back and she slunk into the sitting room.

"Layla." Isam called after her in a loud whisper. Turning to face him, she noticed a strange expression in his eyes. It was a look she had never seen in anyone's eyes, the demeanor of a creature trapped and in pain, of a wounded animal. She could feel tears well suddenly in her eyes and she closed them, biting her lip to keep from crying. She turned back but he restrained her with a gentle hand on her shoulder, as if she were a fragile thing that he feared would shatter at a touch. By the time she turned to face him again, his face had relaxed and his eyes had grown softer, gleaming with a light that transfixed her body and settled somewhere inside. With her sleeve she quickly wiped away the two lone tears that ran down her face, shook her head confusedly, opened the door to the sitting room, and went in.

—

The door to the sitting room had just shut in his face, but Isam did not move away from it. No. No, she could not simply leave him like that—and with tears in her eyes, too. It wasn't possible; she must still be here with him, in his body, his blood, his arms. She was here—her tears wiped away by his kisses, her cheeks, her fine, rosy mouth, slightly open like a budding flower. Isam felt the blood hot in his veins, massing at the back of his head, as if Layla really was pressed to his chest and he was kissing her, his kisses dissolving the deprivation that had lasted four whole days, and assuaging the fever of those four days, too. Yes—he was kissing her, ecstasy, madness, without pause: the curve of that mouth, the curves on that chest, the curved surfaces of that body. Isam shook his head, emerging from his dreamlike state. His face glowed like a beet. He sat down in the front hall, his eyes fixed on the door to the sitting room. He was filthy! How could he even dare to think about her in this way, as if she were . . . as if she were a cheap woman he might stare at in the streets? When she was the daughter of his aunt, the sister of Mahmud. And when her face was still that of a child, or a mother; the face of a sister, a face that would turn the very Devil away from evil. But he had not been able to stop thinking about her once during those four days, thinking about her in this dirty, shameful way.

That day, when his body had touched hers next to the window, he had felt a sudden pang, a sharp pain as if a knife had gone into his back suddenly, and then ... then she had looked at him, and ... and he'd turned back into a child, feeling once again those same pleasurable sensations, those peaceful feelings of contentment that he had not felt for many years—a sensation still familiar from childhood, from that time long ago when his mother's kind face would appear over his bed every night, descending close to his, and his body would bask in a tranquillity that lulled him. It was a pacific state the like of which he had not experienced since, and its sudden return gave him to understand, with an abrupt awareness, that his life was now bound irretrievably to that young woman, that pretty young woman who had stood facing him. Linked forever. Forever.

How had he left the room that day, he wondered later? He had no idea. How had he managed to listen to Mahmud's chattering, and then how had he found his way back to his apartment? He couldn't imagine. Had he walked or flown?

Lying in bed, he felt Layla's presence. In his heart, in his blood, in his body—she was everywhere. But he felt tormented, too, by sensations that somehow, in their unfathomable nature, interfered with his happiness as they thwarted his desire. Lying in bed, his thoughts turned back to Layla, or rather to Layla's body. Here he was, thinking about her again in this filthy, disgraceful way, as if she were no more than ... than a woman encountered in the street. As the agonizing sensations that flooded his body floated slowly to the surface, their outlines became clearer. Isam understood that he was in a painful and consuming dilemma. He could marry Layla—but when? It would be years, long years—after graduation, and after a year's internship, and perhaps not until long after that, once he could stand on his own feet financially. And what about those many long years? His desire, indistinguishable from the yearning one might feel for a mere woman glimpsed on the street, would wrong Layla. His longings would be an outrage against Mahmud and his aunt, too, and against his own mother and sister. For years and years, he would be dishonoring all of the moral values and standards he knew.

For the principles he had been taught—and in which he believed—decreed that two types of women existed in the world. There was the sort in the street, the sort that sparked desire, and then there were mothers, sisters, wives. Any woman for whom he felt desire must be cheap, something to be had that lost its value as that desire vanished. Such a female was prey to be hunted, a thing that a man would pursue and triumph over, taking his booty as happened in any war and parading his pride before others. A man did not feel desire for his aunt's daughter, not even for the sister of a friend, not if one was a proper, polite person. Desire was to do with the body, and bodies were soiled. Nothing, in fact, could be filthier or lower.

Isam's sleep that night was troubled. He tossed as if his bed were an angry sea, waking repeatedly, always to one dream. It tormented and pained him, stupid dream though it was, meaningless yet frightening. As he fled through dark lanes and alleys that appeared abandoned and ferocious, he knew some sort of danger threatened him. He did not understand its import but he was conscious that it was gaining on him steadily. He burst into a broad open space in which stood a group of women, and the sight told him that he was safe now. But he hurried on, cutting a path through the mass of women; once surrounded by them, he fell to the ground in exhaustion.

He was able to look around, and he found his clothing soaked in blood; he saw the eyes of a dead man chasing him, eyes slashing open his head and chest, ripping through his body as if they were sharp nails. The corpse turned, faced him, beckoned him over. It was Mahmud. The blood was his. Isam tried to back away, but the women held him so tightly he could not move. They were nodding at him, their faces suffused with anger, one just like the next, identical faces in fact, the face of . . . of . . . of his mother. With an effort he cleared a path through their midst and now he did back away. But they chased him, they matched his pace, step for step, faces crowding in, fingers trained on his face and chest, poking his body, sharp nails everywhere. Isam wheeled round to find himself on the edge of a deep precipice whose darkness yawned, as the women moved forward, closer and closer, step by step.

Isam shrieked, and bolted up from his uneasy sleep.

The next morning he had made a decision. He would avoid Layla completely. He would consign his feelings to the grave. It would be easier, he also decided, if he were to strengthen his relationship with Inayat, his classmate at the College of Medicine. At the moment that relationship went no further than finding a mutual pleasure in each other's company, but he was quite sure that there were possibilities. He had often felt that her big, black eyes were sending him a message, promising certain things. She might go out with him if he were to ask. She might even allow him to kiss her. Inayat was pretty, he had to admit: her black hair that she let fall in locks across her forehead, her slim waist . . . in fact, she was undeniably one of the most gorgeous females in the College of Medicine. She had been pretty since high school days, prettiest among the Saniya School girls even then.

He was able to hold steadfastly to his decision for four entire days. But now here he was, sitting in the front hall, his eyes and ears—and all of him—spellbound by that door to the sitting room. He was supposed to have left the house by now; there was a tea reception at the college and he was to have met Inayat, as they had agreed. But he hadn't gone. Although he had duly dressed for it, he found himself incapable of leaving. And here he was now, sitting in the same place, as if lashed to the sitting room door by magical ropes. He could not move; he had no desire to move. He waited in patience, as if created to do nothing but wait. Yes, he existed only to wait for her, until the moment when she would appear in the door, coming to him; the moment when she would look at him with her deep eyes, encase him in her gentle loveliness, and return to his heart and body that serenity he had never experienced until those bright eyes had looked at him in that particular way she had.

He heard her voice. "Just a minute. I'll pop in to say hello to my aunt and then we can go." She came out of the room, Gamila close behind, and walked right by without a glance.

"Hey, Isam, you mean you haven't left yet?" asked his sister.

"I have a slight headache," he said shortly, not wishing to encourage anyone to prolong the discussion.

"Well, come in here, then." He followed Gamila into the corridor and toward his mother's bedroom where, he saw, his mother was kissing Layla.

"May you have the same luck soon, honey," she was saying. She caught sight of her son. "My dear, you didn't go out? What happened?"

It was Gamila who answered, as she held out her hand, cupping the aspirin. "He has a bit of a headache. Here's the aspirin, Isam. I'll bring you some water." She left the room.

Isam strode to his mother's chair. Layla, perched on the bed, was facing him. She seemed determined to avoid his unwavering stare. Isam's mother took up a half-finished piece of Aubusson-style needlework. "What do you think of the design, Layla? For Gamila's parlor?"

Layla studied the colors. "It's lovely, Aunt Samira, and the stitching is very fine. You're amazing." She got up to hand the piece back to her aunt, who grabbed her playfully, pulling her close for an affectionate kiss. When Layla raised her eyes they met Isam's, but she quickly turned her head completely away.

"Do you know, Isam," said his mother, "do you know who Layla reminds me of? She makes me think of myself when I was her age, she looks exactly like I did."

Isam smiled. His eyes flickered shut but he returned to gazing steadily at Layla, who was looking at her aunt. Her eyes roved to study the elegantly furnished room.

"That's absurd, Aunt—how could I be as pretty as you? I'm not chic at all or clever either!"

"Now, Layla! You resemble me more than Gamila does. You should have been my daughter, not my sister Saniya's girl." Gamila heard half of this conversation as she entered carrying a glass of water, which she handed to Isam as she broke in.

"What are you talking about? I suppose you're sitting around praising each other to the skies, hmmm?"

Raising aspirin and glass to his mouth, Isam stopped in midair as Layla gave him a sad, questioning look—a reproof, he knew. He gulped the water down and turned to put the glass on a nearby table, deliberately keeping his back to them until he could get hold of himself.

"Excuse me please, Aunt," said Layla.

"Why are you in such a hurry, my dear?"

"I'm leaving with Sanaa and Adila."

Isam turned, a smile on his face. "So, Sanaa and Adila have an errand, but what about you? What do you have to do?"

"You tell her, Isam!" said Gamila. Layla did not look at Isam; her eyes stopped on his necktie.

"Never mind, Gamila. Another time."

———

When the elevator paused opposite Layla's door, she tried to persuade Adila and Sanaa to come in, but Adila protested that it was late. Layla would not be deterred. "Just ten minutes, Adila, come on, please! I want to get your opinion about something."

"Then, go ahead and ask me right now."

"No-o-o—inside."

So the three friends sat down in a corner of the gilt-furnished sitting room. Layla made sure the door was closed and only then spoke.

"Did Gamila tell you this morning about this engagement business?"

"Is *that* your question? You really are a goose! Of course she told us. Otherwise why would we have come to see her? Didn't we come to congratulate her?"

"I mean, I want to know, why was it hidden from me? Why me, in particular?"

Adila jutted her long neck forward and gave the armrest a series of quick taps. Her wide, jet-black eyes studied Layla knowingly. "*That's* your question? Okay, *ya sitti*, I'll explain it all to you. Gamila knew that if she said something to you directly, you'd have sat there philosophizing, going on and on as you always do. The proverb, you know, says, 'Close the door from whence the wind comes and rest.'"

Layla laughed with a shrug. "What do I have to do with it? Why would I go on about it? As long as he pleases her, fine, congratulations to her!"

"What don't you like about him, Layla? Now tell me, what is it?" asked Sanaa.

Layla was silent. Adila stood up, clamped her hands on her hips, and bent forward toward Layla as if to interrogate her. "Is his pocket empty?"

Layla smiled. "It's very full!"

"Does he have a car?"

"Ford."

"And the villa?"

"The Pyramids Road."

Adila flicked her hand toward the ceiling in offhand despair. "Oh please, Layla! All of that and you still don't want her to take him? You've always let the best things pass you by."

Layla smiled. "Sanaa," she asked, "why are you so quiet? Help me out, why don't you!"

Sanaa's delicate lips were turned down in a pout, and she poked her small nose into the air as she queried Adila. "Does she love him?"

Adila put her hand to her head in a theatrical movement that said the question was making her dizzy. "Stop it!" She glared at Sanaa. "This is a marriage, stupid, not a novel."

Layla laughed so hard that tears glinted in her eyes. Sanaa pressed her lips together, trying to conceal her smile, and widened her eyes in feigned astonishment. "So how can she marry him, then?"

Adila knew her friends well. "Get up, you pitiful creature! Come on, let's go."

Sanaa didn't move. "On the Prophet's honor, Adila, how will she go through with this?"

Adila flipped her palm up in a gesture of futility. "You really want to make me say something impudent, don't you? How will she go through with it? Like people do—like your mother when she married your dad."

Sanaa's hand copied Adila's as she shrugged. "Without any love, with no feelings, no desire, no—"

Adila sat down again as she interrupted Sanaa. "Okay, okay, that's enough, you don't have to go through the whole litany—don't we know them all off by heart?"

"It's no joke, Adila," said Layla. "Are *you* just like your mother? Do you think exactly the way she does? Your mother married without love because she could not do anything else. She wasn't in a position to choose. And anyway, if she *had* chosen, she wouldn't have been able to marry the man she chose. Our mothers were the harem—things possessed by their fathers, who passed them on to husbands. But us?—we don't have any excuses. Education—we've gotten that, and we understand everything, and we are the ones who have to decide our own futures. Even animals choose their mates!"

Sanaa gave Layla a loud, enthusiastic slap on the back. "*Ya bitt ya gamda!* What a girl! That's what I like to hear!"

"So who said Gamila didn't choose?" asked Adila coldly.

They could not miss the distress in Layla's expressive eyes. "No, Adila, no. Gamila didn't choose. It was Gamila's mother who decided, and the folks around her, and all their tired old ideas. And—"

Sanaa chimed in. "—And the goods on the lovely man. Son of a good family, a real plum, seemly and solid and reeking with money, no relatives alive to come sniffing around, doesn't get potted, doesn't smoke."

"Don't be so stupid!" said Adila. "You've got to realize that people aren't all alike. Gamila has an idea about what marriage is and she's trying to make it come true. Gamila *wants* the car, she wants that Frigidaire, and the solitaire, and—"

Now Sanaa finished for her. "And the customer who pays the most, right?"

"Gamila wants all these things, yes," interjected Layla. "Because people have told her they're important, they've taught her that a person's value is in the things he owns, that you're not respectable unless you're rich."

"That's not all, though," protested Sanaa. "There's more to it, you know. Didn't Gamila want to marry someone else?"

"Someone else who?" asked Adila.

Adila didn't know anything about Gamila and Mamduh, Layla realized, and it was not a subject that she wanted to broach. "That was just a bunch of talk."

Silence held them for a while. It was Layla who spoke up, first, her voice gloomy. "You know the story of Safaa? I can't get it out of my head. It just convinces me all the more that no girl these days can possibly live the way her mother did."

"The whole mentality has changed," said Sanaa. "There's no doubt about that. For our mothers, marriage was a fate written on their foreheads from the day they were born. No one could change it in the slightest or escape it. You had to accept it as it was. For us the situation is so different, because the harem mentality has changed. Today's girl doesn't accept what her mother took as a given."

"Okay, Your Excellency the Grand Mufti of Islam, now get up and let's go," said Adila. Come on, because its nearly eight o'clock, and your mother will be waiting for you with a cane in her hand."

Laughing, Sanaa got to her feet. Adila stood in the middle of the room and declaimed in a tone of heavy sarcasm, "*Wallahi*, we're the ones in a real bind! At the very least our mothers knew exactly what their circumstances were. But we're lost. We don't understand—are we the harem or not? We don't know whether love is *haram*, prohibited by our religion, or permitted, *halal*. Our families say it's *haram* while the state radio day and night sings love love love, and books tell a girl, 'Go on, you're free and independent,' and if a girl believes *that* she's got a disaster on her hands and her reputation will go to hell—now honestly, is that any kind of situation to be in? Really and truly, now, aren't we pathetic souls?"

Layla closed her eyes. Her lower lip trembled, and on the edge of the chair her finger sketched hard lines that intersected and clashed.

"Hurry up, let's get going," said Adila. "I think you've both philosophized enough for today."

Sanaa laughed again. "And you just sat quietly the whole time and didn't do any grand debating?"

Adila shrugged, smiling. "I mean to say, I don't have the stomach for it. You've been back-and-forthing about things that are already decided for us anyway."

Layla stood up to wish them goodbye. She stayed on her feet until they disappeared from view down the stairs. She closed the front door slowly and headed for her room, but paused in front of her door. No. No . . . she really didn't want to shut herself in alone. So she turned back and went into the sitting room where her mother, hunched over the sewing machine, worked on a nightgown for her daughter.

Her mother lifted her eyes from the cloth. "They've left?"

"Yes, they're gone."

She noticed the lines on her mother's face soften immediately, and smiled inwardly. Her mother was never at ease until all of the guests were gone, no matter whom they were. Layla sat down beside her and reached for a book on the nearby end table. She riffled through it until she found the page where she had stopped earlier in the day. As she read, the sewing machine caught her ears, the steady drone punctuated by an intermittent staccato.

Chapter Five

The doorbell rang. Nabawiya ran to the door. As the maid opened it, they heard footsteps in the hall and Layla's mother raised her eyes uneasily. But her tense features loosened immediately, for Isam stood hesitantly on the threshold, an embarrassed smile on his face.

"Come on in, Isam," said Layla's mother.

"Um—Mahmud isn't back yet?"

"He'll be here any time. Come in."

Isam sat down opposite Layla and her mother. Layla hid her face in the book and pretended to read.

"Congratulations. May you be as lucky as Gamila," said her mother, and went back to work. They were all silent, interrupted only by the sound of the sewing machine. Isam fixed his eyes on Layla. She kept her eyes on her book.

"What are you reading?"

Layla pushed the book away from her face. "A book by Salama Musa," she said, a bit sourly.

He gave her his familiar half-smile. "Why Salama Musa in particular?"

"I found it in Mahmud's library."

"If you want to read old books there are the books of . . . " Isam mentioned a writer.

"I've read him. But Salama Musa's better."

He leaned forward in his chair, speaking to her from across the room.

"Better in what way?"

"Salama Musa says exactly what he wants to say, right away, but the other one beats around the bush, and says I don't know what all before he gets around to making his point." Layla stared straight at Isam and his face reddened as he rubbed his chin and then smiled.

"Layla, you're still young, you don't understand that sometimes there are circumstances that lead a writer to speak indirectly."

The sewing machine stopped. "When's the big day, God willing?"

Isam turned to Layla's mother, a look of confusion in his eyes as if he'd been caught red-handed. "Ummm—the bridegroom wants it sooner rather than later, but my view is that the engagement is enough for now, and then the wedding can happen after she's gotten her high school diploma."

"Of course, that's my girl, Gamila! After all that hard work, what a shame it would be to leave school without a diploma!" The sound of the machine rose again.

"You mean, Gamila won't go to university?" asked Layla.

Isam smiled. "And you *will?*"

"Why wouldn't I go?"

"What use would it be? Every girl's future is marriage."

Layla's mother stopped the machine again, her sweet, short laugh replacing its hum. "Bless your soul. You've always been smart. Not like this crazy little girl and her brother."

Layla began tracing parallel lines down her dress. She raised her head. "You know, Isam, I didn't realize you were such a reactionary." Her voice was grave. The thread escaped the needle and her mother concentrated on rethreading it.

"I'm not a reactionary, Layla. But I live at the university and I know the conditions of being a student there very well. I wouldn't feel happy about my sister being there. Or you. And anyway, you—" His lower lip quivered, his eyes clouding with an anguish that reflected the imprisoned desire trembling deep inside, a yearning to melt into this young woman who sat before him. The thread poked through the eye of the needle and Umm Layla's face lost its tightness. A wave of pleasurable agitation swept through Layla, for she had seen Isam's emotions in his gaze. Tears in her eyes, she snatched up the book that lay open at her side with a semblance of eagerness and masked her face with it.

"I'll call for tea, Isam," said her mother. Once again her words caught him unawares and he spoke in confusion. "Don't go to the trouble, Aunt."

"It's no trouble, I'm getting up anyway."

Isam turned his head to watch until he could be certain that his aunt had disappeared. He hesitated a moment, fidgeting in his seat, and then got up and walked toward Layla, her face still hidden in the book. He stopped at a distance.

"Layla—"

The book tumbled from her hands and she bent to retrieve it, his choked, thick voice in her ears. Slowly she raised her head toward Isam. Now she called to him—her parted lips, her pink cheeks, her eyes throwing an arc of light. Isam came nearer as if pulled to her by some sort of terrific, irresistible force.

"You know, don't you? You know without me saying anything."

Layla couldn't speak. She compressed her lips in an almost-smile, closed her eyes, and nodded again and again. Then she opened her eyes suddenly to their widest stare as a thought she could not repress checked the happiness that had overwhelmed her. She jumped to her feet. "But you didn't come, Isam. All this time, so many days. You weren't . . . here. Why? Isam?" Isam could not bear the obvious desolation on her face, and his arms reached for her. He so wanted to reassure her, to make her understand that he couldn't—even if he had wanted to—he simply could not stay away from her. But his arms stopped in midair and flopped heavily to his sides. He turned his face away. "I was afraid, Layla."

Layla's hand fluttered uncertainly to her own chest. "Afraid—of me? Of me?"

He smiled, looking at her tenderly. "Afraid *for* you."

"From what?"

He hesitated. "From myself, and people, and circumstances, and—well, to be honest, I don't know how to explain it so you would understand, Layla."

"People—what have they got to do with it, or with us? No, I don't understand anything, Isam, nothing at all, and—" Layla stopped at her mother's footfall outside the door. Isam turned to the sewing machine and pretended to inspect the fabric. Heading for the machine, her mother spoke. "What don't you understand, Layla?"

"Oh! a passage in the book," mumbled Layla. "I can't understand what it means."

Her mother sat down to the sewing machine. "Then why don't you let Isam explain it to you?" Layla's consternation vanished. She tilted her head with a sly grin. "Isam doesn't want to help me understand." Isam hid his own smile as he looked at his aunt.

"Did I say no, Aunt?"

"Of course not, dear! All your life, such a fine boy, you've always helped her understand things. Not Mahmud, who doesn't have the patience."

Layla stamped her foot, her eyes glittering with naughtiness. "It's even worse than that, Mama! *He* doesn't understand—he doesn't know how to explain it to me." She broke out laughing and Isam turned to her. How he wished he could give her a hug, could press that laughing face to his chest and stifle those chuckles with one kiss after another! He wanted so much to hold her, to envelop her, to make her disappear into himself, so that she wouldn't laugh at his expense, wouldn't laugh at all except with him. And wouldn't—He heard the sound of a key in the outside door. Layla swallowed her laughter. Isam blushed and slunk to the chair he had occupied earlier.

———

Striding into the room, Mahmud pumped Isam's hand as if they had been apart for years. He gave his mother little pecks on her mouth, across her forehead, over her cheeks, while she tried to fend him off. "Mahmud, you should be ashamed!" Her face was as bright as if she were still a girl of fourteen, and her hand went distractedly over her dark hair, shot through with little streaks of silver. Mahmud protested loudly. "What? You mean a guy can't kiss his mama either? Then who can he kiss?! What do you think, Isam?"

Layla could tell, gazing at her brother's face, that he had gotten over his anxiety. He must have made a decision. She sat down, her eyes still focused upon him.

"Well," said Isam, "you're certainly in good form today."

"Decisions, professor. Serious decisions."

A tremor ran through Layla and right into her head. Mahmud would go to the Canal. To the Canal! The words rang through her brain as if they were an anthem, and a swell of pride poured through her body, followed by waves of affection and then fear. She jumped up and rushed over to Mahmud, her eyes shining. She wanted to hug and kiss him, but suddenly she swerved away from him in embarrassment and spoke instead in a shaky voice, without even looking his way. "Shall I make you some tea, Mahmud?"

Layla knew, Mahmud realized. Trying to hide his reaction, he tugged at her hair, yanking her head to his shoulder. "In awhile, Layla, in awhile."

Layla sat down again. "Was the reception good?" Isam asked his friend.

"What reception?—this is no time for parties! I don't have time to think of such nonsense. But by the way, you left the college without even a 'so long.'"

"I was tired."

"Tired—or was it just so you could come and get dressed and make yourself dandy for the reception?"

"As you can see, I didn't go."

"Then what's all this elegance for?"

"I was going to go, and then I changed my mind."

Mahmud grinned slyly. "But our lovely friend will be angry—she'll really be mad."

Isam noticed that Layla was looking at him, and he could feel his face going red. "Mahmud, you're going to make a mess of things."

Mahmud lifted his shoulders and arms in a gesture of feigned innocence. "Did I say anything? I'll change my clothes and join you. I have some serious news." He left the room.

Layla sat in silence, her face frozen, while her mother went back to her sewing. The machine whirred, echoing in Layla's ears, its sound rising gradually to become a hammer pounding hard inside her head. She bolted up from her chair, her eyes on Isam, who turned his head away. The machine shrilled, the hammer blows knocked insistently, violently, and the blood rose in Layla's body, collecting in her head as she stepped toward Isam, her back to her mother. Her lips formed words and her hands supported those voiceless words with flourishes.

"Who is she? *Who* is she?"

Isam shut his eyes. She's crazy—her mother might turn around at any moment, or Mahmud might walk in. What can I do? What can I do with this crazy girl?

The machine stopped. Layla shook her head as if waking up.

"Now run along, my dear, go see how the tea is doing," said her mother. "It must be ready—it doesn't need stewing!" But at that moment the maid came in, and set the tea tray down on a little table

86

in front of Isam. Layla went back to her chair, her face immobile again. Isam gave her a surreptitious peek. The expression in her eyes confirmed that he was not yet out of danger. He poured a cup of tea and carried it over to the machine, where he carefully put it down. "Have some tea, Aunt."

"No, you have it, Isam. I'm not having anything right now."

Isam dragged over a rattan chair and sat drinking his tea in his aunt's protective shadow. The wheel of the sewing machine began once again to turn; the hammer took up its pounding inside Layla's head and all of her blood seemed to clot there. With a shaking hand she yanked a page from the notebook beside her, found a pencil, wrote something, folded the page. As she stood up, the cup in Isam's hand stopped moving. Layla passed close in front of him, her face on her mother, and bent over the sewing machine as if searching for something.

"What are you looking for?" From beneath the machine the bit of paper fell right into Isam's left hand while Layla straightened up and returned to her place, clutching the scissors. The paper burned like a tiny ice cube in Isam's hand. For a moment he remained hunched over, not daring to open it. Then he put his hand under the machine and read: Who is she? What kind of relationship do you have? Answer right now or I will ask you in front of everybody in this house.

Isam looked at Layla, trimming her fingernails in seeming obliviousness to all around her, the same dangerous expression in her eyes. She might do it. He knew her well, and so he knew how impetuous she could be. She thought with her heart, not her mind, as her father always said. Isam began to sense the sound of the machine in his ears, through his body and mind, as the wheel turned monotonously, turning, striking, striking. Just like a clock. He must leave before Mahmud's return, he must. And the machine's wail rose gradually, with its intermittent knocks; and time passed; and his face got hot and his eyes shifted between the door and Layla, back and forth with lunatic motions. How? How should he handle this? The machine was knocking, pounding. What should he say to this crazy girl? And how could he say it? When the machine was making more and more clamor? He stood up, signs of anger on his face, and walked slowly, heavily, toward Layla. He drew a pen from his pocket and pulled off the top.

"Have you seen one of these, Layla, a ballpoint?" He went up to the table next to her chair and took out a little notebook from his pocket. Putting it down on the table, he bent over it with the pen. "Look—see what a lovely line it makes?"

And he wrote on an empty page a word in English then crossed it out in confusion and wrote in Arabic: You are crazy and I love you. That was exactly what he had intended to write. But when he saw the look that sailed from her eyes he wanted to spend the rest of his life writing while she gazed at him. So he put pen to paper again. I love you, I love you, I love you. With rapid, almost violent strokes he worked heavy lines beneath those words, so heavy and deep that they tore the paper. The blood rushed to his head and the machine pounded against it; he felt a lump in his throat and twisted his neck so that his face was completely averted and she was unable to see the misery of a caged animal in his eyes, the bewildered anguish of a beast just wounded. He straightened up without looking at her, folded up the little agenda and put it back in his pocket. He managed to reach his chair and collapsed onto it. With a shaking hand he lit a cigarette, sucking in the smoke to hold it in his chest, clamping his mouth shut, then finally relaxing it for the smoke to emerge in circles that twined around each other or bumped against one another as he stared. Gradually his face relaxed; he closed his eyes and went on smoking.

Layla sat perfectly still, her body tense. She had no idea what to do with this cacophony swirling across her body, this turmoil so extreme she couldn't stand it, an eruption of joy, tenderness, and pain all at once. If only she could jump up right now, and dance and yell and sing! If only she could tell everyone that Isam loved her and she loved Isam! The mad dance of her elation buffeted her body and mind dizzily. And her mother? There was her mother, sitting right over there, sewing up the hem of the nightgown, just sewing, so calmly, so quietly, such a deathly peacefulness. Layla jumped up and ran from the room.

———

"Mama," said Mahmud, coming into the room in his pajamas, "What's the story, *ya sitti*? No supper tonight?"

His mother jammed her needle into the cloth and stood up, but as she hurried to the door she turned back abruptly as if something had just occurred to her. "Aren't you going to congratulate Isam? Gamila's getting married."

"Married?! Who's she marrying?"

His mother left the room as Isam spoke reluctantly. "The groom. Um, that groom . . . ." Mahmud eyeballed him. "How could you possibly have agreed to something like that, Isam?"

"It's what she wanted, and her mother, too. What was I supposed to do?"

Mahmud sat down in silence. "Shame on you! Marriage without love isn't marriage. That's just—" He stopped. Isam's face reddened, for he knew exactly what word Mahmud had meant to use. It was a word often on their lips, in fact whenever they discussed the subject of marriage in the abstract, without naming any names. Now Mahmud cast about for words to end this strain of conversation before it could go any further. "Of course, I was just speaking in general."

"I'm sure you were," said Isam curtly. "If you please, sir, can we come back down to earth now?"

"Down to earth! What do you mean?"

"I mean: let's talk about the real world. I mean: we don't need to soar across theories and toss around ideas bigger than we are. That's what I mean. If you were in my position what would you decide to do?"

"In your position?"

89

"I mean, about Gamila. What would you do? What can I do as the one who's responsible for her? Release her into the streets so she can find someone to love?"

"No one is saying you should do that! But the girl is still young, and she has lots of opportunities in front of her. There's no good reason to be in a hurry about it."

"Oh, that's all just foot-dragging, it's just a way to try to escape the problem. A good, sound marriage—fine, its foundation has to be love. And for a man to marry he has to love, and also the girl, right?"

"Precisely."

Isam stood up. He was so angry he could barely control himself. As he faced Mahmud his voice was heavy. "Fine. Now suppose, for instance, that Layla was in love. What would you do?"

Mahmud looked astonished. "Layla! My *sister* Layla?"

"Yes indeed, Layla. Your *sister* Layla."

The color drained out of Mahmud's face.

"Just suppose."

Mahmud let out his breath and shrugged. "Suppose why! Layla's young, she doesn't pay attention to these things."

"See—just as I said." Isam's voice was triumphant. "Its all just high-flown talk. Such fine, lofty words! Talk that is completely isolated from reality. It's the one on shore who's the best swimmer." He laughed drily. "The girl *must* fall in love, and *must* get married out of love. Every girl. Any girl. But not my sister, and not yours. Other people's sisters. Right?"

Mahmud said nothing. But Isam, tightening the noose, pressed him even more heavily and harshly. "Mahmud—I asked you a question. You didn't answer it. Why not?"

Mahmud looked away toward the window and hunched his shoulders. "What was the question?"

Layla's head poked through the doorway, unseen.

"If you were to discover that Layla loved someone," said Isam quietly, "what would you do?"

What an entertaining game! Layla laughed. "Hmm, yes, Mahmud," she said, "if you found out I was in love, what would you do?"

Her words came as a complete surprise to both of them. They spun around to face her, Mahmud looking utterly bewildered and Isam, apprehensive. Seeing the smile in her eyes and on her lips, Mahmud was reassured. She did not mean what she was saying, after all.

"So what would you do?" She was still smiling. "Really Mahmud, what would you do?"

Mahmud took a step toward her, grabbed her hair and yanked. "I'd kill you, that's what I'd do. I'd just kill you."

———

When they sat down to supper Mahmud and Isam were side by side, facing Layla. Between them on the table were the *mulukhiya* soup with meat, a plate of rice, some cheese, halwah, and black olives.

"So I'm unrealistic, a man of high-flown theories, is that it, Isam?" said Mahmud.

Isam stretched out his arm, knife in hand, to cut and spear a piece of cheese. "Is there any doubt about it?" he asked, smiling. Layla helped herself to a ladleful of rice, but Mahmud had not yet reached for food. He was so upset that he couldn't. Layla watched him.

"Come on, eat, Mahmud."

"Okay, okay—I *am* eating." Mahmud reached for a spoon, shoved his plate forward to touch the bowl of *mulukhiya,* and dipped the spoon into it. He must tell them his news, but how should he go about it? He must announce it in a manner appropriate to its significance, a manner that would have the proper impact.

"So, any news with you, Mahmud?" asked Isam.

Mahmud's face brightened, his pupils widened, and he rubbed his hands together in pleased anticipation as he allowed a few seconds to pass, heightening the moment's expectant tension. Clutching a spoon, Layla's hand hung motionless above the plate of rice.

"Important news."

Now Isam gazed at him fixedly. Mahmud put a trembling hand in his pocket and carefully withdrew a folded piece of white paper, opened it slowly, and lovingly passed his hand over the creases. He shifted it so that it lay in Isam's line of sight. Isam stared at it as the spoon slipped from Layla's grasp, clattering onto the edge of the plate. Isam shook his head as if unable to believe his eyes, grasped the page with both hands and brought it up to his eyes, and after a pause turned to Mahmud, stupefied. "What on earth is this?"

Mahmud smiled confidently. "What do you think it is?"

"It's a schedule. A training schedule."

"Exactly."

"Whose is it?"

Mahmud raised his head, eyes gleaming, and jabbed a trembling finger at his own chest. "Mine. My schedule."

"You signed up as a volunteer?"

Mahmud nodded. "And I've already started training, too."

"Where?"

"In the university training camp in al-Haram."

"When will you leave?"

"Two weeks."

A knifelike panic sliced through Layla's chest. He had already fixed everything—he had even set the date of departure. Mahmud would go; and he might . . . he might not return. Layla eased back her outstretched arm from the tabletop, gingerly, as if reluctant to let anyone see it move. Mahmud began to eat.

"So what do you think?" he asked.

"Weren't you a little hasty? Wouldn't it have been better to wait a bit until we see what develops there?"

Mahmud stopped eating and clutched the table edge with both fists. He spoke without any hesitation, as if the answer to just such a question lay already prepared in his mind. "We're the ones who will define what develops there, Isam—me, and you, and every Egyptian. Not anyone else."

Layla could not stop the shudder that passed through her like an electric shock; the sensation concentrated in her head so arrestingly that she thought her hair must be bristling. Her hand reached fumblingly across the table to touch Mahmud's.

"Congratulations, Mahmud. Congratulations." Her voice was low, and she sounded as if she might choke.

Isam looked grave as he slapped a slice of cheese onto a morsel of bread, arranging it to fit, then rearranging it. Mahmud was waiting, expecting more of a response, he knew. In earlier conversations, he had asserted that he, too, would go to the Canal. But he hadn't known, had he, that Mahmud would be so precipitate! He had had no idea that Mahmud would even start his training and set a departure date! Surely one must wait and see, wait for events to unfold a bit first. At the moment, the whole business was akin to a suicide operation and it might bring ruin on the entire country.

"But," said Mahmud, "I'll really miss Sitt Mama's *mulukhiya*."

Layla seemed to be laughing and crying all at once. "We'll send you the *mulukhiya*, Mahmud, *mulukhiya* on top of *tirmis*-beans, too!"

The knife in Isam's hand lay stock-still. The two of them were chattering as if no one else was in the room, as if he was not even there with them, sitting at the table beside his friend. And Layla—her eyes were on Mahmud. Not for a moment did they shift to look at him. Did she even know he was there? Perhaps she had expelled him from her range of vision. Dismissed him from her life. We are the ones who will define what develops there. You and me. Me . . . me.

"I wish so much it were *me*," Layla was saying. "I wish I could go with you, Mahmud."

Mahmud laughed. "Wait a bit, wait until all the men are finished off, then you ladies come."

The blood boiled in Isam's veins. He was no less a man, no less inflamed by events, no less a nationalist or a patriot than Mahmud. It was Mahmud who had been so afraid in the 1946 demonstrations, while he had feared nothing at all. But anyway, he thought, this isn't a question of who is a man, who is a patriot. It's a question of who is being reasonable and who is acting rashly.

Layla leaned forward over the table and whispered, with a glance round. "But the important thing is not to let Mama or Papa know. If they knew—"

"I know," broke in Mahmud. "I know they'll give me a hard time."

Layla shook her head dubiously. "They won't understand. They won't be able to understand." A strain of sarcasm crept into her voice. "They'll say, 'Be reasonable. Use your mind. Wait until you see what happens . . . .'"

Isam looked fixedly at the door, wishing he could escape. No. There was no place for him here; the two of them were far, far away, and he was alone. He might as well be standing in a forlorn desert waste, he thought glumly.

"You think that's all they'll say!" Mahmud was chuckling. "Tomorrow they'll be spouting their proverbs and all those cherished words of wisdom they've got."

Layla nodded, suppressing her laughter. "Close the door from whence the wind comes . . . ."

"And rest."

She and Mahmud began batting proverbs back and forth with histrionic enjoyment. "In caution there's safety," intoned Layla, her voice deep.

"And in speed, regret."

"A little snooze and siesta—"

"Are better than carousing."

"If a cur has one on you—"

"Call him 'Master.'"

"The bird whose feathers you clip—"

"Won't be able to fly." They collapsed into giggles like two six-year-olds. Layla dug out her handkerchief and swiped at a tear on her cheek. When her eyes met Isam's she looked stunned, as if she had completely forgotten his presence at the table, and quickly turned her face away. No—she would not look at him, she would not beg. Love does not beg, she thought sternly. Love for Egypt does not demand that. If it does not come from the heart there is no point in it. No point at all. She wiped her eyes and addressed Mahmud.

"Fine, then—but Papa?"

"Papa will scowl, and frown, and wave his hands around, and he'll say—" Layla finished Mahmud's sentence for him, deepening her voice, her theatrical movements exuberant, her pronunciation hilariously clipped. "I know—'This to-do will gen-er-ate only de-e-struction. De-e-estruction, that's all. De-e-estruction and ru-u-in.'"

Isam started laughing in spite of himself and then could not stop. He laughed so hard that he collapsed onto the tabletop. When he was able to straighten his wobbly head and his heaving chest, he discovered that a pleasurable stillness seemed to have engulfed him, giving him more confidence, too. He fixed his gaze on Mahmud and spoke calmly. "I wonder if it's too late to travel with the same group you're in?" This time he was careful to avoid Layla's glances, though he could sense that she was looking at him. This was his decision, his alone. She had no part in it, and she must be made to understand that perfectly.

— — —

As Isam left, Layla ran after him.

"Where are you going?" asked Mahmud. She stammered, "Isam, uh, forgot his pen." She ran after him out onto the stairs and called his name. Already halfway up the staircase, he turned to face her. "The pen! Your pen—you forgot it," she said too loudly, her hand seesawing in a gesture he could not fathom. He felt for his pen; there it was, of course. Layla whispered.

"The piece of paper."

Isam flipped his palm up inquiringly. Layla whispered again, fierce-ly. "The *piece* of *paper* in your *agenda*!" With a sudden smile of recogni-tion, he nodded. How amazing that she had rushed out after him! He came down the stairs slowly, looking her in the eye all the while, and handed her his agenda. He started back up the stairs, step after step; she stayed where she was, waiting. He whirled around. He hurried down the stairs, reached out a hand, fumbling, and ran his palm along her cheek and through her hair, ruffling it. He went leaping up the stairs, out of breath, home.

Chapter Six

It rushes forth, a clear, bubbling spring. The bogs, though, have done their best to block its passage. Intent on sucking that lovely running water dry, they try to absorb it into themselves, to consume it completely, to transform it with their sluggishness into a stagnant pond. The spring is still young, nevertheless, buoyant with life, excitable, and deep; and the bogs are ancient, sedimented over their many years of existence, crouching in quiet defiance across the land of Egypt. Confident that their stagnation speaks of calm strength, the dark-green surfaces glint under the sun's rays.

But beneath that glittering surface lies the swirled mud, ready to dam the spring's flow. The bubbling, ebullient water slowly carves a bed from the resistant mud, losing some of its crystal swells to the voracious throat of the sodden earth, but pounding on, roiling, alive, molding its destination. Yet there, at the end of its way, sits a dam of solid rock.

The bogs lie in sure wait, chiding the stream. There is nothing to be gained by pushing on, young friend, no use in rushing ahead. The stagnant stillness of those glinting patches speaks for itself: quietude is partner to good judgment. The brackish surface glistens; the bogs wink beneath the rays of the sun.

———

Mahmud and Isam announced their decision to the two families the evening before they were to travel. Each one had to face his own family before he could face the enemy. The manner in which their news was received differed according to the style in which each family conducted itself, but it was a divergence more apparent than real. For in essence their styles were one, infinitely multipliable depending on the needs of the moment: an appeal to reason and careful deliberation; a stern invitation to avoid foolishness or any manner of hasty behavior; and finally a bid to end such impetuous action, such a snap decision— now by threat, now through appeal to a man's emotions.

In the home of Muhammad Effendi Sulayman the two families came together in a bloc to face the peril. On the settee sat the two sisters, Saniya Hanim and Samira Hanim, indistinguishable for their equally wan demeanors. On a chair to their right perched Sulayman Effendi, and to their left sat Gamila. Facing them on the opposite settee were Isam and Mahmud, and hovering behind them in the space between settee and window stood Layla.

The news had shaken the two sisters, so fearful of losing their only sons. Paralyzed to the core by her dread, Samira Hanim could not dispel the tormenting fever that gnawed at her head. How? How could Isam have deceived her? He had never concealed anything from her; then how had he hidden this news so completely for so many days? Samira Hanim felt exactly like a beloved and loving wife who, with the sudden discovery of her husband's infidelity, is benumbed by the shock. Stripped of her usual skill—of her array of weapons—she could not but resort to her sister, who had immediately placed the entire burden on the shoulders of her husband. For Sulayman Effendi was smarter and wiser, Saniya thought in relief, more able to resolve such a situation, the like of which her family had never witnessed.

Sulayman Effendi crossed one leg over the other with great deliberation. He told Mahmud and Isam that he would make no attempt to force them to withdraw their decision. They must have the first and last word in that. He wanted simply to discuss the matter. To talk about it as one man to other men. Calmly, reflectively. With intelligence and wisdom. He was no less patriotic than were they, after all; but he had the benefit of more years and greater wisdom; he had a broader understanding of the way things truly were. He did not rush blindly after his emotions as they did, but rather contemplated them with his rational intelligence. And his mind told him that the government was not seriously committed to its position. The army, for example—it had not taken part in the battle. And there were turncoat elements throughout the Palace administration, throughout the parties, and within the government itself. Spies—Egyptian spies—saturated the Canal Zone. Provisions were smuggled to the British troops in full view of the government, and since this had become a focus of public discussion, the government could not possibly be unaware of it. What did they think any amount of courage and heroism could accomplish when weighed against such factors? What could a handful of volunteer fighters possibly achieve, facing a British army lavishly stocked with the latest thing in armaments?

No, indeed. It was a situation that made him despair. It would bring ruin, he declared, ruin alone, on the country. If there were any hope, he would have been the first to encourage them to go. In fact he would have joined them in person, if he were accepted into the commandos' ranks. But there was no point in rushing into this. There was no rationale for such impetuous behavior.

For their part, Isam and Mahmud were mesmerized by the serene voice, the unruffled, composed features, and the judicious logic of Sulayman Effendi. They dove trustingly into the discussion—man to man—each taking up one of Sulayman Effendi's arguments and rebutting it in turn. The popular wave of volunteer activity was more than

99

sufficient to force the government to take decisive measures; if it did not, it would surely fall. The same crest of popular action was enough to reduce the King to silence and wipe out the treasonous elements. Moreover, the struggle would not long remain limited to a handful of guerillas. Little by little it would spread, growing until it comprised the army and the people, all of them. Army officers had threatened to resign—yes, they really had. They would join the commandos, they said, if the army did not join battle.

Sulayman Effendi's voice assumed a new timbre, the honeyed tone vanishing as portents of anger reshaped his features. Mahmud and Isam now detected that they had been deceived. The discussion had not been an innocent or disinterested one as had been claimed, but rather was a veiled attempt to prevent them from traveling. And so Sulayman Effendi was obliged to come out in the open. He shifted the discussion to the purely personal aspects of the issue; there was a new edge to his voice. Only Mahmud answered him now.

"Why the two of you?"

"Why not us?"

"Why *my* son? Why precisely mine, not the children of other people?"

"What if everyone forbade his children to go and so no one went at all?"

"And your studies?"

"They can wait."

"Of course—what do you care? Your father works to the bone and sweats and perseveres·so that your Excellency can become a full human being—"

"There are many things more important than education."

"And what are they?"

"What is the point of becoming educated if one remains a slave?"

"Here's your father, alive and well and getting on just fine, and your grandfather before him—are they slaves?"

Mahmud lost his self-control, and his voice was as cutting as his father's. "Yes, of course—of course they were slaves. Every soul who fails to struggle and fight in order to liberate himself from imperialism is a slave."

His father's face flushed blood-red. He rose to his feet and began flinging epithets at Mahmud—he was a good-for-nothing, he was an insolent cur, he was badly brought up. Then his tone turned to sarcasm.

"Your honor thinks of himself as a hero—right?"

"I'm not a hero, I'm a man. A man who is defending his freedom."

"You're no man. You're a child—a child they've fooled."

"Nobody has fooled me."

"You're a sacrificial lamb, just a dumb beast to be slaughtered by the government, so it can convince people it's a nationalist, patriotic government."

"I don't care what the government's aim is. What concerns me is my own goal, and the people's."

"The people! Will you be serving the people when you fall there, on the first day? When you fall down dead?" His father was barely able to hold back tears, and a wail rose from the vicinity of Saniya Hanim and Samira Hanim. Mahmud averted his face so that no one would make out how deeply this affected him, and fixed his eyes on a distant, mythical horizon as he spoke.

"I know that. I know, and I'm prepared for that possibility."

Layla turned to stare out of the window. Her father, maddened by his rage, was screaming. "Of course it doesn't concern you. What does concern you? You will die a hero, and your mother and father will be destroyed, and so will your sister." Mahmud's face went ashen and a layer of tears welled up over his eyes. His voice dropped to a tone of entreaty. "Please, I beg you, please try to understand. I beg you, Papa, try to understand that I have to go, I can't not go."

His father shook his head, too overwhelmed by his despair to speak, and stalked to the door. There he turned around, his face stiff and still. "If you do go, then you are no longer my son and I do not know you.

You may not cross the threshold of this house again." His lips trembled. "If, that is, you return at all." And he went rapidly to his room.

———

Umm Mahmud walked over to her son. She stood for a moment, silent, leaning toward him, her hands planted on the round table that separated the two of them.

"Use your brain, for my sake. For the sake of your poor mother." Mahmud's face went hard and still as he looked the other way. She turned to Isam in supplication.

"You've always been sensible, Isam, dear. Make him see sense, son."

Isam brushed his hand across his face. His own mother was fixing him with her gaze, her face deathly pale. Her mind was spinning. Impossible—it was simply not possible that Isam would go. Anyone, everyone, but not Isam, her son, her beloved, her man. She could not live without him—not for a day, nor a single hour. What could she do? How could she stop him?

Umm Mahmud was pressing Isam again. "Why aren't you answering, Isam? Talk, son."

He would not look at her. "What am I supposed to say, Aunt?"

Her arms dropped limply to her sides. "Make that madman see sense." To judge by her voice, Mahmud's mother no longer had much hope in anything; perhaps she said the sentence merely because it had formed in her mind.

Samira Hanim laughed bitterly. "So is there any sense left in Isam? I think Mahmud has sent it all flying out of him. Mahmud brings such blessings."

The blood darkened in Umm Mahmud's face as she turned to her sister. "I know—you always put the blame on Mahmud."

"Isam's always been sensible. Your son is the one who's been wild all his life."

Mahmud turned to Layla, behind him, and smiled. Isam stood up and walked slowly toward where his mother sat. He stood before her, his feet planted apart, his voice shaking with anger. "I'm not a child, and Mahmud has no control over my mind—do you understand?" He was fighting to control his voice, trying to modulate it. "And you had better understand, as well, that I am leaving tomorrow. Whatever you do." His mother raised her face to him. He lost the battle to contain his voice; now he was almost screaming. "I'm going, I am going. Understand?"

His mother jumped to her feet and threw herself onto him, clinging in a mad embrace. "I can't . . . Isam, I can't, I just—" Her mouth was contorted, her tongue moving, but as if she had lost the ability to pronounce words. Isam averted his face and gently tried to disengage himself from her arms, but they clung to him all the harder, bracelets made of steel. Roughly, he freed himself and backed away. Umm Isam dropped her head and hid her face in her hands. Gamila ran to her, embracing her from behind, crying. "Shame on you, Isam, for shame!" Her wailing was the only sound to disturb a long spell of silence.

Isam's mother raised her head but her hands still covered her face. Erect, she dropped her hands. Her face was transformed. Those soft features had hardened into a stern rigidity, the worried eyes had settled, unblinking, and the customary soft droop of her mouth had vanished into a razored line. She stared at Isam, as if sizing him up.

"So that's it, Isam?—your final decision?"

He nodded without speaking. Isam's mother disengaged herself from Gamila's arms forcibly and rushed toward the window. For a moment, everyone in the room was too stunned by their terror to move, though Gamila's shriek resounded through the apartment. Then Layla careened over to her aunt as the woman was clambering onto the window frame. Layla gripped her shoulders.

"Leave me alone, all of you," shouted her aunt. "Let me die by myself, I don't want to live."

Isam had followed Layla. He pushed her to one side, yanked his mother down from the window and dragged her back into the room by her shoulders. He pulled her around to face him, bringing her face close to his, and narrowed his eyes on hers. After a few seconds she closed her eyes; the blood seemed to be pumping into her face again, and her muscles relaxed. She returned to the center of the room, her step light and her head high, her face tranquil. Gamila grasped her mother by the arm and said to Isam, "Come on, let's go home."

Isam followed his mother and Gamila out the door.

———

At eleven o'clock that night, Mahmud was packing his things when the maid brought him a folded note from Isam. After reading it he tossed it to Layla, who sat on the edge of his bed. "Have a look, *ya sitti.*"

Layla read.

> My mother has been in a faint for three hours. I sent for the doctor but he has not yet arrived. Mahmud, what can I do? I cannot possibly leave my mother when she is in this state, and after all she has done for my sake and Gamila's. It is not possible, Mahmud. You understand, don't you? When she improves I'll do my best to join you. Go in peace; my heart is with you—with all of you.
>
> Isam Hamdi.

Mahmud flung a woolen undervest into his suitcase. "So what are we supposed to do with his heart? What good will that do us?"

Layla wasn't listening, and her eyes held a vacant look. Abruptly, she focused on Mahmud as he perched next to his suitcase. "Mahmud, do you think Aunt Samira is really and truly ill?"

Mahmud stared at her dully for only a moment before he bolted from the bed, his pupils dilating. "No—can't be! That's crazy."

Layla hid her smile and nodded. Her narrowed eyes gave her a cunning look, as Mahmud came nearer. "Are you trying to say that she's playacting?"

Layla shrugged, and laughed bitterly. "Why wouldn't she act? Did she do a poor job pretending to commit suicide?" Mahmud stopped brusquely, dumbfounded. Layla's bell-like laugh came again. "Mahmud, do you have any inkling of what she did when I came up and tried to pull her back as she was throwing herself at the window?

"What? Layla, what did she do?"

Throwing back her head, Layla mimed what had happened, speaking in a faint voice as if talking only to herself. "She winked at me and pinched my hand."

Mahmud looked bewildered. Layla just laughed. "See—exactly as if she were telling me, 'Don't worry, it's just playacting.'"

Mahmud slapped his palms together and Layla saw in her mind an image of her mother, seated in the front room. "My sister Samira is very clever. She knows exactly how to keep her children tucked under her wing."

———

Dawn. Their mother sat in the front hall, facing the door, silent, grayish, stiff. Across from her sat Layla. Mahmud was bent over his suitcase, trying to close it. A light knock sounded on the door. Mahmud straightened and went to answer. It was Isam, in his bathrobe. Mahmud relaxed visibly, looking pleased to see him. The presence of Isam—of anyone outside their little family—would make the ordeal of saying goodbye easier to handle, simpler and quicker to say.

His mother's eyes rolled. "Isam isn't going?" Her voice was flat and lifeless. Isam's was apologetic. "What can I do, aunt? Mama is ill, very ill."

Mahmud's mother broke down crying, trying to suppress her sobs to keep their echo from reaching their father, who had shut himself into his room. Layla stood up and went over to her mother, patting her shoulder softly as she spoke. "It's all right, Mama—anyway, it's not like Isam was going to be keeping guard over him."

"But why him?" wailed her mother faintly. "Why him, going all on his own?" Mahmud let out an exasperated sigh, and it was Layla who answered her mother, avoiding Isam's eyes. "When Aunt Samira gets better, Isam will go." From her mother's gesture it was clear that she did not believe Layla, but she subsided again into silence, only shaking her head now and then. Isam looked at her, startled, having just realized that she had not inquired about his mother—her own sister—even though he had declared that she was very sick.

With Isam's help, Mahmud finally managed to close his suitcase. He stood up, already grasping the handle. This paleness suited Mahmud's face, Layla could not help thinking; and, wearing his military uniform, he already looked more dignified. But in fact what showed on Mahmud's face was confusion; the case thudded to the floor as he ambled over to his mother awkwardly and kissed her on the forehead. He turned to leave but then went back to her and seized both her hands, bringing them to his mouth and kissing them with warmth. Her tears ran unchecked as he straightened and went over to Layla. He put his arm around her shoulders and kissed her, and then hurried to the door, suitcase in hand. Layla ran after him onto the stairs. He turned round to face her and shook his head.

"Layla, no. I don't want you, of all people, to start crying."

She wiped tears off her face with her sleeve. "I'm not crying, Mahmud. I'm not crying."

"Do you understand, Layla? You do, don't you? You know why I'm going?"

Layla nodded, her face clearer, her eyes glistening.

"Knowing there's someone who understands, someone dear to me, will make me feel a lot better."

Layla smiled. "I understand, Mahmud, and tomorrow, all of them will. Goodbye, and be careful."

Mahmud set his bag down, hugged Layla, gave her a kiss, and started down the stairs a second time.

"We'll be waiting for you!" shouted Layla after him. "We're waiting for you to come back, Mahmud."

She heard Isam's voice somewhere behind her. "Goodbye. So long, Mahmud."

Without looking back, Mahmud raised his hand in a wave that embraced them both. Isam stepped back to let Layla pass in front of him, and started to follow her into the apartment. Once inside, Layla turned to face him; he was still outside the door. She put her hand on the door to shut it, as if preventing him from coming in.

"I'd like to come in and see Aunt Saniya."

Layla shook her head wordlessly. She saw Isam's face change.

"Not right now, Isam. Not now. Go on upstairs to your mother." She closed the door, Isam still standing there in front of it. She stood there for a moment, her face against the door, listening to Isam's steps receding slowly, up the stairs. He had disappointed her, failed her. Failed her?—how could that be? But he had. There was no doubt about it.

Her mother's wail rose, a hammer pounding inside her head, threatening to destroy her with its incessant knocking, and leaving her utterly incapable of thought.

Chapter
Seven

Layla began to keep the mailbox under tight surveillance—on her way to school, on her way home, as the usual mail delivery time approached, and also when it was not even close. Her life had come to center on that inconspicuous wooden box. For Mahmud's letters never failed to send a tremor through her—a prolonged shiver of pride and affection.

He wrote to her twice a week, and sometimes three times. As she read his letters she felt as if he were sitting across from her in his room, recounting everything. In her mind's eye she could envision his eyes, widening now and then as if they were open onto a new world in which all was beautiful and stunningly impressive—people, events, new experiences, thoughts he had never before had, new friends.

One friend in particular seemed to have bewitched her brother, for he wrote about this companion in every letter. It was as if Husayn Amir was the very piper who had led Mahmud into this enchanting new world with his flute. Now Mahmud strode there, reacting keenly to each new encounter, each fresh idea.

"This morning, for the first time," he wrote, "I detonated a bomb.

The first fire bomb into a British camp. I just stood there, far enough away to be safe, watching the outcome of what I had done. When I saw the fire flare up inside the camp I felt like a lighted firebrand was filling my heart—or perhaps filling all of me."

In another letter he said: "I have grown up, Layla. I have truly grown up now. I don't think I was even close to becoming an adult until after I came to the Canal Zone."

"I'm really living," came in still another. "I am so alive, Layla—do you understand what I'm saying, my dear? I feel more alive every hour, touched by everything, every hour and minute of my life. When I was back in Cairo, I considered myself alive. But now, after my latest experience, I realize that I was mistaken. Stasis is death, not life. You ask me if I'm not afraid? Of course I was afraid, at first. Fear is what gives the struggle its savor. You go forward, feeling fear, for sure, but also sensing some strength grander than yourself, greater than your fear, a force that pushes you on and makes you do what you have to do. It keeps you steady and precise all of the time. And when it is all over you feel so refreshed, because you realize that you have prevailed over yourself, over your weakness as just one puny person. Time after time, a person is liberated from the selfishness that governs everything in our lives. You feel like you are one in a collective, that your life is significant as long as you are serving this collective, and that if you were to lose your life the world would not stop turning. To the contrary—others will continue the work you start, the work for the sake of which you might lose your life. And at that point one is freed of one's fear, liberated from one's concentration on 'me.'"

"Layla, I'm starting to go mad. I haven't been able to find a single chance to work things out with you. What's going on? Aren't you going to explain anything to me?"

They were standing in Cicurel, between the main door and the elevator, waiting for Gamila and her mother to finish paying at the *caisse*. It was the first day of the sale, and the swinging glass door did not pause once.

Layla did not answer. Isam spoke again, this time in a whisper. "Layla, what is it? Don't you love me?"

A heavily made-up elderly lady came through the door. Layla focused her gaze on the glass as it swung behind the woman, the reflection of the neon breaking on it. "I believe you know perfectly well, Isam."

"I don't know anything, and frankly, it is driving me mad. Are you angry because I didn't go with Mahmud?"

Layla studied Isam, loaded down with packages.

"Why would I be angry at you? Did I try to force you to go?"

"Well, then, why have you changed? Why do you act so differently toward me?"

The elevator doors opened wide and a crowd spilled out, moving toward the door that led outside. Layla watched them. "I haven't changed at all."

"Not true. You're not your usual self."

Layla faced him. "What do you want me to do? Sing? Dance? When my brother is off fighting?" Her voice was rough.

"You don't love me," said Isam dejectedly. "You don't love me even the tiniest bit."

Layla opened her mouth to say something, but people thrust themselves between the two of them and the crush forced Isam to step back; it was all he could do to maintain his balance as he clutched the purchases that weighed him down. A man in a gray suit spoke to his wife, who was setting a hat with a large feather in it on her head. "They cheated us! That isn't the real thing, that cloth—it's just a cheap imitation." Two women hugging their new belongings to themselves, expressions of triumph sketched on their faces, pushed him from his path.

"It's just a cheap imitation," the gray-suited man muttered again, his voice swallowed in the welter of other voices.

"What a buy! It's the chance of a lifetime!" This was a woman in a black gown. "What about that woman in pink who wanted to snatch it from you!" another voice answered. The woman in black laughed. "I would have killed her."

"Just not the real thing, that cloth. Cheap imitation." His wife was straightening the feathered hat on her head. "Shh, don't make such a fuss," she said. "I saw the label with my own eyes, it's the real thing, from England."

"Oof, I felt like I was going to suffocate," a young woman with a swan neck and arched eyebrows grumbled to another young woman who was with her. "This is no sale, dear, this is war! We're the real guerillas in the struggle!"

Her companion laughed. Layla jumped when her aunt came up suddenly from behind, clapped her hand on Layla's shoulder, and spoke. "Fess up, Layla—don't you think we did well with all of these bargains?"

———

As his mother and Gamila finished their shopping, Isam did not drop his glance from Layla once. In fact, his eyes were fixed on her as if pulled that way by an invisible cord. Layla noticed the accusing look in his eyes, the mutely wounded expression. What had happened to Isam? Had he really gone mad? Where had all of that calm reason and self-possession gone? Didn't he understand that his mother was with them, and so was Gamila?

Samira flagged down a taxi for the trip home. She sat in back with Gamila, heaps of purchases between them. In the wide car's front seat sat Layla and Isam. Isam shifted closer to Layla; now his thigh was pressed against hers. His breaths slapped her cheek, heavy and fast, and he put out his hand to hold hers gently. She tried to pull her hand from his grasp but his hold grew fiercer. She tried to draw her hand out slowly and his hold became stronger still. She bit back a yelp of pain. Tears came to Isam's eyes and his grip loosened. He took a pen and pad of paper from his pocket. He scrawled some words and let the bit of paper fall into the pocket of her overcoat.

He stood paying the fare. Layla said goodbye to her aunt and rushed in bewilderment into her family's apartment. In the living room she read what Isam had written.

"I beg you, my love, don't leave me. I beg you not to leave me."

Her hand shook as she returned the paper to her pocket. Her hand was still shaking when she pressed it on the doorbell to Isam's apartment.

———

Gamila opened the door.

"Oh good, here's Layla. Come in, *ya sitti*, come and help us solve this problem." Layla followed Gamila to her mother's room. On the bed sat Samira Hanim. Lengths of cloth were spread out before her, a spattered sea of bright and clashing colors. Hardly did Layla's eyes settle on one hue before they were pulled to another. Her eyesight was overpowered.

"I am so glad that you came up, my dear," said her aunt. As Layla came nearer, Samira Hanim pointed to the patterns arranged along the edge of the bed.

"Here is the cloth. There are the patterns. Now you decide what goes with what."

"I think the red lace does best for this draped dress," said Gamila. "What do you think, Layla?" But Samira Hanim gave Layla no chance to speak. "No, Gamila. The red lace absolutely has to be sewn up into a simple gown. *Drapee* in lace? No, that needs *chiffon*. Or what do you say we do the *drapee* in that *chiffon*?"

"What *chiffon*?"

"That one—the color of a pistachio nut when you break it open."

Gamila scampered over to her mother, her mouth puckered. "Mama, you are so incredible! It'll be out of this world!"

Layla threw an anxious glance at the door. Gamila's face fell, and she straightened, facing her mother and pointing. "But on one condition, Mama. *Not* for the engagement party."

"But it will be absolutely beautiful, sweetheart. Real *chiffon*—superb!"

Gamila's shoulders jerked upward. She looked as though she would burst into sobs, and indeed she sounded tearful. "No, Mama! How can you? I told you I want *Gibere* lace for the engagement!"

"Honey, I'll *get* the *Gibere* for you! But that's for when we write the marriage contract, for *that* party, not the engagement."

The tears coursed down Gamila's cheeks now. She could barely speak, her voice choked by sobs. "Fine, okay. Okay, Mama. I don't want to get married anyway. That's it." She dragged herself to the door. Her mother got up and hurried after her, her arms wide open.

"Honey! Why upset yourself so? Okay, then, I'll get whatever you want. What color do you want the lace to be?"

Still sniffling, Gamila said, "*simone.*"

"And the shoes?"

Gamila wiped away the tears with the back of her hand. "Satin, same color as the dress."

"So that's it. Tomorrow morning I'll go out and get the lace and order the shoes. But come tell me what you think about this now so we can finish up. Time is going fast and we only have a week until the engagement." Samira Hanim dragged Gamila by the hand, her gaze distant as if dreaming as she spoke. "Anyway, after the engagement you'll really need all of these dresses. One day at the Auberge, one day at the Mena House, and then the Hilmiya Palace . . . ."

Gamila giggled. "Mama, that's enough. But I just don't want that gray. It's a dead bore."

Dropping into the armchair, her eyes steadily on the door, Layla spoke. "No, Gamila, it's just the opposite. It's a restful color, and very attractive."

Her aunt perched on the edge of the bed. "Not only restful, Gamila, that gray shows off a woman's shape really well. It's not the color the man'll look at—he won't even notice that. What he will notice is the body—your figure."

Layla tried to keep from smiling, while Gamila laughed. "Mama, you see everything, don't you? You are so *au courant*!"

Samira Hanim chuckled and gave her daughter, sitting across from her, a little slap on the thigh. "So where is Isam?" she exclaimed. "He has very good taste in dresses. Go call him, Gamila. No, wait, help me roll up the cloth so it won't wrinkle, and Layla can call him."

Layla stood up.

"You'll find him in his study, Layla," said her aunt.

As she closed the study door behind her she felt a swell of aching affection surge over her. Isam was at his desk, head buried in his hands. Layla paused, observing him, then tiptoed closer. She patted his shoulder gently but, as if he were submerged in a deep sleep, he did not react. She bent over him and whispered. "Isam."

The voice startled him; he twitched and raised his head. Layla shot up, alarmed, but he seized her arms with both fists before she could step back. His face seemed different, as if its outlines had partly dissolved: the nose seemed broader and flatter, the cheeks sagged. His chin was slack, his mouth loose; his eyes were vacant, as if he were not wholly conscious. He seemed to lift his body ponderously; his tight grasp fixed her to the floor. Now his features began to sharpen, to gain both strength and harshness, while his blank gaze settled and gradually took focus, but with an expression of threat and determination; she wondered if he was going to slap her. His hands were tight on her upper arms, his body towering over her, his clouded face touching her face, his lips falling heavily on to hers. Layla threw her head back and let out a choked scream. "Isam—"

He gave no indication of having heard her. His face did not relax; his eyes remained hard. Layla backed away—one step, another—but Isam followed her step for step. She glanced over her shoulder and tried to alter the direction she was moving, but Isam held her arms more tightly and directed her toward the empty space between the chair and the wall, forcing her against the wall.

"Let go, Isam. Let go!"

He still seemed not to hear anything. He lowered his hands slowly, still on her arms, and seized her hands. He brought his body close to hers. Layla jerked her head as far back as she could, to the wall. A cold shiver ran through her limbs and her lips trembled. "Isam, I'm going to scream. I'll scream, I will, Isam."

Isam crushed her body with his and brought his parted lips down over her eyes. He stroked her cheek slowly, then suddenly moved his lips to her mouth. Her lips froze; Isam's tears wetted her cheeks. He fell into the chair, jammed his elbows onto his thighs, supported his face in his hands, and broke into sobs. His sobbing rose gradually as Layla stood rooted to the spot, her body and mind vacant, desolate, as if she had just awakened from a dream, her mind blank. Isam's crying, loud in her ears, reverberated with the terror and embarrassment that overwhelmed her. Had she committed some awful deed, entered a sacred place where she had no right to be, seen something inviolable that she had no right to see? She longed to be away from this place; she yearned to escape. Isam's wailing filled her ears. She reached out a shaking hand that stopped, hesitant, in midair and then came down gently on Isam's shoulder. He spoke, his voice interrupted by sobs.

"You despise me, don't you?"

"Shh, Isam," Layla whispered. "Shh, quiet down. Please. That's enough."

Isam pushed her hand from his shoulder and looked at her in loathing. When he spoke his voice had grown steady. "Go away. Leave me alone. I don't want to see you. I don't want to see you at all."

Layla pressed her lips together and ran out of the room.

She sat in her bedroom, busy with a jacket she was knitting. Her father was out; her mother was upstairs, visiting her sister. The maid came in. "Mr. Isam is outside, *ya sitti*."

Layla's face grew hard. She dropped her knitting, walking toward the window, her back to the maid as she spoke. "Tell Isam that Mama is not at home."

"I told him that, madame; he said he wants to see you."

"Tell him I'm asleep, Fatima."

"Careful, Fatima," said Isam, pushing the young girl gently away from the doorway as he entered. Layla did not move. She held her head straight and absolutely still, her back to Isam. After a moment's silence, she spoke coldly. "What do you want, Isam?"

"I—" She could hear him come nearer. "I'm sorry, Layla, about everything that happened."

Layla turned around slowly. Isam's pale skin was blotchy and sallow, and deep black circles shadowed his eyes as if he were recovering from a long illness.

"Okay, Isam. Consider the subject closed." Her voice was flat.

Isam's nostrils trembled. "What subject?"

She did not answer. She sat down on the edge of the bed and put out one trembling hand to her knitting. She slipped the needle into the stitch, brought the yarn round it and pulled the new stitch over the old. She slipped the old stitch from the needle and began again. Isam came nearer.

"What do you mean, Layla?" His voice was gentler now. Layla pulled the yarn so hard that it broke. She threw the knitting down on the bed, irritated.

"The relationship between us. Consider it ended."

Isam narrowed his eyes on the knitting. He leaned down and started to pick it up with both hands, but his grip loosened and he let it fall back onto the bed. He turned and shuffled, his shoulders slumped, to a small table. He leaned his palms heavily on it and spoke faintly, as if talking to himself. "I knew you wouldn't forgive me if I didn't go with Mahmud."

Layla yanked the piece of knitting back onto her lap and nervously slipped it off the needle. To reattach the broken yarn she began to undo part of what she had knitted, her right hand jerking from left to right repeatedly. Then she discovered that she had unraveled more than she had intended and she dropped her hands into her lap, folded motionless over the piece of knitting.

"Isn't that what you wanted?" Her voice was bitter.

Isam was silent, motionless, his back still to her.

"So, you have nothing to say?"

Isam turned to face her; his skin seemed even paler. "If you could only imagine." His voice got fainter until it was barely audible. "If you could only imagine how much I love you." Tears glistened in Layla's eyes. She averted her gaze and tried to speak, her voice choked. "You don't love me. If you loved me you wouldn't have done what you did upstairs." Layla got up, the knitting falling from her lap to the floor. She faced Isam.

"Why?" Her voice was sharp, threatening. "Why did you do that?"

"Because I love you."

Layla's laugh came out more like a moan. She walked to the window and pressed her forehead against the pane until it hurt. "Do you know, Isam, what I was feeling, the whole time? I felt like you wanted to hit me." She turned to him but stayed close to the window. "No, Isam, that isn't love. Call it anything you want, but not love."

Isam sat down on the armchair across from her bed. "You're still too young to understand anything."

"I'm not too young," said Layla, stalking toward him. "And I do understand. Everything. And I still say it isn't love."

Isam raised his head. "What do you understand?" His voice was quiet and bitter. "That love is this thing you read about in novels? That I can't sleep, can't study, can't live? D'you understand the agony I feel when you're next to me and I can't even look at you, can't touch you?" Again his voice grew fainter and fainter, and he bent over, his eyes on the floor. "And when I'm away from you, I tell myself, Layla was with me but I didn't see her, not enough, and then I feel like I'm going mad,

I feel like someone shut up in his cell. So then I come back, and what happened before happens again." He raised his watery eyes. "You know, Layla, what it's like? Like you're in the desert, digging just so you can find a single drop of water, and you go on digging, and then you say, now, now I'm there. No—just a bit more, and I'll be there. Next time. And the further down you get, the more imprisoned you become in the hole you have dug, and you never do get there. And the water never appears. It just never does." Isam struck the chair with his fist. He jumped up to face Layla, still speaking, his voice full of anger and sarcasm. "Can you possibly understand those feelings?"

Layla fixed her eyes on the floor. She caught sight of the knitting, fallen there. She went over, bent slowly and picked it up, straightened slowly, and put it on the bed.

"Isam," she said calmly. "You did kiss me one time before, didn't you? Can you tell me why I wasn't afraid that day?"

"Because that day you loved me. Today, you don't."

Layla made a gesture of disavowal. "Nonsense. My feelings about you haven't changed. Do you want to know why I wasn't afraid that day, Isam?"

Isam compressed his lips and sat down again. Layla was pacing the room.

"That day there was something. Something in your hands, in your face and eyes and movements. Something that made whatever you did okay—and not just okay. Okay and very nice." She stopped right in front of Isam. "That day, there was love. But today—today you were looking at me as if I was your enemy, as if you wanted to win some victory over me. Why? Why, Isam?"

Isam covered his face in his hands and did not respond.

"Why did you treat me like that?" Layla asked, her voice unsteady.

Isam got up and walked toward the window. Her outcry seemed to exhaust Layla, and she collapsed onto the edge of the bed, repeating in a faint voice, "Why? Why?"

Isam turned and walked over to her. He leaned over and rubbed her shoulder gently and whispered. "I'm afraid, Layla. Afraid. Since the day Mahmud left, I've been afraid. From the moment you closed the door in my face, afraid, afraid you'd slip away, afraid I'd lose you. That fear has been driving me insane. It puts me in a state where I have no control over my actions."

Layla averted her face again but he went on doggedly. "You can be sure that if I'd been in my right mind I never would have gotten that near to you. You can't imagine how hurt I am by what happened." He paused. "Maybe if you knew that from the day we began to love each other, my conscience has been tormenting me, and all the time I feel like I'm doing something wrong, that I'm betraying a trust people have put in me—maybe if you realize that, you can imagine how awful I feel now."

Things began to fall into place. Isam's behavior had so bewildered her at the time, but now she realized why his face would go red whenever her father came into the room where they were, or Mahmud, or her mother. He considered her their property, and so he felt embarrassed, ashamed, as if he were wronging them by loving her. The feelings that had filled her with pride and happy expectation and a new desire for life—with a belief in herself—filled him with a sense of guilt. Her face darkened. "If you feel like you are wrong because you didn't go to the Canal, then why don't you go now, Isam?"

Her question startled him. He quickly raised his hand from her shoulder and straightened up, his demeanor angry. "I'm not wrong. You know perfectly well the circumstances that prevented me from going."

Layla cut him off coldly. "Mahmud had circumstances, too, yet he went."

"So that's what you've been wanting to say to me all along, isn't it?"

"Me?—" Isam interrupted her. "Tell me. Talk. Say that you have stopped loving me because I'm not a hero like your brother."

"I didn't say anything stupid like that."

But Isam was now so angry that he could hear only his own voice. "Who do you think you are, to be able to insult me like that? Who do you think you are, to despise me like this? I'm not your slave and I'm not your brother, either. I'm free, do you understand? If it was because I love you—because I did love you, then consider the subject closed. Totally closed." Isam stood up, trying to regain his breath. "I'm sick of this. I want to love a regular girl, who thinks like girls think, and feels like they do. I'm sick of you, and of your philosophizing, and your moods."

Layla bent over and hid her face between her hands. "Fine, Isam. It is all over. You can go now."

"Of course I'm going. What do you think? That I can't live without you?"

Layla pulled her hands from her face and stood up, her color gone. "Go."

Isam looked at her, hesitated a moment, then went out and slammed the door behind him.

———

Her face set, Layla sat down again on the edge of the bed and pulled her knitting over. She tried to jab the needle into the undone stitches but her hand was shaking so hard that they kept slipping out. Stubbornly, she tried again, defiantly, as if her whole self was concentrated in this single attempt.

The door opened. Isam stood in the doorway rubbing his chin for a moment before he spoke in a faint voice. "There's just one thing I want to know, and I think it is my right to know. It is my right to know exactly where I stand at the moment."

Layla didn't answer; her eyes remained fixed on the piece of knitting, her hands busy trying to put the stitches back on the needle, as if she had not even heard him. Isam stepped inside the room.

"There is one question I want you to answer. And if the answer is no, I promise you you'll never see my face ever again."

Still, Layla said nothing. Isam walked forward until he was directly facing her.

"Layla, do you love me or not?" He seemed to choke on the words, and turned his face away. Layla pressed her lips together and tears blurred her vision. She set the knitting down on her lap. Isam bent over her and put a hand on her shoulder.

"I'm sorry Layla. I'm sorry about everything. I really can't do without you. I can't live without you. Please, please reassure me."

Layla closed her eyes and the tears spilled out.

"Just one word, Layla, I don't want any more than that. Did your feelings about me change because I didn't go?"

Lips pressed even harder together, eyes still closed, Layla shook her head hard.

"It's just like it was before? Just like before, Layla?" Isam's voice shook.

Layla nodded, without saying a word. Isam's face cleared and he bent over until his face was close to hers. "Just as much? As much as I love you, darling?"

Layla smiled and opened her eyes. Isam looked at her for a moment, tenderness shining in his eyes, and then he brushed her hair with his lips.

Chapter Eight

For the next fifteen days Layla felt as though she was trying to live at the vortex of a whirlwind, or as if she could not emerge from an intensely disturbing dream. But everything that conspired to keep her in this state of extreme nervous tension ended. All of it—thank God.

For the whole period leading up to Gamila's engagement party, Isam acted like a madman, and Layla felt nothing but fear and terror toward him. On the eve of the party his insanity reached new heights; and then he stayed away from her for five entire days.

At first she truly thought she could be understanding. He seemed so afraid of losing her, and whenever she gave him a simple reassurance of her love, his fear would vanish. So she tried to reassure him at every opportunity. But she soon realized that her words were no use. He would sit like a statue, only his eyes harboring determination and threat; she feared constantly that he was about to hit her. Her mother noticed his odd behavior, and her aunt began to perceive something as well. Gamila, too; but he didn't sense any of that. It was as if he were completely unconscious of the world around him. The bizarre expression never left his eyes. In those moments when they were alone together, he would act like a man going under, exclaiming in despair, "We *must* find a solution."

Then he thought he had found the solution, and at once he appeared more self-possessed. He suggested that they get married immediately. He said he had been thinking about it for a long time and had figured out that it was indeed possible. He could take on some extra work on the side, in addition to his studies; and the added income, on top of his present stipend, would be enough. From the practical point of view nothing would change, really. All that would happen would be that she would move in. The apartment was big enough for all of them, especially since Gamila would be getting married and moving to her husband's home. It was all very natural, simple, and reasonable.

Layla agreed that the matter was natural, simple, and reasonable, but she questioned whether it would appear that way to her mother or to his. Her mother wanted her to marry as soon as possible, but with a dowry equivalent to what Gamila had gotten, and to a man no less well-off than Gamila's intended. And his mother? She did not want him to marry now. His mother wanted him to graduate, to open his clinic, to prosper and then to marry the daughter of a pasha or at least a bey. His future was all sketched out in the clearest possible lines and with utter precision, and so was hers. Therefore, her mother would never agree to it, and neither would his. The sisters would work to separate them by all reasonable means and maneuvers, and by less reasonable ones, too. Why should they face this possibility if they did not have to? Why should they make themselves vulnerable to this danger? Yes, she knew that his mother loved her, very much in fact—but on one condition: that Layla not spoil any of her designs, that she not become attached to Isam as he was ascending the ladder, that she not stop him at the apartment of Muhammad Effendi Sulayman before he was able to reach as high as the home of a pasha or bey.

But it would not be easy to convince Isam of this. He could not get it into his head that from the very day on which every baby is born—

boy or girl—the family has its plan already sketched out. And one has to follow through. If you do, you enjoy the love, affection, and accord of the family. But if you do not, thought Layla, if you contravene that design and violate the family's principles, the family will strike you down, as her father had done when she joined that demonstration. The family would withhold its love, as her father had done to Mahmud when he went to the Canal Zone front. Indeed, the family might go so far as to kill its offspring, as had happened to Safaa.

Isam protested and accused her of simply parroting Mahmud. He told her that he would prove this to be nonsense. He was so sure of his mother's love for him; he was entirely confident that she would only want for him what he wanted for himself.

Well, then, did his mother love Gamila, too, or was this love restricted to him? Of course she loved Gamila. Then why did she want for Gamila something that Gamila did not want for herself? Gamila had known whom she wanted to marry, but her mother had married her off to someone else. At that point Isam, thunderstruck, demanded to know whom this person was? It was their neighbor, Mamduh, who loved Gamila. And Gamila had had a liking for him. He had asked Gamila's mother for her hand. No, he had not known, he'd had no idea! Why had his mother refused? Wasn't Mamduh an excellent young fellow, and an accountant in a respected company to boot? Why, the future was wide open before him!

Yes indeed, Mamduh was a fine young man, and his future looked promising. But he would never own a villa on the Pyramids Road, nor a Ford sedan. He would never be able to buy his wife a solitaire, or to pay the kind of dowry that Gamila's bridegroom had paid—a bridegroom who couldn't even make out a single written sentence if it were shoved under his nose!

But how could it be? How could he have lacked the slightest inkling of this? Why had his mother concealed these things from him? Well, it was natural that he not know, and that his mother hide it all from him, for perhaps he would have interfered and spoiled the plan that was all drawn up for Gamila.

No. It was not easy at all to persuade Isam of the necessity of waiting until he had graduated, and had developed some independence from his mother, if the matter demanded as much. He resisted; for if he were convinced of her reasoning it would demolish the only solution he had found to resolve the crisis he was trying so hard to surmount.

But the signs that this solution would so likely fail were too many and too clear to ignore. He had to let himself be persuaded, and he did. And then that stubbornly menacing look returned to his eyes, where Layla constantly faced it. She saw it as well in her mother's glances, those confused, embarrassed glances, and also in the mirror. In the mirror in her own room, as she was trying on her white dress, with her aunt making the final adjustments. And in the mirror at the beauty salon, as she had her hair done—that glass also reflected his determined and threatening gaze. And then, the same evening, in the mirror in Aunt Samira's room, Layla saw that look again. It was the evening of Gamila's engagement.

———

She felt good that evening, in her white dress, as bright a white as the full moon that peered through the slits in the tent erected on the roof in preparation to celebrate the engagement's announcement. She toyed with the folds of her dress, the delicate, massed pleats, as the servants removed plates from the tables and a band took its place on the platform to play.

"Your dress is so pretty, Layla," said Sanaa. "You know what you look like? An angel."

Adila touched her mouth delicately with a napkin. Sketching circles in the air with her hand, she gestured at the curves in Layla's body. "All that, an angel? That's pretty curvaceous for an angel."

Layla laughed as Sanaa protested. "But her face, really, isn't her face just like an innocent baby!"

Layla caught sight of her father on his way out, now that dinner was over. He had informed her aunt that he would attend out of respect for her. But he could not under any circumstances stay through to the end of the party. He could not observe the forbidden things that God had prohibited.

Gamila moved among the tables, greeting the guests. Her black-suited fiancé followed close behind, the large gold watch bouncing over his belly, suspended on a gold chain with the thickness of manacles. Gamila was stunning in her lacy gown, thick with panels like the leaves on a fecund tree, the tips worked in tiny white pearls that shone in the lights that twinkled from the roof of the tent. She was a gorgeous sight—her long, pale neck and abundant black hair, swirled along her temples and swept upward to show her small ears; her shining eyes like crystalline pools, just like her brother's eyes.

"That handsome fellow must be in love with you, Layla," said Adila, leaning toward her friend across the table. Layla turned toward her. She had been observing her mother, who sat hunched and small, next to Dawlat Hanim; she seemed almost lifeless, which was her usual state now that Mahmud had gone.

"Who?"

"Isam, Gamila's brother. His eyes never leave you."

"You're terrible!" said Layla, trying to suppress her smile. Adila's long neck and large black eyes craned toward her.

"Then what do *you* think it is? I pick these things up pretty easily, you know."

It was Sanaa, though, who was always fishing for the next love story. "Is it really true, Layla, is he in love with you? Now tell the truth, girl, on the Prophet's honor!"

Layla was silent. Seeing Sidqi, Samia Hanim's son, she waved.

"So you're going to play it cool with us then? That guy isn't just interested in you—he looks like he wants to eat you up!"

Layla stood up, laughing. "I'll be back in a minute, I'm going to speak to Mama, she's been trying to wave me over forever." She made her way amongst the tables, heading toward where her mother sat. Several guests smiled at her and she returned their smiles, noticing the looks of admiration that came her way. A woman she did not know grabbed her hand and pulled her over to give her a hug. "My stars, what a sweetheart you are! Whose your mama, remind me, dear?"

She resumed her way with a light tread, hardly sensing the floor. The thin, white folds of her dress spread like the wings of a bird, parting, closing, and opening again.

"Come here, sweetie pie," called out Dawlat Hanim. "Come over and show me! Now, anyone who's got on such a pretty dress—shouldn't she show it off to folks?"

Layla laughed, a series of little trills. She wished she could just go on laughing, for no particular reason.

"Are you going to sit over there, plastered to your chair, all evening?" exclaimed her mother softly. "Move about a little, greet people—they're all from the family."

Layla recognized immediately that Dawlat Hanim and her mother wanted to present her to the guests; perhaps sitting among all these people was a suitable husband-to-be. She did not feel at all irritated. She laughed again, a stream of bubbling little sounds, and began her rounds at Samia Hanim's table. She had every intention of going on to all of the other tables, but a sudden desire propelled her in a different direction. She was like a kitten searching for warmth. She wanted someone to cuddle and tease her, to pat her on the shoulder, to rub her hair, to repeat that she was pretty. She headed toward Isam, standing near the tent opening that led to the stairs from the roof, speaking to one of the servers. Layla put out her hand. When she laid it on his shoulder he turned to face her. Her eyes were a gay, flippant gleam, and her lips were parted in a half-suppressed smile. She seemed to shimmer—where did it come from? The glimmer ran from her lips, from her face and body to Isam; it settled in the space between them, a gaze that remained incomplete, a touch that was not quite there, sentences that had no periods. The light cocooned them, a single image, apart from all around them.

"Come, let's go outside for a few minutes," he murmured, his voice thick. He turned, Layla made as if to follow, and the perfect harmony of their image was broken. Isam collided with his mother as she entered the tent, having filled her obligation to serve food to the waiters and drivers.

"Isam! The dancer, she is absolutely insisting on sixteen pounds. Even though she and Ali Bey already agreed on ten. Go down and see what the problem is."

"Ali Bey can go down, *sitti*." Isam could not keep the irritation out of his voice.

"Please, just this once, love, for my sake. Tell her twelve. Because I said not a millieme more, and I don't like to go back on what I've said." She patted Layla on the shoulder and disappeared into the tent. Isam looked at Layla. "Come with me."

He knew that now she would not. The beam of light had gone from her face and body. She shrugged playfully, the teasing look still in her eyes. Isam stopped, his shoulder to hers, and whispered without looking at her. "Do you know what I'll do if you don't come with me?"

"What?" She was looking into the distance.

"I'll kiss you right in front of all these people."

She glanced at him from the corner of her eye. "If you're clever enough."

Isam turned to face her, his eyes fixed on the deep shadow between her breasts, visible at the neckline of her dress. Layla blushed.

"Isam, don't look at me like that. Everybody can see us."

He gave his head a shake. "You look beautiful today, very beautiful, my love." He turned and almost ran out of the tent.

———

129

As Layla strode toward Adila and Sana, Sidqi stopped her.

"What? Not even a *bonsoir*? Fine, so we don't even know each other, is that it?"

Layla shook Sidqi's hand, smiling in embarrassment. She noticed the playful admiration in his eyes.

"Will you allow me to say something to you?" he asked.

"Go ahead."

"You are overpowering today."

Layla laughed and her face went rosy. She angled her head. "Overpowering? Meaning what?"

"Meaning, *fatale*. And that's *haram*, too."

Layla gave him a sidelong glance, letting a restrained smile show, and walked away.

"Now who's *that* one?" asked Adila.

"That's Sidqi—Sidqi al-Maghrabi, Samia Hanim's son."

"Wow, he sure is a dish," said Sanaa. "He looks just like Gregory Peck. Why don't you marry him, Layla?"

"*He* wouldn't marry *her*," declared Adila.

Layla bristled. "As if I want to marry him?"

"What, is Layla such a bad choice?" asked Sanaa. "It's obvious he thinks she's pretty wonderful."

Layla laughed. "That's right, Sanaa, and mules get pregnant, too."

"Even if he has fallen for her," said Adila. "Fine, he goes with her for awhile, no problem, but marry her? No. There is something called a class system, remember?"

Layla looked at her in amazed admiration. "You really know what you're talking about, Adila. Listen, one time he said to me—"

"Shh!" said Sanaa. Layla sensed a man's hands coming to rest on her bare shoulders. She stopped talking, her body rigid. She turned her head. Sidqi's eyes were staring brazenly and confidently into hers.

"Aren't you going to introduce me to your friends? Or is this table a monopoly for all the beauty at the party?"

Layla introduced him to Adila and Sanaa. Sanaa extended her hand with a mechanical movement that compensated for what she was feeling, while Adila's hand rested firmly on the table as she nodded curtly. Layla felt discomfited with Sidqi's hands still pressing her shoulders; she felt that all eyes must be on her, and she saw Isam standing at the tent opening, a dangerous look in his eyes.

"Do sit down, Sidqi Bey," she said awkwardly. Sidqi was pulling out an empty chair when Isam stopped in front of Layla and said in an angry voice, without looking at either of her friends, "My aunt wants you."

Adila winked at Sanaa. Layla got up and Isam followed her. Sidqi said something that caused Adila and Sanaa to laugh. Layla walked toward her mother's table as the strains of music were muted in noisy *zagharid*, the ululations of the women. The dancer burst running from the tent opening, a red chiffon wrap floating on her body. The guests stood up as she entered, and Isam seized the chance to take Layla's hand and drag her outside the tent.

"What's happened, Isam?" asked Layla, leaning against the wall that encircled the roof, out of breath.

"What is there between you and that boy over there?"

"What boy?"

Isam shook his head violently. "The guy who was pinching you on the shoulder! I didn't think you could be so cheap."

Layla shut her eyes tightly and her face convulsed, as if she had just been slapped.

"Say something," Isam said ferociously. "Don't you have anything to say?"

Layla opened her eyes. "You're incredibly impertinent and bad-mannered." She turned to head inside the tent, but Isam yanked her back.

"Am *I* the bad-mannered one, or are you? You must have encouraged him. You must have!"

131

Layla turned to face him, her hand still in his grasp. She spoke quietly.

"Yes, that's right, I encouraged him. And I love him, too. What more do you want to hear?"

Isam could say nothing, and his grip suddenly loosened. She seized her chance, snatched her hand away, and ran inside.

Sashaying directly in front of Ali Bey, Gamila's fiancé, the swaying dancer had thrown herself onto his lap. He tried haplessly to shift his body back so that no part of him would touch her. Gamila was smiling and tugging at her mother's hand, and laughter rose from all sides of the tent.

Adila waved, but Layla ignored her and went to where her mother sat, hunched and alone. She sat down opposite, tapping her fingers on the table nervously.

"What's the matter?" asked her mother.

"Nothing."

"Nothing—what do you mean? Your color is completely gone—looks like a bird snatched those pink cheeks away."

Layla went on striking at the table without feeling anything.

"I have a headache."

Isam entered the tent. Layla shoved her hand down to her side, stood up, and walked straight over to where Sidqi, Adila, and Sanaa were sitting. Isam hurried forward and intercepted her halfway. He whispered into her ear. "If you know what's good for you, you'll go back to where you were."

Layla's face darkened. She tossed her head and kept walking.

"What happened, Layla?" asked Adila. "We've been trying to get your atttention for ages. We're ready to go."

"Now leave Layla alone," said Sidqi slyly. "Seems she is a very busy lady."

Layla wished she could slap his face. She sat down between Adila and Sanaa. "It's early."

"No, *ya sitti*, it isn't early at all. We'll just barely get home in time. Let's just go and say goodbye to *Tante* Samira and Gamila, and then leave."

"Really, we have stayed awfully late," chimed in Sanaa.

"Please allow me to accompany you," said Sidqi. "*Wallahi*, that would be a great honor, indeed."

Sanaa smiled. "You are so kind, Sidqi Bey," said Adila. "But there is really no need. We live just around the corner."

She stood up and Sanaa immediately followed suit. They shook Sidqi's hand and Layla led them over to where her aunt stood next to Gamila. Sanaa and Adila both kissed Gamila and shook her fiancé's hand in turn.

"What do you think of the bride, girls?" asked Samira Hanim.

"Marvelous, *Tante*! Just incredible! What a dress!" This was Sanaa.

"And what's *inside* the dress," added Adila. "And the whole party, everything, so beautiful. May you see the wedding soon, *in sha' Allah*."

"And may you see one soon, too, my dear."

Sanaa gazed at Gamila's fiancé for a moment, her small, aristocratic nose high. She addressed him coolly, almost reproachfully. "Gamila is a bride who deserves the most loving care."

Gamila laughed very loudly. Samira Hanim embraced Sanaa.

"Did we suggest anything but, *madame?*" exclaimed Ali Bey. "By my head and eye, whatever you say, *madame*, your wish is my command."

Adila leaned close to Layla so that she could whisper. "What a creep."

Handing Layla the ring of keys to the apartment, Samira Hanim said, "While you are here, my dear, bring your aunt the fur jacket from the wardrobe. I am so-o-o cold! Obviously your aunt has gotten old— she just can't take the cold any longer."

Ali Bey twisted his moustache and gave her a big smile. "Well, I do hope you recover, *sitt hanim*, I do hope so!"

———

"He's repulsive!" said Adila, putting on her coat.

"A real lout," agreed Sanaa. Layla twisted an imaginary moustache and danced about.

"May you see the same, both of you, *madame, madame, ya sitt hanim*, may you have the same fine luck."

She waved as their laughter rose from the descending elevator and headed to the apartment to retrieve her aunt's jacket. She tore it from the hanger, draped it over her shoulders, and shut the wardrobe. She stood looking at herself in the mirror, stepping back as she gathered the fur to her chest with her fingers. But her hands froze over her breasts as, in the mirror, she saw Isam at the door, a monstrous look in his eyes. Realizing that Layla had seen him, Isam came into the room and shut the door behind him. He folded his arms across his chest. Layla turned to face him slowly. Feigning calm, she said, "My aunt is cold and wants her jacket." He didn't answer, or move. There was a frightful stillness in his face, a murderous one, she could not help thinking.

"What do you want, Isam?" A strain of alarm had crept into Layla's voice.

"I'll kill you."

"You're mad!"

"I know I'm mad," said Isam, without losing the note of deadly calm from his voice. "But I told you—I said, don't go over to where he is." He walked slowly toward her, his head jutting forward, like a cat stalking its prey, step by careful step. She moved back until she was hard against the bed. Her voice held tears in it. "I was just seeing if I could make you angry. Isam, I was just trying to annoy you."

He got so close that he could almost touch her. She slipped from his hands and stood facing him, the bed between them.

"Don't wear yourself out trying to get away, Layla," he said in the same voice. "You won't escape from me."

"Please, Isam. Please, leave me alone."

Isam wiped his hand across his face violently. "So why didn't you leave me alone, since you love someone else?"

"I was playing a trick on you, trying to tease you. That's all."

She tried to steer for the door but he caught up to her, grabbed her by both shoulders, and turned her roughly to face him. He leaned her forcibly back against the door.

"I know you were playing a trick on me. But you won't do it again." He put his hands on her bare shoulders, where they stayed, fingers splayed out near her neck bone.

"No, I won't. Ever." Layla rolled her head back and closed her eyes as Isam spoke viciously. "So how long have you been playing tricks on me? How long have you been with that beast?"

Her head straight and still, Layla said calmly, "Go ahead and kill. Go on, now, show me."

His hands still on her neck, the middle finger of his right hand moved toward her chest.

"As long as that is what you think of me, it's better if you just go ahead and kill me."

"Why? Am I mistaken?"

She didn't answer, but tears rolled from her closed eyes. The finger of his right hand moved back to her neck and he bent his face to her, repeating it. "Am I mistaken?"

She spoke without opening her eyes. "You know—you know you are wrong!"

His lips fell onto hers and stayed there, but without movement, in a sort of exhaustion. Then they went rigid as his hand clenched her neck. He moved his face back and said in a choked voice, "I told you not to go back, and you did. You did." His body shuddered and so did his voice, and his eyes rolled as he shouted like a madman. "You belong to me! You're mine! My property! Understand?"

His grip tightened on her neck and she yelled, her voice hoarse. "Get away!"

She put her hands out and, with a strength she didn't realize she had, she tore Isam's hands from her neck and ran to the sofa, where she stood facing him like a bristling cat. "If you know what's good for you, you'll stay away from me! Totally! Understand?"

Isam hung his head while her voice got sharper. "I am not your property, I'm not anyone's property! I am a free person! Understand?"

Isam attacked her, his face glowering; a violent, wordless struggle began. Isam got the upper hand and threw her down onto the sofa. His body was like a rock on top of hers, his hands clenching her arms like iron shackles, his mouth pressed over her eyes, her mouth, her neck, her chest. The tap-tap of footsteps on the roof; the women's *zagharid*; music; a heat breaking out on her face and body; Isam's uneven breaths, his feet, crushing hers; the trilling louder and louder; the music. The sound of footsteps stopping in the corridor, and a knock on the door, and a voice calling, "Mister Isam—Mis-ter Isa-a-a-m!"

The knocking got harder, the call came again; Isam heard nothing. Then, the sound of her teeth on his cheek and his scream. He suddenly awoke to the rapping on the door and the voice, and his fists abruptly relaxed around her arms. Blow after blow came down on her shoulders, and his stifled wailing, his steps as he moved away, and the screech of the door as he opened it, shut it, and his mad shriek in the corridor.

"Enough! Get away from me, get away, before I kill you!"

The sound of the maid's drawn-out voice, as she said, "Oh, sir!" and her steps receding, Isam's footfalls, loud in the corridor, coming, going, slowly growing distant. The outside door slamming, shaking the whole apartment; the sound of her breathing, deep, as it dawned on her that she had barely saved her neck. The coldness of the dark room, biting her feet as she tiptoed out of the apartment and ran down the stairs, still in darkness, feet bare, as if she were dreaming.

———

Yes, a dream, a leaden one—and over, now, praise be to God. It had not ended that evening, though, but rather five days later. Five days—after which Isam came to see her. It was the Isam she knew, the one she loved, not that stranger who had sent fear and chills into her heart and body. He came to her, his face shining, peaceful, in control of himself, tender—as if somehow he had been reborn.

"Okay, Layla, okay. No more problems. I've found a solution. I will never again touch you, or bother you. I will only look at your pretty face and listen to you talk. I will love you and I'll wait until we are married." His features relaxed, his eyes softened, and a steady light came into them that burned Layla's body and settled inside her. It did not occur to her, in the joy that flooded over her, to ask Isam what solution he had found to the crisis that had made her suffer so.

———

"The solution?"

Mahmud wrote to Layla: "There is only one solution. The solution is for something amazing to happen, something that will shake those people to the core—all of those respectable, complacently settled folks. It has to be a miracle—only that will compel them to tear their shrouds to bits. Otherwise the situation will not change. The shrouds will not be torn apart because those folks will be holding so fast to the cloth and hiding themselves behind it. They will reckon that those shrouds are protecting them, strengthening them, when in fact the shrouds just fetter their ability to think and act. Behind these shrouds they go on living, each one saying, 'No, I will not risk it, I will not put myself in danger, I will not move outside of the circle that has been sketched out for me. For then I might bring harm on myself, and I might damage my own interests. I might hurt my future; I might harm my children. No, I will think only within the confines of what my society finds acceptable. I will have no desires except for what those around me desire, and I'll act only as they do. I will feel only the same emotions. And I will not react, for that is the other half of pain, and I want to spare myself all pain. I will do only what is in my own interest.' So they go on living under their shrouds. They never experience a

137

grand love, nor do they ever make great sacrifices. They do not linger in the world of the intellect, the imagination, the senses. They marry; they have their children, who are all in the same molds. They think alike, the same things impress them, and they have identical preferences and make identical choices. Repeatable patterns and identical molds—that is what it all is, Layla. Masses of people, without any extraordinary spark, people without any distinction, without any special skills or abilities, without any powers of invention, and without any readiness to really love."

In the three months that Mahmud had spent in the Canal Zone, his writing had never stopped or been interrupted. But his letters, long at first and so wonderfully packed with his feelings and reactions, became shorter and more matter-of-fact week by week, until finally they consisted of only a few lines asking after the family's health. Layla sensed that he was hiding something from her. More than once, she prodded him in her letters. And despite her blunt persistence his responses always skirted around her question. When she insisted, he wrote saying he was terribly busy; the small number of guerilla fighters meant added work, he said. Their number meant that a fellow had to focus his thinking—indeed, his entire existence—on this work. Therefore, his aim in writing was simply to reassure the family.

Layla had a hunch from the allusions in these notes that Mahmud and his mates were feeling lonely and isolated. She sent asking whether this was the truth he was hiding from her. In his last letter to her before leaving the Canal Zone, he wrote:

"Yes. We certainly are isolated. I'm not the only one who feels that way, everyone here does, but it does not affect us so badly that we are incapable of fulfilling the mission for whose sake we came here. But no—and even the betrayals and the spying are not particularly important, they do not make a big difference. In fact, those who are betraying us, and those who are spying on us, are really the exception; and they can be rooted out. The ones who have truly isolated us are not the traitors and the spies, but rather the millions of good people who love Egypt, but only as long as this love does not clash with their own selfish interests. The true betrayal is the betrayal of those folks who love Egypt with their hearts and mouths but not with their limbs and blood."

That letter contained painful news of conditions at the Canal. In addition to feelings of isolation, arms and ammunition were running short, organization was deficient, uniforms were lacking, and food was wanting. The great majority of freedom fighters were laborers, poor folks from city and village who had left behind their work, children, and whole families that they had been supporting. The government was procrastinating unforgivably about giving the fighters weapons and money for essential expenses.

In the same letter Mahmud informed Layla that he was coming to Cairo with his buddy Husayn on an official mission. They would not stay in Cairo more than twenty-four hours, he told her, and they would return directly to the Canal Zone.

Mahmud's language seemed emotional, angry. It was as if—as if he were implicating her as he cast blame for the situation! But what could she have done? Yet, wasn't it the truth? Wasn't she one of the good people who loved Egypt but not enough to tear apart their shrouds and jump to its rescue? Layla felt mortified, as if she had committed a crime; the sense of humiliation had still not left her as she extended her hand to greet her brother.

Chapter Nine

He had changed enormously. His father noticed the transformation as they sat down to lunch. He gazed at his son in awed alarm for a few moments but said nothing. His mother filled his plate with helping after helping over his protests, as if he had fasted throughout his time at the Canal.

He tried to start a conversation; he asked the usual questions, about everyone's health, about his aunt and Isam and Gamila; about his cousin's wedding plans. He learned that she would be married within the week. But periods of silence between one sentence and the next were long, and they were uncomfortable silences, as if he were a stranger. No one tried to find another topic of conversation. His mother wanted to ask him whether he was eating well there, and were there enough blankets, and had he been in any danger? But she knew that her husband did not want to hear a single word about any of these worries, and so she made do with gazing at her son, her eyes watering from time to time.

His father had one thing on his mind. One specific issue pressed on him, he could think of nothing else, and did not want to talk of anything else. But every time he was on the verge of saying something he would look at Mahmud's features, newly stern and rugged, at the traces of lines on his forehead, at his eyes that had lost their old sparkle, as if something in them had died; and then he would lapse into silence again. It was no use. This person in front of him would never listen to him, would not heed his words, and would never retreat from what his acts had set in motion. For he had indeed changed. He had left the space of filial obedience entirely. His father turned his eyes away, before there could be any risk of meeting his son's gaze.

As Layla stole glances at Mahmud, an indefinable fear trembled inside of her. He was sitting rigid and straight, his left hand gripping the table edge, his face stiff. He seemed tense in the extreme, all of him, more tensed than reasonable caution would demand, as if obliged to always remain at the ready, never allowing himself to relax even slightly.

Layla began warily to eat. The sound of spoons hitting plates jangled her nerves, as if she dreaded that at any moment something would happen to irritate Mahmud, some word, some noisy interruption that would threaten his fragile, concentrated poise, that would cause him to put his head down on the table and break out sobbing. The thought bothered Layla terribly, and she tried very hard to get it out of her mind. Wasn't this fear of hers laughable? Because she herself was weak, did she consider everyone as weak as she? Such a thing could not possibly happen to Mahmud. He was strong, he had fought the English for three months, and tomorrow he was returning to the Suez Canal to renew the fight. Mahmud would never let himself go; he would never collapse, ever. Such a thing was unthinkable. And it was natural for commandos to be in such a state of wariness. For they were fighting, not playing at it as she was, and as were those who remained far from the Canal Zone, satisfied merely to observe the outcome of the struggle.

Layla waited patiently for the meal to be over. Yes, Mahmud had changed. But everything between them would return to normal once lunch was over, once she was able to be alone with him in her room, or in his. Then they would talk to each other, really talk, as they had always done. She waited and waited for the end of the meal, her patience running out.

Finally they were alone in his room, and they did indeed talk to each other, as they had always done. They told each other things, yes; but something seemed to have come between them. She tried hard to reach Mahmud, to climb over the barrier he had put up between them, but her attempt failed. What had happened? Was he hiding something? No, he wasn't hiding anything from her, for he had told her everything, everything it was possible for one human being to convey to another through words. But even so, that prohibitive barrier remained in place, coming between them, as if . . . as if things had indeed happened to him, things that had put him at a distance from her, that had caused him to age so that the gap between them was now much greater. Those experiences had turned him into someone who was no longer Mahmud, her brother whom she knew so well, but rather a person she could not intuit, whose moods she would not recognize.

But could so much occur in a mere three months? Impossible! It must be that something was causing him pain and she was simply not doing a good enough job at distracting him to cheer him up. Maybe Isam would be able to do something? Yes—Isam, after all, was his friend, his dear friend, who always knew his secrets. Then, too, he was a man, and men were more able in such situations. Yes; she would summon him to come down here at once.

Layla stopped the elevator, yanked the door open, and dove inside— and stopped cold, smiling in confusion. She had collided with a tall, brown-skinned young man as he emerged. The young man stepped back inside the elevator.

"I'm sorry," he said. He smiled at her and Layla noticed an immediate change coming over his face. His angular, prominent features melted into a pleasant roundness as he grinned, so that his brown face almost reminded her of a suckling baby. Layla could not resist his smile, and she smiled back.

"Are you going up or down?"

The young man put up a hand to touch his soft black hair. "Neither. I'm getting out on this floor."

Layla stepped back to make room for him to pass. She stepped into the elevator and closed the metal door. But he did not head for either of the two apartments. He stood watching her, in his eyes a bewitchingly commanding expression. As if he were ordering her to stay where she was. About to close the inner glass door, Layla asked, "Is there something you need?"

"Can you wait just one minute, please?" His voice did not have the same suggestion of command that his gaze held; to the contrary, it was quiet and utterly controlled. "Where is the apartment of Mr. Mahmud Sulayman, please?"

"Oh—Mahmud? Um, it's right here."

Layla pointed to her own home as it dawned on her that this young man standing before her must be Husayn Amir, her brother's fellow soldier at the Canal. Her realization filled her with enormous relief, as if her worries and her brother's cares had dissolved under the full smile that faced her. Had God just answered her prayer, sending Husayn deliberately at this particular moment to cheer Mahmud up, to stand beside him as he always had at the Canal? Her face lit up with delight.

"Welcome, welcome!"

She flung the steel grating open and rushed out to lead Husayn to her apartment. Before her hand reached the doorbell, Husayn spoke.

"Layla."

It wasn't a question. He was addressing her. She turned and faced him.

"Husayn."

"How did you know?"

"How did *you* know?"

Their eyes met and they laughed. Layla turned and pressed the doorbell. "Mahmud has talked about you a lot," said Husayn.

"He's written a lot about you," she said without turning.

"So then we know each other pretty well. That means we're friends."

Layla turned to face him, a serious look in her eyes. "You're Mahmud's friend, right?"

Husayn nodded, smiling, and Layla went on. "And a friend helps his friend if he needs it, right?"

Studying her face, Husayn said, "Right."

Layla knew instinctively that she could rely on him, and that Mahmud could, too. Her face broke into a big smile. "Fine, then. Excuse me."

She left him there and returned to the elevator. As it moved, she gestured to him and waved, and then disappeared. Suddenly Husayn remembered the bad news that he was bringing to Mahmud. Now he felt like he was the one who needed help. They all needed help. The building began to sway before his eyes, the edifice they had all built, brick upon brick, with their sweat, their nerves, their blood.

———

Gamila opened the door. Her face was rosy, her eyes sparkling, and no sooner did she see Layla than she threw herself into her cousin's arms. She dragged Layla inside by one hand.

"The wedding dress arrived," she said, breathlessly happy. "And what a dress, Layla! *What* a dress!"

Layla disengaged her hand. "Just a minute, Gamila. Mahmud's arrived, and I want to tell Isam to go down and see him."

"How can you?" said Gamila, her enthusiasm suddenly flagging. "Aren't you going to see my dress first?" Then she smiled. "So, how is Mahmud?"

"Fine. Where's Isam?"

"In the study. Anyway, it's better this way. I'll be putting on the dress so when you come back you can see it on me."

Isam was sitting at the desk, a book open before him. Sayyida, the maid, was kneeling on the floor, wiping traces of coffee off the carpet with a damp rag. The offending coffee cup was still lying overturned at the edge of the desk. Isam got up, an embarrassed smile on his face.

"Hello, Layla."

"Mahmud's come." Layla was still standing near the door.

"Really?" Isam's voice carried no enthusiasm. Layla walked further into the room.

"Aren't you going to come down to see him, Isam?"

"Right now?"

Layla stopped right in front of him. "Yes, right now. Unless you're busy."

Isam shrugged and smiled. "No, I'm not busy at all." He turned to take his jacket from the armchair next to his desk chair, and as he walked forward he passed Sayyida. She raised her eyes, large and round like those of a cow, as she went on striking the carpet with the edge of the wet cloth.

"I want to tell you something before you go down, Isam."

Isam was putting on his jacket. "What is it, Layla?"

Layla pressed her lips together and nodded slightly in Sayyida's direction, trying to tell Isam with the set of her face that she would not talk in front of Sayyida. They stood waiting for her to finish what she was doing. There was no sign of the coffee on the carpet now, but Sayyida was still kneeling in her place, hitting at the floor with one end of the rag.

"Aren't you finished, Sayyida?" Layla asked gently. Sayyida raised her puffy face to Layla and pressed her full lips together without saying a word. She went on hitting the carpet. The repeated movements bothered Isam, and he shouted warningly.

"Hurry up, that's enough."

Once again Sayyida raised her eyes, giving him a bold look but staying crouched on the floor. Then, slackly, she got to her feet.

"*Yoo*, Si Isam, you mean I should leave the carpet dirty?"

Layla took a relieved breath when Sayyida was nearly out the door, but then she came back in, her large body moving indolently, taking the cup slowly from the desk, and then leaving the room again, letting her full hips sway slowly, heavily, a half-smile on her lips that was not directed at anyone, as if she were smiling at something that had just come into her mind—a secret, something very private and significant, something that gave her a sense of importance.

"Isam," Layla started. Isam walked quickly toward her, took her hand, and bent over to kiss it gently, quick little kisses she could hardly feel, as if he were trying to placate her, to make something up to her after hurting her in some way.

"Isam, for my sake, be nice when you are with Mahmud. Just be really nice." She looked away. "He's changed, Mahmud is different, completely different, Isam."

"I know he is sensitive, more so than he should be."

Layla placed her hand on his shoulder. "That's exactly it, Isam."

"Do you remember how much he suffered during the '46 demonstrations? But you were small then, so small, my love."

Retrieving those days in her mind, Layla whispered. "But I do remember, Isam. I remember it all, as if it had just happened this morning." She seized his hand and they walked together toward the outside door.

"I won't go down with you, it's better that way," she said. "I'll go see Gamila. I don't want Mahmud to think that I got you to come down." Layla pressed Isam's hand, smiling, then released it, turned toward Gamila's room, and opened the door.

———

Gamila's back was to the door. Layla stopped short in the doorway and sucked in her breath. Wasn't this her own white dress—the same chiffon, the same accumulating folds like a white bird's unfolding wings? As Gamila straightened and turned to face her, Layla gave her head a shake, bemused by her foolish thought. Gamila's dress was entirely different. The white chiffon was not actually part of it, but rather a flowing veil that cascaded down the back of the dress. The gown itself was of white satin, embroidered with artificial pearls, sequins, and beads.

"What do you think?" asked Gamila triumphantly.

"Marvelous—it's beautiful, really gorgeous! Fit for a princess, and you look better than the best." But she felt some sort of inner strain, as if Gamila had taken something from her, something that belonged specially to her. Her white dress, her lovely white dress.

Gamila walked toward the mirror. "Wait—this isn't the whole effect. Right now you can't properly see its fit. The zipper's still open."

Layla sat down, across from the mirror. "That Sayyida of yours is really annoying. There I was wanting to talk to Isam about Mahmud, and she was standing there, just hanging around. We even told her to leave and she still stayed."

Gamila was zipping up the dress. "That's because she has a crush on Isam. She's his girlfriend, *ya sitti!*" The zipper closed with a harsh sound.

"His girlfriend? What on earth do you mean?"

Gamila gave Layla a sidelong glance and put her hand down to straighten the bodice of her dress. She gave it a sharp tug downward. "Layla, you are *so* naïve! Any fellow his age, and not married—you know—he has to do that. If he doesn't, he isn't much of a man."

Gamila's hands went up to her hair. She gathered it in back and piled it on top of her head. She turned her head to one side and tilted it, studying the effect, and then turned to Layla.

"What do you think of this hairstyle, Layla?" But when she saw Layla's bewildered face, her mouth open stupidly, she broke out laughing.

"You know something, Layla? You know what you just made me

think of? The night I saw them in the kitchen. That was the night of my engagement party. I got up in the middle of the night because I had an awful stomachache. I went into the kitchen to fill a hot-water bottle. When I turned on the light, I had to flick it off right away. And I was as stupid-faced as you are right now. I stayed that way for two whole days, too. Until Mama explained everything to me."

Gamila sat down next to Layla, a sad look in her eyes. Layla wiped her face and stood up.

"Where are you going?"

"Downstairs." Layla's voice was carefully level.

"Shame on you, Layla!" Gamila's voice was disapproving. "Obviously the dress doesn't please you. Why not, Layla? It's so stylish—the skirt alone took seven meters. Look."

She jumped to the middle of the room, threw her head back proudly, steadied the heels of her shoes and swirled around. The dress flared, the skirts forming a widening circle. The room whirled before Layla's eyes—the ceiling was the floor, and the walls were leaning in toward each other. Gamila came to a stop, breathless.

"Now what do you think? Really, have you ever seen a dress like this? Even in the cinema?"

Layla muttered something without even a glance at the dress.

"Stark naked. Completely exposed."

"The chest, you mean?"

"All . . . exposed."

Gamila reached for the bolero that was the dress's finishing touch and put it on. She turned around, smiling lightly.

"Does that satisfy you, *ya sitti al-shaykha*, my fine cleric?"

Layla shook her head despondently. Her voice was almost a whisper. "It's no use. Exposed, bared—and from within. Exposed, Gamila, stripped completely naked."

Now Gamila stared at her—and shrieked, for Layla's face was ashen, her pale lips trembling, her eyes unfocused as if she were in a coma. She could not still her hands—clutching the neckline of her dress as if to force it closed, dropping to grasp the hem, yanking it as if she wanted it to stretch down to cover her toes, then rising again to clutch at the throat of her dress.

"Layla, what's the matter?"

Layla gave her head a bewildered shake and collapsed onto the nearest chair.

"Layla, what's wrong? What is it? Tell me!"

"Nothing."

"I'll call Mama."

"No!" whispered Layla. "Don't call anyone, because . . . because I have a stomachache."

"Can I make you tea?"

Layla nodded. Gamila left the room. Layla heard her order Sayyida to make tea, and then she could hear her cousin's footsteps moving in the direction of her mother's room. She jumped to her feet and tiptoed cautiously to the door. The lost look in her eyes once again, she strained her ears and moved forward, crossing the front hall to open the outer door.

She pressed her hand to the wall for support and made her way to the stairs. She froze in place as the whine of the elevator forced itself into her ears and head; her whole body seemed to vibrate with it. The elevator passed her on its way down; she saw its cable straining slowly downward. She stretched her head forward over the wall that separated the stairwell from the elevator shaft, her eyes clinging to the cable as it was pulled downward. She hung her torso into the emptiness that the elevator had left behind, and stared at that cable, letting herself be dragged by the eyes. She steadied her hands and lifted more of her body away from the floor until she lay stretched along the top of the low elevator wall. The cable was pulling her downward, downward. Her grip on the wall grew slack, and the cable pulled her on.

"Layla!" It was Gamila, shrieking. A hand shot out to grab her.

Pulled off the wall, Layla turned and found herself on the stairs face to face with Gamila.

"Layla, what are you doing? You're crazy!"

Layla stood motionless, the same expression of empty loss in her eyes. Now a terror cold as ice swept over her body as it suddenly struck her: she had just barely been pulled from her death.

"Gamila, come downstairs with me." Her voice was choked. She stumbled down the stairs, Gamila close behind her. She kept going, passing the door to their apartment, not realizing it until Gamila said something. She turned and retraced her way, up the staircase, her steps sluggish. Her room? No—not even her room. Down—she wanted to go down, down, where she would feel nothing, where she would not even be able to think.

———

She went in, shuddering as she noticed the open sitting-room door. Isam. Isam was there, with Mahmud. She headed directly to her room, swiftly, as if someone were giving chase. But as she reached her door the urgency in Mahmud's voice, calling her name, stopped her. Gamila, she realized, was tugging at her. Her cousin pulled her into the sitting room, as if she'd been stripped of the will to move her own body. She came to a dead stop in front of Mahmud, who sat not far from the door, as if she did not even see anyone else in the room. At the sight of his sister, Isam jumped to his feet, waving at her dress. "What on earth are you wearing?"

"The city's burning," Mahmud said to Layla. She echoed him, a flat statement of fact, no reaction on her face. "Yes, burning. Burning." But another face gazed into hers, smiling broadly—a true, sincere smile, unrestrained by any caution. A strange face, the face of a stranger. Suddenly Layla yelped as if only in this moment she had regained consciousness and realized what Mahmud had said. "Burning? What d'you mean, burning?"

Mahmud noticed that Husayn was standing next to them, a smile on his face. "Oh—this is my sister Layla, and—" His gaze turned to Gamila, encased in her white dress, he paused, and finished his sentence in wonder. "And—my cousin. Gamila."

Husayn's hand hung in the air for a moment before Gamila's met it firmly. She turned and whispered something into Isam's ear, and, his face solemn, he immediately returned to the settee opposite Mahmud, Gamila close behind. Layla's eyes remained fixed on Mahmud. She mumbled, her lips trembling. "What, Mahmud? What do you mean?"

Mahmud's face grew stony as he gazed into the distance. His voice seemed to catch on something, to have difficulty leaving his throat. "People. People burned the cinemas, and Fuad Street. The whole city is on fire, it is all flame and smoke."

"People burning the city?" Layla wailed. "Why? Why would we burn our own city?"

Mahmud, biting his lower lip, said nothing. He shut his eyes; he left her alone; a stranger. Layla's eyes wandered. Gamila was perching gingerly on the edge of the settee so she would not crush her dress. Isam was huddled at the other end. Her eyes came to rest on Husayn, who responded with his customary, broad smile.

"The truth is, the people have been wronged. Folks went out to protest the Ismailiya massacre, and then the Palace and reactionary elements took advantage of the situation in order to discredit the nationalist movement."

With a shaking hand Mahmud took out a cigarette. "The betrayal didn't start today, you know. It's been there since the beginning, and now we're seeing the upshot of it all. The end. This fire, it's the end—the end of the battle for the Canal."

Layla flopped onto a chair; she could see herself in the grand mirror that crowned the sitting room, despite the tears that blurred her vision. Across the mirror's blank face broke the late-afternoon sun's tapering rays, imprinting a blaze of redness on the glass. Layla tried to bring the flaming mirror into focus: before her blurring eyes tongues of fire slid across the sheet of glass, fusing her to its surface as if an act of sorcery lured her there. A painful droning drummed into her ears, as if thousands of old kerosene burners had all been lit at once.

"For a country boasting heroes like the soldiers of Ismailiya," exclaimed Husayn, "this can't possibly be the end. They were cut off, isolated—more important, they knew full well that the entire country had washed its hands of them. Sure, they could've surrendered—they knew that. They could've raised a white shirt, waved a white handkerchief, anything. But they didn't. No, they died in their boots instead."

Mahmud mopped his face slowly, heavily. "So, what's the use? What's the use, then? All that blood—it went in vain."

Layla's hand went up to her collar; she tugged it away from her neck, her eyes still held captive by the mirror. Blood and fire! She staggered between them. Blood and fire—she was hit, and now she was trying to save herself. Blood surrounded her on every side, and the flames rose. But there sat Gamila, impassive, a cold stone statue in her pure-white dress. The word "betrayal" torched through Layla's ears. Fire—it enveloped the city, choked the city! Fire, choking her! She jumped to her feet and tore from the room, from the apartment, out, onto the stairs—up, up to the fire. She must see that fire; she must witness the flames gripping the city, the crimson cloud that choked Cairo. She must see it all. As she climbed furiously she could hear her cousin. Gamila had leapt from her serene pose, shouting hysterically. "The stairs! The stairs!" But it was some moments before she could regain enough control of herself to make them understand Layla's alarming state of mind. Mahmud took off at a run toward the stairs, Isam pressing forward after him and Gamila behind them both. Husayn, pausing on the threshold, noticed the elevator's slow ascent and stopped it.

On and on hurtled Layla, bounding up the stairs, propelled by a curious strength that pushed her, dragged her, urged her on toward the fire. She did not see Husayn as she burst onto the roof, not even slow-ing down until she came right to the edge of the low encircling wall that ringed the roof and toppled onto it. By now the fire had subsided to the point where it was visible only as scattered points of light, its feeble remains nearly vanquished. But the smoke stubbornly held out, crouching in the sky, enormous, stupefying, appalling masses of blackness everywhere—in the air, on the ground, a crushing weight on her chest.

When Husayn touched Layla's arm gently, she started and stared at him in fear. He stood beside her, his back to the wall, his hands bracing him, his broad smile full in her face. Her features relaxed as she turned her gaze back to the masses of smoke.

"What's the matter?" His voice, too, was gentle. She raised her eyes, staring dully at him for a few seconds before she returned her gaze to the viscid black smoke.

"What's wrong, Layla?" His voice was even softer this time. She sighed deeply, her eyes still on the acrid smoke as she spoke. "Why does everything good always turn out badly in the end?"

Husayn perched on the wall edge and bent his head toward her. "This is not the end, Layla. *We* determine the end; we *make* it—me, you, Mahmud, everyone who loves Egypt."

Layla gave a short, hard laugh that came out more like a howl as she gestured toward herself. "Me?" Her face changed completely, taking on a look of contempt as if she was speaking of a mortal foe. She stood up and walked heavily toward the door that gave onto the rooftop. Husayn caught up to her and put out his hand to pat her shoulder. His voice shook with feeling. "This isn't the end. Don't believe Mahmud. Believe me." He turned her toward him and looked hard at her, his expression one of sympathy and entreaty. "Believe *me*." He seemed to pour his entire being into the attempt to persuade her. As their eyes connected she found a confidence there, in that frank, direct, gaze that spoke of goodness and an acute understanding. That gaze seemed to promise her a more pleasing tomorrow, and her tense face softened.

But she tipped her head forward suddenly to listen as footsteps and voices approached the roof: Isam's voice, calling to her. She studied Husayn for a moment.

"I don't believe anyone," she said flatly. She turned again to walk toward the door, but stopped dead as Isam burst through the doorway, followed by Mahmud and Gamila. Isam ran toward her, his arms extended, his hands reaching to touch her, moving rapidly and with mad desperation from her face to her shoulders, all the while whispering her name. Layla felt as if something had died inside of her. She put out her hands calmly, pushed him away, and marched right up to Mahmud, who had stopped cold, bewildered by Isam's behavior.

"Come on, let's go—right now." She plodded to the door, brushing right by Gamila, who stood motionless as a statue in her white dress, her back to the sky, a portrait framed in the ropy, ugly masses of smoke.

———

That evening, Mahmud went to jail. With many other irregulars, he would stay in detention for six months. As the sentence wore on, Layla's father intoned an unchanging refrain. "I knew it. I knew this would be the end of it all."

———

And as the sentence wore on, Layla's entire existence was concentrated in her effort to conceal her turmoil from all of them. She went on as usual: talking, laughing, behaving as she normally did. At the end of each day she would return to her room in utter exhaustion, an actress whose spell onstage had gone on far too long. Stretched full-length on her bed, she ached through every part of her body. It was a pain whose source she could not exactly pinpoint. Her mother always referred to this sort of fatiguing ache—whose exact location you could never really figure out—with the same phrase: "My body is defeated." Yes, that's what it was; her body was defeated. And not just her body: everything. Everything inside of her was defeated, as if she had hefted a load that was really far too heavy for her capacity, and it had fractured her spine.

Wasn't that what she had done, in fact? For she had challenged her father and posed a threat to her mother. She had flown in the face of their accustomed practices, had rejected their most fundamental beliefs. She had fallen in love. And then, she had been so determined to abandon their narrow world for a world that was alive, a world vast and wide and full! She had wanted—had willed—that she and Isam would build a world of light. In their world all would be beautifully transparent, authentic and basic, so unlike the world she knew. Theirs would be a world of love; it would be the beautiful world of truth. And then what had been the result of it all? Coffee spilt on the carpet; a darkened kitchen; a defeated body; earth, mud—nothing but the soiled surface of that world she had tried to flee.

And Mahmud? Mahmud had challenged and threatened them, too. He had gone, he had left, he had broken defiantly out of their world to sail, laughing and sparkling, into a world of . . . of love, that world of love, truth, and beauty. And he had returned crushed, cowering, withdrawn, his wings more than clipped. Filth had filled his eyes, filth and mud; the mud from which he had fled. And a fire encircled the city, the country—black, acrid smoke, and a darkened prison, and a world narrower than the one he had burst from so determinedly to sail beyond, laughing and sparkling. No. To sparkle was not the lot of her brother, nor was it her lot. To sparkle was the province of Gamila alone.

———

With radiant triumph Gamila's eyes made a slow, careful circuit. "Really, Layla? Does the dining room set *really* please you?" She did not bother to wait for an answer; Layla, she knew well, had never in her life seen the like of this. Her aunt, she was well aware, was staring round in stunned delight—like a woman just come in from the village, thought Gamila with a flash in her eyes, visiting Cairo for the very first time. Her aunt's husband was silent; this was the only way, she was certain, that he could hide the embarrassment and agitation he must be feeling.

From the huge window, the sun's rays cascaded in, setting the redness of the carpet on fire, and glinting against the marquetry work of the mahogany buffet. An almost painfully intense greenness pulsed upon them from the garden beyond the window, breaking the carpet's ardent red. Sitting at the head of the table, Gamila beckoned the *sufragi* lightly, naturally, as if she had been doing so her entire life. The man walked all the way around the table to her side. Gamila spoke to him in an undertone, relaxed, smiling, animated, her hand toying with a diamond collar that circled her neck. At Layla's arm, the *sufragi* bowed slightly as he offered her the plate—a pyramid of *cassata* sheathed in preserved fruit. Isam's eyes flashed as he looked at her with a smile. "Take another chunk, Layla," he said. "You've always loved ice cream."

He sat down to eat his own *cassata* with relish, at ease in his chair. He no longer felt any discomfort in her presence. At first, when she had ended their relationship—and before he'd understood why—he had felt vexed indeed. When he realized that she knew, his chagrin vanished, though, for why should he feel at all embarrassed now? His conscience was clear and clean, his thoughts as transparent as the crystal goblets gleaming on Gamila's table. He had done what he truly believed expressed his obligation to her; after all, he had saved her from something that made death look positively bearable. Anyway, there had been no other solution; and if he had acted any differently, then inevitably he would have harmed her. And he would find it infinitely easier to die than to harm her, when he loved her so, and always would.

But what Layla found so painful was Isam's behavior. Why, he acted still as if he sincerely loved her! It bewildered her. How could he possibly love one woman with his soul and another with his body? And anyway, what about that other woman? Had it never occurred to him that she was a human being, too? That he had harmed her bodily and emotionally, that he had threatened her humanity? No, clearly it had not occurred to Isam, not at all. He seemed completely confident and at peace with himself. His face bore a new expression—the grieved look of the martyr to duty.

Yes, indeed, Isam was confident and at peace. And Gamila—well, she went far beyond confident! Gamila was proud; she was splendid; she was smugly victorious. *She* had accepted life as it was, and simply, without creating any complications. Gamila had not stopped to philosophize. She had listened to her mother and she had followed sanctioned practice. She had followed those fundamentals. And therefore life had been good to her. Life had offered its bounty, its contentment, its security.

There had been a time when she had regarded Gamila with a touch of disdain. She had considered herself stronger than Gamila, than her aunt, than her father—and stronger than their beliefs, their rules, their traditions. She had laughed with a certain superiority when her mother had said, "The one who knows the fundamentals does not suffer."

Yes. She had existed for a time in the shadow of this silly illusion. But in truth it was she who was silly, trivial, conceited, and despicable. She was the doormat beneath people's soles.

Chapter
Ten

July 23, 1952. Morning. The army had shaken Egypt to the core. Awe, disbelief, a belligerent joy and pride; as news of the revolution spread, new sentiments trembled on millions of lips and shone through the tears in people's eyes. New words sobbed from throats choked with emotion. Egyptians poured from their homes to fervently clasp the hands of the soldiers, hearts sheltered in their cupped and shaking palms.

Muhammad Effendi Sulayman sat at home, riveted to the radio, listening again and again to the declaration of the Revolutionary Leadership. He was petrified by the conviction that something would intervene to thwart the revolution and postpone Mahmud's release. At first he had not believed his ears. He simply could not accept that men like him—Egyptians just like him—had successfully challenged the authorities—all of them!—and had overturned the government. When it finally dawned on him that the thing had really happened, a wave of pride in himself, in having been born an Egyptian, engulfed him.

But a different reaction followed all too soon. An agonizing fear throbbed through his body as he heard that the revolution had moved into a new stage, and it mounted as he heard that they were talking about dethroning the king. Wasn't the earth still turning? he asked himself. Well, then, mustn't the king still be on his throne, the Egyptian people bowing as always to his sovereignty? How could those revolutionaries change the course of destiny? Glued to the radio, Muhammad Effendi Sulayman listened to the news of the king's expulsion from Egypt. Tears collected in his eyes, reflecting the blend of alarm and pride he felt as the paramount icon of the old Egypt was demolished before his eyes.

———

As Muhammad Effendi Sulayman heard the momentous news, Layla was walking along Qasr al-Aini Street. She noticed a blue-overalled worker on a bicycle coming in her direction; still at a distance, he was waving his hands wildly, turning first to one side and then the other, flinging out words that Layla could not make out. She could see, though, that people were coming together, forming little groups and chattering. A few meters from Layla the bicycle rider stopped, his swarthy face wreathed in smiles as he looked at her. Gesturing wildly, he yelled, "The king has left the country!" and then turned away immediately to offer the same news to a barefoot boy who was dashing toward him. Layla felt a quaking in her body and took off at a run after the worker. People darted from their shops to crowd around him, asking for more details. "The king has left the country!" The worker's ecstasy encompassed his whole face. Layla's hand shot out and he shook it vigorously with a simple "Congratulations!"

"Congratulations!" The word resounded as if people were incapable of finding any other. Spaces between bodies vanished as one person clapped the next on the shoulder, as people chuckled and whooped and told jokes. Layla could not move; she stood among them, enjoying her sense of oneness with the crowd, the companionable sensation that they had all contributed in one way or another to expelling the king. A mood of sympathy, of ease and belonging, swept over her, a sense of confidence in herself and others; how she wished she could stay among them, stay on and on! But the moment passed; the bicyclist straightened on his seat, warning people that he was about to move on; folks tried to detain him but he would not stay. He moved forward, waving his hands, laughing, to go on to others, to tell more and more people that the king had been thrown out. Forward he went, from one group to another, as if propelled by a crying need inside of him to connect with the greatest number of people possible at this precise moment in time.

———

It was a pounding forceful enough to shake even the massive doors to the Aganib Prison, where many of the guerillas were imprisoned. It was like the blow of a single man, in unison like the shouts with which it mingled: "Long live Egypt! Long live the Revolution! Down with Imperialism!" It was a moment when those young people surely could have broken down those doors, but there was no reason to do so. They understood that the prison doors were as good as open; they knew they were all but free. It was just a matter of days. Yet those young souls could not bear it! At such a moment, were those doors to keep them apart? At *this* moment, for which they had waited all their lives, indeed for which they had *lived?* They were determined to be together, united, and the prison shook with their blows and cries. It was not the usual time to organize themselves into rows for the officers; but the prison superintendent issued his order to open the huge doors. Prisoners and jailers—they hugged each other, laughter and tears mingling. A prisoner twisted a jailer's belt around his middle and began to dance. A crowd gathered round him, clapping in time, while other prisoners split into groups, talking and laughing. A voice rose in song.

> *My country, my country*
> *My blood I've offered you*
> *I'll sacrifice my life*
> *For the peace that is your due.*

Silence—and then other voices rose, and still others joined those, as their youthful owners stood tall and the circle widened to embrace them all. The voices combined to become one voice—a single, strong voice of celebration that arched across the land of Egypt to embrace every one of its folk.

———

Mahmud and Husayn strolled through the yard that lay behind the Aganib Prison. "Didn't I tell you?" exclaimed Husayn. "Now maybe you'll start believing what I say!"

Mahmud smiled, shaking his head in wonder. "But who could have imagined it? Who could have foreseen that things would develop like this? And so fast?" As the friends approached a wooden bench, Mahmud dropped onto it and stretched. He felt deeply refreshed, as if an enormous responsibility had suddenly been lifted from his shoulders; as if he had delivered that burden to another and dusted his hands of it; and now it was his turn to rest.

"What's on your mind right now, Mahmud?"

Mahmud's hand, no longer tense, stroked his growing beard. "A good shave, a warm bath, and a clean mattress."

Husayn snorted. "What a lucky guy you are! *You're* going back to an orderly household, all waiting for you—to your mother and sister. Speaking of your sister—she's awfully nice."

Mahmud looked at him. "Why don't you get married, Husayn? Instead of living by yourself like this."

Husayn started laughing. Then he raised his head. "I'm broke, *ustaz*."

"Two years an engineer in a good, solid company, and you're broke! You've got to be kidding me. How much were you getting?"

"Thirty-five pounds."

"You didn't save any of it?"

"I saved."

"So?—"

Husayn smiled and shrugged. "I married off my sister—got her off my back."

Mahmud leaned over and clapped a hand on Husayn's thigh. "But you're no ordinary guy. And can't you take up the scholarship your sister did the paperwork for?"

"I don't want to leave the country right now."

Mahmud pulled himself upright. "Oh come on, Husayn, what's the matter with you? Sure, the first time around you pulled out of the scholarship, and your excuse was perfectly reasonable and acceptable, and they knew that. There were circumstances, and a guy couldn't leave the country at such a time. But now—it couldn't be a better time. So—?"

"A month or two, that's all, until things settle down. Mightn't they need us?"

"They? Whom do you mean?"

"The revolution."

"Why?" Mahmud's voice was sarcastic. "Are they going to appoint you as a Minister of Public Works, or what?"

Husayn began to laugh but stopped short as he leaned toward Mahmud. His voice was serious. "Mahmud, we've got to be alert. The English aren't going to take this lying down. They aren't going to watch the country slip from between their fingers like this without putting up a very big fuss."

Mahmud did not seem bothered. "In any case, our responsibility stops here. Now it's up to the army."

Husayn was silent for a moment, gazing toward the horizon. He spoke quietly, as if thinking out loud. "We're all responsible. As long as one's alive, his responsibility toward his country never comes to an end."

Mahmud got to his feet. "Fine, then, just stay here and languish, lazybones," he said, irritated. "Anyone with your attitude doesn't deserve to travel, anyway."

Husayn's face reddened at the sudden, unexpected insult. He bit back the sharp words on his tongue. He truly loved Mahmud, and he knew how intense had been Mahmud's transformation while in detention. His friend had sketched such a rosy picture of life in his head that confronting its rawness shocked him. Death he could face with courage, but he had not been able to face treachery so peaceably. He had witnessed betrayal at the Canal, and in the burning of Cairo, and in the wave of arrests and detentions. The world had frightened him and he would never quite recover. Now, he turned to his friend.

"I'm sorry, Husayn."

Husayn gazed into his companion's gaunt face, aged by deprivation, the eyes permanently bewildered, the look of a child unthinkably deceived. He smiled, stood up, and put his arm around Mahmud as they headed toward the prison's reception area, trying all the while to think of something to say that would dispel Mahmud's worries. Husayn knew he had clubbed his friend in a sensitive spot at the worst possible moment. He had reminded Mahmud of responsibility at a time when his friend believed he had finally rid himself once and for all of that burden. The revolution had come as a salvation from on high for Mahmud, a rescue that lifted from his weary back the necessity of facing life in its merciless realities; a salvation that gave him to believe that he could finally stand on shore, a mere observer, without the slightest feeling of guilt. Husayn smiled and leaned toward Mahmud.

"I'm bad news, aren't I?"

Mahmud broke out laughing and disentangled himself from Husayn's grip. But Husayn grabbed his arm again and quickly went on. "Mahmud, there's something I want to talk to you about, something personal."

Mahmud stopped laughing and looked straight at Husayn, his eyes showing interest. "What's going on, Husayn?"

Husayn hesitated a moment. The smile disappeared from his face, his hand dropped from Mahmud's arm, and he took a rapid step forward.

"Husayn, what is it? Come on, say something, brother."

Husayn would not meet his eyes. "Later, Mahmud. Later on." His voice dwindled. "It's my problem, and I'm the one who has to solve it."

Husayn tossed and turned on his straw pallet, settled on his back and lay still, thinking. Why had he used the word "problem"? Why not, for example, "subject," or "issue," rather than "problem"? But wasn't one-sided love a problem indeed? Especially when you didn't even know if the girl you loved was attached to someone else or not. No—she isn't attached; she was, she really was, but everything ended. That was clear, very clear from the way she had pushed Isam's hands away from her body, as if they held some filth that she absolutely could not bear to have within reach. No—this was no ordinary quarrel! It could not have been. It was the end of their relationship, an end that bastard deserved.

Husayn smiled lightly in the darkness. What right did he have to cast names at a person he knew only by sight? Someone of whom he knew so little? Wasn't this madness? But wasn't the whole story madness and more madness? What did he know of the girl who had occupied every moment of his life in this prison? A girl to whose image he fell asleep and wakened? Who filled his heart with her radiance and an enthusiasm for life? Nothing—he knew nothing at all. Yet the sensation persisted that he had known her all his life—and would never know her any better than he already did today, because it would be impossible to know her any better. He was sure that he could finish whatever sentence she started, could turn automatically in the direction she wanted to go even before she could do so. And he had known this after spending no more than half an hour with her! Well, perhaps it was the prison. It was this solitude, this loneliness, that had constructed from one fleeting meeting a whole legend to consume him, a fairy tale that started to fade whenever the light of day brushed over it. If he were to leave prison, perhaps his feelings would change? No, never—that would never happen. He had sensed the extent of his attachment to her even before prison; in fact, he had known it the moment he saw her. What had happened was beyond anyone's understanding. You couldn't explain it to anyone; it could not be subjected to any logic or rational explanation. But it had happened, and it had happened to him—to someone who was never convinced by anything that wasn't completely logical or rational or scientific. When she had rushed toward him in the elevator he had barely been able to keep back a shout. She had stopped and apologized, and into his mind had sprung a wholly-formed question: "Where have you been all this time? I've been waiting for you all my life!" Meanwhile, his tongue had formed meaningless utterances that had absolutely nothing to do with the thoughts coursing through him. And then he had left her, he had come out of the elevator. But when she had shut the iron grille between them he realized that he could not just leave her and go away. She was his fate and he could not let go of that. Then, when he discovered that she was Mahmud's sister, he realized that he would see more of her. Still, as the elevator ascended he had felt that a part of him was going with it. When his eyes had met hers and they had laughed together he imagined that perhaps she, too, had understood that he was her fate, but he'd been wrong. The two of them were worlds apart.

With the back of his hand Husayn wiped away the drops of sweat that had collected on his brow. What had happened to her in the meantime, as brief as that interim had been? What had made her despise life so, to lead her to think about suicide? And then cause her to submit so passively, so that she faced people with a stiff body and even more severe face from which all life seemed gone? Yet during that short time, when she was not with Isam, hardly would he sit down with Mahmud before the guy would appear—ten minutes later, maybe a quarter of an hour at most—to sit composedly with them. No—it didn't appear after all that anything had happened between them. True, Isam was one of those emotionally detached people whose actions and reactions, comments and feelings, were always so calculated. You encountered people like that every day—there were thousands of them just like Isam. Husayn had recognized the signs the first time he'd seen Isam. But after all, the fellow was a human being. It did not seem possible that something could have come between him and Layla that would shatter her so and yet leave him so completely unruffled. It must be as he had first thought. Layla must have heard something about Isam, perhaps from Gamila. Whatever it was, she had seen her world devastated before her eyes.

So Husayn tossed and turned. He doubled over his pillow to cover his face. How had he come to be so certain of this? How could he have grasped the situation so precisely, and so rapidly—indeed, the moment he had seen her bewildered face as she entered the room? Even before he had seen her on the roof pushing Isam's hands away from her body in disgust, he had understood. He had seized the situation fully, immediately, as if she had spilled out every detail, telling him, for instance, that she loved Isam, but that Isam had committed an act so horrible that it had eliminated all possibility of her loving or respecting him. He understood it all, swiftly and exactly, even though she had not so much as glanced his way. She had not even sensed his presence, leaving his hand—reaching toward hers—suspended in the air.

Lord, how had he been able to size the situation up so readily, in that room, before Layla had made any sort of telling gesture? A simple guess? There'd been no preliminaries that would have made it a reasonable deduction, he puzzled. Yet he had understood perfectly, as if whatever barrier kept him from knowing what was in her mind had vanished. And she had not even turned his way, had not even sensed that he was there! No, no it was impossible. She had to have been aware of him. How could he possibly feel so strongly about her—how could he have these feelings that destroyed all logic, all limits, and penetrated him from body to soul—if she did not have something of the like, even just a bit, even one part in a thousand?

Husayn flattened his pillow and rested his palms on it. When she had waved at him from the elevator and smiled, he had sensed a current run between them. On the roof, when he had whispered into her ear, "Believe me," and she had turned to face him, and their eyes had met, he had said all he wanted to say in a single gaze—and she had understood everything. Hadn't she? Then the current had been cut: Layla had heard Isam's voice and her face had regained its hard lifelessness.

Husayn closed his eyes, trying to banish Layla's image as she stood there on the roof. He did not want *that* picture to form his memory of her. He wanted to see her as she had been the first time, when they stood at the stairs, the joy of life dancing in her eyes and face. Six months had passed. Surely she had gotten over the shock of that incident by now. And when I see her, he thought . . . . He shot upright in bed. Yes! He would see her, a few days from now at most. She would enter the room where he was, happiness dancing in her eyes and face, through her body. That wondrous, lovely buoyancy that had almost made him shout in the elevator would envelop him again.

Chapter Eleven

Husayn perched on a chair in the sitting room of Muhammad Effendi Sulayman's home listening to Mahmud's mother, feelings of bitterness knotting his chest. This was his first visit to Mahmud's home since their release; he had been in the apartment for about an hour, but there had been no sign of Layla. Mahmud was putting on his outside clothes so that they could leave the house together, and there seemed no hope that he would see her today. Perhaps he would never see her again.

A shy smile played dimly on Mahmud's mother's face, giving it even more sweetness. Husayn swung his head toward the door of the room, as if in impatient expectation; his eyes went blurry. Before his gaze was the image of a kind-looking, fair woman, her full body stooping before a bread oven, face glowing in the flame, and a dark-skinned little girl hanging onto her hem. It was his mother, at home, in the Delta town of Sambalawin, his sister Samiha clutching at her gallabiya. It was the first time in many years that Husayn had seen his mother's image clearly. He had lost her at the age of nine, and her image had always appeared in mid-movement, out of focus. But now he could see her clearly, and the tiny house, too—the door bearing its huge wooden bolt, the single date palm that always shook in a strong wind, those delicate, sweet layers of pastry still aglow from the oven, the thick cream and molasses. And the diffident smile, one soft hand rubbing his forehead and tidying his hair, light kisses over his eyes, quick and awkward.

Her faint, shy smile still hovering, Mahmud's mother spoke. "And so you live by yourself, son?"

Husayn murmured something inaudible, his eyes still in the distance. He saw women swathed in black crowding into the house, and his young sister's eyes, wide and round and confused, moving from face to face, searching in vain for her mother's lineaments; and himself, burrowed into a mound of dried clover a little way from the house. The women's wailing reached him like the muffled barking of village dogs on a storm-filled night. And his father, after the women had gone: he remembered his father dragging him with an unusual roughness then collapsing in sobs when they reached the threshold of the empty house. Then there was an unfamiliar woman before the oven, offering him the pastry, the cream and molasses. There were new brothers and sisters, strangers, and a father who was now a stranger. He had journeyed, a long voyage among strangers—in the city of Mansura, at secondary school, and then more strangers, in Cairo, at the College of Engineering. Even his sister Samiha had become a stranger, he thought, as he recalled their life together in Cairo after their father's death, their struggle together as he tried to complete his studies, and then so he could put together enough money to buy the expected trousseau for her after his graduation. All of that was no more than a memory, and now the words got stuck on their tongues whenever he and his sister searched for a subject on which they could converse. It was never easy to find a topic that interested them both, for each had gone his own way, becoming utterly distant from the other, and the gleam of love in her eyes that had been his share had gone to another man. A strange man, a stranger.

Husayn shook his head, trying to extract himself from his musings. These sorts of thoughts bothered and upset him. It was so cheap and easy, so self-pitying, to wallow this way. Undoubtedly deprived of a mother's love, he had found people who cared wherever he had gone. He had found affection in deep, enriching friendships, but he had known it also in passing encounters with strangers who did not remain strangers for long. A bond of shyness with a curly-headed youth at the Mansura school; a sentence on his tongue one day that he had been unable to complete; a shared glance with an elderly man on Tram no. 12; a smile exchanged with a stern-faced worker in the Canal Zone, who gave him ammunition for his suddenly empty machine gun. And now, a reserved smile on the face of this woman who sat before him—a smile that meant she, too, was no longer a stranger. And he had managed to live to the age of twenty-four without this cheap self-pity. He knew, of course, why this bitterness had clouded his thinking just now. Yesterday he had spent the entire night dreaming of the moment in which Layla would come in and raise her radiant face to his, extend her hand, her eyes laughing, and say in her strong, resonant voice like that of a country flute, "Welcome."

Mahmud stood in the doorway, cutting an elegant figure in his navy-blue suit. "Come on, let's go."

Husayn tried to conceal his agitation with a smile as he rose to his feet. "Whoa, you look very official! Or are you a bridegroom already marching in the wedding procession?"

Mahmud gave him a worried look as he tugged at his white shirt-collar to bring it away from his neck. "I shouldn't be wearing it in this heat, should I?"

It was a new suit. Mahmud had had it tailored just before the battle for the Canal had begun. He had never worn it. He had gone to the Canal Zone, and after the Canal Zone, straight into detention, and there he had imagined himself wearing it, so that it had become linked in his mind to freedom. It had not been a conscious decision to put it on today; it had not occurred to him that it was totally unsuitable for the August heat.

Husayn patted him on the shoulder. "Don't worry. It cools off in the evening anyway."

Mahmud's mother stood up to say goodbye to Husayn, who responded with his usual broad grin. The mother extended a tentative hand to give him a gentle pat on the shoulder. "Goodbye, son." Husayn crossed the living room with Mahmud behind him, as a voice rose from behind the door to an adjoining room, calling Mahmud. Then the door opened and there was Layla.

———

Husayn whirled around. Layla's face flushed, but she quickly composed herself and bobbed her head in his direction.

"Mahmud, someone named Hamdi was asking for you earlier when you were napping. He says he'll be waiting for you at the Rex Café at eight o'clock." Mahmud looked at Husayn, shaking his head in wonder. "See? See—Mr. Hamdi and his one-sided appointments?"

Husayn did not answer. He was staring at Layla with a bewildered expression on his face, as if he had no idea who she was.

"Of course, you know Layla, my sister, don't you, Husayn?"

Husayn did not answer. He took a few hesitant steps toward Layla and put his hand out, gazing into her face as if he were searching for something. As if asking a question, or perhaps uncertain of the response, he ventured, "We've met before?"

Layla's eyes flitted from place to place before she extended her hand to Husayn and raised her face to him, cold, hard, empty of expression, on her mouth an artificial, tight little smile.

"Yes, we have met."

Husayn noticed that the timbre of her voice had changed, too. It no longer came from deep inside, singing like a flute. Now it seemed to issue just from the tip of her tongue, a restrained, imprisoned voice. Husayn kept her hand in his, and his eyes on her, searching in despairing entreaty for whatever it was that had gone, whatever comprised that beautiful glow that had shone from her face and body. He dropped her hand crossly as if it were guilty of stealing one of his possessions. His eyes went blurry. He saw his sister Samiha, a child of five, crying and saying, "Let it fly away, Husayn, let it go." And he, in his white gallabiya, shifted his gaze in confusion from his sister to the pretty butterfly pressed in the notebook, while Samiha cried hotly, "Let it fly away, Husayn, it will be so pretty when it flies!" And he was hugging Samiha to his chest, kissing her hair, telling her, "It can't, Samiha, it can't fly . . . ." Husayn looked at Layla again, and without saying a word he turned and practically ran out of the apartment.

———

Though he returned to that apartment, never could he locate the elusive quality that had attracted him to Layla at the start. His throat choked with bitterness; he would leave again—to come back yet again. Why, he did not understand; perhaps it was because whenever he was not with her, the vision of her he carried was that image he had seen the first time. Or perhaps it was because he believed that with the force of his love he could return her to what she had been. Or maybe it was simply the result of that incredible, irresistible feeling, completely unsupported by any logic or evidence, that she was inevitably his and he was inevitably hers no matter how long the wait might be. He had to be very cautious. He had to change his approach, to think differently about how he might proceed. Alert always to what he wanted, he was accustomed to getting there by the shortest and most direct route. He detested stealth; he had always favored frontal attack. Had this been a normal situation he would have declared his love on the first possible occasion and proposed marriage. Then he would have waited for her to answer his love with her own. If it had been a normal situation he would not have given much thought to the fact that he was unemployed and broke, nor would he have worried that she might give these facts undue attention, if indeed she loved him. For he was an engineer, after all, and was sure to find work. He would begin on the bottom step, with her; they would begin together, side by side.

But it was not a normal or a natural situation. And he had to step with the utmost caution, to move furtively around the protective shield she had imposed on herself, seeking an entrance, to reach those depths, somehow.

He tried very hard to get her to converse; he worked to draw out her laughter, to stir up her enthusiasm, even to elicit some anger. But she would only talk with great reserve and laugh with guarded politeness. She seemed careful to avoid outbursts, whether of anger or enthusiasm, no matter the subject, as if she had lost the ability to summon either emotion. When her gaze met his searching, desperate eyes, she would smile apologetically as if to excuse her very existence. And then Husayn could no longer keep his doubts at bay. *Were* there any depths behind that shield? Or had Isam drawn Layla with him to the very bottom, into the filth, and lashed her there? Had he made of her a carbon copy, a mere one of the thousands of people who talk only after making their calculations, and open themselves to feelings only after deliberation? Was this shield really a mask to conceal her capacity to love, to feel, and to react, a bulwark erected in her fear of making herself vulnerable once again? Or was it no more than the characteristic expression of a truly inflexible and unfeeling human being?

Was the self-loathing so apparent in her movements and words a temporary sentiment imposed by events? Or was it so firmly fixed in place that it had put out roots around her heart, choking out all sources of self-love and as a consequence all possibility of loving others? Did she grasp so tightly to rules of behavior and ancient traditions out of conviction, or were they a route to self-protection, the only solid ground she could find after the violent tremors she had passed through? Did she really believe the opinions she repeated? Did she truly think that love was nonsense, that all men were alike, and that to enjoy a respectable social status was paramount? Was she as admiring of Gamila and her marriage as she seemed? Did she really see her cousin as a paragon of wedded life?

Her brother always remarked that Layla had changed, and so did Sanaa; and when Sanaa saw Husayn's searching, despairing look focused on Layla's face, she realized why he had wanted to know.

———

As soon as she managed to be alone with Husayn, Sanaa touched his arm.

"Layla wasn't like this before, you know. She's changed." Husayn raised his eyes to her and said questioningly, "Isam . . . ?"

Sanaa blushed as if the conversation had taken a sudden direction that implicated her personally. "Then you know . . . ?"

Husayn nodded. "But I don't want Layla to know that I know."

"Are you in love with her?"

Husayn lowered his head and smiled weakly, and Sanaa knew. He jerked his head up immediately and spoke abruptly. "But what exactly happened?"

He assumed that Sanaa would hold back, but she did not hesitate. She told him briefly, in stinging words, as if she were whipping not only Isam but all men. Sitting down again, her back rigid, she said heatedly, "You're the only one who can help her."

"Why me?"

"Layla likes you," she said shortly.

Husayn's broad smile lit up his whole face. "You'd never know it!" He hid his face for a moment. "Did she tell you so?"

Sanaa shrugged and laughed sarcastically. "No, of course not."

Silently, Husayn raised questioning eyes to her.

"Layla can't possible admit that, not even to herself. She can't possibly acknowledge a liking for anyone at all." Sanaa stood up, still talking. "Layla has suffered enough. She doesn't want to go through any of it again. She doesn't want to fall in love with anyone."

Husayn's voice was choked with feeling. "But it's different. *I* love her."

Sanaa faced him, her expression and voice sardonic. "And Isam loved her. And to this day he says he loves her." She went toward the door.

"Please, please see. The story is so different. Isam—"

"You know what? Sometimes it seems to me that none of you can really love. That the ability to love and to make sacrifices is just not there when it comes to men."

"I beg you to stop making such generalizations! Now, look—you, first of all. Do you trust me? Me? Or not?" Sanaa gazed at the tall, broad man before her, pointing to himself determinedly as he awaited her answer, like a child waiting for his mother to reassure him that he was a good boy. Her face relaxed into a big smile.

"The important thing is for Layla to trust you, right? Not me."

"But how? How can I make Layla trust me?"

"If you love her enough you'll figure it out."

Husayn's face darkened. She was so silly! He wanted to tell Sanaa that if she were to live a hundred years she could never love anyone as much as he loved Layla. But Sanaa just smiled sweetly into his face and said gently, "Don't give up, and don't get tired of the whole thing. Just be patient."

Husayn took her advice. And then at a certain point it seemed to him that his attempts had almost worked; he was almost there. Layla would laugh at one of his jokes, his eyes would meet hers, and suddenly the old spark would flare for a second before she turned her face away and it faded. But whenever that spark appeared, he knew he would wait—all his life, if he had to—to see her eyes shine steadily again.

———

But suddenly matters slipped from Husayn's grasp with a bewildering rapidity. He had stopped by the scholarships administration office to ask for news of the overseas scholarship to which he had applied. The official who had responsibility for the program looked intently at him from behind piles of papers, his glasses slipping down his nose, and in a whispery rasp asked what he wanted. The old man took a long time searching slowly for the relevant scholarships file, and opened it with the same deliberate indolence. He turned the pages, one at a time, page after page, until he came to the report of the Higher Scholarships Committee. He stared at Husayn in silence, looking him over carefully, it seemed. Husayn was convinced that luck had betrayed him this time round. He had not been awarded the scholarship place. He let out his breath—and, startled, realized it was a sigh of relief.

But the official, still taking his time about it, adjusted his glasses over his eyes and eventually informed Husayn that he had been selected as a recipient of the original scholarship to which he had applied. It was imperative that he quickly complete his papers so that he could be in time to start classes in the first term. The official grew quiet again, as if this speech had exhausted him. Again he stared silently at Husayn from behind the glasses that were once again slipping down his nose. Husayn tried hard to avoid that gaze; strange feelings swept over him. This old man, hunched like a cat, was stalking him, lowering a trap over him.

As Husayn reached the street, Layla's face came into his mind and his heart lurched, leaving an empty space in his chest. He took off at a run. He must see her. He must ascertain for himself that she was not just a mirage in his life but rather a tangible fact, a presence to which he could stretch out his hand, something he could embrace and never let slip away. Only then would he be able to tame that sea of thoughts raging through his head. Only then could he take the practical steps necessary to face this new set of circumstances.

———

He rushed into the building just in time to see the elevator door opening. Layla stepped out, dressed for outdoors. She stood mutely before the elevator as Husayn came over to her and took her hand, holding it without saying a word. Layla's face grew pink as she raised her eyes to him; his pleading gaze arrested her. She dropped her eyelids; something serious had happened, she could tell. Husayn seemed to be struggling, tired, at his wit's end; she had never seen him like this before. "They've given me a scholarship—three years—Germany."

When she raised her face this time he saw a deep sadness in her eyes, as if she had just become aware of how deep was her own misery, how crushing her sense of loneliness and alienation. She did need him, he could see that, perhaps as much as he needed her, despite all the barriers she raised in his face. Tenderly he pressed her hand, and Layla realized that she had given herself away. She pulled her hand back violently.

"Mahmud's upstairs." She walked toward the outside door.

"Where are you going? Stay here."

Layla was astonished at the sudden change in his voice. The tone of despair had gone completely to be replaced not by his normal, everyday voice but rather by a tone of command, as if he were ordering her to wait. But when she turned to face him his features had relaxed into a captivating smile, one of those smiles that just could not be resisted. Even so, she did not return his smile. Welling up inside her was a fear of that confidence she glimpsed, of that smile that filled his face.

"Come here, I want to talk to you about something."

The vague apprehension in Layla's chest took a more lucid form. She was afraid: Husayn might say something to disturb the ordinary tenor of her life. He might say something that would strip away the repose she had acquired after the very hard effort she had put into convincing herself of her own self-sufficiency, her invulnerability; no individual could truly harm or wound her now, she felt. Her mind was working, but not very well. She must escape—but into the street? Husayn would merely follow her. To her room? If she locked the door, no one would be able to reach her; no one could cause her pain. In order to gain time, to prevent Husayn from speaking, she said, her eyes on the stairs, "Where?"

"Upstairs," he said simply, his face still one broad smile. "Or we could go out somewhere, anywhere."

"That's impossible," Layla said in confusion. "Husayn, I can't." She hurried to the steps and began to charge up them. Husayn, following her, pressed his hands on her shoulders to restrain her.

"Just a couple of words, Layla. That's all." He caught sight of her face; the fear clearly etched there shook him to the core. "Don't be afraid, Layla. I want you to trust me. Please."

Layla's voice was thin and high, almost a sob. "Leave me alone, Husayn. Please, leave me alone."

"What if I'm incapable of leaving you alone?" His voice was perfectly calm and steady. "What if I love you?"

Layla slipped from his grasp, and with two or three long strides was at the door to her apartment. She put her finger out to punch the doorbell, but Husayn's hand gripped hers before she could ring it. His voice was a whisper, a strong and deep one, as he pressed on her hand. "I love you, Layla."

She jerked her head downward as if a blow she had anticipated had arrived. Husayn had confronted her with a *fait accompli* that she could not simply ignore. She must pull herself together to face it. She raised her face, cold and rigid, empty of all expression. Husayn let her hand drop.

"You're still attached to Isam, I guess," he said bitterly. His eyes met hers; he turned his head away. He felt as if a knife had gone straight to his heart. She stood there, obviously defenseless, a wounded animal, bleeding; she could not hide the waves of astonishment, fear, humiliation, and loss that washed over her eyes. He wished he could retract his words. Layla, slumping against the door, held tightly to the doorknob, as if afraid she might fall. Husayn came nearer and put his hand on her shoulder, quivering all over with a desire to take her in his arms, to kiss her eyes. Layla felt his touch and straightened immediately, her body tense. She pushed his hand away fiercely. He saw an expression of such vehement loathing in her eyes that he unconsciously stepped back until he was pressed against the opposite wall.

"I am not attached to anyone," she said quietly. "And I will not become attached to anyone."

"You know what you need?" he said roughly. "You need someone to shake you hard until you wake up. Until you understand that the world has not ended. And that what happened was going to happen no matter what, because you chose badly."

Layla started pounding on the door. Husayn looked at her for a moment, then shrugged and pressed the bell. "But unfortunately I don't have the time to wake you, since I will be traveling soon." He turned and left her, realizing as he descended the stairs that he had taken a final decision on the subject of the scholarship.

—

But Husayn was not at peace with that decision, he knew, for it meant erasing Layla from his reckoning. Yet events conspired to convince him that his decision was a sound one. Layla avoided meeting him whenever he stopped by her home. He considered seeking Sanaa's help, but when he asked Mahmud for her whereabouts he learned that she had traveled with her family to the seaside resort of Ras al-Barr, where they would spend a good part of the summer. In fact, Mahmud told him, his own family would follow in a few days' time.

Husayn hurriedly completed his papers, chose the books he would carry with him, and reviewed the program of study at the university where he would be enrolled. Meanwhile, his relationship with Samiha, his sister, grew stronger, closer than it had ever been since her marriage. He spent many evenings at her home, and they stayed up very late talking. He had told her about Layla, and she could tell that he was suffering, even if he refused to acknowledge as much to himself, let alone anyone else. One time, busily straightening a tablecloth to hide the awkwardness she felt, she asked him, "Would you like me to pay a visit to Layla, Husayn?"

He shook his head without a word. Samiha looked at him inquiringly.

"This is the way Layla wants it, Samiha. There is no point in trying to force her."

"You know what, Husayn? My heart feels that you are fated to have her. Her future is yours, too, once you are back from Germany."

Husayn laughed sarcastically. "Has your excellency gone into the fortunetelling business?" But his sister's words, as naïve and illogical as they seemed, twisted the knife further. Her words roused feelings that had never been so clear, a sense that something, *something* bonded him to Layla, something stronger than either of them, a force that would bring the two of them together someday. This intuition helped him to endure the harshness of the present.

But he returned home that night weighted down by feelings of wrongdoing. He had just come from the Sulayman home, having wanted to wish Layla farewell. She was to travel to Ras al-Barr the next day. During his visit she had avoided him, as she had ever since he had broached the subject of his feelings. He sat with Mahmud the entire time. But as he left Mahmud's room for the front hall he came upon her, standing amidst a pile of baggage—some cases closed, others still open—talking with her mother. Husayn shook her mother's hand and then turned to Layla, his eyes fixed on her face as he took her hand in both of his. Her eyes flickered around the room before she withdrew her hand and smiled her cautious smile as she said "goodbye." She turned back to her mother. "Mama, by the way, the wool jackets—we forgot them."

Husayn stood there, unmoving, his gaze on Layla's back. She sensed his eyes burning into her spine and turned slowly to face him. Her voice was an agitated whisper, as if she were passing on a secret. "Because it can get cold there, cold and dark at night." Her lower lip trembled. A layer of tears pooled over her eyes.

Chapter Twelve

For a space of fifteen days Layla's tearful eyes chased Husayn. Each day's passing brought him nearer to his day of departure for Germany, now set, and intensified his feeling that he was abandoning Layla at a time when she was most in need of his aid. Her eyes summoned him, clung to him, until one day he found himself sitting in the train heading for Ras al-Barr.

He leaned his head back against the seat, feeling deeply peaceful, as if he had just emerged from a long struggle, finally released. He had offered his love to her; when she had rejected it, he had drawn back furiously, like a big baby, even though he knew that she was in a state that did not permit her to love him—or to love anyone. Perhaps if she were in a normal state she would have returned his love. Maybe she would love him after a time, if she could stand on her own feet and regain her confidence in herself and in life. Or perhaps she would never love him; perhaps she would fall in love with someone else. But none of this kept him from loving her. Nor, he admitted to himself, did it exempt him from his obligation to her. He must exploit all possible means to help her. He had fancied that he could help her only as a husband or beloved, but perhaps he could help her just as much if he were her friend. Just a friend, nothing more. He had to try all means possible, but . . . then her eyes would be there, remaining with him, summoning him, cleaving to him in despair, waking him from his sleep. He would not escape them, even if he put thousands of miles between them, yes, thousands of miles, thousands. Thousands. The train echoed the word. Thou-sands, thou-sands. Husayn got up to open the window. His eyes took in the fields, extending as far as he could see, as if he wanted to carve them into his mind with every detail intact. Here he had been raised, here he had grown into adolescence, in a village like that one over there. The fields amidst which he had grown up were a mirror image of the fields he saw beyond the window, with a *saqiya* turned by the water buffalo, its water irrigating the fields; a little irrigation canal; people like those he could see, working so hard, sweating, the sight of them so rough and hard concealing their overwhelming ability to love, to give, to sacrifice. Husayn felt a rush of compassion; he wished he could stop, could stroll, the breeze slapping his face amidst the green fields, could sniff the scent of the earth, could clap his hand against those rough, hard palms.

But the train raced across the land, its rhythmic chant driving into his ear the word thousands . . . thou-sands . . . Yes, he would go thousands of miles from these fields, far from the homeland. In foreign lands he would live by himself, would work alone, would eat alone, would sleep alone. His day would be filled with a lonely aching, and his night, an ache for the homeland. If she had been going with him . . . . If she were to be with him . . . . Husayn's chest flared with a wave of anger. Why couldn't she stand on her own two feet like everyone else? Why couldn't she return the slap of whoever had slapped her, pick herself up, and go on her way? Why had it been so easy to shatter her, as if she were made of . . . of . . . .

Sitting on the train, Husayn tried to find something with which to compare Layla. Glass. Crystal. Yes, that was it, crystal—beautiful and so easy to shatter. And crystal was hard, too, like her. It reflected light but produced none. If you put it in the light it would glitter, but if you put it in a dark place it would give off no glow. The light sat not in her heart but rather on the outer surface. No confidence came from within her; she had always taken it from others. That was why Isam had been able to crush her, to make her hate herself, and therefore hate others.

She was good-looking, intelligent, outstanding in every way, yet she could not stand on her own feet. She always had to lean on someone or something. First it had been her brother, the hero of her childhood. Through his eyes she had seen the world; she had thought it vast, beautiful, boundless, replete with love and sacrifice, with loyalty, truth, sincerity, and beauty. Then Isam had shown her another side of life, one she had not known, an unsightly, exposed side, and the earth beneath her feet had turned to infinitely yielding sand. So she gazed yearningly, despairingly, at her brother, trying to see mirrored in his eyes the life he had sketched for her; but he had closed his eyes, afraid she would see in them what he had seen. It was as if Mahmud had seen only betrayal, had never seen . . . Husayn noticed the palm trees that heralded the approach of Damietta city's train station: standing in line, thickly clustered, row after row, towering, victorious, heavy with fruit, clusters of red dates gleaming in the sun's rays . . . as if Mahmud had never seen any beauty at all. It was as if Mahmud had seen none of it: heroes who stood up to their enemies—towering, victorious—before they died, standing tall and proud to the end; or the deep joy shining from the eyes of that youth as he raised his head for the last time to witness the fire as it broke out in one of the British camps; or Usta Madbuli crawling forward, already wounded, already inside a British camp, burning down the petrol stores with a hand grenade—and burning along with it. It was as if Mahmud had not heard Madbuli's yell— Down with imperialism!—ringing out in the silence of the night, shooting tremors into the hearts of everybody there, making the earthquake, setting the fires of revolution.

The train shuddered and came to a full stop in the Damietta station. Husayn crushed his cigarette butt under his shoe, picked up his suitcase, and climbed down onto the platform.

The car left the main agricultural road and plunged toward Ras al-Barr. A breeze saturated with water vapor slapped Husayn's face gently, calming his anxiety. He felt an overpowering sympathy for Layla. Who was he to cast blame on others for their weakness? Who was he to issue judgment on their behavior and deeds? He had almost cried like a child as he saw Cairo burn; he had nearly broken down in sobs when he saw the end of the battle for the Canal, and only faith had saved him. His was a faith in the people; feeling their emotions, never sensing himself isolated from them, he had not himself weakened.

Mahmud, though, had withdrawn from all of that. So had Layla, isolating herself, a captive to her individual concerns, alone and scraping the scabs from her wounds. The whole world had become concentrated into one small "me," and Layla's only concern now was to protect herself from the aggression of the outside world. She had leaned on her mother, on the rules—the fundamentals—with which she had grown up, on the traditions of those around her. And so she had seen life through her mother's eyes: it was a restricted existence with no reach beyond the four walls within which she lived. It was a frightening apparition against which you were supposed to fortify herself, making extreme efforts to avoid rather than embrace it. You armed yourself with the old rules: speak with care and forethought, act with caution, react only after deliberation so that you do not inflict fatigue or pain upon yourself. You might never know great happiness but at least you would never suffer intense pain. The walls were there to surround you, to protect you from the fierce beast that crouched in wait outside . . . from life!

The sand dunes rolled far under Husayn's gaze. It was an arid, withered wasteland without vegetation or trees. From behind the dunes stared Layla's eyes, the pools of tears stagnant within.

———

Lying full length on a beach recliner, shaded by an umbrella, reading a book, Layla felt a hand on her shoulder. "Layla—Husayn's arrived." It was Mahmud.

Layla's face broke into a smile, but it froze as she became suddenly aware that her body lay extended, in full view of Husayn. She scrambled to her feet, greeting him embarrassedly. "Hello—welcome."

Mahmud pulled the towel from his shoulder and put it on the back of an empty chair. "Husayn leaves for Germany in two weeks."

Layla's pupils darted around but she said nothing. She took the towel that was in Husayn's hand, put it on the seat back and began to tug it straight.

"Aren't you going to congratulate Layla, Husayn?"

Husayn's face fell. Mahmud went on. "She got her secondary diploma and she'll be starting at the university." Now Husayn beamed and he embraced Layla with his gaze. "Congratulations!" Mahmud headed toward the water. With a quick, quizzical glance at Layla, Husayn followed him. She sat down again, but not on the recliner. This time she sat stiffly upright on a bamboo chair and tried to engross herself in her reading, but she could not. The voices of the vendors seemed to spoil her concentration, and the waves, pushing forward to lap over her feet, interrupted her.

"The sea's nothing today," said Mahmud as the two of them turned their back to a high crest.

"Nothing?—it's atrocious."

"Probably better out further."

"Further?—further where? I don't even know how to swim."

Mahmud burst out laughing. It delighted him to discover an area in which he bested Husayn. "So tall and husky, and you don't know how to swim?"

A high wave nearly sent Husayn into a somersault. He righted himself, laughing. "Hey, that's enough. Come on, let's get out." But Mahmud plunged further in, plowing a path through the waves, gesturing to Husayn to follow. Husayn shook his head and turned toward the beach.

———

He approached Layla, drops of water flying from his hair and face. She handed him the towel without a word. He dropped to the sand beside her chair. "Are you still quarreling with me?" he asked, smiling at her as he dried his hair. Layla shut her eyes and smiled.

"Well, it's one of two things," he said, his voice teasing, "either you're angry at me or you're afraid of me."

"Afraid of you? Why would I be afraid of you?"

"That's a respectable question," he said lightly. "Why does someone feel afraid of someone else? I suppose, either the other person must be harmful, or—"

Layla looked at him uneasily. Husayn looked right at her and said in a deep voice, "—or else that someone is afraid of loving the other person."

Layla whipped her head away to gaze distractedly at the ocean. Crowned with white, the waves towered, crashed, and—now subdued—slunk back from the shore, humbled, into the sea. "I'm never in my life going to love anyone," she whispered.

Husayn flung himself onto a vacant chair, stretched out his legs, and leaned back into the shape of the chair. "Are you so sure?" he asked, a strain of disbelief lacing his voice.

"Of course I am."

"Well, if you ask me, I'm not so sure of it."

"What are you getting at?" Layla's voice was edgy with irritation

Husayn shifted, smiling and jabbing his finger at his chest. "What I'm getting at is that you *will* love *me*. You will. One day you'll wake up and discover that you love me."

Layla gazed at him, bewildered, then burst out laughing.

"What are you laughing at?"

Layla shook her head in wonder, still laughing hard. "I wish I had the kind of confidence in myself that you have, Husayn."

Husayn's face was that of a petulant child. "I don't understand any of this."

Layla smiled. "What makes you so sure, as if I personally had told you . . . had told you that I . . . I . . . loved you."

Husayn spoke as if he was simply repeating an established fact. "You did tell me, you really did."

Layla opened her mouth dumbly, as Husayn smiled. "You did, really, you told me, more than once."

She smiled and waved her hand in despair. "No—you're insane. You're completely insane."

Husayn crept toward her. "Do you think these are things one says only with one's voice? No, on the contrary, such things are said more fully with the eyes."

"So what did my eyes say, sir?"

"Your eyes, they may have lost their shine, but they still shine for me, and only for me. And your face, its glow may be gone, but it lights up just for me."

"You're imagining things—that never happened at all."

Husayn moved even nearer, until his head was almost touching her thigh. His voice was as soft and gentle as it could possibly be. "Layla, take me seriously, okay?"

Tears shone in Layla's eyes. "I'm sorry, Husayn."

"No—please, please, today I want to see you looking bright and happy, like the first time I saw you." As he raised his face, his features seemed to melt in that bewitching smile of his. "Do you want to make me happy, so that I leave happy?" Layla nodded. "Good. Then let's imagine, let's imagine together." Layla wiped her eyes and smiled. "Okay, just supposing that you were to wake up tomorrow morning and discover that you love me."

"And then?" Layla caught the spirit of the game.

"And then you'll go to the telegraph office, and write out a telegraph, and you'll send it to my address in Germany."

"What will I say in it?"

Husayn picked a stone and began to write letters in the sand, pronouncing the words slowly as if dictating. His eyes wandered and his voice grew faint. "Start making arrangements to get a marriage contract, and I will tell you in the next telegram the date I'm to arrive, and I'll send details by post." He lifted his head to her, his hand still tightly around the little rock, and he gazed steadily at her as if to test her strength. Would she accept this role that he wanted her to perform? Under his searching gaze Layla fidgeted. The conversation had shifted so rapidly out of the joking spirit in which it had seemed to begin; she could see that it was about to take a very serious turn indeed. But she held fast to the game, though her voice, still light, held a note of uneasiness. "And then?"

"And then you'll take passage on the ship and you'll come."

Husayn's voice suggested that it was no longer the words that interested him but rather his attempt to reach this young woman. To what extent could he count on her, when his future was so dependent on hers? She spoke in a low voice, beckoning toward an imagined distance. "All that way by myself?" Husayn straightened in his seat and spoke slowly. "That's the road you have to travel by yourself, Layla."

Once again she felt his searching gaze close in on her; she felt she had revealed how weak and unable she was. She shifted to stare at the sea. Her lips trembled. "Well, suppose the sea is stormy, the waves terribly high."

"To reach shore," Husayn said with deliberation, "we have to face the waves and the open ocean."

Layla gave him a long look, and then narrowed her eyes and laughed, though it came out more like a wail. "And then on shore what would I find? Husayn, what would I find? Spilt coffee?"

Husayn stared at her, bewildered. It took him a moment to realize that she must be alluding to a detail from the story of her relationship with Isam. His face tightened and he said nothing. Layla covered her face in her hands and shook her head despairingly as she spoke. "I can't, Husayn, I just can't." She took her hands from her face and stood up. So did he, facing her.

"Don't waste your time, Husayn." Her voice was calm. "There's no point, the way I'm feeling." She walked slowly toward the cabin. Husayn caught up. She heard him behind her, calling, "Layla." There was no anger in his voice; nor was there despair or even pleading. But his voice, commanding her with masculine duty and compassion to stop, was compelling.

"Layla, do you know what you'll find on shore?" Layla just looked at him mutely. "You'll find something more important than me, more important than anyone else, too. Do you know what that is, Layla?"

She raised questioning eyes to him. He spoke slowly. "You'll find what it is that you've lost, you'll find yourself, you'll find the true Layla."

She did not understand at first what he was getting at. Then she blushed as she realized for the first time how much she had changed, and how deeply Husayn understood it. She fled to the cabin.

At lunch, Layla sat across from Husayn, her mother to her right, Mahmud to her left. Her father was in Cairo. She bent her head low over the plate to avoid Husayn's eyes. She feared his searching gaze, for it seemed to pierce her, to reveal everything that was there. She did not want to see the despair in his eyes, knowing that he was in despair of her.

But when her eyes did meet his by chance, her fear vanished, for she found neither despair nor fear. He was not searching her, testing her, but merely offering her the affectionate touch of his eyes; he was summoning her gently in desire and regard, and she brightened up.

Husayn, for his part, was taking in the smallest details of Layla's face as if to sculpt it whole in his memory. It was a delightful pursuit; he loved this slope of Layla's face, from one fine ear to her cheek. He loved her upper lip, its deepening redness at the center revealing a tiny triangle, pulling her whole mouth upward as if she were smiling even when she was not. He loved those light, honey-hued eyes, so intelligent, so expressive, just like a sensitive camera lens; and the wide forehead that hinted a lofty pride; the soft, short, very black hair; her ivory skin with its pinkish tint at the cheeks—soft skin, like a child's; and . . . . He loved all of her features, each in itself. But he truly loved the manner in which they came together, for in her face's composition he found a startling beauty. It did not simply flow from the features, nor just from the harmony they formed, but from . . . well, from what? Perhaps it was the contradiction between a soft, child-like innocence and that broad, adult forehead over eyes that sparkled with the intelligence of a mature and highly aware woman. Or perhaps it was the inconsistency between that childlike face and a mature woman's body. Or was it simply the result of his feelings, his love for her? Never had he caught sight of her face without feeling a lovely peacefulness cradling his whole being, submerging him in a lovely sense of reassurance and well-being, pushing him gently and affectionately forward. These were moments in which he felt that suddenly he could comprehend the most elusive secrets, find solutions to all of his problems, accept that his dreams might take the concrete form of events. He had only to extend a hand and these chimeras would be in his grasp. After all, what could possibly remain beyond him if he were to wake up every morning to that face?

But he would not be waking up every morning to that face. Tomorrow he would depart without having accomplished anything, unable to change anything. All he had in his grasp was her image, to be saved in his mind and preserved in his psyche; and then he must live on the memory throughout the years of exile. If that were to happen, her face must be the last thing he would see when the ship put distance between him and the homeland, the last thing he would see of the homeland—a symbol for all he loved in his nation. An idea flashed into his mind. Tomorrow, as he left, he must bid Layla farewell as he crossed the Nile on his way to Damietta. He would stand in the boat and she would stand before him on shore, filling his mind and his eyes with her face. He could imagine . . . could imagine that he was actually leaving the homeland, and would return—to step onto that beloved land again. But how would he convince her that she must be there to say goodbye? And when? And would she be able to go by herself? Would she be able to overcome her fear of herself, of him, of others? The idea took possession of Husayn; its importance grew to enormous proportions with every minute that passed. If she did go to the riverbank to say goodbye to him, the import of it all was that she was taking the first step toward him—and that he would not have taken leave of her before she took that first step. All that Husayn could think about was how to draw Layla aside so that he could tell her of his plan. The sun was setting before he found his chance.

———

He was strolling along the beach with Mahmud when they caught sight of Layla and Sanaa watching the sunset. Layla appeared melancholy, as if she were thinking that the sun would not come up tomorrow. Sanaa's face, to the contrary, sparkled with life, as if she had taken into herself all the rays of the sun that she could catch as it lay on the horizon, about to sink.

Mahmud and Husayn joined them. The four walked slowly, a purplish tinge enveloping them, a moist breeze invigorating their skin. Layla's feet almost touched the water; Sanaa was to her left, then Mahmud, and then Husayn. Mahmud and Sanaa fell into conversation; Layla and Husayn were silent. Layla's eyes were fixed straight ahead, and Husayn was dawdling. He turned suddenly and switched his place; now he was walking practically in the water to Layla's right. She blushed, but her pace did not change. Husayn's arm bumped her shoulder now and then, sending an electric quiver through her body. Hardly would she recover before she would find herself anticipating—her throat dry, her heart jumpy—the next one. From the corner of her eye she saw Husayn's face, tense, tight, as if something pressed down on it.

Husayn noticed her glancing sidelong at him, and he pressed his arm to her shoulder, deliberately this time. His eyes seemed to melt, they were so tender; he stuck his lower lip out slightly as if he were kissing her. Her ears reddened and she stared straight ahead. Husayn smiled to himself, and his tense features relaxed. The buzz of conversation between Mahmud and Sanaa dropped to a whisper, and their pace quickened as if, without being aware of it, they were trying to be by themselves. Husayn noticed and slowed down. Here was his chance, and he was not about to let it escape. Layla, though, was determinedly lengthening her stride to catch up with Sanaa and Mahmud. Husayn put out his arm and drew her back, his face laughing as he whispered, "Come here. Where are you going?"

Layla stopped cold, so surprised was she by his unrestrained boldness. She tried to disengage her hand, but when Husayn raised her hand to his mouth and kissed it, with Mahmud and Sanaa just a few steps away, she was too appalled to even pull away.

Husayn let go of her hand when he could be sure that Sanaa and Mahmud had increased the distance between the two couples. Layla's lips were trembling. "You're mad. Suppose Mahmud—" She could not even find the words to finish her sentence. Husayn laughed. "Yes, suppose. I love you, and I am proud of it, and I want Mahmud to see. I'd like the whole world to notice that I love you." Then his face clouded, and he practically pressed against her as he spoke in a shaky, deep whisper. "I'm just waiting for you, waiting for you, darling." He ran his finger along her arm lightly, and his voice grew softer, almost like a child's. "And I know that you will love me. I know your future is me, just like my future is you."

Layla felt a lump in her throat, and her eyes swam under a cloud of tears. Husayn told her what he had in mind. He tried very hard to dispel her fears. They could meet somewhere away from the family's cabin—for instance, at the government building that overlooked the Nile. She could go on ahead of him, and he would join her there after he had given Mahmud the slip. But her eyes were still wide and fearful as she stared at him—more as if he were asking her to murder someone!

"You aren't going to come." A note of despair had crept into Husayn's voice. She did not answer. Husayn plunged forward, staring straight ahead. Layla's stride lengthened to keep up with him, and she put out a hand blindly, knocking against Husayn's hand. "What time?" Her voice was shaking. Husayn seized her hand, his face brightening immediately, his eyes embracing her. Layla pulled her hand away as she saw Sanaa and Mahmud, still at a distance, turning back to walk toward where they stood.

Layla stretched out in bed. A young man like him, who was excellent no matter what perspective you examined him from, wanted to marry *her*—and despite his knowing the details of her relationship with Isam. A wave of relief and serenity ran through her body; it was exactly the way she felt when the dentist had finished removing a bad tooth, or when she covered an infected sore with a layer of soothing balm. She felt as if he had returned her self-regard to her by asking her to marry him.

She turned restlessly in bed. No. It wasn't marriage for which he was asking. He wanted her love first, as a fundamental condition for a marriage that would depend on that love. He could have proposed marriage right away, but he had not done so. He did not want a cold corpse, and that is what she was. He wanted her love. But she was incapable of love. She was afraid of it; and there was only loathing in her heart, loathing for the world, and for Isam, who had deceived her, who had broken her. Isam, who had . . . Layla tried to launch her usual train of thought. Normally she could summon it without much effort. It would come to her compliantly, one image after the next, bringing tears to her eyes and a hot lament to her heart as she lost herself in pity. But at the moment the way seemed blocked. Normally, the merest echo of the name "Isam" made her boil and long to break something.

But now, he seemed far away—so far away that she wondered for a moment if he really existed. Had she really known him? Had there really been a relationship between them? Layla discovered suddenly that her anger had vanished, that she no longer hated Isam. Her body was not aching, either, as it usually did; her muscles were relaxed, as if she had just emerged from a steam bath that had sucked out a poison running through her body. She fell into a deep sleep uninterrupted by dreary thoughts or bad dreams. But she was careful to wake up early so that she could say goodbye to Husayn.

When she came out of the bathroom everyone was still asleep. But even if someone in the cabin had been awake, there was nothing out of the ordinary in this. Usually the first to awake, she would go for an early walk.

She slipped off her nightgown and stood in her underclothes before the mirror, combing her short hair. She noticed that her skin had dried from the rigors of the sun, and found her bottle of lotion, which she had not bothered to use even once this summer. She leaned toward the mirror, rubbing the lotion into her face. Suddenly her hand stopped on her cheek. She went nearer to the glass and contemplated the face that gazed back at her: the gleaming night eyes of an untamed cat, the lips full and red, a face alight with a healthy glow, chest rising with a suddenly more vigorous heartbeat. She stepped back. Where was she going? What future were those gleaming eyes, that throbbing chest, rushing toward? Ruin? Her father always said so: she was heading to no good, he would frown.

Layla put up her hand to wipe away the sweat that was breaking out on her forehead and tiptoed back to collapse onto the mattress. She might as well have had no experience, learned nothing, never suffered before from her impulsiveness! For here she was, slipping out behind her father's back, behind Mahmud's back, behind her mother's, stepping outside of those rules to meet Husayn; stepping outside with her feet, with her will, to encounter more pain, more loss. Today she would be walking alongside Husayn. Before Husayn it had been Isam; tomorrow what man would it be? Any man who whispered honeyed words into her ears, as if she was a puppy that trotted after anyone who beckoned?

But Husayn! Husayn was different, Husayn loved her. Yet—hadn't Isam loved her, too?

Love! Hadn't she already suffered enough from the fantasy of it? And hadn't she been happier in those days when she felt content to be by herself, when no one was able to cause her pain or hurt? Yet here she was heading into the flames of her own accord, as if she had not already tried it, as if she had learned nothing, suffered nothing.

She leaned her head to one side, listening to footsteps in the cabin. Mahmud was awake, and Husayn was getting ready to leave. Layla hung her head and chewed on her lip. Let him go back to where he came from, and leave her be. She was not going to sacrifice herself for anyone, lose herself in anyone, abase herself for anyone. She would not put her neck between anyone's hands. She would remain as she was, her own mistress, happy in herself, no one able to hurt her.

As voices reached Layla, she began listening again. Mahmud was determined to accompany Husayn, and Husayn was trying to extract himself. She heard Husayn's voice ring out triumphant, as he asserted a final ruling in the argument. "That's what I want, Mahmud. I want to leave on this gorgeous morning by myself." Layla's eyes narrowed. He had won. He was sure that she was there, waiting for him. He had beckoned, and he was confident that she would follow. But she wouldn't be there. She wouldn't follow. She wouldn't—a shiver ran through her. Husayn's voice came, deep and low, warm, as he said, "I'll miss you, Mahmud."

"You'll write to me, of course, regularly."

"Of course."

She heard Mahmud's spoon in his tea as silence descended on the two friends. "Husayn, you are more than a friend." Mahmud's voice was trembling. "It is you who gave me reassurance, who helped me to understand that everything is more or less okay." Layla felt blood rushing into her head, and she jumped to her feet. She must . . . she must thank Husayn, she must say goodbye to him.

Husayn got to his feet. "I'll see you, Mahmud. Keep well."

Layla ran to the door of her room, and put her hand on the doorknob. But then she realized that she could not go out there. She could not put out her hand to Husayn. She was not ready. She was still in her underclothes.

She heard Mahmud shouting from the veranda, putting all of himself into those few last words. "'Bye, Husayn. Goodbye." And behind her closed door, Layla's hand tightened on the doorknob.

Chapter Thirteen

In the days that followed Husayn's departure, Layla felt nothing. It was as if her senses had been numbed. Whenever he came to mind she shrugged him out of her thoughts unconcernedly and went about whatever she was doing in the cabin, or picked up whatever book she was reading. She went about her life for two weeks, until there came a day when she was stretched out in a recliner on the veranda, reading the morning paper. Her brother stood at the wall gazing at the sea, extending as far as one could see. He stretched and turned to face her. "Lucky Husayn, he must be at sea by now."

She said nothing, but straightened up in her seat and let the newspaper fall from her hand. She got to her feet. She had lost the ability to stay in one place or to concentrate on one thing. "What has happened to you?" her mother would snap, while she fidgeted and tossed as if in a fever. About twice a minute she would straighten up in her seat, stand up, sit down, to stand up again. She would open a book then clap it shut in boredom a few moments later. She ate when it was not meal-time and drank without being thirsty, just to find something to do. She would go out for a walk, but hardly would she be outside before she would come in again. She would go down to the water and come out after moments. She always found an excuse for her behavior. This chair wasn't comfortable; that book was stupid; the sun was too hot; the water was full of muck.

"If the sea doesn't please you," Sanaa said, "let's go tomorrow morning to al-Girbi." Mahmud applauded the idea of trying out the popular beach on the Nile, and Layla assented.

———

The sail cleaved the air and the boat pushed forward toward al-Girbi, on the Nile just before it met the waters of the sea. Sanaa listened attentively as Mahmud talked, her head supported on her hand, her eyes fixed on Mahmud. Layla did not make much attempt to follow their conversation. She was gazing at Nile Street as the boat slipped by: the cinema, on its façade a huge poster of a woman in *décolleté* with a silly smile on her face; hotel lobbies, one just like the next, and no one was visible around any of the tables; heaps of shoes, sandals, and slippers forlornly awaiting buyers; store windows gleaming in the sun's rays, piled with Damietta's famous pastries and sweets—*harisa, basbusa, mashbak*. They passed kiosks—Coca-cola, *ful*-beans, *ta'miya*—and an advertisement saying, "Stop! Here you'll find fish roe sandwiches." It was all laid out, so carefully prepared, waiting. And no one stopped; no one bought; the woman on the poster went on smiling stupidly. At this time of morning the famous riverside *suq* was empty of people, even of merchants, deserted as if it were a city of ruins.

Sanaa glided to the front of the boat, took off her robe, and stretched out on her back, her body on show. She covered her face. Layla studied her. Sanaa had positioned herself with premeditated care that described her every movement, as if she had pondered all the angles to ascertain how her small, fair, well-contoured body would appear to best advantage. Aware that her body was attractive, she loved and cared for it; she always rubbed it with oil before exposing it to the sun and with lotion after bathing. She measured her waist every day,

200

and if it grew the slightest bit thicker she fussed, started exercising, and denied herself food until it had reverted to its former slimness. Sanaa did not try to hide this preoccupation of hers. Whenever Adila made fun of her, she just smiled self-assuredly and said, "Why do you want me to feel so shy about my body, Adila?" as if it was natural for one not to feel any shame or embarrassment where one's body was concerned.

Sanaa stretched and said without uncovering her face, "The weather is so nice today." Layla looked at Mahmud, expecting to see his eyes on Sanaa's body. But he was trailing his hands in the water and, a dreamy look in his eyes, gazing at a knot of fishing boats piled on the sand. Layla's eyes followed his. They were ruins of boats, no longer fit for the water; on the desert sand they sat, alone, unused, crippled, cut off from the water. Mahmud gave a sigh of contentment as he took in the sight of the boats, storing it in his memory. Their white coatings of paint, he mused, gleamed in the rays of the sun like huge, beautiful, white birds, perched on the shore to rest, so as to resume their flight soon enough.

"Did you see those boats?" he asked Sanaa. She uncovered her face and sat up to examine the boats, gently, as if patting them fondly with her gaze. Then the beach at al-Girbi was there before them, rolling out beneath their eyes, crowded with people. Some swam in the river and others were sitting around scattered tables beneath huge umbrellas.

"We're here," said Sanaa, delight dancing in her eyes.

———

The boatman picked out a relatively quiet spot, tied up the boat, and laid a board across to land. But Sanaa, now on her feet, jumped straight from the boat into the water. "Come on," said Mahmud to Layla. Without waiting for an answer he dove into the waves. Layla put her hand up to ward off the spray. Sanaa appeared, reaching up a hand to grasp the side of the boat. "Come on, Layla, hurry up, the water is great."

"Not now. I'm cold. Maybe in a bit."

Mahmud joined Sanaa, holding onto the boat too so that it tipped toward them. Layla shrieked. "Mahmud—what are you doing? Watch out," she said crossly. Mahmud gave his shoulders a shake, turned, and began to swim away. Sanaa caught up with him. They were swimming very gently, as if they were afraid to slap the water that encased them together in a delicious peacefulness; they seemed to be resting more than swimming.

"I could swim like this all the way to tomorrow," said Mahmud. Sanaa laughed.

"How did you know? I had just the same thought." A current seemed to flow between them, connecting them, now that they had become better acquainted, left to themselves in Ras al-Barr. It was a calm, pleasant current, making its way unhurriedly from one to the other, strengthening as the days passed. There was a sense of repose to it, of belonging and mutual need; it seemed a protective shade, surrounding and enveloping the two of them. There was nothing fiery about it, nothing to instigate sleeplessness, no agonizingly overpowering emotion. Whenever Mahmud peeked at Sanaa's small face—her delicate lips compressed in such resolve, the tip of her little nose perked upward in pride, her small eyes, steady in their assurance—a feeling came over him that he had after struggle reached safe shore. Sanaa, contemplating his lustrous green—and often unsettled—eyes, the abashed smile on his lips, the pride that showed in the turn of his dignified, bronze-hued face, would long simply to take him quietly in her arms, rub his hair, rock him and tease him until those uneasy eyes grew peaceful and sure, until the uncertain smile broadened into a grand laugh.

———

Layla observed the two of them as they moved off. Something bound them together, she could see, and distanced her to a place where she was isolated, lost, adrift. She tried to call out to them, but the call froze on her lips; she closed her eyes and huddled there, in the boat, as if she anticipated the approach of a dreaded event. To the surface floated a consciousness of how lonely she really was. She had been able to suppress that feeling throughout the past weeks, but now it refused to stay hidden; it tyrannized her.

She kept her eyes closed as if afraid to open them—afraid she would see only an unending desert. A shower of spray hit her face; she opened her eyes to a face dancing with the joy of life, a childish face teasing her. Angrily, she seized an oar and brought it down over the figure, but he dipped under the water to escape, waving as he slipped away, a laugh ringing out over the water, reinforcing her sense of loneliness and isolation. The sight of people teeming on the beach made it even worse: those children racing each other through the water, their eyes intensely serious as if their futures hung entirely on this race; that woman, not at all shy, who rested her head on her man's lap and relaxed into sleep, in complete security as if sleeping in her own bedroom, as if the eyes of passersby were not devouring her. And there was the girl over there, spilling out an endless succession of giggles, as if she had entirely and happily lost control of herself, or as if her young male companions were actually tickling her. Layla came to as a soft-sided object struck her on the side of the head, and she saw a rubber ball flying back into the water. The boy who had teased her was catching it, around him a whole retinue of young swimmers, whispering and laughing at her, as if they knew instinctively that something or other separated her from all the other human beings who filled the beach. Layla's blood boiled.

"Hey *rayyis!*" But the boatman, sitting at the other end of the boat, paid no attention, in his eyes a naïve delight as if he were sharing in the vacationers' games. Layla spoke again, her voice harder. "Hey—" He turned to her, a look of surprise on his face.

"Put the plank down and get out."

"And the boat?"

"I'll take it out."

"By yourself?"

"Yes, by myself," said Layla sharply.

———

She sat in the exact center of the boat, her body rigid, and tightened her grip on the oars. She began to strike the water, slap after slap, swiftly, powerfully, with everything in her, as if she were in a race—and as if fleeing a danger that pursued her. She went further and further, into the deepest stretch of the river, as far as she could get from any sign of humanity. There she stopped, catching her breath, drops of perspiration shining across her face. She turned to look about her. Water, nothing else; water surrounding her on all sides, imprisoning her, choking her breathing as if she had ingested it straight into her lungs. Her grip on the oars loosened. Where was she going? Where might she flee? From whom was she escaping? If she was fleeing from people, she was as lonely by herself as in the company of others. The loneliness was inside, in her very soul, in her depths. It was in her blood: like cancer it ran, growing, swelling. Layla put her head on her hands as she kept hold of the oars. Husayn was the cause. Yes, he was responsible for all of this. Before she had known him she had been self-sufficient, secure, and confident; and she had been happy that way. She had implored him to leave her alone, to get out of her path; but he had not stepped back. And now he had gone, and had left this loneliness for her, a loneliness that gnawed at her body, a sense that something precious had been lost to her, something she could not replace. Husayn had said that she had lost the shine in her eyes, the brightness in her face. But in fact she had lost more than that, far more. She had lost affection, affection for people, and security and stability. Nothing was left to her but lonelenss, and feelings of terrible loss.

If he had not gone away; if he had stayed by her side . . . Layla shook her head in despair. What was the use? She was alone when he was with her, too, even when he was expressing his love. Only once had she felt truly close, truly together: when, his hand running lightly along her arm, he had said, "I'm just waiting for you, waiting for you, darling." But even that sense of intimate harmony had been short-lived, seeming now a mere dream. Fear had gotten the better of it. She had been afraid of Mahmud, of Husayn, of the whole world; and that had woken her up.

Layla woke from her reverie to see the oar sliding out of her right hand and over the frame of the boat. Suddenly an extraordinary strength shot through her, a totally unaccustomed energy she never would have dreamt to possess, a toughness that made her challenge the Nile as if it were a rival, as if they were two equally muscular forces engaged in struggle. In a trice she pulled the left oar hard with her fist as she leaned her body heavily to the right to grab the other. The boat dipped sharply with her sudden movement and the water rose to meet the rim while she tried to raise the oar. The river's surface was now even with the side of the boat. Layla straightened up, the right oar firmly in her grip. She let her breath out and slumped over. Only then did she sense a massive shiver of fear seize her body.

She swung the boat round in the direction of the beach. She rowed slowly, rhythmically, as the current pushed her forward. Her gaze wandered along the distant horizon as she considered this latest of incidents. Where had that ability to handle the situation come from? How had she acted with such determination, such muscle and swiftness, without hesitating at all? Where had it come from? She shook her head wonderingly, almost unable to believe that she had faced her encounter with the Nile so courageously. Usually, she reflected, she became confused when faced with the simplest matter and lost the power to think or act; usually, she covered her face in her hands and submitted to her fate. So how had she been able to act when a crisis faced her—and to act precisely as she should have? With utter speed, precision, and force? As if the person acting was not her but someone else. Another person! Another, stronger person seemed to reside deep inside her.

"What happened, Layla?" asked Mahmud. "We were really worried about you." He and Sanaa had swum toward her when they noticed her heading the boat toward shore. Layla shook her head as if awaking from a dream when she saw a look of accusation replacing the anxiety in Mahmud's eyes.

In the boat as they headed back to Ras al-Barr, Mahmud's face was rigid. "You just can't stop doing stupid things, can you? You always do exactly the wrong thing! You could have drowned, out by yourself like that." Layla felt a shiver go through her body and turned her face away. "I really might have drowned," she said in a whisper, as if to herself.

Chapter
Fourteen

All three of them—Layla, Sanaa, and Adila—enrolled in the Department of Philosophy, Faculty of Letters, Cairo University. From the start they comprised a little clique; hardly ever were they apart at the college. They mixed with the other students, of course, women and men, but within limits that were well understood by all, so that they remained always a clearly defined little group. If a student wanted to approach one of them, he must approach them all; if one among the three made him uncomfortable, he would have to avoid them all. If he wanted to talk to one of them, he must have his say in front of the whole clique or not at all. For there were no secrets among the individuals of that little set, and if one girl were to be invited to a party or group activity without the others, she would not attend.

The other students treated them like a clique and referred to them that way. "The *shilla* likes such-and-such." "The *shilla* can't stand that." "The *shilla* is going to do something-or-other, but it won't do that." It was as if they were a single person, not three nearly full-grown girls each of whom had a distinctive personality and moved in a personal world whose features she could reveal and hide at will.

Adila was the tallest among them. Big-boned, she had a large frame without being at all plump. Her skin was light, her eyes big, dark, and shadowed by silky black lashes. She had such a forceful personality that an observer would understand as much with a first glance. She voiced her opinions firmly and backed them with unassailable arguments; she let no one escape her skill at imitation, invariably drawing a great deal of laughter. Not a shade of the humor in human behavior or in any social situation ever escaped her; she would give it her attention, develop it, make it a source of great amusement within the *shilla* that might go on for years.

She was highly realistic, too; Sanaa described her down-to-earth practicality by saying that Adila had only to touch the most awe-inspiring poem for it to be immediately transformed into an arithmetic problem. She had not wanted to join the philosophy department, but rather the department of "earning bread," as she would say, but her unremarkable examination results left her no choice. Adila it was who always explicated what the set favored and frowned upon, what was suitable for the *shilla* and what was not; she it was who chose and rejected new acquaintances. She guarded the group's good name, and made its life inside the college and outside one continuing peal of laughter.

But Adila's own laugh was not untouched by bitterness. Her practical bent derived from a necessity that circumstances had imposed. Under this hard, recalcitrant, sometimes aggressively hostile skin beat a heart that longed for affection no less than did the hearts of other girls, but Adila hid this verity with stubborn persistence. She would always say that love was how the leisure class wasted time, and she had no time to waste. She had to help her mother with the house; she must work hard so as to graduate quickly, to find a job and earn money to pay off her widowed mother's debts, and to support her siblings, all of whom were younger. Life was no rosy dream, nor was it a romance. Life was an unvarnished fact: open mouths demanding nourishment, clothing, education; and a meager pension, seven pounds and no more, ever; and a father who had died suddenly after losing—on behalf of himself and their mother—all the assets they had had. That was not to mention a certain social position that one must try to maintain so that relatives and enemies would not be able to derive malicious pleasure from the situation.

Sanaa was as different as could be; it was as if she and Adila stood at two opposing poles of existence. Sanaa loved poetry, music, literature, exquisite works of art—everything that had beauty. Not only did she monitor the shape and size of her body, she took great care with how she showed it off. She took time choosing her clothes, and she took care to make her appearance distinctive—the particular tying of her sash, the flower she might wear, a delicate scarf she knotted round her neck, leaving its ends to ripple on her shoulders in the breeze. She was never sparing with herself. She loved pretty little trinkets, a tiny golden fishnet change purse, a watch in the shape of an icon dangling from her neck, sweet *parfum* spreading from her handkerchief. Compared to Adila and Layla she was well-off, and so she could wrap herself in the beauty she loved, which she managed to preserve even after her financial situation changed. She was enamored of the power of imagination, too, and relied on it whenever reality did not satisfy her; she could live in an imaginary world for hours at a time. And she was positively in love with love.

Before falling in love with Mahmud she had been enamored of Robert Taylor. Fourteen years old, she had taken a razor and carved the first letter of his name into her hand. She let the blood well from the cut so that the letter "R" would still be there when the wound dried. And whenever the scar began to disappear she cut herself again.

Sanaa was more of a listener than a talker. Her small, pale face rarely reflected the vehemence of her reactions. People always assumed she was shy. In fact, she had a great deal of self-esteem. It was not arrogance but rather a quiet sureness that came from an unshakeable belief in the rightness of her actions. As she tended to give in without argument to Adila and Layla on small matters, they assumed she was easily led, mistaking this elasticity for weakness and failing to see that her flexibility came rather from the generosity of her firm desire to please those she loved. Observing this small, easily led girl with her superbly delicate features, who dwelt in her imagination, neither Adila nor Layla imagined that an unyielding will was encased in those tiny ribs, together with a totally practical bent no less serviceable than Adila's. She knew precisely what she wanted and how to get there; and how to preserve whatever she acquired.

———

And so after the sojourn in Ras al-Barr it was Sanaa who discovered that she could not live without Mahmud—some months before Mahmud was able to discern the same thing for himself. The relationship that had grown between them was unlike love as she had always imagined it: an emotion that would inevitably draw in its wake a burning agony, jealousy, doubt, sleeplessness—the sort of love she had gotten to know through novels and films. This, to the contrary, was a peaceable sensation, a sweet something that as it grew severed her from that all-encompassing imaginary world of hers, securing her instead to the earth. It gave her the unprecedented sense that now she walked on ground that was not only solid but also—and to her surprise—remarkably appealing. And she intended to stay there all her life.

Back in Cairo, Sanaa could see Mahmud at home whenever she came to visit Layla. Sometimes she could even be alone with him, for occasionally, Layla deliberately left them together. But these fleeting encounters could not satiate Sanaa, and she suggested they meet somewhere else. Mahmud, his astonishment mirrored in his face, stammered something about her reputation and the imperative of preserving it. She fixed her narrow eyes on his.

"Do you want to see me or not?"

"Of course I want to."

"Then that's that." And Sanaa meant what she said. Having fallen in love with Mahmud, she found all else meaningless; it was as if she could see only from one perspective—Mahmud's. His thoughts and notions became hers; she adopted his reactions and his projects. They began to meet regularly in the lobby of the Metropolitan Hotel. They had a preferred corner; in dim light they sat, Mahmud mostly talking while Sanaa listened and her eyes embraced his words. Day after day her presence in his life grew, until one day he realized that he could not do without her. She had known all along that such a day would arrive, but when it actually came, she discovered a novel emotion trembling inside, a love stronger and vaster than the earlier sensation, a love encompassing the yearnings of the martyr.

"You know, Mahmud? I must do something to prove to you how much I love you—I want to die for you."

He took her hand tenderly. "I want you to live for me, Sanaa. Without you I am worth nothing." And he meant it. He felt genuinely strong when she was with him; he found himself capable, excellent, and handsome; he marveled at the world around him, full as it was of love and fidelity, sacrifice and beauty. The uncomfortable ties that had bound him to the earth, his fear and doubt and confusion and worry, had suddenly come wonderfully unknotted. Now he could move freely; he could have soared into the air, were it physically possible! Sanaa, studying him, could see those bewildered eyes settling, beginning to shine with a smiling confidence. With her gaze she embraced his—his eyes, his dreams, the joy that flared in his heart, enfolding its wings about her, living with her, for her, in her. Sanaa was cocooned in a world she concealed from Adila, and of which Layla only knew a fragment. Layla had no idea that they were meeting outside the apartment, nor that they dreamt of a future that would hold the two of them in its singular embrace. Nor did she know that they had begun to discuss the finer points of that future. It would have been natural for Sanaa to

relate these details to Layla, but she did not. It was not for lack of trying, but the words always seemed to stop on her lips. Exactly why this
was so she did not know; but she had an inkling that Layla would not
be overjoyed at her happiness, would not react as she had, would not
share her dreams and dream them together as the friends had always
done. She perceived that something had separated Layla from her, had
brought Layla closer to Adila than to her, contrary to how it had always
been in the past.

———

Layla had always felt closer to Sanaa than to Adila; within the confines
of their little clique the two of them formed a true unit, nourished by
a correspondence in mood, in emotions and taste, in the ways they
understood life. But Layla's encounter with Isam had altered this. She
had drawn away from Sanaa, pulled wholly toward Adila.

"You know, Sanaa, Adila is the most intelligent one among us. If I
had really listened to her, it never would have happened. She always
used to say to me, 'Don't latch on so.' Well, I hung on like a block-
headed sucker."

In Adila's cold reality Layla found consolation. Adila made life
appear so simple—no complications, no fantasies, no pains. Life was
just an arithmetic problem: all you had to do was to follow the basic
rules and you would come up with the solution. And no one would dis-
agree about what it was. The important thing was to follow the rules,
step by step, precisely, rationally, cautiously, after forethought and
without any impetuousness. Otherwise your vision could get clouded
and the numbers would get mixed up. All would become entangled in
everything else, and you would be burdened with a bewildering situation from which there was no way out.

Moreover, the rules were all clearly laid out. And Adila knew them
perfectly. Everyone knew them. If you knew them, then you knew the
difference between right and wrong. If you followed them, you walked
the right path, where you would find stability and assurance and peace

of mind, not to mention respect and confidence that you were right. After all, it was not simply your own, personal sense of right, but that of others. All others—and that meant you were never alone or vulnerable. You did not have to face life alone and vulnerable. The others would always be there, supporting you at every step, offering backing and protection, as long as you followed the fundamental rules—their rules.

On this firm, hard ground, next to Adila, Layla stood. On this solid foundation she stood, after her experience with Isam, and within the bounds of those rules. There she existed, fortifying herself against life, so fearful; and suppressing all the wellsprings of spontaneity and lively inquisitiveness that were in her nature. She faced life with a cold face and a colder heart, with chilled feelings, with a studied behavior the consequences of which she always knew in advance. She constructed a shell of emotional serenity from her certainty that she was acting correctly, that she was perfectly self-sufficient, and that no one could harm her or cause her pain. Then Husayn passed through her existence and a vibrant current touched her, setting off the sort of animated reactions that anyone who followed the rules and was clever at reckoning consequences would hardly dream of. Layla paused on the bank, observing life's current as it pushed forward, and something in her heart rebelled. Something was willing her to join that current. Yet something in her mind pulled her back, enveloped her to imprison her on shore. And there she remained. But as that current deepened her feelings of solitude and isolation, her ties to Adila grew firm and taut, as if she drew from their bond the very ability to stand on her feet. She felt more and more distant from Sanaa.

Adila stood on ground that Layla could touch, from which she could draw reassurance. Sanaa hovered in the sky, in an open space toward which Layla was afraid even to glance. In her mind, too, Husayn was linked to this amorphous space, for he lingered there waiting, waiting for her. But she could not do it; she did not want to voyage upward, to meet him where he waited. For that was a space where one lived in perpetual fever. You never knew exactly where you stood; you saw things not as they really were; you felt a strength you did not really possess, a beauty you could not really claim, and a happiness bigger than one person could sustain. For the thread that connected one to the sky was fragile; it might break suddenly, and you would tumble to earth and shatter.

Embracing Adila's view of life, Layla managed to conceal her feelings for Husayn even from herself. Layer upon layer of emotion, of warmth—those feelings settled so deeply inside that they were no longer visible, along with her compelling desire to embrace life. On the surface floated only the deception that was Layla's existence.

———

Entering by the monumental front gate, Layla glanced at the enormous university clock. The chime announced 9:45. She headed toward the main building of the Faculty of Letters, hesitating as she started up to the second floor. It would not be seemly for the lecturer to catch sight of her, for then he would know that she was in the college yet had not attended his lecture. On the other hand, how could he possibly be aware of her absence when such a crowd of students filled the lecture hall? Taking extra precaution, Layla stopped some meters away, waiting for Sanaa and Adila to come out.

The door opened and a horde of students poured from the room. A small, dark-complexioned young woman with tiger-like eyes laughed. "Did you see Suzy—did you see what she did to herself?"

"I wasn't paying attention," replied her classmate.

"She uncovered half her chest, she'd drowned herself in perfume, and she was making eyes at the professor the whole time he was talking."

Her friend doubled over with laughter. "And our dear professor might as well not have been in the same room. Just as likely to be moved as a mountain would be." Her companion pinched her warn-

214

ingly on the arm as the fast-moving wave of students parted in the middle and Dr. Fuad Ramzi appeared. He strode with measured slowness, followed by Suzy and her fragrance and then by a knot of students, male and female. Dr. Ramzi stalked on, his tall frame absolutely straight and rigid, his pale, sober face empty of all expression, his frosty eyes ahead, as if no students trailed him, as if none were attempting to engage him in discussion, as if he heard nothing of what they said. To Layla he looked like a solitary walker, as if he had slipped into a glass case that set him apart from everyone else. Dr. Ramzi approached the spot where Layla stood. His eyes moved round her and then came to stop on her. She could not understand how he could have seen her in the first place, when his eyes were fixed so steadily forward. But now those eyes measured her, weighing her, not with any desire or curiosity, but slowly and with disinterested calculation, as a person might eye a coin in his hand to make sure it was not forged. The eyes shifted away, and Layla let out her breath in relief. But Dr. Ramzi stopped right in front of her, his eyes straight ahead again as if he did not see her after all. "Where were you, Miss?"

Layla's face grew bright red. The students behind Dr. Ramzi peered at her in delighted curiosity, as if they were watching a mouse just fallen into a waiting trap. She tried to regain her poise and said weakly, "I arrived late."

"And then?"

Layla realized that his question was meant to embarrass her into becoming a target of attack and censure. She said nothing.

"Next time, get your timing straight. Anyone who wants to get educated has to be sure of his schedule." The professor said all of this without looking at her. His chilly voice seemed to confirm to her and the others that it was all the same to him whether or not she got her schedule right, or perhaps whether or not she went up in flames. His valuable piece of advice was crowned by a chuckle from one of the students, and then the professor moved away, leaving Layla motionless, her forehead beaded with sweat. She looked round in vain for Adila and Sanaa; instead, her eyes met those of the student who had laughed—bold, wicked eyes, intensifying the sensation that she was truly alone. She left the corridor almost at a run.

At the female students' lounge she stopped, shoved the door open, and collapsed onto the nearest chair. She put down her book bag, keeping her diary on her lap, her head down, and peered covertly at the room's occupants. At the table in the center sat a student copying lecture notes. To her right sat a girl shining her shoes with a scrap of wool. Facing her was another, drinking tea with a spectacular show of disgust, as if she had just found a scorpion in the glass. Before the mirror stood her classmate Nawal—"the bee," as the first-years in philosophy all called her—poking into place her needle-like eyebrows with the handle of a comb. Layla's eyes met Nawal's in the mirror, and Layla jerked her head away. Adila had ruled that Nawal's name was mud in the college, and that to mix with her would sully their little set's name; from that day Layla had avoided her, except to exchange brief greetings.

Nawal moved the comb to her other eyebrow. "Good morning."

Layla returned the greeting but could not overcome her discomfort. Noticing, Nawal assumed it was directed at her and arched her eyebrows. She smiled lightly. "You have a letter on the board."

"A letter!" Layla was surprised and disconcerted. "For me?"

Nawal's smile broadened and her eyes narrowed, giving her a sly air. "A letter—there—" Her hand waved toward the message board and she turned back to face the mirror, smoothing her dress over her petite body, pulling the belt tighter around her startlingly small waist. Layla stood before the board. A foreign stamp: the letter was from Husayn. With a trembling hand she snatched the envelope, stuffed it into her diary, and hurried to the door. Nawal called after her, twisting and drawing out the syllables in her name with delicious mirth. "La-ay-laa!" Layla stopped cold in the doorway as if caught red-handed. She turned slowly, noticing that the glass of tea had paused at the lips of its drinker, while the young woman shining her shoe had sat back and swung one leg over the other, ready for the entertainment. Nawal, her hand now on her waist, in her eyes the same sly look, was speaking, "Your bag—you forgot your bag."

Layla leaned down to pick up her bookbag from the floor, and stayed bent over as she worked to hide her confusion. She straightened and ran from the room. A student stopped her in the corridor. She caught only the word "Adila," muttered something unintelligible, and hurried on her way.

———

An empty classroom: she chose a seat at the very back. She opened the letter with shaking fingers.

Dear Layla,

I say "Dear Layla" even though I would rather use another word that better expresses the truth of my feelings for you. But I am afraid that I might scare you; I know how easily you are frightened—painfully easily. It is painful to me, anyway.

For the same reason, I hesitated to write to you. But my overpowering longing for the homeland left me no choice. For you have become a symbol for all I love in my nation. When I think of Egypt, I think of you; when I long for Egypt, I long for you. And to be honest, I never stop longing for Egypt.

I can almost picture you smiling. You do not believe me, do you? You do not trust me; you put up barriers between yourself and me. You are not willing to let go, to let your true nature have its way. You are afraid that you might really become attached to me—might lose yourself in me. You are afraid that from me you might develop some confidence in yourself and in life, and that then you might discover yourself spilled, like coffee, in my room.

I love you, and I want you to love me. But I do not want you to lose yourself in me, or in anyone. Nor do I want you to draw your self-confidence and your trust in life from me or from anyone else. I want you to have your own individual, independent self, and the confidence that can only spring from the self, not from others. Then—when you have achieved that—no one will ever be able to crush you. Not I, nor any creature. Only then will you be able to volley back whatever blows come to you, and go on your way. Only then will you be able to link your own existence, the core of yourself, to others, so that the real you will flourish and bloom and renew itself. Only then will you be happy. You are miserable now, my love. You tried to hide that from me, but I saw it. You have imprisoned yourself in the minute space within which most people of our class keep themselves: the province of the "I," of apprehension and stagnation, of social rules, the same rules that made Isam betray you, and made Mahmud feel isolated in the struggle for the Canal, and has made our class, as a class, stand motionless for so long, on the sidelines, merely observers to the nationalist movement. The very same rules that you despise and that I do too, and all who look toward a better future for our people and our nation.

In the space of the "I" you have been living, miserable, because deep down you do believe in liberation, in letting go, in sacrificing your selfish desires for the larger whole, in love, in an ever-renewing, fertile life. You have been miserable because the current of life inside you has not died but has remained alive, fighting to get out. Don't let yourself stay imprisoned in that narrow sphere, my love; that small space will close in on you more and more until it either strangles you or transforms you into a completely unfeeling and unthinking creature. Let go, my love, run forward, connect yourself to others, to the millions of others, to that good land, our land, to the good people, ours. Then you will find love, a love bigger than you and me, a beautiful love that no one can ever steal from you. A love whose echo you will always find resounding in your ear, reflected in the heart. It is a love that makes one grow: love of the nation, love for its people.

So let go, my love, run forward, fling the door open wide, and leave it open. And on the open road you will find me, my love. I will be waiting for you, because I have confidence in you. I know you can get out. And because all I can hold onto is to wait, to wait for you.

Husayn Amir.

P.S. I wanted to write a light letter, but I found myself philosophizing in spite of myself. (This is another one of the shortcomings you can add to the list.) But you like philosophy too. And you like . . . all the things I do. Believe me, Layla, we were created for each other.

Fondness and grief chased across Layla's face. Putting down the letter, she leaned forward, her gaze sternly ahead. Her face lit up; it was a lovely vision, but a rather incredible one. She saw herself walking steadily to a closed door and giving it a push. She stood on a threshold meeting the rays of light that flooded across her in a warm embrace. With a final glance at the dark room in which she had been held, she walked forward, light welling up around her, afraid of no one, returning the blows that came her way, and then walking on . . . . The university clock chimed the hour. Layla got up, fumblingly, as if she had just awoken. She folded the letter and left the room. She descended the back staircase slowly, and almost collided with Adila at the bottom.

Chapter Fifteen

A stern face confronted Layla. Her lips pressed together, Adila dragged her by the hand to an empty niche under the stairs.

"What was the letter that came for you?"

Layla stared at her in astonishment.

"I could have beaten Miss Eyebrows to a pulp. I go into the room, asking if anyone has seen you, and she says—in front of twenty girls— she says, 'Your friend got a letter in a blue envelope, and ran out in a complete tizzy.'"

Layla swung her face away with a little gasp, as if she had just been slapped in the face. She noticed Sanaa crossing the garden, coming toward them.

"There's no reason to make such a big fuss about it, Adila."

"If you had seen all the laughing and winking, you'd know I wasn't exaggerating."

Sanaa had joined them without Adila noticing. "What's the matter? Why so grim?" No one answered her. "C'mon, why so grim?"

Layla's voice was faint, her shoulders slumped. What came out was, "A letter came," but she might as well have said, "The worst disaster came." Sanaa burst out laughing. Adila threw her a dark look.

"It was a blue letter, my dear," said Adila emphatically; this was too serious for laughter.

Sanaa's eyes sparkled. She was still laughing as she spoke. "You're kidding, *shaykha*." Her hand shot out to grasp Layla's. "Good going! Shake my hand—" But her hand, stretched out for a knowing handshake, hung in the air. Adila looked at her suspiciously, and Layla pinched her side in warning.

"What's the story?" asked Sanaa. "Explain what's going on! All this grief about a blue letter?"

Layla directed her words at Adila. "By the way, all the letters that come from Germany are blue, not just that one."

Sanaa's face lit up and she threw her arms around Layla. "From Husayn? Was it from Husayn, Layla?" A genuine delight shone in her eyes, as if *she* had received a letter from her beloved. "What does he have to say? Layla, what did he say in the letter?"

Adila gazed at Layla, waiting for an answer. Curiosity, for the moment, erased the scandal she had sketched out in her mind. Layla blushed. No—Adila would not see Husayn's letter. Nor would Sanaa, nor anyone; what that letter said was a secret between her and Husayn. No one else knew about it, and no one else ever would. It would embarrass her to have Sanaa read the letter, or Adila; she would feel as if she had undressed before them. She closed her lips firmly; and Adila understood that she would not speak.

"Anyway, what would he have to say?" remarked Adila. "It's the same old thing. I love you, I'm crazy about you, I have nothing but you— then you find him mooning over every German girl he meets."

Layla's lips got white.

"Shame on you, *shaykha*," said Sanaa. "You think the world's that bad? That there's no such thing as loyalty any more?"

Adila laughed mockingly. "Sure, Madame Sanaa, sure there is—in those novels you read. You tell me: if Mr. Husayn loves Layla, why didn't he go to her family and ask for her?"

"That's enough, both of you," said Layla, her voice low. "I don't want to hear any more of this." But the argument between Adila and Sanaa had flared too strongly to be easily extinguished.

"How could he marry her, just like that?" demanded Sanaa. "Is she a parcel you buy? Now if Layla was the shrinking violet type . . . so he says, 'I love you,' and she says, 'But I don't love you,' then what is he supposed to do? Buy her? The guy is waiting for—"

Layla felt like screaming, but she just steamed, "Enough!" It pained her that Adila and Sanaa could discuss such a personal subject, right in front of her, as if she were not even there, or as if she were some useless, lifeless object, a pebble under their feet or the like. But Adila paid no heed to Layla's protest as she countered Sanaa in her most sarcastic voice. "Poor, wretched Husayn? Fasting, I suppose, like it's Ramadan? And the guy is just waiting for the cannon to go off, telling him it's finally time to break his fast? Right—oh well, I guess you can't break a fast with blonde hair and blue eyes."

Layla's lips were trembling. "Anyway, it makes no difference to me. Blonde hair, tarand pitch. The subject of Husayn doesn't interest me in the least, and I don't want anyone to talk about it."

Sanaa's sidelong glance at Layla brimmed with regret. She gave a disconsolate shrug and trudged off. Adila was not so easy to fend off. Her mind was busily joining all the threads as she rapidly considered the practical measures that Layla must take to tackle this state of affairs.

———

Late that afternoon Adila visited Layla at home. Layla received her with noticeable reserve. She knew quite well that Adila would do her utmost to pull the noose tight by forcing her to take an immediate, practical step. And she could not handle practical steps at the moment. Adila narrowed her eyes on Layla.

"So what are you going to do about this?"

Layla averted her gaze. Adila went on and on. Her duty as a friend forced her to warn Layla of how dangerous the situation really was, she declared. As a friend, she must remind Layla that there was only one solution, and no alternative could be considered. Layla must write to Husayn, asking him please to stop writing to her, because to receive his letters subjected her to gossip that ruined her reputation in the college. Layla jumped to her feet. But Adila just went on talking in the same calm tone. Indeed, it would be even better if she—Adila—were to write the letter, in her own handwriting, and then to sign it on behalf of Layla. That way it could not possibly be used as a weapon to threaten Layla's stability in the future, at the point when she decided to become engaged or married. How many, many homes had been brought down that way, sighed Adila.

Layla was appalled, and her face showed it. Her voice was faint. "Impossible. Impossible, Adila. You don't know Husayn at all."

But Adila brushed off Layla's words with a wave of her hand. All men were alike, she said. Husayn was no better or worse than any other. And extreme caution had never harmed anyone. Layla collapsed back into her seat. Adila went on. Was there any other solution? she asked. She did not stop to consider that Layla might desire a relationship with Husayn, might want to correspond with him. After all, she was not one of those cheap girls who had disdained principle. All that those girls won in the end was a man's scorn, anyway. So what could the answer be? There was no alternative to the solution she had proposed, which would settle things quickly and decisively. And if Layla did not answer Husayn at all, he would take this as encouragement to write again. Then, instead of writing once he would write again and again, and the scandal would widen in the college, day after day, until Layla's name was fodder for every tongue. Was she really prepared to sacrifice her good name? To give up the most precious of a young woman's possessions?

Adila paused after this presentation and observed Layla narrowly. "Well?"

Layla leaned her head back against the chair and closed her eyes. "I can't . . . I just can't, Adila."

"Why not?" Adila's voice was harsh. "Are you in love with him?"

Layla shook her head in despair. "No, it's not like that. It's not."

"So what is it then?"

Layla opened her eyes and sat up straight, leaning toward Adila, palms open as if she lacked the words to explain things. When she finally spoke she could barely keep back the sobs. "What can I say? You won't understand."

Adila stood up. "Because I'm a donkey, right? Anyway, I've done my duty. And you're free to do what you want. It's your life." She stalked out.

———

For a week, Layla was too bewildered to do anything but cry. On the tram, in the street, at home, wherever she could be alone, she tried to think it over, but thinking just led to more thoughts, and more tears. She could not give in to Adila's point of view, but she could not dismiss it either.

She was still giving it thought as she sat between Adila and Sanaa in Dr. Ramzi's lecture, the professor's voice reaching her as if from very far away. Adila's arguments were clear and persuasive, but she could not throw Husayn's love back into his face. She could not stab him so, when he had opened his heart and his life to her. She could not strike the hand he had extended to her, or cut off the single ray of light that shone into her life. For this would be the end. It would mean she would remain forever in that vicious circle, inside the dark room.

Vicious circle? Dark room? It was all such nonsense! The vicious circle was the one in which Isam had imprisoned her, and in which Husayn would enclose her, too, one day. It was that mocking smile with which Nawal met her when she greeted her in the corridor; it was Adila's coldness and the denial etched on her face. This was the closed circle from whose confines she must exit.

But she could not do it. She could not cause Husayn pain. Layla's whole body throbbed with affection as she envisioned Husayn's strong features softening into his beautiful smile, his face transformed almost into that of a suckling infant. No one, ever, would treat her with the same tenderness, and no one would know her, really know her, as he did, know her as if the curtain of separate selves had vanished between them, as if he could see into her depths. "Believe me, my love, we were created for each other." No, she could not cause him pain, even . . .

Layla came out of her reverie abruptly as Sanaa poked her arm. "Miss Layla Sulayman—" It was Dr. Ramzi, calling out her name. She realized immediately that he had directed a question to her. She had not even heard it. She jumped to her feet. "Please repeat the question." She tried to keep her voice calm.

He repeated it. He stood waiting, his eyes drawing the noose tighter to elicit her confession. She spoke in a faint voice. "I'm sorry. I wasn't following the lecture."

"Of course not. You were daydreaming." Laughter rose from the room, and the professor directed the same question to a young man on the other side of the lecture hall. Nawal leaned over to Suzy and said something. Suzy laughed and turned to look at Layla, sitting in a row behind her. "Whoever has stolen your mind away should be congratulated," she whispered with a grin. But her smile faded quickly as Adila, staring at her, hissed, "If you know what's good for you, you'll straighten up. Stop talking nonsense."

Suzy turned. Layla looked out of the corner of her eye at Adila, but her friend had turned her head away in anger.

Some days later, Layla was walking along the big vestibule that fronted the college with Adila and Sanaa when Nawal stopped them. In her insinuating voice, she said, "Layla, there's a letter for you in the girls' lounge." Adila smiled bitterly, triumphantly, as if saying to Layla, "I told you so."

When Layla went to pick up Husayn's letter, she found the room full of students. She walked to the board with some unease and extended a shaking hand to the letter. It seemed to her that all the eyes in the room were leveled on her, and she felt the letter burning into her hand. She stuffed it into her bag and turned, making sure not to meet anyone's eyes. On the way to the door she bumped into the table, lost her balance, and fell. She heard laughter, some of it loud and open, some of it suppressed, but imperfectly. Her eyesight blurred as she collected the scattered contents of her bag, feeling the ground with both hands as if she were blind.

———

Late that afternoon Layla dropped in on Adila unannounced. She sat waiting in the living room, her body rigid, her face unmoving. After the usual greetings she pressed a folded slip of white paper into her friend's hand.

"What's this?"

"Husayn's address." And so Adila knew that Layla had accepted her solution, and she knew as well that this was costing her profound emotional pain. Sadness came into her eyes as she said, her voice unsteady, "I'm doing this for your own good, Layla."

"I know that."

"Would you like to be the one who writes, Layla? At home, by yourself?" Layla shook her head. She had already tried. Adila proposed that she write the letter later, when Layla was not there with her.

"*Now*," said Layla, her voice muffled.

Only after she began to write did Adila understand Layla's insistence on facing the painful situation immediately. Layla did not agree to the first draft, nor to the second.

"Something gentler. It has to be *gentle*, Adila."

Adila's natural inclination was to respond sarcastically, "You won't be happy, Layla, unless I write a love letter to Husayn. Even if it is me doing the writing." But the words stopped on her lips. Layla's emotions seemed stretched so tautly that she would need only the slightest poke with a needle to pop. So Adila merely asked, "Gentle like what, Layla?"

"Thank him."

"Me?"

"Aren't you writing the letter in my name? So I'm the one thanking him."

"For what?"

"For everything, all the things he has done. Write that."

In the end, Layla dictated the letter to Adila. The tears stood in her eyes as she said, "I thank you from the bottom of my heart for what you have done for me. For everything you have done." This turn of phrase did not please Adila, but she was afraid to protest. She was aware that the slightest opposition might cause Layla to reverse her decision, to cancel the whole idea of the letter once and for all. So Adila thanked Husayn.

When Layla reached the street she sighed with relief, as if she had just left a battle that had exhausted her forces. She felt like someone who had finally faced a long-awaited disaster and realized that the worst was over.

Chapter Sixteen

Dr. Ramzi's campaign to distress Layla continued in class and outside the lecture hall as well. He pressed so hard that, alone with her friends, she would cry out in desperation, "What does that man want from me? That's all I want to know—what does he want from me?"

As each term ended she hoped from her heart that she would not be re-assigned to his classes, but her hope was continually dashed. He taught her regularly through her years at the university. If it was not one subject, it was another. She felt as if he were drinking her blood drop by drop, in anticipation of the moment in which it would have all dried up.

He began by focusing his attention on her in class; he seemed to direct all of the difficult questions to her as if there were no other students in the lecture hall. Lobbing a question at her, he would stand waiting, ready to discredit whatever answer she gave; waiting, his distinguished, pallid face empty of expression, speaking to her but as if he were addressing anyone but her, listening to her as if he were paying no attention, his very presence oppressive, constricting every breath she took, but as if he were not really there, as if he stood alone in a glass case that set him apart in grand isolation.

So she would answer; and invariably he would disparage her response. It was not this that angered her, though, for most of the time he belittled whatever any student said. But what did infuriate her was the impression he gave of taking especial pleasure in ridiculing her responses. Launching into his mockery, a sardonic smile would gleam on his thin, pale lips, and those cold eyes would flash with victory as if he had just aimed a wholly accurate and vicious blow at his worst enemy. He would push aside the glass case and the students would feel that life was beginning to pulse within their professor; a spark would be triggered between teacher and students. Laughter, comments—the god would suddenly turn into a human being who actually made jokes—at Layla's expense, of course. "No, you still don't get it. You're philosophizing, but philosophy isn't a pot of stew on the stove, Miss." "Do you know what it is you need? You need brakes—brakes on your imagination. Philosophy is not a figment of the imagination. Philosophy is principles, firm principles; and rules, strict and fundamental rules." "The philosophy department is not where you belong. You should have gone to one of the literature departments. Maybe your imagination would have served you well there."

So a silent struggle began, imbuing Layla with its outlines, a struggle she felt compromised her very existence and sucked the blood from her veins. If she did not comprehend at first what Dr. Ramzi wanted from her, it was not long before she understood perfectly. His attitude to life diverged from hers in sharply defined ways. The source of that was not difficult to locate: his whole nature differed from hers. So, she realized, he wanted to humiliate her—precisely her—and to bend her to his will; he must hear her parrot his opinions. The only view he could brook was his own. Indeed, no response one might offer could please him; to be more accurate, he could not regard *any* answer with pleasure, for as far as he was concerned, pleasure was a vulgar emotion wholly inappropriate to the intellectual, who must at all times impose on his feelings an ironclad structure of thought. No, he could not consent to any answer unless it conformed to his own personal opinion—unless his merchandise was returned to him in full!

This was not a phase of her life in which Layla felt any particular need to assert her will. She resigned herself to a great deal, and tended to yield without argument; but in this case, something led her to put up with the disparagement, the commentaries, and the jokes without crumbling. It almost seemed as if she did not dare to capitulate, for if she had, a danger she could ill define awaited her.

"Just say what he wants to hear and be done with it," Adila would say.

"He wants me to be a parrot."

"Parrot, parrot, isn't that better than having him always picking on you? What's the big deal about making him happy, hmm?"

Layla had no convincing answer to offer. If she were to tell Adila that something within her warned her not to yield, deterring her from buckling under, Adila would laugh at her. If she insinuated that some sort of danger threatened from the direction of Dr. Ramzi, a danger she could not pinpoint at present, Adila would think her insane.

Layla did not surrender. Dr. Ramzi went on drinking her blood, his words like a hammer in a worker's fist, demolishing whatever resisted, day after day. His presence filled her with a fear that paralyzed her senses and yet at the same time attracted her. She could not take her eyes from him.

———

Layla stood up. Dr. Ramzi had asked her a question. His eyes narrowed; a smirk played on his face. Not a trace of surprise: he knew she would cave in. It was just a question of time, patience, and persistence, nothing more and nothing less. Layla spun out her response. She was alert; she attended to all that occurred around her; she was perfectly capable of perceiving what he wanted and batting his view back to him in words that almost echoed his and in a style that closely imitated his. The inexact parallel was not lost on the professor.

"Are you really convinced of what you are saying?"

Layla pressed her lips together in irritation and said nothing. A new operation was mounted. He was a sculptor plying his chisel, now delicately, now almost violently, and always with studied care. Here a light touch, here a deep furrow, here a chunk that must be dislodged entirely, and here a segment that required only refining and polishing. The lineaments of the statue emerged gradually, notch after notch, dent by dent, cut away by the artist's will.

Layla understood nothing of this. She knew only that Dr. Ramzi had changed his manner. He had come to consider her a proponent of his school of thought, one of his followers. He had become more patient with her, more charitable of her lapses, even if he still did criticize her now and then. After all, he wanted her to learn from her errors. Layla began to chime in with Adila, defending Dr. Ramzi whenever Sanaa denounced him.

In Layla's second year at the university Dr. Ramzi's authority seemed to extend into areas she had considered her own personal province. One day she was turning in a paper in his office. She put it on his desk and turned to go out.

"What's that?" he said.

Layla sensed that his gaze was fixed on her face, specifically on her lips. Gamila had invited her the evening before to an evening party and had insisted on coloring her lips. In the morning there was still a trace of it, so she had added a light layer of color. Now her face grew pink. "What's what?"

"What's on your lips."

She spoke faintly as if confessing to a crime. "Lipstick."

He concealed a smile. "I know that. But why did you put it on? You've never used lipstick before."

"All the girls use it."

"That's descending to the gutter. Just because a wave of vulgar behavior has engulfed the city, does that mean we are all obliged to act immorally?"

His reference to immoral behavior provoked Layla. "I'm not immoral!"

He spoke coldly, apparently unmoved by her anger. "I am saying the opposite. I'm saying that you are far superior to the girls who act that way."

"I'm not superior to anyone," said Layla obstinately.

"You are certainly superior."

She met his gaze for the first time since entering the room. "Superior why?"

He smiled directly at her, his eyes coldly confident. "Because I believe you are."

————

It did not stop at that. His eyes followed her everywhere. He would appear suddenly, as if the earth had split to let him emerge, and his eyes would rove across her before fixing intently on her, as if taking her measure, as if weighing her. There was no desire or emotion in his gaze; his calculation was slow and precise, an inspector evaluating a coin for possible forgery. Under Dr. Ramzi's gaze Layla shivered. An obscure fear paralyzed her senses, and she always let out a sigh of relief the moment he pulled his eyes from her.

Even when he was not in sight his presence seemed to corral her. Standing with Adila and Sanaa, sharing a joke with a male classmate, she would thank God that Dr. Ramzi had not seen her. If she gave a paper in class that won another professor's approval, she wished Dr. Ramzi could have heard her so he would have to admit her exceptional ability. Submerged in the library for hours on end, she would ask herself why he had not happened to see her devoting herself so fully to study. Why was it that he only seemed to see her when she was giggling or hanging behind to chat in a corner of the college? Why did he catch sight of her only when she was doing something she ought not to be doing? Yet occasionally she found herself able to forget his existence. That was what happened on one particular morning.

———

In the library's main reading room a classmate approached Layla's table. Would she loan him that reference book she was reading as soon as she had finished with it? As she raised her head she thought immediately of Husayn. Yes, when Husayn smiled his eyes had exactly the same look: the boldness, the fierce hardness seemed to melt, and his eyes became as soft and dream-filled as these big, black ones she saw before her now. Smiling, she promised her classmate the book. He pulled out the chair next to her and sat down. He admired the way she spoke in class, he said, and he liked what she had to say. He wrote poetry, and he would be very pleased if she would agree to read some of his poems. He began to chat about the future, the poetry he hoped to compose, his ideas about poetic innovation, and how he could steer clear of the chasm that now existed in Arabic poetry between form and content . . .

Layla sat back, at ease, listening to him; lowering her eyelids, she tilted her head to one side, a diminutive smile on her lips. She could so easily imagine that it was Husayn she heard. When he talked of the future, Husayn's voice rang out richly, too, a dreamy timbre creeping into it. Husayn's words pulsed like this, with a life of their own, an energy his listeners could not help taking in, their thoughts inevitably soaring with his as that voice bore them upward.

"Have you seen this book?" The voice was icy, sharp; a book appeared from nowhere, shoved across the table toward the two of them. Layla's eyes flew open; Dr. Ramzi faced her. Her classmate jumped to his feet but she could not. In fact, she could not even see; she was dizzy, as if she were falling from a great height. Her classmate leafed through the book; could he borrow it? he asked Dr. Ramzi. No, said their professor; he had put a copy in the library but it was not yet catalogued. He would not loan this one; it was his own personal copy.

"And I like my books to be very clean. I do not appreciate having anyone touch them. When that happens to a book I can no longer read it; I cannot feel that it is truly mine." As he spoke, Dr. Ramzi fixed Layla with his gaze. But if his words were to carry more than one meaning, Layla was not in any condition to perceive it. Fear numbed her, as if she had been caught red-handed in a capital offense.

Dr. Ramzi tried to get her to meet his eyes. "Miss, have you seen this book?" But Layla did not raise her eyes. She put out trembling hands and slowly drew the book to where she sat, and tried to focus her eyes on its cover. Dr. Ramzi turned to the bookshelves lining the nearby wall. Her classmate excused himself and left the reading room.

She longed to leave, too. But she could not; she must wait until Dr. Ramzi retrieved his book. He stood at the shelves for what seemed a long time; ponderously, he went to the librarian's desk. Layla could almost feel his slow, heavy steps crushing her nerves; he was drawing out his conversation with the librarian to lengthen her torment, she was certain. He returned and saw at once that she had not touched the book.

"You did not open the book? And why not? Are you that embarrassed?" This time Layla did pick up his double meaning. Her face reddened.

———

Dr. Ramzi's treatment of Layla underwent another perceptible change. Encountering her in the corridor, he would turn his eyes unhurriedly away, no longer confronting her with that calculating gaze, as if he had discovered that the coin was forged after all and did not even deserve to be assessed. In class, he turned on her; his tone was markedly harsher, as several of Layla's classmates, female and male, commented.

"What is that man's problem?" Sanaa asked. "Can't he leave off?"

"I can't stand any more," said Layla. "Enough abuse! And anyway, I'd really like to know what it is he wants from me?"

Adila stopped in her tracks. Her voice hinted that the thought that had just come into her head was nothing short of brilliant. "Mightn't he be in love with you, Layla?"

"Get out of here. Have you lost your mind?"

Sanaa laughed. "What kind of lousy love is that? That's hate, not love."

But the idea had captivated Adila. She was ready with one of her poses. "Why not? Did not the famous philosopher Schopenhauer say that love, deep down, is really hatred? And hatred, in its depths—is it not love?"

Layla and Sanaa burst out laughing. Choking back her tears, Sanaa said, "Right—just like when you open a barrel from one end and it's honey. Then you open it from the other end and you've got tar."

"That's enough clowning around," exclaimed Layla. "Come on, let's find a place to sit. We've got to think of some way out of this." The friends headed for their preferred spot on the grass behind the library. Adila, her face serious now, turned to Sanaa. "But I really don't think I'm crazy. Can *you* tell me why that man chases her everywhere? And why he is so fond of upsetting her?"

"Do tell, madam cleric."

Adila tried to hold back her triumphant smile. "I swear, he's in love with her." She turned to Layla, her eyes gleaming. "He ought to be! If he marries you, Layla, now that would be some marriage!"

Sanaa's response was a theatrical flourish. "God preserve us!" Adila tilted her head quizzically and addressed Sanaa again, enthusiastically, as if Dr. Ramzi had indeed proposed to Layla. "So? What's wrong with it? Is he so bad? Fantastic professor, good looks, has a car, people know who he is, he gets respect. A groom any girl in the college would hope for."

"You're awful," said Layla. "Now come on, girls, be serious. What are we doing? Stay on the subject. I *have* to find some way of handling this."

"It's simple," said Sanaa seriously. "There's only one solution."

Layla looked at her curiously.

"Marry him."

Layla burst out laughing. Adila seemed less pleased. "What's your problem? Why are you in such a tizzy? Now, this match isn't—" Layla interrupted her, tears of laughter still pouring from her eyes. "Adila, stop it! What on earth brought the subject of marriage and all that nonsense into this? How ridiculous can we get?"

But Adila was entirely elsewhere. Her notion had graduated to firm belief, and she began defending it as established fact.

"Fine, tell the truth, *ya sitti*—now wouldn't you want to marry him?"

"Perish the thought."

"Are you going to find anyone better than him to marry?"

"Of course."

Mahmud's image shot into Layla's head. Next to Dr. Ramzi he seemed a midget next to a giant. She was not at all happy about this unbidden comparison.

Sanaa leaned over toward Adila and said quietly, "You know something, Adila? Whoever marries Dr. Ramzi—now what kind of life do you think she will have?"

A look of interest came into Layla's eyes as she listened to Sanaa.

"Whoever marries him will be put in the deep freeze and locked up. Jammed in a tin of sardines and sealed." Layla shivered. But Adila slapped her own cheek melodramatically. "Horrors . . . "

Sanaa went on. "And personally, I have no desire to live in a deep freeze. I want to sail . . . ."

"Sail? Through the air? Like this?" Adila spread out her arms and flapped them up and down. Sanaa tried not to smile. "Yes."

"Okay, girl. So he might make you soar. What's the flaw in him?"

Sanaa's voice was flat. "Make me soar—he would smother any woman to death."

"Oh stop being ridiculous. By God, tomorrow the whole college is going to envy Layla."

Layla laughed. "Adila, you're the one who should stop being ridiculous. So we can find a solution to this."

"I have a suggestion," said Sanaa. "Adila can talk to him when she goes in to deliver her paper."

"What is she going to say to him?"

"She can say, 'Why the mistreatment, apple of my eye? Release her, I beg of you for God's sake, and for the sake of love.'"

Now it was Adila who burst out laughing as she tried to imagine herself standing before Dr. Ramzi's solemn face and saying these words.

"I'm leaving," said Layla in irritation as she got up. Sanaa pulled her by the arm. "That's all, now I'll be serious. Adila can say to him, 'Layla apologizes if she did anything wrong, and she begs you to forgive her.'"

"That's more reasonable," said Layla. "But forget about the 'forgive her' part."

"And who said I'm going to talk to him about this anyway?" said Adila, cutting Layla off. Layla's face fell.

"Don't get upset," said Sanaa. "I have another suggestion."

"What?"

"Adila can marry him."

"You're really on your toes today," Layla said bitterly to Sanaa.

Adila seemed to be thinking. "Frankly, it wouldn't do."

"What wouldn't do?" asked Layla.

"Me marrying Dr. Ramzi. Either he would break my skull the first week or I'd break his. Because we're so alike. Birds of a feather."

Sanaa laughed. "One *ful* bean split in two."

But Adila was still reflecting. "No . . . I definitely wouldn't suit him. He wants someone soft and gentle, like Layla. That's what he needs. And calm, and sweet."

"And obedient," finished Sanaa. "And who puts up with a lot, and is as pliant as the ring on his hand, that he can move from finger to finger!"

238

"So all I can get from you two is teasing?" said Layla, showing her annoyance. "Anyway, this is my problem, and I'm the one who will work it out."

"What are you going to tell him?"

"I'll say what I say. What matters is not getting trounced in class like that."

When Layla headed toward Dr. Ramzi's office on the pretext of picking up her marked paper, she had worked out exactly what she wanted to say. But when he raised that waxen face from the desk, every last word she had prepared evaporated from her brain. She stepped forward until she was almost against the desk and said, the tone of her voice mingling dogged challenge with frailty, "My paper, please."

He opened a desk drawer slowly, staring at her all the while, and drew the paper out with no hesitation, as if he had been expecting her. He sailed it across the desk in front of her, still looking at her. She blushed as she picked it up and started to turn away, toward the door.

"Wait."

She froze. She did not look at him.

"Open the paper and look at the mark."

Very good. She was sure he knew it was a 'very good' but even so, he asked her, "What did you get?"

"Very good."

"You might have gotten 'excellent'—do you know why you did not?"

She did not answer. His cold voice showed impatience as he said, "Answer me."

Still she did not answer, and his anger erupted. "Because you waste your time. Because you use the library for purposes other than for what it was intended."

Layla's hand gripped the edge of the desk tightly. She wished she could slap him. But she was too afraid to move. She was silent, absolutely still, staring at the desk; a wave of profound loathing swept over her, tensing the muscles in her face. When Dr. Ramzi spoke again, his voice had regained its customary dead calmness.

"You despise me, do you not?"

She said nothing but this time she did raise her eyes, and fixed them on his. Ramzi's eyes twitched, betraying a dim apprehensiveness. Had he, uncharacteristically, forgotten to prepare for something? Neglected a certain detail? Layla's eyes hinted an arresting blend of revolt, bold readiness, and loathing, a strength he had never imagined thinkable for this meek, gentle child to harbor. The moment was a crucial one, Dr. Ramzi realized, a moment of crisis in his exchange with the person who faced him. He managed to overcome the shock, meeting her eyes again with all of the authority he could summon. Their eyes locked in a protracted, silent struggle; his icy gaze attacked, threatened, then feinted to become more gentle, subduing and taming her, deepening to match her depth, as if stripping her of the sources of her strength drop by drop. Layla felt the blood sucked from her body; she closed her eyes slowly. Smiling lightly, Dr. Ramzi said, "Why are you angry with me? Because I want you to follow the proper path? Because I want you to become the college's finest young woman?" Layla's eyes remained closed; she said nothing.

"I want you to answer just one question. What you did—was that right or wrong?"

She did not answer. He repeated his question in the same, deadly calm voice and was silent. The waiting filled every moment, every atom of air in the room, as if the whole world had paused, lying in wait for her to speak. Silent tears ran from her eyes, and her grip on the desk relaxed. He put out his hand on the desk and touched her fingers, speaking gently.

"There's no need to cry."

Her eyes flew open. She stared at him, astonished, as if she had just beheld a freak of nature. Then his face was again hard and empty of expression, his hand gripped tightly on his desk—as if he did not see her, had not touched her hand just then, had not said just one gentle sentence. Layla turned to leave, wiping her tears. Her hand on the doorknob, she found the words in Husayn's letter coming into her mind. "So let go, my love, run forward, fling the door open wide, and leave it open."

"One moment, please." said Dr. Ramzi. "There is a small matter to which I want to draw your attention before you leave." Layla faced him, staying near the door. He stood up, gazing down at her for a moment before speaking. "Many people call themselves intellectuals yet mock and belittle the principles and traditions that are ours. But you must realize that these fundamentals are what bind us to the land. Without them we would be like a tree without roots—the slightest breeze could sway it, and even knock it to the ground."

Layla stood absolutely still as she listened, and remained still after he had finished. She stared at him as if her eyes were pulled to him by invisible cords. She could not take her eyes away. She could not move; she could not walk to the door. He towered there in front of her, his head high, very pale, near yet remote, his striking face shrouded in a fog of ambiguity, gazing at her as if he were a god looking down upon her.

A god? Yes, one of those gods belonging to the Greeks, one who never, ever weakened; who stood erect, believing himself always in the right, wanting her to be in the right. To be in his shadow. He never erred, never let down his guard, never relented, never softened. If he were to soften, perhaps . . . ? If stone were to soften! Her heart screamed out, "I beg you, I beg you, do not torment me. I will walk in your shadow. I will follow you. Just do not torment me." Her eyes reflected how deep was her pain, her despair, how desperate her pleading. His face softened into a smile.

"That's all, Layla. You can go." His voice was gentle.

She realized he had called her by name for the first time. He had not said 'Miss' as he usually did. He had called her by her own name.

Chapter Seventeen

From that day, Layla's association with Dr. Ramzi acquired a newly personal tone. Meeting her by chance in the corridor, he would give her a special smile, one that he reserved for her, a smile that singled her out and made her feel superior to her classmates. At the end of the school year he loaned her some books from his personal library to read during the summer vacation. As she embarked on her third year at the university he began asking regularly to see her papers, initiating private discussions on their weaknesses and strengths. As firm as he was with her—in class and outside of the lecture hall, too—something glimmered beneath that stern surface to distinguish her from others, to make her feel that this must mean she was a cut above the rest.

But it all took its toll. Forlorn, apart, drained of energy, Layla had sought the shade of an immense wall whose shadow could easily encompass her. To remain in that shadowed space could not be called a conscious decision; she merely leaned back against the wall to rest. She felt all right as long as she supported herself against the wall while it spread its shadow over her; the shadow itself seemed to lend her the massive solidity of the wall, to offer her its strength, to infuse her with its hardness. She clung to that wall, seeking its protection, wanting its strength. She reined in her own behavior—indeed, her very thoughts—so that they remained within the radius of Dr. Ramzi's approval. What was right was whatever he thought right; wrong was whatever he considered wrong. And it was never difficult to distinguish one from the other. For what constituted wrong was very clear and well defined, and so was what was right. Black was black and white was white, and there were no intermediate shades. He knew the boundaries, and so did she; moreover, so did her mother, Adila, everyone.

But Dr. Ramzi towered above them all, for his commitment to what was right did not parrot other people's commitments but rather expressed his beliefs. And when he avoided what was wrong it was not because he feared the judgments of others but rather because of his superior strength, and because he was an extraordinary person, an intellectual. A true intellectual imposed stringent controls on his emotions, his likes and dislikes, his acts and his words. Such self-control prevented him from acting before thinking; hence he could not err. Such a system distinguished the civilized person from vulgar folk, whose impulsive embrace of the basest emotions led them inevitably into wrongdoing.

Layla adopted Dr. Ramzi's views and stayed within their confines. He noticed this development and was careful to show his support. After she had presented a research project in class, he commented, "The research was good, and you have almost succeeded in ridding yourself of the personal flaws that were preventing you from being objective. That is, from following scientific method. You still have a long road in front of you, but you are making progress."

———

One day after the lecture Adila took Sanaa aside. "So now do you believe me? Look—he's always lending her books, he congratulates her right in the lecture, and everything's just A-okay—see, didn't I tell you he's sweet on her?"

"Why wouldn't he be?" said Sanaa sarcastically. "God's up above, and he's just one step below as far as she's concerned."

"You're jealous," teased Adila, trying to provoke her friend.

"*Ya shaykha*, don't make me sick. Are you happy about the strait-jacket she's in? I can't speak to that fellow, she says. I can't do this, that posture is not proper. And the long-sleeved dresses, the principles, the tree with its roots, the beast and superman! Now really, tell me the truth—are you pleased with all this nonsense?"

"Tell you the truth? She's overdone it a bit."

"A bit? It's sickening."

Sanaa did think Layla's transformation was lamentable. Her friend had become unbearable: self-absorbed, judgmental and self-righteous, rigid, dry, emotionless, as if she had lost her powers of sympathy. Her horizons had narrowed terribly; she only saw as far as the palm of her hand, as if she were literally near-sighted. And then what she noticed excited only disgust and disdain, for she seemed able only to see others' lapses. Everything that came from her mouth was a stern reproach, issued confidently and insolently as if she personally balanced a set of infallible scales. Anyone who took her words seriously might just as well go off and commit suicide! Roots had shaken loose, dissolution was upon every household, corrupt moral behavior had engulfed the entire country, and the intellectuals—those demigods—must stand firm against them. And of course there were no intellectuals except Dr. Ramzi and, by extension, her.

Sanaa was very troubled by it. What had happened? What had changed this young woman from whose face—from whose whole being—affection had once shone? How had she become so filled with rancor, bitterness, rigidity, petrified ideas? Who could ever have believed that she was the sister of Mahmud, whose eyes radiated love for people and for life? Sanaa knew full well that soon she and Layla must come to blows. Mahmud had graduated and was about to complete his internship year. The two of them were waiting only on the announcement of his appointment to a hospital to make their own announcement to the two families. She and Mahmud were not going to let anyone stand in the way of their marriage. Only a month now, and she would surely face Layla head-on. Sanaa dreaded this even more than the inevitable clash with her father and mother. It would be very hard to confront Layla openly, to face a quarrel that would end a friendship that was once the most precious thing in her life. But what could she do? With her newfound rigidity, her cold inflexibility, there was not a chance that Layla would understand.

In fact, something happened to bring Layla and Sanaa together, almost returning to their bond the strength it had had in the past.

—

The blackboard at the college entrance announced that the door was now open for female students who might want to volunteer for the National Guard. The announcement remained posted for a week, to be replaced by an invitation to all female college members to meet in lecture hall 71 with the detachment commander of the National Guard.

At the appointed time the glass door of the lecture hall swung without pause, filling the room with hundreds of young women. Some students had come to register their names on the rolls of the National Guard, others were propelled by curiosity, and one group seemed to have come simply to present a collection of the latest fashions. Sitting between Layla and Sanaa, waiting for the officer to arrive, Adila complained, "See, in the time we've been waiting I could have gone and washed my hair and—" She broke off as the officer entered the lecture hall and stood facing them—three hundred young women. The room was silent for a moment while all eyes examined the young officer as he began to speak, his voice barely audible and his face going scarlet with embarrassment. The whispering soon picked up, resuming interrupted stories. A girl who looked almost Chinese positioned one leg over the other and declared to all in the vicinity that she had accepted the hand of that young man who had been courting her just to stop his pestering. A plump young woman complained to her classmate that her hair had dried out all of a sudden so that it now felt like straw; the classmate advised her to take a steambath, adding oil to the water. The officer's hand went up to his shirtcollar in confusion, and a little knot of young women at the back of the hall chanted to a regular beat, "We can't hear! We can't hear!" The officer slapped his hand down on the table and yelled sternly, "Quiet!"

This time nothing broke the silence but the sound of breathing. Realizing that he finally had the upper hand, the officer was able to raise his voice. He stepped forward into the aisle that divided the sections of seats, speaking in an everyday, conversational manner—no formal oratory, no flowery expressions. His speech flowed from feelings unfamiliar to these young women, sentiments about the value of women, the true equality being given to them for the first time, since they were now being given the right to defend the nation. Tears stood in many eyes; others widened in amazement, as if the door to a strange world had opened before them.

And some eyes moved upward, bored, to look at the clock in the lecture hall. But the silence triumphed, broken only by excited breathing. As Layla sat listening, scenes from her life passed before her: herself as a little girl, jumping in rhythm and raising and lowering her right hand, and chanting as the demonstrators were doing, "Weapons, weapons, we want weapons." Her image as a young teenager, on the shoulders of other demonstrators, women this time, calling out in a voice that was not her own but was the voice of thousands. These memories seemed so distant to her, as if they had happened to someone else.

Sanaa took a pen from her bag and wrote on a bit of paper, "I'm going to volunteer."

Layla's lips formed a sardonic smile that faded as she watched Sanaa, leaning over the paper, lips pressed together and eyes shining. Sanaa drew line after line beneath her words, lines heavy enough to rip the paper. A tremor ran through Layla's body and collected in her head.

Standing before the officer to have her name recorded as a volunteer in the National Guard, she was still unsure. As the officer waited for her to say something, all she could do was to sketch lines with her hand along the table edge. Finally she spoke. "Layla Sulayman. Philosophy, third year." She ran, her cheeks flushed, to catch up with Sanaa.

—

At first it seemed an entertaining game: the long lines they formed, the military movements, the army's phrases and slogans; the lieutenant with his commands and prohibitions; the early morning breeze slapping against their faces and ruffling their hair. And the collective spirit, again, as if the detachment was a clique of friends organizing a plot, exactly as it had been in secondary school. Layla enjoyed every minute of the training; she began to regain the feeling she had lost at the university, that feeling of being part of a whole. But when the lieutenant ordered her to raise her head, she began to feel remote, alienated. Every time she tried to lift her head, only her shoulders came up. It would require an enormous effort, she thought forlornly, to achieve what the others seemed to do so easily and naturally, as if they had been born with their heads straight and high. The lieutenant never failed to remark on it; she tried, but every time, she failed. She would be on the point of giving the whole thing up, but then she would come back.

"I can't. I just can't do it, Sanaa."

"It's only because you've gotten used to walking with your head bowed."

"So what can I do?"

"Raise your head and relax your body. Tell yourself whenever you are walking, 'I am pretty. I am intelligent.'"

Layla laughed.

"I'm not kidding, Layla. Anyone has to feel a certain amount of pride inside. Pride in yourself."

Layla smiled wanly. She tried again, and this time she succeeded. Everyone around her noticed that her posture was straighter and her walk steadier. But then Layla faced a new difficulty. The lieutenant said she was holding the rifle as if it were a broom. This comment stirred up a great deal of clever joking. But Layla put an end to that when they started target practice. She astonished all of them, including the lieutenant.

After the first shot, her body, which had been completely rigid, relaxed. Her whole being had felt as if it were concentrated in her eyes, and with a steady hand she had pulled the trigger. She had hit the bull's eye. She took aim, fired, and hit, time after time, day after day.

The feelings that had abandoned her flooded back. She was capable and strong after all. It was not the words of encouragement and approval; it was the realization that she had worked her will, and that she could always do it again. She could desire something and then she could succeed in achieving it. Moreover, there was no time-lag between the desire and the act, which made the achievement all the more powerful.

Almost finished now with her military training, Layla had a new sense of self that never left her. The pleasure of it pulsed through her body and shone in her eyes.

———

Layla raised a smiling, rosy face to Dr. Ramzi. Her military uniform swinging from her arm, she said, "Good morning, professor." On her way back from the training field, she had come face to face with Dr. Ramzi at the main entrance into the college.

Astonishment appeared on his face. This was the first time that Layla had ever raised her face to look him squarely in the eye or had taken the initiative in speaking to him. He noticed the training uniform on her arm.

"Where are you coming from?"

"From training."

"What training?"

"The National Guard."

He took a drag on his cigarette, giving her a searching look all the while.

"Forget that nonsense. Just concentrate on your studies—much better."

Layla looked at him, a light smile playing around her mouth as if she were humoring a child. Her expression angered him.

"I guess you think you are quite important? You are going to fight, is that right?"

Layla's smile broadened.

"When will we grow up? Outgrow these childish ideas? When will we understand that everyone has his own sphere?"

Layla looked at him inquiringly. He went on. "Intellectuals are a select group. It is not a group that goes into combat. Every country is composed of two population groups—one group that thinks and the other that wars. Defending the country is a duty that must be limited to those who are not intellectuals."

The smile on Layla's face faded, and she spoke with trembling lips. "Defending the country is everyone's duty, whether an intellectual or not." She muttered something to excuse herself, turned, and hurried in the other direction, feeling that some sort of danger slunk after her.

A week had passed since this encounter. Dr. Ramzi sent a message summoning Layla to his office. As she extended her hand to open the door, the courage and determination with which she had begun to face others deserted her. Whenever she stood in front of Dr. Ramzi, the feelings that had tormented her the first time she had entered his office came over her again, a blend of fear and awe, of dread and attraction.

He was standing, his back to the desk, searching for a book in his bookcases. He turned his head when she opened the door, simultaneously noticing her and snatching a book from the shelf. Without another glance he said, "Please make yourself comfortable."

She perched on the edge of the chair by the desk and yanked the hem of her dress down over her knees. He let her wait for a few minutes while he flipped through the book. Then he turned and sat on the edge of the desk. "I want to meet your father. Would you be able to set up an appointment?"

Layla's face reflected her astonishment. "When would you like to meet him, sir?" Slowly, Dr. Ramzi took his diary out of a desk drawer, opened it, and, again slowly, leafed through it, concentrating on each page. Layla's mind began to whirl. Why did he want to meet her father? He did not know her father; there was no connection to link them. This was what a man said to a woman when . . . Layla peered at Dr. Ramzi out of the corner of her eye. He seemed very distant, isolated as usual in his glass case.

No. It was not possible. No, it could not be. He must have some interest to pursue in the Ministry of Finance and he had heard that her father was employed there.

He raised his head to look at her. "Would Monday be good, Layla?"

"Fine, Doctor." She stood up.

"When will you give me an answer?" he asked, smiling.

"Tomorrow, God willing." She stood a moment, hesitating, but she did not dare to ask him why he wanted to meet her father. Contrary to his usual practice, Dr. Ramzi stood up and shook her hand before she left the room.

Sitting at lunch, her mother said, "I swear by the Prophet, my heart senses it, he wants to marry you, Layla."

"Don't you have anything in your head other than marriage, Mama?" shrieked Layla. "Do people get married just like that, with a snap of the fingers?"

Her father gave her a stern look. "What do you mean, 'just like that'?" He turned to her mother. "In any case, there is no reason to put such nonsense into the girl's head. A man with his position, his status, his name—when the time comes for him to think about marriage, he'll be looking high."

"And is Layla so bad?" said her mother protestingly. "Si Mahmud al-Atrabi says—" She went on to relate a story she had told perhaps a hundred times before, the upshot of which was that if the Faculty of

251

Letters could boast three students like Layla, it would be the top college in the whole university.

Layla waited until her father had left the table. She leaned over to her mother and spoke in a low voice. "I wish you wouldn't start with these guessing games. If it were a question of marriage he would have at least given me a hint. It just is not!" She got up from the table, exasperated.

———

It was a question of marriage. After Dr. Ramzi left the apartment, her father put his arms around her, in such a transported state he could hardly stand still. "Congratulations, Layla! We read the sacred Fatiha together—the word of God in the sight of God."

No one consulted her; that was the first thing that came into Layla's head. No one—neither her father nor Dr. Ramzi, as if the marriage concerned someone other than her. But she forgot this observation in the flood of self-pride that submerged her. Once the news got around the college, her pride increased, too; she enjoyed the looks of envy and curiosity that came her way. She felt constantly as if she were the target of pointing fingers, and that whoever had not known her before knew her now, because she had become Dr. Ramzi's fiancée.

Adila gave her a hug when she saw her. "You scoundrel! What a marriage! The whole college is rocking with the news."

Sanaa kissed her. "Congratulations."

"I told you so," Adila said to Sanaa once Layla left them. "I pick these things up, you know."

"Who would have believed it?" Sanaa's voice was melancholy, her face grave. But Adila's response made it clear that she had missed the import of Sanaa's words. "Really! Who would have believed that Layla would hook that grim man, before he even had a chance to realize what was going on! But remember that proverb—Still waters run deep."

"Don't be so dumb! *Wallahi*, he's the one who hooked her and pulled the wool over her eyes. Not the other way around." Sanaa sounded disgusted.

Chapter Eighteen

The battle between Dr. Ramzi and Layla's mother began early, even if it wasn't a conflict in the usual sense of the word. Layla's mother did not dare even to speak in front of her daughter's betrothed.

When the subject of the engagement party came up for discussion, Dr. Ramzi gave his opinion simply, swiftly, and concisely. He thought it should be "on a small scale"; moreover, the ceremony of the contract signing and the actual wedding should be collapsed into one, scheduled for the summer vacation following Layla's graduation. Her father concurred. Her mother opened her mouth to say something but closed it without a word. But after Dr. Ramzi's departure, she did say something. And as usual she put the blame on Layla.

"Now, why did you just sit there like a wretched lump, as if he hadn't just trampled all over you? Does he think you're an old spinster who'll take anything? On a small scale! I might swallow that if the wedding itself was coming up soon, but it's a year and a half away! Happy the one who lives *that* long!"

"Okay, okay, Mama. What do you want?"

"I want to celebrate! Don't I get any joy out of this?"

She was so happy; finally, finally, she had found a bridegroom for her daughter—and one whom she could flaunt in front of her sister. So how could she possibly let this opportunity fizzle, she moaned?

Her sister always had better luck than she did! Her sister had married a judge, while *she* had married a low-level civil servant in the finance ministry. Then, Gamila had married years before Layla. And what a marriage! A marriage to end all marriages! *Such* a respectable match, that fetched her the finest clothes and put her in the company of all the best people! Samia Hanim's children, and Dawlat Hanim's, were part of Gamila's set. She went out with them and came in with them. Sidqi, Samia Hanim's son, and his sister Shushette, were always over at Gamila's home. Isam, too, of course—and what made *him* so special?

He had graduated a year ahead of Mahmud, because he was clever and bright and had not wasted an entire year on the war or other such nonsense. Now he was a deputy at the Qasr al-Aini Hospital. Meanwhile, Mahmud was unemployed, having finished his intern year but still waiting for a permanent assignment. He might or might not get an appointment; even if he did, it would be as a general practitioner, not as a deputy like Isam. Moreover, he would certainly not get a place in Cairo but rather would be appointed somewhere out in the provinces. He would live far from her, in exile, while Isam went on living in his mother's embrace.

And Isam knew the best people and socialized with them, too. Her heart told her that behind Gamila's social contact with Samia Hanim's children there was a story. No doubt her sister had her eye on Shushette for Isam. After all, when her sister struck, she always aimed high. She knew her sister so very well.

She herself had requested Mahmud to please be attentive to Shushette, but her son had paid no heed, shown no interest. She was too much like a boy, he had said. He was so thick-headed; he had no sense of what was in his own interest. His fate would be to fall into an unlucky, wretched marriage, she just knew that was what would happen.

And there was Isam, so wise to things around him, so sharp. No doubt he was at this very moment hovering around the girl. Otherwise, why did they mix so much? What was the point? And why did Sidqi and Shushette stop by Gamila's house so often? There must be a secret behind it all. And if a match between Isam and Shushette really did take place, then it just would go to show that her sister's luck was as high as the skies.

And they were not even willing to give *her* the chance to celebrate her own daughter's fortune, as if such a thing was not for her! The grumbling in that household went on for days. Layla's mother complained to her sister and to her niece, to Isam, to Mahmud, to her husband. She repeated the grievance so often that Layla's father finally blew up in her face.

"Stop it! That's enough—we said it would be that way and that's the way it is going to be."

She said nothing, but her tears streamed down. Layla gathered her courage and began to broach the subject cautiously with Dr. Ramzi. But he blocked her way immediately.

"Enough, Layla. Is she getting married or are we? We don't like fusses and large crowds."

Gamila came to the rescue with a proposal that mollified Layla's mother. They could hold the engagement party "on a small scale" at home, to satisfy Dr. Ramzi. But then she would throw a grand party at her house to celebrate, inviting all the relatives and friends. It was Layla's job to convince Dr. Ramzi. She hinted her way round the subject; finally, she tackled it directly, begging Dr. Ramzi to accept Gamila's proposal. He gave her a long look.

"What is important to me is the way that you see things. Are you persuaded by my perspective, or not?"

"Of course I am. But for Mama's sake—" Her eyes reflected a pleading urgency: a child's entreaty, a cherished demand, a father's reply in the balance.

"All right, Layla," he said, smiling. But, as if in self-reproach for giving in at a time when he should have been firming up the rules of engagement for their relationship, he added, "But you must understand, Layla, that if *this* time I gave in, it is for your mother's sake. I do not expect ever to have to give in again. In the future, my opinion must be yours—one and the same."

She told him that she understood his position perfectly and respected it, and took a deep breath. She was so ready to be rid of these trivial matters—the engagement, Gamila's party, everything. She wanted to free herself for him, to be alone with him, to open her heart to him, as he would open his heart to her. Their feelings would become uppermost, and the barrier that separated them would vanish. The professor-student relationship that had brought her into his circuit no longer satisfied her. She wanted to feel that she was his fiancée, his beloved.

Yes, his beloved. Otherwise, why had he proposed? She was not beautiful, not rich, not from a family of great social position; she wasn't distinguished in any way. So what would cause a man like him to marry a young woman like her, other than love?

Up to this point she had lived in the shadow of his strength; now she craved the shade of his warmth. She dreamed of the day when he would remove the mask that enclosed his emotions toward her, when an effusive, resplendent affection would envelop her—would envelop them together—and would erase the awe she felt for him, and the fear she felt in his presence. She longed to feel that she was not merely accepted as a person but also loved as a woman, and desired. This longing kept her awake at night, although in the days preceding the formal engagement announcement there was much to distract her from it.

The house hummed with people; wherever she turned, Layla saw faces dear to her heart: her mother, her aunt, Gamila, and sometimes Mahmud. Her brother's term of residence at the hospital as an intern had ended, and he was living at home again while he awaited his appointment. If he spent most of his time out, the moment he came home life seemed to erupt everywhere in the apartment, as if a freshening breeze had blown in with him—as if he were so happy that his joy must overflow into the lives of others. For he seemed very happy indeed; he was barely capable of staying still, like a foaming fountain, or like the bubbles rising to the surface of soda water. He would breeze in to give Layla an affectionate kiss, or fling his arms exuberantly round his mother, or pat his aunt breezily on the shoulder. He would praise Gamila's taste in clothes. And whenever he looked in the direction of Sanaa, the bubbles would disappear, the eyes would deepen, the lips would soften, all concentrated into a long, deep gaze, weighted by his overpowering feelings. Then the bubbles would stream out again, and Sanaa would drop her eyelids as if she were under the irresistible influence of a powerful drug.

Didn't Sanaa worry that people would notice her? Layla asked herself. And how did she know when Mahmud was going to be at home? He must be calling her on the telephone, and they must be meeting outside the house. But how? For Sanaa was watched very, very closely. How did she manage to escape that strict observation? Sanaa was playing with fire, thought Layla. The flames must inevitably burn her, and Mahmud, too.

It was clear, though, that they found fire to their liking. Mahmud, utterly happy, seemed reborn: he seemed stronger, more manly, more handsome, more confident in himself and in the future. And Sanaa did not even touch ground in her daily life; she was flying. They had become bolder and more confident these days, as if they had agreed on a specific step—one that would demand all the audacity they could muster. They were so bold that it could not possibly escape Gamila's searching eyes. Nothing could get by those eyes now.

Over the past three years Gamila had changed startlingly; sometimes her transformation seemed hard to believe. The young, unstudied, impulsive girl had become a mature, clever, practical, and extremely worldly-wise woman. Her figure had filled out, and her curvaceous body moved with stately elegance. That handsome face was steady on a long, white, slender neck, no longer dancing about, turning this way and that like the whirlwind that Gamila had once been, so like Mahmud's impetuous energy. The jet-black plaits now circled that placid white brow proudly, all strands carefully in place, as if drawn by an artist's brush. Those lustrous eyes that had flickered and shone like a pure spring now had a gaze that was hard, cold, and intrepid. The shy grin had become a carefully sketched, studied smile. Gamila appeared more like a breathtakingly beautiful marble statue than a live, warm human being; but below the tranquil surface simmered fire. Those veiled flames were the sort that kindle men's desires, provoked further by a tranquil surface that fueled their sense of masculine contest, a trial of strength against this beautiful woman who was perfectly aware of her appeal. Confident of drawing any man she had the slightest desire to attract, Gamila enjoyed every moment she spent at every party she attended. But she returned home from her evenings out to an engulfing depression as she passed her husband's closed door and his snoring reached her ears. She would stretch out in her own bed and dream that she was once again seventeen years old, still young, still unmarried, and in love. With whom? Someone who was not any of the men she met at her parties. They passed time pleasantly enough, those men, as she did, no more and no less. But flirtations were not what she wanted. She longed for a profound love, a quiet, true love that would not encase her in a heated battle but enfold her in a tender peacefulness.

—

When Gamila learned that Layla was about to become engaged, her eyes clouded with anxiety and she quickly found an opportunity to be alone with Layla in her room. She asked immediately, "You love Ramzi, Layla, right?

Layla nodded. The worry faded from Gamila's face and her frame relaxed as she let out a short, nervous laugh. "I knew as much. All your life you've been wiser than me. You waited until somebody came along who loved you and whom you loved."

Layla leaned over to Gamila and seized her hand. "And you—you're happy too, in your marriage, aren't you, Gamila?" A sad look came into Gamila's eyes but it soon disappeared. She stood up. At the window she turned. Layla could see her profile; the usual cold, hard expression had returned.

"Ask Mama, she'll tell you. She'll tell you the kind of happiness I have." She turned to face Layla. "In any case, we are on the subject of you at the moment. We have to give this some thought. What shall we do for the party?" She was very involved in the subject of Layla's engagement, in the party, in all of the details. She was dropping by to see Layla almost every day. Her perfume would announce her entrance; as she sailed in, wearing her stunningly simple, luxurious, perfectly composed outfits, everyone would sigh in relief. Now they could turn everything over to her. She was the one who knew everything; she made the suggestions, and then she it was who arranged things, seemingly without any complication or confusion, as if she had been mounting weddings and engagement parties all her life. In the beginning she usually came in the company of her husband, but soon she started coming by herself.

"Well, where is Ali Bey?" her mother would ask.

Gamila would shrug. "If I bring him, what will he do? Sleep, like he did yesterday?"

Layla held back her laughter as the image of Ali Bey came into her mind, a body draped over the sofa, more or less filling it, his head dropped onto his shoulder, his mouth open, his breathing successively louder and louder until he was snoring, the fat gold watch chain hanging massively down as far as his paunch.

"No," said Gamila's mother. "It's not right, Gamila. Aren't we his relatives?" Gamila shrugged her words off. "By the way," she said to

Layla, "Isam apologizes for not being here. He's coming by tomorrow to congratulate you."

Layla had been uneasy at Isam's silence. She wanted to see him, to make sure that he bore no feelings of bitterness and to show him that she had none either, as if she wanted to clear all outstanding matters before she became officially engaged.

———

Isam came to their home with Sidqi. They had become inseparable companions. Seeing them together Layla smiled, recollecting Gamila's engagement party. Isam had wanted to choke her merely because Sidqi had spoken to her. Isam noticed her smile and understood immediately. When a seat next to her was vacated he sat down and said, smiling, "What were you chortling about?"

"So, you've become friends, you and Sidqi!"

Isam laughed. "Do you remember?"

"Like children playing, weren't we?"

Isam didn't answer. Layla noticed Sidqi whispering something into Gamila's ear. Her cousin blew cigarette smoke straight into his face and laughed, a series of curt, broken sounds. Isam raised his face to Layla and smiled, but shamefacedly this time. "You know, Layla, what I'm planning to do when I get married?"

Layla looked at him questioningly.

"The first daughter I have, I'm going to name Layla, after you."

Layla felt embarrassed. She was so inconsequential, so paltry. Isam, for whom she had felt so much contempt, seemed a better and more courageous person than she was. Isam had no wish to conceal or deny true feelings that had once filled his heart. Those feelings had gone, but he still preserved them in his heart as a beautiful thing of which he was proud. She, on the other hand, had been suppressing and denying emotions that had once filled her with happiness. Harshly, meanly, she had labeled them "childish play."

Whom was she trying to please by denying those sentiments?

Herself? Ramzi? Layla could not continue her line of thought. Gamila interrupted it, clapping her hands. "Come on, will the men please leave. Women, we have work to do."

Isam stood up, but Sidqi did not move from his seat. Elegant, attractive, handsome, bold, he was attacking Gamila with his eyes, as she sat beside him. Before he would leave, Sidqi teased her. He just loved women's work, he said. But Isam dragged him out by the hand, laughing.

Gamila began to outline the details of the party she was planning to give for Layla. Their discussion came to center on what Layla would wear. When Layla mentioned the material she wanted, Gamila objected. It was the pattern that determined the material, she said firmly. In front of everyone, she announced that the party dress would be her gift to Layla on the occasion of her engagement.

The next day, Gamila took Layla to her seamstress. "I want the best thing you have, *madame*," she said.

"Something *spécial, madame*?" smiled the seamstress, alluding to the high cost of the dress she would present for their inspection. Gamila said stubbornly, "I told you, the best." She showed them a "model in gauze" that she described as a Christian Dior design. Layla and Gamila stood before it, stunned speechless. The seamstress spoke again, in French. "That is no pattern, *ma cherie*—that is a dream."

She was not stretching the truth. Layla had never seen anything prettier in her life, not even at the cinema. She could almost picture herself in this dress of white chiffon. No doubt it would make her loads prettier than she was now. Then, no doubt, Ramzi would think her pretty.

But her face tensed. "Do you have anything else, *madame*?"

"Are you crazy, Layla?" asked Gamila in astonishment. "Can there be anything more lovely than that?"

"I want something with a higher neckline."

The seamstress shrugged disdainfully. "*Non!* A high-necked cocktail dress?"

Layla was silent. Gamila begged the seamstress, who refused stubbornly, and said in French, disparagingly, "I am an *artiste*, not a seamstress. I do not make high-necked cocktail dresses."

Gamila sat in her car, her body rigid, tears of anger glinting in her eyes. Layla patted her thigh gently. "I'm sorry, Gamila."

Gamila made no response. Layla leaned over and kissed her on the cheek. Gamila turned to her and said furiously, "I just want to understand, that's all. Why do you want to keep yourself all buttoned up? All your life you have worn things that are open."

"Because, well, because Ramzi doesn't like them open."

"He can go to hell, my dear. So men think they have something to say about what women wear now, too?"

"I can't, Gamila."

Gamila leaned over to Layla and spoke slowly. "Indulge me, Layla. Look, I have more experience of the world than you do. When a woman goes down on her knees from day one, the man will just climb on top of her and ride her hard with his legs firmly on either side."

Layla felt a sharp pang in her heart. She realized suddenly that what Gamila was warning her against had already happened. But, whether or not it had, the dress had to be very modest. Otherwise, Ramzi would not accept it.

Her aunt made a dress for her to wear for her engagement. It had a very high neckline.

———

Layla stood before the mirror. Her aunt was putting the final tucks into place. "It's gorgeous, sweetheart, absolutely gorgeous." She stepped back. She narrowed her gaze as she studied the dress from a distance, and laughed abruptly.

"Layla, do you know what your dress has turned out like?"

Layla turned her head. "Like what, Aunt Gamila?"

"Like Gamila's wedding dress, except this one has a closed bodice and hers was low cut. Exactly, though—same cut, same lines, same material."

Layla's eyes blurred. She saw Gamila standing on the roof, on the day of the Cairo fire, her back to the skies, still as a statue in her white dress, the masses of thick, acrid smoke surrounding her like a frame. Husayn's voice echoed in her ears. "This is not the end, Layla. Believe me, this is not the end." Layla turned to her aunt and said in a feeble voice, "Are we finished?"

Chapter Nineteen

Layla sat in the car between her father and her fiancé, on the way to Gamila's home. Her father sat stiffly upright. Ramzi had shrunk into himself as if afraid that his body might touch hers. Layla felt a cold shiver brush her despite the July evening. She tried to think of something to say, to dispel the embarrassment that seemed to dominate all three of them. She turned toward Ramzi.

"Is the dress nice?"

Her father looked at her disapprovingly. Ramzi suppressed a smile, and spoke as if humoring a little girl. "It's just fine."

Neither the smile nor the comment satisfied Layla, but she respected Ramzi's circumspection, for no doubt it could be attributed to her father's presence. Silence pressed on them again, and Layla began to toy with her engagement ring, staring at it. Just the day before, Ramzi had come with his mother to Layla's home and had put the ring on her finger, along with a gold wedding ring. Layla had loved his mother the moment she saw her. She felt as if something brought her close to this woman and attracted her, as if they shared something. She kept looking at the woman's face. There was a sweet prettiness there that the years had not erased, a gentle fragility. In her eyes shimmered a faint sadness that would suddenly vanish when she looked proudly at her son.

Ramzi noticed Layla playing with the ring. He broke the heavy silence.

"And do you like the ring?"

She raised a smiling face to him. "It's absolutely beautiful."

"What is valuable is always beautiful," he said. Layla felt uneasy at this allusion to the price of the ring. Her father said, "Yes indeed, what is expensive holds its value."

Silence pressed down on them again until the car came to a stop in front of Gamila's house. The door opened and a wave of heat swathed Layla.

———

From among the waiting crowd, Mahmud pushed his way out and ran toward Layla. He had meant just to greet her but when he got close and took her hand in his, he pulled her to his chest and hugged her. Layla clung to him. He seemed very, very close, closer than at any time in the past. When the brother and sister moved apart, tears shone in her eyes. Her mother stood to one side, her lips trembling. Gamila shouted enthusiastically as she held Layla by both shoulders, "You look stupendous today, Layla! Fabulous!"

"My dear," said her aunt. "God protect you. A bride like no other, you are!"

Isam shook her hand, smiling his shy smile. "Really, it's enough to make one decide it's time to get married."

Ali Bey was there to shake her hand, too. His stomach quivering, he said, *Ma sha' allah, sitt hanim*! Wonderful, *sitt hanim*, absolutely wonderful, God be praised!"

Dr. Ramzi stood apart, waiting for the little demonstration to end. Then everyone turned to him, shaking his hand, congratulating him. Layla walked over to her mother, leaned down, and kissed her, tears welling up in her eyes once again. The music began. Ramzi seized

Layla's arm and strode into the garden. Layla felt uncomfortable as she began to move among the tables scattered across the garden and already filled with people, but her embarrassment soon passed. The men stood up to wish her well as she went by; she sensed their eyes gently studying her face, as if those eyes were patting her quietly on the cheek. A woman let out a warble of celebration and opened the way for other voices, a woman's—"O my soul, she's as pretty as a new moon"— and then a man's—"Just like a peach, a pretty little peach." Layla straightened her back and raised her head, blushing. Her small mouth was rounded, and her eyes fluttered with a lovely gleam. She felt so pretty; she felt loved and desired. She felt intoxicated.

When she drew near the head table she took off her gloves, tilting her head a trifle, coquettishly. She put out a hand to cut the huge cake. The tea party had begun.

As the knife plunged into the cake, Layla remembered suddenly that Ramzi was beside her. She threw him a glance, laughing, and offered him a piece of cake, with a mischievous expression on her face. Tonight. Tonight . . . He would say something lovely to her. Yes, tonight. Something that would move her and would draw them together, above the crowd of guests, bearing them upward to circle together, alone. Tonight, she was so pretty in her white dress! And he looked handsome in his dark blue suit. Tonight was their night, which they would always remember, when they were alone together in their home. He would muse about it to her, and she to him.

Tonight he would reach his hand under the table, and take hers. He would whisper something in her ear. Something that would make the blood run hot in her veins. Tonight he would gaze at her, as if his eyes were touching her, were caressing her, were drawing her to him. Then he would pull away, painfully, when he realized that to look was not enough; it would not satiate his desire, his longing to surround her, all of her, with himself.

Tonight, the words would stop on his tongue, broken, incomplete, unable to convey the love this illustrious man held for her, somewhere deep inside.

She tilted her head and spoke lightly, trying to move Ramzi toward the moment she awaited.

"You never did say whether you like my dress or not."

"I did say."

Layla pursed her mouth, still chewing on a bite of cake.

"So, you do like it?"

He smiled. "I know what you want me to say. But I think that sort of thing has been said enough tonight. It will go to your head."

"What do I want you to say?" she said flirtatiously, her eyes sparkling.

He laughed. "That you're pretty."

Layla's face went crimson, and she lowered her head in embarrassment.

"You mean, I really am pretty today?" she whispered. Her heart fluttered as she waited for a reply.

"Is there any doubt?" But his words had a note of disdain that made her uneasy. Her grip tightened on the table edge as if she needed its support. She shook her head like a stubborn child. "Anyway, I must be pretty, to you anyway, or else you would not have decided to marry me."

"In any case, I do not choose my wife for vulgar reasons." The fork dropped from Layla's hand and clattered into the plate. He added, "Outer appearances really do not interest me very much. What concerns me is rectitude."

Layla pushed her plate away. Her face tightened, and her eyes circled round the garden. She noticed that Gamila had arranged everything exactly as it had been on the night of her wedding. The tables placed across the garden, on either side of the walk. The colored lights glinting among the trees, the orchestra in the same spot, near the entrance to the garden. The same faces gazed at her; the head table, as before, sat near the main entrance to the villa. There was only one difference. She was sitting at the head table, instead of Gamila. And Ramzi was sitting where Ali Bey had sat.

———

Gamila leaned over Layla and Ramzi. "What do you think of it all? Is everything to your liking?"

Layla made a reference to the elegance of everything and said weakly, "All this for me? For me, Gamila?" as if she deemed such luxurious surroundings too elegant for her. Gamila laughed. "My goodness, my dear, how many Laylas do we have?"

She straightened up and spoke, laughing provokingly. "And for Dr. Ramzi, too. I pray to God he's pleased. We know that he does not like parties and all that nonsense, but what can we do? He has to humor us, doesn't he?"

The strain of sarcasm in her voice did not escape Dr. Ramzi. He gave Gamila an irritated look. She withstood it, only partly suppressing her smile. His displeasure melted in a smile. "Whatever the case, we thank you." Gamila made as if to leave them, then stopped, as if she had just remembered something. Waving her hand across the garden, she said to Layla, "Did you notice, Layla? I made everything to look the way it did the day I got married. Exactly."

Layla gazed round, gravely. Turning to go, Gamila added, "Exactly, Layla."

Layla's face grew still more somber. "Truly, it is exactly like the day of your wedding." But Gamila did not hear her. She had turned her back, heading for the tablefuls of invited guests. As she walked away in her close-fitting dress, Ramzi's eyes focused on her back. She was wearing a black dress that, as it rigorously held in the ebullient fullness of her body, left bare much of her back. The clean waistline showed off her small waist, and at her buttocks the dress seemed to pause, interrupted, as if sculpted there as she dressed. The skirt precisely, barely, covered her slender but very round thighs. His eyes went from bottom to top, where the black dress parted to reveal her shoulders, round as the tops of apples, and then a long, marble neck. Then Ramzi was submerged in blackness again, the deep black of her hair, now cut carefully into a short round cap.

Layla observed Gamila as her cousin drew near the table where Sidqi, Isam, and Shushette sat. Sidqi was sitting at ease, playing with a gold chain in his hand, but his face was not as relaxed as his posture suggested. He was giving his full and wary attention to Gamila as she approached him.

Occupied with Sidqi's sister, Isam did not sense his own sister's approach. He was giving Shushette his bashful look, smiling his half smile, trying—in vain, it seemed—to reach her. She sat absently, submerged in the smoke from her cigarette. She was very thin, and the only beauty in her face was in her eyes, large and dreamy as they gazed into the distance, toward where the smoke wafted. Isam kept trying: the poor fellow was attempting to fulfill the role of gallant rake he had set for himself. She was right there, beside him, but she seemed very far away indeed, as if imprisoned in the rings of smoke that her cigarette produced.

Gamila, Layla saw, was bending over Sidqi, offering him a piece of cake. He straightened up in his chair and whispered something in her ear. She shook her head. Gamila was saying no, and now she was returning to the table at which her husband sat, paunch and all; now she readied herself to circulate among the other tables. Layla moved her gaze to the table where her mother sat. Mama looked anxious; her shoulders seemed to hang as she raised her eyes cautiously, even fearfully, as if she wanted to have a look at something but was apprehensive lest her fears be confirmed. But what could her mother fear? Was she afraid that her daughter was not happy? No, she was not looking in Layla's direction. She was looking to the right, toward Mahmud and Sanaa.

Sanaa was sitting with Mahmud, the two of them alone. What audacity! Sanaa, her face pink, was whispering something into

Mahmud's ear, and Mahmud's eyes sparkled like twin chunks of turquoise. Layla leaned forward, as if magic threads pulled her eyes in the direction of Sanaa and Mahmud.

———

Ramzi touched Layla's arm. She realized that Sidqi stood just behind her, offering his congratulations. As Sidqi walked away, toward the villa, and then stepped through its front door, Ramzi watched.

"Gamila's brother?"

A sarcastic laugh burst from Layla, as if she had been waiting for just such an outlet for her irritation.

"Sidqi—Gamila's brother? Of course not, they don't resemble each other in the slightest."

"Maybe not in outward appearance, but their personalities are one."

"No, there's no comparison. Gamila is a good girl, very simple and straightforward, but Sidqi—"

Ramzi interrupted her. "You mean, Gamila's personality is, well, like yours, for instance?"

"Just about. We were raised together—it might as well have been one house."

Ramzi shook his head as he continued to gaze narrowly at Gamila.

"No, she is altogether different. And you will never be like her."

Layla stared at him, with a confused, embarrassed little laugh.

"What are you laughing at?" he asked.

"Because you said that sentence in an odd way, as if you were angry that I'm not like Gamila."

Ramzi looked at her for a long moment, drawing on his cigarette.

"If you were like her, I would not have thought to marry you."

"Why? What's wrong with Gamila?"

"I didn't say that anything was wrong with her. Maybe she is the best young woman there is. But she is not the sort that would do for me. As a wife, I mean."

"Do you mean the way she dresses and makes herself up?"

"No, something deeper than that. Her personality—it would never work with mine."

Layla hesitated a moment, then threw out the question that had been plaguing her. "And you want to marry me because my personality does work with yours?" She looked at him, waiting for his face to soften, for him to tell her that he loved her and always had.

Not a muscle twitched in Ramzi's face as he said simply and without a moment's hesitation, "Of course. Because you are compliant and quiet, and you listen to me, and you do what I say."

Layla clung to whatever hope she had left. "And that's all?" She seemed to stop breathing as she waited for his answer.

"What else could there possibly be?"

—

Layla lowered her head and stared at the blurred table surface. In a half-finished cup of tea she noticed a drowning fly, trying desperately but hopelessly to free itself. Instinctively her head jerked upward and she focused her undivided attention on Mahmud and Sanaa, as if she could pour her whole self into watching them. A sudden pain gripped her heart; it felt like a hand were squeezing it. As the pain intensified, so did her absorption in the pair; she took such pleasure in her pain, it seemed, that she sought to make it heavier. Her eyes wide, her head swiveled to watch now Sanaa, now Mahmud. Her brother's lips had softened so that now they were hardly visible; Sanaa was blushing and turned her head away teasingly as Mahmud leaned across the table and whispered something. Sanaa bit her lower lip to keep herself from bursting into laughter. Mahmud's gaze caressed Sanaa as if his eyes were the hands of a blind person. Sanaa's eyelids dropped and she groped for Mahmud's hand under the table. But he put both hands squarely on the table with a mischievous chuckle. Startled, Sanaa stared at him, unsure of his intent, but as Mahmud said something and motioned with one hand, her eyes sparkled. Her delicate lips pressed together, giving her a look of determined readiness, she put her hand on the table, and Mahmud took it in both of his—right there, in front of everyone, in broad daylight! It was as good as announcing to anyone who did not yet know that Sanaa and Mahmud were in love.

Ramzi touched Layla's arm. "What's the matter? I said, what you are mooning over?"

Layla gave him an odd look, as if she were just waking up from a dream, as if she had forgotten that he was beside her. But he was indeed there, in every atom of the air; very much there, as if in fact he was the only person present. Layla felt a cold shiver go through her body. "In the deep freeze . . . locked up." That was what Sanaa had said. "Whoever marries him will be put in the deep freeze and locked up." She leaned toward Ramzi, laughing, for all the world as if she were on the point of telling him a story to which she attached no importance, an amusing tale that no one of sound mind could take seriously.

"Can you believe it? Sanaa and Mahmud are in love! Imagine that!"

Now Ramzi became absorbed in watching the pair as Layla went on, her voice a series of staccato phrases as if she could no longer draw more than a shallow breath. "Child's play! Isn't it—just a game, child's play. Children!" But her voice dwindled into a huskiness that seemed to promise a sob. Ramzi paid no heed; his attention was fixed wholly on Sanaa and Mahmud. Observing them seemed to afford him some sort of special pleasure.

It was very clear by now that Sanaa and Mahmud were deliberately goading those at the party into noticing them, broadcasting their determination to marry in a manner that brooked no doubt. Ramzi straightened up and asked distastefully, "There's an official engagement?"

Layla laughed—short, feverish laughs, as if he had told a good joke. She leaned over to him as though she would divulge a startling secret. She whispered, her eyes widening, "There's love. Imagine?" She laughed—or sobbed—again, straightened in her chair, and went back to watching her brother and Sanaa as if those invisible threads pulled her gaze involuntarily toward them. But she could not focus her eyes.

Ramzi's voice reached her from far away as if he spoke from inside a glass-walled chamber.

"There's no such thing as love. It is just the word that a civilized person uses to tame his instincts. What you see in front of you is mere impulsiveness, like an animal pouncing to satiate his instinctual appetite." It was a relief when that voice stopped. Now she could concentrate, could focus, as that pain squeezed her heart. Sanaa, her face rosy, whispered into Mahmud's ear, and his eyes twinkled like chunks of turquoise.

———

Layla nearly sprang to her feet in surprise when she felt two hands clapped on her shoulder. She came to her senses when she saw that it was Gamila, standing behind her, pressing slightly against the back of her chair.

"What's the matter, Layla? Are you just going to sit there like a gutless jellyfish? Aren't you going to come and greet your guests?" As Gamila turned to face Ramzi she angled her head to one side. Her eyes flashed, her voice was sinuous, her tone coquettish, provoking. "So is Dr. Ramzi one of those men who do their best to frighten folks away?"

Layla's heart pounded as the words left Gamila's lips. She worried that Ramzi might answer insolently or coldly, even after all the effort that Gamila had made for her sake. But to her wonder she saw Ramzi's face go crimson. His confusion lasted only seconds, though, as he let out the smoke from his cigarette and then visibly relaxed in his seat. His eyes sparkled with a bold, challenging look and his face took on an animated brightness as he leaned toward Gamila and smiled. "And you? You don't *get* frightened?"

Gamila shook her head and tossed off a series of quick, tiny laughs, her whole body quivering. Dr. Ramzi's eyes roved across that ripe, effervescent figure as if his hands cupped a precious glass of ice water after a long spell of thirst. He leaned back in his chair again; his eyes narrowed and his legs shook rhythmically as he spoke. "Never? Never?"

His words came out thickly, heavily, as if something weighted them down. Gamila pushed her chest forward, pressed her palms to her thighs and said, her whole face shimmering, "I do not get frightened. I only frighten others, Dr. Ramzi."

Layla could see Ramzi's eyes fixed avidly on the shadowy line between Gamila's breasts, his lips rounded in a smile that she found disgusting, reminding her of the grimace of a predatory animal. The strains of the orchestra reached her ears in rapid, wild beats.

Dr. Ramzi ran his tongue over his lips. "That's what you think." But his voice insinuated something else: "Just wait. You and I have a long way to go." Gamila noticed his gaze trembling on her breasts; he could not sit quite still, she saw, and the thought exhilarated her. She straightened and laughed knowingly. "In any case, Layla's enough—you can frighten her." She turned and walked away, unmindful of what she had come over to do. Her body swayed more than usual, her buttocks seemed to take on a life of their own, an impassioned, independent existence that nothing could tame or restrain.

Gamila paused before the front door to her villa. Layla's lips parted to call her, but no sound came out. Gamila's hesitation did not last long. She disappeared inside, her bottom still in perpetual movement. Layla caught sight of the fly in the teacup, now limply afloat on the cold surface of the tea. She followed it with her eyes, her mind empty of thought and feeling, her body a vacuum.

There was a murmur among the guests, a suppressed gust of noisy movement. A dancer ran lightly into the space made by the ring of tables, her body wrapped in a long red sash. The music picked up, growing more feverish; clapping rose and settled into a rhythmic embrace as wild shouts sounded from the audience. The dancer unrolled her red sash and began to whirl. Things lost their balance; the tables began to jump before Layla's eyes, people and trees whirling; the wall that encircled everything seemed to buckle. She raised her hands to her head as if to ward off a looming blow.

Ramzi was shaking his shoulders to the music. "What is it? What's the matter, Layla?"

Objects regained their positions; her senses began to right themselves. She felt a chilling fear as she heard a voice she recognized as Ramzi's. "All of the noise and to-do must have tired you out. It really is tiresome." Layla's face tensed as she moved to brush a fly from her cheek. But somehow she did not dare to move her arm; it stayed limply at her side like a heavy metal rod until Mahmud seized her hand.

———

Layla clung to that hand insistently and squeezed it so hard that Mahmud nearly yelled. "Layla! What, Layla? What is it?"

"Take me inside."

"Why?" asked Ramzi.

Layla's voice was feebly apologetic. "Just for a little. Just a little." The words echoed through her as Mahmud led her into the villa. Sanaa caught up with them in the hall, her face bright, and grabbed Layla around the waist.

"Layla, congratulate me! This is the moment I've waited for all my life. Congratulate me!"

Layla moved her lips, trying to smile, but looked as though she would cry. The image of Husayn rose before her, touching her arm as he spoke. "I'm waiting for you, darling." She ran up the stairs as if closely pursued. Sanaa tried to follow, but Mahmud pulled her back. "Leave her alone, Sanaa. She's a bit upset."

———

Layla opened the first door she came to on the second floor and flopped down on the first seat that presented itself to her eyes, panting. This was the bathroom that adjoined Gamila's bedroom. She sat there, her chest heaving, trying to collect her thoughts. But there was a faint sound stopping up her ears, fracturing her nerves, breaking her attempt to concentrate. Looking around, she realized that it was the sound of water under pressure, welling up inside the faucet. She tried to ignore it. But the water made a raspy gurgle, like a death rattle, she thought, that irritated her and interrupted her attempt to think. Layla pulled herself together, went over to the basin and with difficulty opened the tap. The suppressed water surged out with frightening energy before it quieted to a calm trickle. Layla felt a quiet softness pervade her wracked and sore body. Her confusion of thoughts seemed almost physically to drain from her mind. Suddenly the whole situation was clear before her, a panorama in all its details: the curtain was yanked open, removed abruptly from before her eyes and her mind. She whispered in despair, "What am I going to do? O Lord, what can I possibly do?"

She could hear strains of music from the garden, mingling in her senses with the aroma of jasmine. She caught sight of her face in the mirror. Corpse-like. She wiped her hand across it. She had her whole life before her, a whole life to devote to these thoughts. But for the moment she must conceal that deathly face from everyone. She must go down there, she must face Ramzi and all of those guests. She must face the future that she had chosen for herself. It was all very simple: a touch of face powder, a bit more rouge, and no one would know. No one would realize that beneath the makeup was the set, white face of a corpse.

She went over to the door that led into Gamila's bedroom, her step heavy under her sluggish body, as if she had been an invalid for months. She pushed the door open and went in.

—

Gamila was stretched out on the chaise-longue, her eyelids drooping as if she were dozing. On the floor knelt Sidqi, his back to Layla, his torso over Gamila's body, his face buried between her breasts, as if he, too, were asleep. Gamila saw Layla first, her eyes flashing open as the bathroom door swung closed with a little screech. Her eyes flared; she gave Sidqi's shoulder a sharp slap to get him off, but his arms tightened around her. Her disgust now including him, she shoved his arms away with a muffled screech.

"Get up!"

Sidqi turned, still kneeling. Confusion and then embarrassment spread over his face when he saw Layla. He jumped up, a half-smile hovering on his lips, as if he had just come upon something terribly amusing but was keeping back his smile out of a barely-acknowledged respect for others. Gamila scurried to her dressing table, her back to Layla, while Sidqi stood in the middle of the room, running his hand through his hair. Gamila spoke with the same muffled anger. "Get out!"

Sidqi shrugged and walked to the bedroom door, turned the key in the lock, and went out. It had not occurred to Gamila that, with the door locked, someone might enter through the bathroom. Gamila opened a wooden box on the table, took out a cigarette, and lit it with a shaking hand. She inhaled and turned to face Layla.

"Be my guest. Call me names, lecture me on virtue, on deception, on corrupt morals." Layla said nothing. She looked at Gamila as if she did not really see her but was looking right through her. Gamila began pacing like a caged tiger: a few steps, wheel round, a few more steps. She stopped suddenly. "So go on, talk! Why don't you say something? Or would it be improper? Not suitable for you to even talk to one like me?" She crossed her hands on her chest. "Right, I know! Someone like you, so respectable, the professor's wife. The respectable professor who—" But Gamila could not go on. She burst out laughing, laughs empty of mirth, nervous little laughs in quick succession that threatened to choke her. She doubled over, a hand on her stomach to quell her laughing. But her laughs simply grew longer and sharper, and thinned into a wail, and then she was quiet. She stood up very straight, speaking with what sounded like a vicious joy. "That professor of yours, he's just like a dog. He'll salivate and let it drip onto any set of bones he finds." She pulled her body taut as she came right up to Layla and jabbed a finger at the door. "You know, Sidqi there, who just went out? Sidqi's more honorable than that professor of yours. At least he doesn't act like he's a god. At least he doesn't try to hide what he really is."

Gamila raised the cigarette to her mouth and inhaled deeply. She gazed at the rings of smoke, one curling round to embrace the next, then continued in a whisper that came from deep in her throat. "What do you know about the world? What? What do you know about what a woman suffers when she lives with a man she despises? Did they teach you anything about this in the books you've read? Did they explain this to you?" Gamila's voice collapsed as she spoke the final sentences and her eyes filled with tears. Her voice shook as she went on. "Do you know how a woman feels when she realizes that she's become like an old rag? She's all dried out—her body has dried out, and her heart, too, because no one looks at her with a glow in his eyes, no one says to her, 'I love you.'" She paused, and then her voice rang out, shaky, hoarse, despairing. "What can I do? Tell me, what can I do?"

Layla's face twitched; she was trying to speak, but when her mouth shaped the letters no sound emerged. Gamila, smiling bitterly, spoke again. "Divorce—right? So simple?" She gestured with a shaking hand to the bed. "That bed, there, in front of you. I slept there for three days between life and death. I'd swallowed a bottle of aspirin. My mother said, 'I don't want any scandals.' And she knew perfectly well what it meant for me to stay with a man who doesn't love me. One I don't love. But it didn't make any difference. She was absolutely determined." Gamila was quiet again, and then began to laugh hysterically. "My mother! My own mother! 'I don't want any scandals.' My mother. My mother doesn't want any scandals!" She stopped laughing suddenly and her eyes narrowed. "And you? What about you, Miss Respectability, you and your principles—if you were in my place, what would you do? What would you do?" Gamila's voice was high, full of challenge, and then it dropped lower and lower, and the threatening overlay disappeared, as if she were asking Layla an ordinary question. "What would you do?" It was as if she knew instinctively that Layla was in the same situation and would inevitably come to the same end. Layla felt her whole body shake with a loud scream. She rushed toward

Gamila, seeing nothing, feeling her way as if blind, to collapse at her cousin's feet.

———

Some time later, Gamila and Layla crossed the threshold into the garden. Layla returned to her place, while Gamila plunged among the guests. No one noticed anything. Both had put on a great deal of makeup. But anyone who looked closely would have noticed something that makeup could not conceal: the sad, resigned expression in Gamila's eyes, and the frightened, uneasy searching in Layla's gaze. But no one did look closely. No one was that interested.

———

A few days later, Layla received a letter from Husayn.

Dear Layla,

I received Mahmud's letter informing me that your engagement to one of the professors has been announced. Yesterday I wrote an insane letter to you but then I tore it up. Do you believe me when I say that I still love you?

Today I feel somewhat better, at least enough so to think properly. I write to congratulate you. In spite of everything, I am happy for your sake, my dear. I am happy because you were finally able to push that door open and to walk through it. He was able to do what I could not. He was able to free you and to return your self-confidence and your trust in others. Is that not so? I am sure that now you are walking on the open road, your eyes shining, your face bright—the radiance that almost caused me to shout in the elevator.

Do not worry about me. I am well. I did not collapse when your dry letter reached me, nor when I heard the news of your engagement. I am working and living for the sake of a greater love than my love for you: my love for Egypt and its people. As long as that love fills my heart I cannot be destroyed. And I will not stop working. What is difficult for me now is that my love for my nation has become totally intertwined with my love for you, so that you became a symbol for everything I love in the nation. And now I must try to uproot you from my thoughts, my imagination, my blood.

Do not feel any hurt on my account, and do not blame yourself. You gave me no encouragement; to the contrary, you did all that a gentle, sensitive person like you could do to dampen my feelings. But what can I do? What can I do about the mad idea that took possession of me? The idea that you were for me and I was for you no matter how long it might take? The only mistake you made was to let me see you, to see how lovely and gentle you are, and that you are . . . you.

If you wish to make amends for that mistake, let me see you just once, one time, when I return to the nation. Let me fill my eyes with you one last time, as you walk down that road, your face shining, with that wonderful glow in your eyes.

Husayn Amir.

Chapter Twenty

Mahmud was appointed as a staff physician to the government hospital in Port Said. A few weeks after he had taken up his position he visited Cairo. Sitting at the Friday afternoon meal with his family, he raised his head from the plate.

"By the way, I'm getting married."

Layla's heart beat fast as she observed one reaction follow another rapidly across her father's face. Stiff and still at first, as if he had not understood Mahmud's words, that face seemed to collapse. Both corners of his mouth hung down and a deep sadness came over his eyes, then his eyelids came down over them. He reached for a towel, hiding his face behind it as he pretended to wipe his mouth. When he threw it aside his face had returned to its accustomed rigidity, although a measure of congestion seemed to overlay it. He let a few seconds of silence weigh on those around the table before speaking, his voice artificially calm.

"What did you say?"

Layla looked at her brother. His lips were quivering. She waited impatiently for him to say something, as if her future hung on the words that would come from his lips.

"I said, I'm getting married."

Layla slumped back in her seat. Her eyes glistened with tears. She felt intoxicated, as if she were the one who had faced her father with such bold, straightforward simplicity. After all, it was such a simple thing. All she would have to do would be to move her shoulders as Mahmud did and to train her eyes on those of her father, and say . . . What would she say?

Her father's voice rang out, sending a shiver through her. "So your excellency has already arranged everything and now you've come to inform me? Why? Why are you giving yourself the trouble? I'm just an old fool, anyway."

"Please, Papa, please understand me."

"I am not your father. I do not know you. I have no responsibility for you."

Mahmud lowered his eyes in despair, striking his right hand against the table.

"All my life—all my life I have been raising you." Now a strain of resentful blame infused the voice. "I've spent my heart's blood on you so that when you grew up you would be able to stand on your own feet, and to help your mother, and your sister, who is on the point of being married. Now, the minute you become a full human being, you want to kick us in the face. You want to get married." Their father's face was red as he listened to the strain of weakness that had crept into his voice. The tone of censure immediately became one of sarcasm. "Instead of helping me, now you want me to help you so you can get married. Right?"

Mahmud faced his father proudly. "I do not want help from anyone."

His father became even more upset; this was a declaration not to be borne! A bitter, bitter sarcasm shaped his words. "So who are you going to marry, esteemed Doctor?"

Mahmud ignored the sarcasm in his father's voice, preferring to implore him in a way that might reach his heart. "Papa, the girl I am going to marry is wonderful, and very goodhearted and caring. She's well-educated and comes from a good family. You can even ask Layla about her."

Layla shrunk into her seat as her father's gaze came to focus on her, harshly inquiring, as if he held her responsible for this catastrophe that had befallen them. Her mother struck her hands together as if she had given up on both of them.

"It is her friend, *ya sidi*. Our own Lady Layla here is our beacon of happiness. All my life I've said this mixing between girls and boys brings only disasters, now here's the end of it all!"

The father pulled his gaze from Layla to settle coldly on Mahmud. "This family, then—on what basis will they accept you? How much dowry will you pay? How heavy a gold bracelet will you give her?"

Mahmud's voice was low. "I am going to marry the girl, not the family."

His father slumped back in his chair. "That's what it has come to, then? So she is one of those? One of those girls who let down their hair and do whatever they please?"

Mahmud covered his face in his hands, trying to gain control of himself. He had expected all of this, and more; and he must stanch the flow of wounding words that were forming in his mind, he must keep them from bursting out.

"*Wallahi,* I swear," his father's voice rang out, "if this were my daughter I'd kill her! I'd just kill her." His eyes settled on Layla, sharp, threatening, and she felt another tremor pass through her body under his gaze. Had he guessed something? Impossible. How could he? Maybe . . . his fatherly feelings? What feelings?! A huge wall seemed always to sit between the two of them, as if they did not speak the same language, as if they . . .

Mahmud took his hands away from his face and in a polite, restrained voice he announced that the discussion was over. "I am sorry, Papa, but it seems, sir, that you will not be able to understand me." But he could not escape so lightly. His father was determined to continue the discussion.

"Who can understand you? Who can understand that a person in your circumstances, penniless, graduated day before yesterday, wants to marry and set up a household and raise children and bear responsibilities?"

Layla felt her muscles relax. No, he had not guessed. He could not possibly guess what was going around in her head, nor could anyone else. Even she could not describe her overpowering feelings of disgust these days in words that would seem understandable and reasonable to people. What would she say? That the mask had fallen, and beneath it lay filth? That Ramzi's gaze crept like a snake up the chest of . . . ? Her mother spoke in a trembling voice. "Son, there are ways of doing everything, rules, principles. Everything has its rules. He who follows the fundamentals will not suffer."

Layla shut her eyes. What *would* she say? If she told her mother how Ramzi's eyes had slithered over Gamila's breasts, her mother would only laugh and say, in all simplicity, "All men are like that. So what did you think they were like?"

What would she say? And who would understand her when she said that it was Ramzi's eyes creeping along like a snake that had revealed his depravity and weakness? Indeed, no one was free of immoral behavior, as those eyes had shown her. Consenting to this marriage, she was not free of it; nor was Gamila, nor Isam, willing to play the role of clown, nor Sidqi, searching daily for prey so he could prove to himself that he was a man, and to the outside world that he was a daring hero. And then there was the corruption of Umm Gamila, and of her own mother, who had bowed to living in a state of fear—the dread of what other people would say—and of her father, believing himself ever in the right. And the immorality of all of their principles—their fundamentals! Every last one.

"Mama," said Mahmud, "the fundamentals have changed, rules have changed. The times are different, ideas are changing. Please, both of you, try to understand." But they could not possibly comprehend him. Their father kept to his room, having threatened to cut off all communication with Mahmud. Their mother resorted to tears. Mahmud went to Port Said, and on the following Thursday he came to Cairo, but did not visit his family. He did visit the week after that, and found Dr. Ramzi waiting for him.

Mahmud's mother had requested Dr. Ramzi's intervention to bring Mahmud to his senses. Perhaps Dr. Ramzi would straighten him out. Ramzi and Mahmud sat alone in the sitting room, for the father still kept to his own room. The mother—with her daughter—sat in the front room, waiting.

———

Layla paced the front hall, her eyes staring anxiously at the shut door, a shadowy fear constricting her heart. Would her brother give in to the force of this man who sat with him alone? She was gripped by an irresistible desire to hear every word her brother might say, as if her own future depended entirely on what he would say. Still pacing, she veered toward Mahmud's room. Her mother asked sharply, "Where are you going?"

"To get a book from Mahmud's shelves."

She entered his room and crept to the glass door that separated it from the sitting room. She pressed herself to the wall and tried to make out the exchange between the two men. Though a sudden embarrassment about her spying seized her, it went away as soon as she distinguished the cadences of Ramzi's voice. She had never heard him speak this way; she had never heard his voice sounding honeyed, low, pleasantly mellowed—the voice of one friend talking to another. No doubt his features, too, were relaxed, mellow; perhaps the glass box that encased his face had vanished. How many faces did this man possess? With her he acted the god; with Gamila, he was a child, saliva dribbling from his mouth; and now with Mahmud he was an old friend, relating tales of the past.

"I'll tell you a story, Mahmud, one I have never told anyone before.

But you are my little brother, and I cannot be niggardly about sharing any of my experiences with you. When I was a student at the university I fell in love with a girl who lived in an apartment on the floor below mine. Evenings, I would sit in the dark, listening to Umm Kulthum and weeping. I'd stay up all night, writing a love poem to my darling. I'd go downstairs and find her waiting for me on the staircase in her school pinafore. I'd give her the poem, every inch of my body trembling. The days passed; I started to see more of her, to be with her outside the building. It seemed like my feelings for her were getting stronger every day—the world was so completely beautiful to my eyes. I intended to marry her the minute I graduated. I could not imagine myself living a single day without her."

Layla's eyes widened in astonishment and she swallowed. Ramzi went on.

"One night, when her family had left on a trip, she opened the door to me . . . And later, when I got up from the sofa, I just looked at her, lying there, and I knew suddenly that my love for her was gone. It went just like that, at that moment. The next evening I found the door open a crack; I shut it, I went out, and I got drunk. I came back early in the morning, packed all my belongings, and left the neighborhood."

Layla barely managed to suppress her scream. She longed to flee from the room, from the apartment. But she remained where she was, transfixed, pulled to the closed glass door as if to a huge pit, pulled with a force she could not repel. Ramzi began to speak again. "Since that day I've known that there's no substance to what we call 'love.' There's desire, which is gone the minute you get what you want. Anyway, desire is one thing and marriage is another."

A single thought resounded through Layla's head, a single question that bore into her skull like a nail. The girl? What about the girl? What had happened to the girl?

Mahmud's voice was cold. "I do not understand why you've told me this story."

288

Layla covered her face in her hands. Mahmud's words bore no echo of the questioning in her head. The girl's fate was not on anyone's mind, not even Mahmud's. It was as if these two men had some prior agreement that the girl who had transgressed the rules did not deserve any further consideration.

Ramzi spoke tentatively, slowly, his careful words implying more than he said. "I mean, Mahmud, is it really necessary to get married? Is there no other way? Couldn't this be a little dalliance which will pass? If you marry her you'll be paying dearly for it, you know."

Layla bit hard on her lower lip. The scoundrel! She wished Mahmud would slap him; his poisoned suggestion deserved no less than that. But Mahmud did not move. Perhaps the intended meaning had sailed right by him. He spoke stiffly. "I am not a child, Dr. Ramzi. I am capable of making my own choices and sticking to them."

"It's clear that our conversation is over," Ramzi said. "But before I leave I want to tell you about a memory that just came back to me as you were talking."

"Go ahead," Mahmud said politely, his voice indicating not the slightest interest in what Ramzi had to say. Layla, on the other hand, sharpened all her senses like a mouse staring out of a newly sprung trap. Her body stiffened and her face grew absolutely still and hard, as if she were the one who sat there with Ramzi as he spoke and was reacting visibly to every word. And his words did stir up in her imagination a mass of images and expressions, from the past, from the future, from here and there, crowding together, piling up, intermingling until they lost their meaning. A painful sorrow pressed inside her chest as if Ramzi's words were fingers slowly closing around her throat, her lungs, minute by minute.

"This is a story about one of my colleagues, who got married five years ago. He was very ardent, very eager, just like you, and he married for love. The woman he married was also intent on it, and rather radical, and they overcame all the obstacles that faced them, stood against all the social pressures around them, and got married, and lived in an apartment with only a table and a bed. And, of course, love and new values. They applied all of their theories, all of your theories: husband and wife are one, no secrets between them, their relationship is based on affection and on sincerity and openness."

On fear; I will live in fear of Ramzi. Day after day, my blood will go dry with fear. The fear gone by and the fear to come.

"And even their theories on sex. Sex and marriage as one, body and soul united. And the more time that passes, the more he loves her and feels she is a part of him and he is part of her. My friend's eyes shone all the time when he was with us, he was so happy. And whether there was any excuse to do so or not, he was always mentioning his wife. 'My wife said this, my wife thinks this . . . ' He was happy and everyone knew it. 'Well, a new sieve is always strong!'—that is the way they saw it. But a year passed and his eyes were still shining, and he was still saying, 'My wife this, my wife that.' People began to feel that something odd was happening, something not in accord with the rules of the society they were living in. Something laughable. They began hiding their smiles in front of him while laughing at him behind his back."

Scandals! We don't want scandals. My mother does not want scandals.

"So this friend of ours—it was as if he didn't notice a thing. He took his wife and went to Europe. He was determined to share every experience he'd ever been through with her. And after he came back, he and I, we used to have supper out, in this one restaurant, with a few other friends. And after we'd eaten our fill we'd start talking, about women of course. One would talk and the rest would listen. It might be a true story about something that was going on at the time, or maybe something that was going to happen to one of them, or something that had happened in the past, something of the like."

In the kitchen. The darkness, the couch.

"And one story would draw out another, and we'd take turns doing the talking, and everyone was in tune with everyone else, just as if we all were members of a society and knew and agreed on its tiniest regulations, or the gears of a clock moving at exactly the same pace and in the same direction, all the time, one direction that everyone knows, clear, logical, in sequence."

He who knows the fundamentals will not suffer.

"So our friend's turn came. His eyes grew soft, and his features, as he told about an experience in one of England's loveliest wooded spots—with his wife!! And after three years of marriage! We were speechless."

Scandals! She doesn't want scandals! My mother doesn't want scandals.

"We were all stupefied, we really were. Something in the clock mechanism stopped; a gear quit, or reversed direction, messed up that logical, clearly understood direction. One of our group summed it up when he said, 'After three years of marriage? Impossible!' Another couldn't stop laughing until the tears were coming from his eyes. We resumed our conversation but our friend there sensed he was an odd man out, not part of our circle, and he got up and left."

"Don't let yourself stay imprisoned in that narrow sphere, my love. That small space will close in on you more and more until it either strangles you or transforms you into a completely unfeeling and unthinking creature."

"From that day on, our friend stopped talking about his wife, and began feeling discomfited in our midst, in our sessions, in all sessions. He began to feel that he was unlike us, maybe of a different species or something, and that he was isolated from the larger scheme of things. He became confused . . . "

"Okay, Layla, I've found a solution. I've found a solution, my love." "The servant? Well, she's got a crush on Isam. His girlfriend, ya sitti!"

"And after some time had passed, when he started bringing in his wife's name again, he found people who would listen to him, who found what he had to say reasonable. He'd started talking about wives and how tiresome they can be. 'Anyway, what does any woman want besides a house and children and a husband who fulfills the duties of marriage? What?'"

She dies like Safaa, or . . . does as Gamila has done.

"And just a few days ago I came upon that friend of ours, right there in the middle of a group of fellows, talking so confidently, his eyes shining, everyone listening to him. So I pulled up a chair. He was talking about the last little adventure he'd had."

Layla stood in the middle of the room, shaking, helpless, disgusted, in a rage. When Ramzi resumed, there was a tone of sadness in his voice. "There's no way out. Believe me, Mahmud, there is just no way out."

This time, Layla could not keep back her scream, and madly she ran from the room. Ramzi went on, rising above his tone of sadness. "We're all cogs in a big wheel, and that wheel keeps moving and anyone who tries to stop it is crushed. But the clever guy is the one who recognizes the reality of things and profits from it."

Mahmud had the melancholy look of someone watching a sunset. But he was still smiling, and as he got to his feet, he said, "I assure you, Dr. Ramzi, that I will not let myself be defeated as your friend was."

Layla attacked her father's bedroom. At the sound of her hoarse shriek—"Papa!"—her father jumped up from his bed, startled and frightened. "What is it? What?" Worry palsied his limbs; he stood there shaking, looking at her changed demeanor, at her eyes, blazing from her face. He stood waiting for her to speak, to tell him what disaster had struck them now. Layla gestured hysterically to discount this possibility. "Nothing. There's nothing."

For a moment her father looked as if he would faint; then the blood began to circulate again. When his eyesight began to return to normal and things took on their customary appearance, he spoke. "If there's nothing, then why are you rushing in like this? How can you come in here without asking permission?"

Layla flung out the sentence that had formed in her mind in one rushed breath, as if she feared it would never come out otherwise.

"I need to speak to you about my getting married."

Layla heard her own words one by one as if someone else were saying them. Fear clutched Muhammad Sulayman's heart. This was indeed the brink of disaster, one more serious than any he'd faced in the past. He must do his utmost to get past it. His grey eyes narrowed and gleamed terrifically as he stared at his daughter.

"What do you need?" There was no anger in his voice, not even the suggestion of it. It was an icy voice, the cracked, metallic tone of a tired old radio.

"I need—" Layla could not go on. He was walking toward her with short, mechanical steps, face hard, body rigid, a weapon trained on her, coming nearer slowly, nearer, ready to fire. "What do *you* need?" His voice sounded a despair far deeper than anger, that despair of someone who has lost everything and has nothing left to lose, a man who would not hesitate to do anything at all. Layla saw a murderous look in his eyes, murderous but empty of anger; coldly murderous. She spoke in a choked voice, putting her hand to her neck as if she were protecting it from him. "Nothing. Nothing at all." She wanted to back away, but she could not move. The fear stopped her dead, and she went on murmuring, "Nothing. Nothing at all, Papa. Nothing, Papa."

With that pleading call the murderous look was pulled from her face. He shook his head as he turned, as if he were waking from a particularly terror-ridden nightmare. Layla stepped back toward the door, wiping her face with both hands and murmuring, "Nothing, nothing at all."

Ramzi filled the doorway, speaking to her father.

"It's no use."

Layla shivered from the top of her head to her toes. She gripped the back of a chair in time to keep herself from collapsing to the floor. Her father turned to face Ramzi, a weak smile on his lips, and spoke in a shaky voice. "I knew as much. I knew it was no use. May God compensate us." Shifting his gaze to Layla, her father's eyes were sharp. "Our Lord is Generous, our Lord has truly compensated us. We lost a child and gained a man." His gaze settled on Ramzi.

"We gained you, my son."

Chapter Twenty-One

That night, lying in bed, Layla wished she could die. She longed to close her eyes and sleep; morning would arrive and she would not open them. She would go away, leave, escape whole and in peace—no problems, no roughness, no quarrels. But that is not how people die. They do not simply close their eyes and die. There has to be a cause of death. Illness? How about typhoid, for instance? Yes, typhoid was an easy sickness to have, a pleasant, lovely illness that anesthetized you. She could go to sleep, lose consciousness gradually, day after day, slipping off in calm and quiet. Around her bed would gather the tearful faces, trying to hold fast and hard to her as if they were barriers keeping her from slipping into her dreams. Then the faces would vanish and a cloud would envelop her, would thicken, would make those barriers disappear. Layla slipped off to sleep, to her dreaming. At first, she slept a peaceful sleep full of calm dreams. Here she was, stretched out on the deck of a ship afloat, with no idea of where she was going or whence she had come. She did not know who she was even; she had no past, no future. She understood nothing except that she was lying on her back, a lovely stillness in her heart, blue sea-like eternal space surrounding her, the sun's rays dancing on the azure water, sparkling like diamonds, dancing across her body as it lay there, teasing it, subjecting it to a lovely numbness.

Now she was pushing on a door, entering a garden. She had never seen the like. It was a white garden; all the flowers were white and the trees were crowned in whiteness. It was a sea, widening into the distance, a sea of white flowers, strange flowers, tall, as tall as a human being. Tall and white, towering, beautiful, one leaning gently toward the next to pat it tenderly, to almost whisper to it as if it were a human being. Layla pushed her way through the flowers; they bent over her, waving, caressing her cheek, intoxicating her with their scent. She ran, laughing short, breathless laughs. She reached the garden's end, refreshed, exuberant, filled with a bubbling happiness that she could barely endure. She sat on a bench surrounded by a jasmine tree whose petals fell on her head. She reached out her hand, and there was the jasmine, arranged of its own accord into a crown over her hair. She leaned back softly, the sea of flowers filling her eyes.

The blooms parted to reveal a child running toward her. Her child. Layla hugged her son eagerly and lifted him onto her lap. The furious joy in her body subsided, transformed into a lovely tranquility. In silent adoration she rubbed her child's arm gently, his pale arm, translucent as if light shone from it. She yearned to spend the rest of her life sitting there, gazing reverently at her son as he sat in her lap. But the child did not want to sit still. He wanted to play, to run, to take off, to discover the beautiful world around him. She kissed him on his soft little mouth one last time, and let him go.

The son stood facing her, and an astonishing thing happened. Before her eyes, it happened. Her son was growing, older and taller, and changing into a man. A tall, brown-skinned man from whom light shone as it had from the body of her son. Who was this man? Who was he, this man who looked at her with a smile not to be resisted? She must know him; of course she did. But who was he? She knew them;

she knew those black eyes, she knew them when they were full of strength and spine and readiness. She knew them, too, when that bold hardness melted and they became so soft and gentle, so full of sympathy. Whose were they? If only she could recognize them! Who was this man who gazed at her with an irresistible smile?

Layla strained her mind to figure out his identity, as if her life depended on the knowledge. A rumbling reached her ears, the sound of a storm, and sent a shiver into her hands. Darkness had come over the garden; her son had disappeared, swallowed up by the murkiness. Now a ray of light gleaming on the horizon was all that was visible of him. Layla sat there, tortured by a vague sense that she had done something wrong. The feeling grew, crystallized, floated on the surface. If she had been able to figure out who the man was, her son would not have been lost to her. The storm would not have risen; the darkness would not have descended. The wind grew stronger, stronger, a whip lashing the garden, the beautiful white flowers. They swayed and bent, clearing the way for the chastising storm but returning to their fullness, as tall as they had been, more beautiful, more defiant, until even the darkness could not drown them. The branches crowned with white cleaved that darkness as if they were the first signs of dawn, scattering the darkness. The storm died, and all was still.

Then the door swung open and a crowd of men and women came into the garden, led by a man in a black suit. In slow, measured steps they approached, their heads high, bodies taut with readiness as if they had come on a mission. Layla tried to slip away, to flee; she hid behind the jutting branches of the jasmine tree so that she could see them without being seen. From a distance she saw the man in the black suit motioning silently to the group. She saw the crowd break apart, moving with the same measured, firm steps, to form a circle that encased the white flowers. Amidst the flowers stood the man, and he gestured to them to begin. Suddenly there flashed in the gloom shiny new sickles that quivered in those figures' hands. Where had they gotten them? There had been nothing in their hands a moment ago.

The men and women began to tear out the flowers one by one, rhythmically, purposively. Blow by blow, row after row, tall stalks fell to the ground, lifeless. Men and women moved forward, row by row, hard faces and sad eyes, as if performing a duty that weighed heavily upon them yet must be done. Every time one of them slowed down, the man in the black suit pointed and smiled, grimacing, an animal stalking prey as he watched each row of stalks fall, as if he could not rest until all of the flowers had fallen beneath his feet, to become cold, pale corpses.

In the distance a bird keened. A woman straightened up, the scythe gleaming in her right hand. With her other hand she wiped away a tear that had escaped from her eye before she bent to tear out another flower. Layla swallowed her scream. That woman—she knew her. She knew her. It was Safaa's mother. It was Dawlat Hanim, Safaa's mother.

Now Layla saw all the faces clearly. The men's were close-shaven and the women's gleamed with makeup. Among those many faces looking so alike, she could now make out some that had features she recognized. There was her father; there was her aunt, Umm Gamila. This man in the black suit, his back to her—it must be him. It must. Ramzi turned his face toward Layla, as if to confirm his identity. Layla compressed her lips so she would not scream; she held tighter to the jasmine tree that hid her. When the sea of white flowers lay like a carpet over the ground, the men and women tossed their sickles aside. The men arranged bricks in the shape of a big circle while the women bent over the flowers, gathering them into bundles. Every woman hugged a bundle to her breast as she would embrace her newborn and walked to the circle the men had constructed. Gently, they all let go of their bundles, putting them on the ground, and stepped back. The black-suited man lit a fire amidst the bundles. The men and women stood in a vast circle watching the flowers burn. In the brightness of the flames their faces appeared convulsed with pain; sweat stood out on their brows. It was as if a part of them burned. But not a single one moved. They muttered prayers, supplications; they seemed fixed to the ground, leaning on each other for support. The branches began to dry and splinter, they began to wail.

From behind, a woman with flowing hair broke the ranks and pushed forward, trying to throw herself into the fire. An angry murmuring rose from the crowd. Some men returned the woman to the circle and stillness prevailed, as if it was necessary to their peace of mind that no one move, that they stand like that, held to the earth, shoulder to shoulder, one supporting the next.

The flowers turned to ashes; the fire flared, trilling, and began to die. It could only be seen in scattered spots, a weak glow. But the smoke crouched in thick, horrid masses across the faces of sky and earth, pressing down on the earth's breast to crush it. And Layla awoke, frightened and unable to breathe.

Chapter
Twenty-Two

Time passed. And time blunts the sharp edges of our experiences, and attenuates the threads that bind us to them, day by day, so that the most wounding of events becomes ordinary, indistinguishable almost, part of what defines daily life, to be embraced rather than pushed away.

Layla did not do as she wanted; she did not kill herself. Nor did she flee as she had been so determined to do, nor did she blow up in Ramzi's face as she had feared she might. She no longer even cried in bed every night. She did not run through mental scenarios of fights with her mother, her father, and Ramzi. Her emotions seemed numb, as if she were under the influence of a permanent anesthesia; she no longer reacted to anything. Even Ramzi could no longer spark her loathing—as violent and blazing as it had been—for, with the passing of days the sharpness of her animosity eroded. She began to endure him as she endured the commands of her father and the rebukes of her mother. All that remained was a bitter taste that never left her throat, a bitterness to which she awoke every morning and with which she went to sleep every night, and a vacuum in her chest, a sense of want that she felt at times of particular loneliness. It was the resigned emptiness of discovering a sudden and permanent loss, something cherished that will never be replaced or compensated. These were moments of acute awareness, when she found herself muttering unconsciously, "Strengthen me, Lord, strengthen me."

Where was this plea coming from? From what depths did it suddenly spill out like this? It was always the same entreaty. But why did she beg God's help? So that God would strengthen her to bear her fate? Or to change it? Layla did not stop to ask herself these questions or to contemplate the answers, for it was of the utmost importance right now that she avoid any tendency to stop and think. Without being aware of it, she guarded herself against pain. It was like shrinking from touching a bad wound, for the pus might erupt, bringing a worse pain to which her normal human power of endurance was not equal. Without being aware of it, she organized her life in such a way that she was not able to stop and think. She would go to the college and return with her arms full of books from the library, mostly short story collections, not because she preferred short stories but because they required less concentration than, for instance, novels. Hardly would she finish her memorization homework for classes before she was off, reading and reading. Like any addict, she would go on reading, reading, without necessarily drawing pleasure from it, without reacting one way or another, emotionally or aesthetically. But it did not matter: she read. Page after page, story after story, forgetting each one as she embarked on the next. No matter how hard she exercised her brain she could not recall the plot without going back and skimming the story. Like a robot she read, her eyes exhausted, her head spinning, something indefinable constricting her chest as she read—fast, greedily, breathing unevenly, as if someone stood over her, whip in hand. The book would fall from her hand; she would turn out the light, sleep, wake, like a patient under anesthesia, to face life again.

And day after day, the apartment filled with furniture—the furnishings of her future home. Day after day she made the rounds of shops, endless rounds, behind Gamila and her mother, interfering only to halt their spendthrift progress. She felt guilty, as if she were stealing every penny that her father paid to furnish the new home.

Standing dazzled before some piece of merchandise or other, Gamila would say, "What do you think of it, Layla?"

Layla would shrug. "Whatever."

Gamila's voice would grow sharp with annoyance. "Don't you have any opinions about anything at all?"

In the past, she had had her own views on things. She had had a clear idea of the home she would want for herself; she could even envision exactly the way it would look. There would be only a few rooms, but they would be spacious. The sitting room would be carpeted, not strewn with fancy rugs, just carpeted in gray. The chairs and sofas would be comfortable, upholstered ones, with pillows scattered across the sofas in bright and varying shades. The furniture would sit discreetly in the corners, leaving restful spaces where one could draw a good breath. But now it was all the same to her. Everything—whether or not after graduation she worked in journalism, as she had always wanted, or teaching, as Ramzi wanted. Becoming a journalist no longer seemed to have any great importance. She had always wanted writing to be her profession; she wanted to give rein to her ideas, and to express the thoughts of those around her. She really had begun to write, and she had been told that she could write well. Even when she spoke, people noticed her meticulous powers of expression. One of her classmates had always been very enthusiastic whenever he heard her speak. "You must write," he would say. "You are a born writer." And she did write, and dreamed of the day when she would become a real writer.

But that had all been a long time ago. Now, nothing interested her. Anyway, she was incapable of writing now; she could not even speak clearly. The words would stop on her lips; she would stutter, stumble, completely unable to finish a sentence. Sometimes she would respond to questions put to her with a quirkiness of which she was not aware until she saw the look of astonishment in the eyes of her listeners. Moreover, the teaching profession was an easy one; it would not require deep thought or any special ability, she was sure. A teacher prepared the lesson, delivered it, and then her task was done; it was all the same to her.

It was all the same to her—whether her wedding took place after she began working as a teacher in September of 1956, as Ramzi preferred, or in July, immediately after graduation, as her father wanted. Her father was urging a speedy wedding. Ever since that day he had been trying to rush it; ever since that day his life had been an anxious one.

A few days after Mahmud's wedding, her father intimated to Ramzi that he was ready and anxious for the contract-signing ceremony. But Ramzi did not take the hint. Her father tried again, more openly this time. Ramzi replied that he preferred the contract signing and wedding itself to take place simultaneously. Moreover, to even think about setting the date before Layla had graduated was premature. Reluctantly, the father said no more; from time to time, he gave his daughter searching looks, as if trying to gauge the extent of her strength. If his gaze always moved away satisfied, not for a moment could he forget the day on which she had burst into his room like someone gone mad, screaming. He kept his worry well hidden, yet it came to the surface whenever Mahmud arrived from Port Said to pay them one of his brief, terse visits. Something was gone between these two men; a link had been severed. Gone was that rare and lovely flash of understanding, whereby words on the son's lips could bring tears to the father's eyes, whereby the son would understand the thoughts of the father immediately and wordlessly. Now they were strangers to each other: simply two men, civil but distant. The father would inquire about his son's health and would ask how his work was going; Mahmud would answer politely. Then the father could think of nothing more to say to his son, nor could the son find words to exchange with his father.

The flow of conversation would stop as it might between strangers, although each would try to set a trap for the other. What never left the father's mind was the one subject that conversation never touched, for if it did not come up at all, it must not be real or heartfelt. He had forbidden all of them to mention Mahmud's marriage to Sanaa, just as if it had never taken place. In the father's mind and in the son's, whenever they were together, was the same thought, the same topic, the one that conversation could not address, and that could not be real if silence surrounded it.

These sensitivities hurt Mahmud. He loved his father, perhaps more than he loved anyone else. On the day of his wedding, when his father had called him to his room at the time of the contract writing and had stuffed into his pocket two hundred pounds, he had cried like a little child and had tried to embrace his father. But the older man had pushed him away coldly. It was like being stabbed, at a time when his heart and soul felt so open to his father, at a moment when he was far more in need of his father's love than of his father's money. It hurt him deeply, his father's refusal to give him love even though that would not cost anything, when the money had been so difficult to scrape up. Only God knew how much that had cost him!

And then, on the day he was to travel to Port Said with his wife, at the moment when he was to start a new life, he stood before his father's room, knocking on the door to say goodbye. But his father had left the door closed. He had left it in place that it might divide and separate the two of them, and to this day it remained shut.

Each time his father had asked, "Son, do you need money?" Mahmud had always answered, "Thank you, Papa, no." But what he really wanted to say, each time, was: "I don't want anything—except for you to love me the way you used to love me." But words like these were not to be uttered. And love was not something that could be summoned at will. Either it was there or it was not. His mother's love for him, for instance, had not changed at all. She was exactly as she had ever been, her beaming face, her vast love that she was so shamefaced about demonstrating, her shy touches, the little eyes that a mixture of worry and tenderness always governed. And his sister. His sister Layla loved him. Indeed, it seemed that her love had doubled in recent days. But she had changed. It was as if the water of life had dried up in her.

Had there been some development in her relationship with Ramzi? Sanaa said that she loved him, and had much esteem for him, and that Our Lord was above and Ramzi just below as far as Layla was concerned. But then why did she avoid any mention of him? And why had she changed? Had she discovered that Ramzi did not love her? That he was incapable of love? Ever since that conversation with Ramzi, he had been uneasy. He wanted to intervene but Sanaa told him not to get involved. She said that any demolition of Ramzi was equally destructive to Layla, because she had such a deep-seated belief in him. But what had happened? Had her conviction been shaken? Had the god been shattered before her eyes? Had she come to recognize in him the individual who hid his scorn for himself under an appearance of strength, and who justified his weakness by means of profound theories? The person who grew at the expense of others—like a creeping vine—and who felt confident only when he had crushed any will that might oppose his own, the opportunist who consecrated his own intelligence and the humanity of those around him to achieve his own personal, self-interested aims—had the veil been stripped off? Had she seen him for the person he truly was?

But then why was she so utterly compliant? Why had she submitted, without saying a word? He had tried hard to make her talk about herself, her coming marriage, and future life. But she fled from him every time; she made him talk about himself and Sanaa. When he did so, her behavior bemused him. She would take his hand between hers; squeezing it, she would smile and cry at the same time. She would look at him in mute adoration as if he were a legendary hero. One time, fear in her eyes, her smile had faded suddenly. She had leaned close to him and whispered. "Take care of Sanaa, Mahmud. Watch out for her."

"What are you afraid of?" he asked her in bewilderment. "Layla, just tell me what you are afraid of."

She straightened up and said bitterly, her eyes gazing into the distance, "It's not enough that you are building something beautiful, Mahmud. What is important is that you preserve its beauty." She leaned toward him again, as she said brokenly, "Always, Mahmud . . . always."

She seemed almost to choke on her affection for him, as if her whole life depended on his happiness—his and Sanaa's—and as if her own happiness did not concern her at all. She acted as if it were no one's concern. And she ascribed the change in her health to stomach pains. "I'm not digesting, well, Mahmud, that's all."

"What do you mean, you aren't digesting well?"

"Whenever I eat, right away I get a burning in my chest and a headache."

"Are there any particular foods that bother you? Eggs, for instance, or milk?"

"Everything, even dry bread."

He examined her more than once but could find no specific physical cause for the pains she felt. Her gall bladder was fine; her liver was not inflated; there were no colon cramps that would suggest chronic intestinal or bowel problems; there was no . . . But she would moan in pain whenever he probed her stomach wall even lightly.

He yanked the stethoscope from his ears and stared at her. "It's nerves, Layla. Your abdominal nerves are suffering." His gaze revealed dozens of questions. Layla's lips trembled and she turned her face away. She sat on the bed and said, laughing as she straightened her clothes, "Nerves? So now doctors don't have any tricks up their sleeves except to say it is nerves? Or is this what you say, Mahmud, when you don't know how to diagnose an illness?"

He did not laugh. He was determined not to let her slip from his grasp this time.

"Layla, what's wrong? What is it? Tell me—I'm your brother."

Layla closed her eyes. Her face convulsed as if someone had just slapped her. Their mother entered the room. Mahmud tossed his stethoscope angrily into his bag. His mother always came in at precisely the wrong moment, as if she were delegated to do so. Maybe his father was afraid for him to be alone with Layla.

"So what is there, son?" she said. "What did you find?"

Still angry, Mahmud said, "Nerves, *ya sitti*. Her nerves are a complete wreck."

"Nerves?" His mother's tone of voice made it clear that she did not believe him. "What do you mean, nerves, son?" And his father waved off his diagnosis with the word "nonsense!"

But the father's anxiety was growing. He must broach the subject of setting a date with Ramzi. Layla was approaching her final exams, and there no longer seemed any justification to put it off.

He sat listening to Ramzi, waiting for a gap that would allow him to launch into the subject. But it was not easy to find one. Ramzi had an amazing ability to focus the conversation on himself; on the plots that had been mounted against him and how he had foiled them; on the plans he had sketched out and how they had succeeded; on the books he had written and on the ones he intended to write; on the victories he had chalked up, and the ones yet to come. He was equally skilled at enveloping his words in an aura of importance that reached almost the level of sanctification, as if the fate of the entire world depended on the point he was about to make or on the next step he would take to crush his adversaries. It was impossible for his future father-in-law to interrupt; that would certainly be outside the bounds of polite exchange. So Ramzi went on and on while the father fidgeted. When Ramzi paused to collect his thoughts, the father could no longer contain himself. The words rushed out.

But, no, no—there was no reason to rush things. Everything required due preparation; everything had to be given sufficient consideration. Choosing a place to live, for instance, was a very important operation and must be mounted on a firm foundation. That could not happen until Layla had started her new job. Their residence must be as close as possible to her place of work so that she would be able to take care of all domestic matters. Good organization was the basis of married life. He could not make any compromises on the question of organization, because he intended his home to work like a well-oiled machine—everything in its place, everything in its time. How could Layla possibly undertake all of these duties if her workplace was far from the home? No. Getting married in July would be premature indeed. It wasn't like boiling an egg. It must be studied from all angles.

What would he suggest? He proposed that all the necessary preparations be made, and then they could leave the question of setting the date until after Layla had been appointed to her post.

This time, though, the father did not comply. He would set that date, even if it was to be months away. They must set the date. He could no longer stand to leave it up in the air. So they agreed on the first of October 1956 as the date for the wedding of Layla and Ramzi. The father was not content with this postponement, which seemed so unjustified. It meant waiting three months, more than three months. And who knew what might happen in three months? Layla was a good girl, but she was under bad influence, that of Mahmud and the other woman. Had her father known that Layla had begun to meet Sanaa daily and to spend as much time with her as possible, his worry would have been even greater.

Chapter Twenty-Three

Sanaa had settled in Cairo so that she could take her final exams. After each one she and Layla headed for their old corner behind the library. On the grass, in the shade of the big tree, they sat. Suddenly, everything was as it had been so long ago: everything was good. Layla was the fun-loving girl, laughing from deep in her heart, until tears would spring from her eyes.

Abruptly Sanaa would ask, "And how's Ramzi?"

Still laughing, Layla would say, "He's crushed half the world and has the other half still ahead of him."

Sanaa gazed into the distance and began yanking out handfuls of grass. Without looking at Layla, she said, "So why don't you leave him, Layla?"

Layla sighed. Her voice was calm. "Everyone has their own lot in life, Sanaa."

Sanaa straightened up and faced her. "There is no such thing as a 'lot in life,' Layla. We make our own fates."

"Well, I made my own fate, with my own hands."

"Okay. But that's no reason to destroy yourself."

Layla bent toward her and spoke in a whisper, as if to reveal a secret. "Believe me, Sanaa, I don't deserve any better."

"You're wrong. You are a girl who—" But Layla put her hand firmly over Sanaa's mouth and said in a decisive voice, "Don't trouble yourself, Sanaa. I know myself very well."

Sanaa pushed Layla's hand away from her mouth gently and took it between her own hands. "And Mahmud? Mahmud can't help you out, Layla?"

Layla snatched her hand away. With a bitter laugh, she said, "Mahmud? Can he raise the dead after they've rotted away?" But Sanaa grabbed her knees and almost shouted. "Why? Why, Layla? Why are you so full of hate for yourself?"

"Because it is all the truth."

Sanaa and Layla walked toward the university's main gate, their faces somber. As they passed by the tables in the courtyard Sanaa stopped suddenly and turned to face Layla. "Guess what, Layla? Do you know who visited us in Port Said?" Her voice had softened musically and her eyes shone.

A tremor ran all the way through Layla, as if an exposed electric wire had touched her. "Who?" Her voice was a whisper. She did not really need to ask, though, since she already knew. The blood rushing to her heart knew; like that sense of electric shock, it collected in her head.

"Husayn," said Sanaa triumphantly. In silent accord the friends headed toward one of the tables. Sanaa ordered two Cokes. She changed the subject immediately, as if she meant to keep Layla in agony. Layla's hand trembled on her glass, and questions crowded into her mind. But she did not ask them. She waited, her heart pounding, for Sanaa to come back to the subject of Husayn.

Sanaa did return to the subject, eventually, and she answered all of the questions Layla had wanted to ask but had held back. All except one, the most important one.

Yes, Husayn had returned from Germany, two months ago. As usual, he looked splendid. He had changed a bit; he seemed more attractive, more manly; he had acquired a quality that was hard to pinpoint, but it was visible in his walk, his voice, his eyes. A new contentment, as if he had undergone a trial and had discovered that he was stronger than he had believed. He was so pleasant, Sanaa exclaimed. He had spent two days with them in Port Said, which had been among Mahmud's happiest days, she thought. Mahmud was astonishingly attached to him, so much so that Sanaa could not help but feel jealous. And Husayn had an amazing amount of influence on Mahmud, but Sanaa did not object to this at all; in fact, she welcomed it, for Husayn made Mahmud feel that all was well with the world, that people were good, and that everything was within reach. He convinced Mahmud that dreams really could become realities.

He had joined the army and was working in the munitions factories. He still had dreams for the future, of course, he always did. He had spent three hours sketching blueprints and explaining them to Mahmud, who had been dazzled, while she had been on the point of screaming, she had gotten so tired of hearing the details.

"And you know what he was sketching out? The High Dam, *ya sitti*." Sanaa laughed. "And the way he was talking about it? You'd think he was talking about his beloved."

Layla smiled fleetingly. Sanaa looked at her and said mischievously, "And can you believe it, Layla?"

Layla stopped breathing.

"Can you believe that Husayn is still in love with you?"

Layla felt her eyes water and she blushed. She bent over the table and tried to say, "That's ridiculous." But instead, what came out was "How did you find that out?" Sanaa burst out laughing. Layla's face was a study in bewilderment, for she felt completely undone by this. It had been a long time since anything had been able to shake her. And here she was, trembling away, as if she were just a young teenager.

Everything, everything inside her was trembling. And Sanaa was laughing at her. Layla spoke with an anger directed more at herself than at Sanaa. "What are you laughing at?"

Sanaa went on laughing. Then she pulled herself together and extended both hands in a theatrical flourish. Imitating Layla, she said in a heightened stage voice, "Can he raise the dead after they've rotted away?"

Layla could not keep from laughing. "You're a disaster!"

"God's truth, the only disaster around here is you. Acting as if you are on your deathbed without any justification at all. You? Dying? You have enough life in you for ten people." She started laughing again. Then both were silent, Sanaa suddenly despondent, as if she had grave matters to contemplate. She leaned forward over the table toward Layla, her face calm. "Go on, Layla, marry Ramzi, since that is what you want to do. But face the truth first, the truth that you keep on trying to escape." She stopped talking as Layla's hand crept across the table, trembling like a tiny, wounded animal. In her friend's eyes Sanaa saw a look of supplication, begging her not to speak, as if the facts, the truth, would not be real as long as she did not speak, as long as the truth was not shaped into living, breathing words. Sanaa hesitated, but then she flung out her words roughly, as if slapping someone out of a faint. "The truth is, Layla, that you love Husayn. You have always loved him and you always will."

Layla felt dizzy, as if she were suddenly bleeding inside. She put up her hands to cover her face. Without looking at Sanaa, without saying a word, she took her bag from the table and got up. As she walked away Sanaa called after her, but she would not stop. Her steps were long and fast, as if someone were chasing her. She threw herself onto the first bus that stopped in front of the university gate, not even looking to check where it might be going. She sat down, head bowed, shrinking into herself, clutching her book bag. Husayn's words echoed in her ears. One morning you will wake up and discover that you love me. The words stopped in midair, they swam together, they piled atop each other. But they were always the same words. One morning . . . you will wake up . . . one morning . . . But that morning had come so late. So late that it would have been better never to wake up, better if that morning had never come. Everything was so clear now. Clear, sharp, rough; and now it was not all the same to her. Her love for Husayn was sharp and rough, and so was her loathing for Ramzi. And her disgust with her own inabilities and weaknesses was even sharper and rougher. And there were the facts, the truths, bared. And Layla faced them, her eyes open, but feeling absolutely powerless over her own affairs.

Chapter
Twenty-Four

At her desk, Layla rested her head in her palms. Her eyes were bright, gazing into the distance; her ribs could barely contain that astonishing fire that, so long absent, she had thought would never return. She had been pacing the room, pacing, pacing, yet the flames still burned, the embers glowed, still called her to cry, laugh, scream, jump; to kiss someone, anyone, to talk with someone, with anyone and everyone she could find.

She heard a murmur that grew until it was like the crashing of waves at the shore. She ran to the window and flung it wide open. She longed to be part of one of these human waves that passed below, rejoicing and triumphant, along the boulevard. She began pacing the room again, not knowing what to do with the tumultuous fire burning in her chest. She turned back to her desk and took out a piece of paper and a pen. Without stopping to reflect on what she would say, she started writing to her brother.

Dear Mahmud,
For a long time, a very long time, I have not felt what I felt tonight as

I listened to Gamal Abd al-Nasser's speech. I felt strong, I felt as if I could do anything, anything at all. Do you understand me? And the feelings of pride that had left me—had forgotten me—have come back, and a sense of belonging, too. Mahmud, I'm not alone any more. In that moment I felt I was right there, with the thousands rejoicing in Alexandria, and with you, and Sanaa, and with . . .

Even my father seems no longer a stranger. He almost hugged me as we listened to the speech. Can you imagine that? All of us—even my father—all of us have nationalized the Canal. And the pride that abandoned me—I have it back again, and the feeling of wonder, because there is still strength deep inside me, alive, even if it has been imprisoned for so long.

Layla stopped for a moment, tears blocking her vision.

Is this the miracle you promised me? The miracle that would shake all of us, would make us shake off our shrouds and rise, free and strong? Tell me that it is that miracle, please, Mahmud, please tell me that . . .

No, this was not the miracle. In Mahmud's view, "the miracle will happen when we can protect the Canal, when we can preserve all the gains we have made as a nation. When we rid ourselves of our passivity, and stand firm together until death—firm against imperialism."

That was out of the question, maintained Ramzi. Nationalizing the Canal had rallied all the forces of imperialism against Egypt, at a time when Egypt was too weak to confront them. The balance of power is not in our favor. We could have waited. We could have waited until things were set up more propitiously, we should not have been in such a hurry. Only a very fine line separates courage from stupidity.

"But we're not standing alone," said Layla. "All the free peoples in the world are standing with us, and the balance of power—" Ramzi cut her off roughly. It had been a long time since she had opened her mouth to voice an opinion that challenged his. And here she was now, talking confidently, brashly, as if she understood world issues better than he did. Layla bit on her lower lip and was silent. Ramzi exchanged a few words with her father. She seized the opportunity afforded by the pause in conversation, leaning toward Ramzi as she spoke.

"If people live their whole life scared, measuring every step, thinking about the consequences, civilization would never have been built, nothing would have ever been invented, and people would not have demanded their freedom and taken it. Nothing good would have been achieved, ever."

Ramzi's face tightened, and then returned to its usual grim set. He spoke sarcastically after settling back. "Such eloquence—why didn't you pass with high honors?"

That caught Layla unprepared; her face flushed with anger. She had not anticipated that Ramzi would resort to such low tricks to avoid the discussion. But he had, so that he would win. There was nothing he would not do to win! Even in a simple conversation.

He was upset, riled not because she had passed 'acceptably' but because Sanaa had passed with a final mark of 'very good'—Sanaa, whose failure he had predicted, swearing in the crudest way that she would not succeed. Now, Ramzi shot Layla an angry look. He had given her everything a man could give a woman—his name, his position, his property. He had given her the respect of others; she had been a nobody, but everyone now respected her on the grounds that she was his future wife. He had given her an organized, secure life, free of anxiety; and he had given her his books, his advice, his instructions and guidance. Everything, everything a man could give to a woman, and a professor to his student! And despite it all she had let a smutty girl like Sanaa surpass her.

"I don't understand what you didn't have," he said maliciously. "You had all the help in the world. Everything to make it easier. Everything."

Layla bent toward him, her face rosy, her eyes dancing, as if she were about to jump off a high diving board and the adventurousness of it bewitched and frightened her at the same time.

"Would you like to know what it is I didn't have?"

But her father intervened hurriedly in the conversation and spoiled her sudden exuberance. He wanted to know what influence one's final evaluation had on appointment to a teaching position. Would it mean trouble in finding a place for Layla in one of Cairo's secondary schools?

Yes, trouble was a real possibility. In fact, getting Layla a post in Cairo would have been close to impossible were it not that Ramzi—and praise be to God—had a lot of influence in the Ministry of Education. He knew all the deputies personally, and they all yearned for an opportunity to be at his service. He could even get an appointment to see the minister at any time. He really did not like to use his influence. He had always made his own way, cut his own path; he had always prevailed over others by means of his natural superiority. But in this case there was no help for it.

———

Ramzi took Layla to meet the General Inspector for Social Studies, who had jurisdiction over the government's girls' schools. Layla found herself in a vast office. Behind the huge desk in the center of the room sat a woman, probably in her fifties, her silver hair pulled back to reveal a lofty, pale forehead tinged by the wrinkles of age. Layla sat on the edge of the settee that faced the desk at a distance. Ramzi leaned back and threw one leg over the other as he explained the purpose of their visit.

The inspector listened without looking at Ramzi, a light smile on her handsome face, as if her mind were on an entirely different subject that had nothing to do with the man sitting before her—one leg flung over the other as if he were in his own home—nothing to do with the subject that so passionately engaged him. Without a word she gazed at Layla and held out a folded piece of paper. A bit embarrassed, Layla jumped up and walked over to the inspector. As she stopped across from the woman at the desk, the inspector smiled at her as if she had just recognized her and spoke gently. She had a very sympathetic look. "Write out the request, Layla." She waved at a table at the other end of the room, still smiling.

With a firm hand Layla took the request form, as if that confident, serene smile had lent her a measure of its own assured calmness. With firm steps she went over to the table and sat to write the requested information, far from Ramzi.

Name, address, diploma, final mark, requested position, location.

Ramzi did not stop talking. Cairo, it was absolutely necessary that Layla be posted in Cairo. No, he could not be satisfied with a mere attempt. He must have a clear promise from the inspector. If that were not forthcoming he would be obliged to fall back on his influence. The ministry's deputies were all anxious to be of help. The minister personally would not fail to grant such a request, promptly, and . . . Layla stopped at the line where she was to write a location: her first choice, her second choice. Ramzi was still talking. Cairo, it had to be Cairo. Cairo was where his work was located, and thus it must be where his future wife was appointed. The inspector must promise him that Layla would be appointed in Cairo. There was no alternative to Cairo.

The inspector was smiling her light smile, gazing at nothing, as if she were thinking about a completely different subject that had no link to this man who threatened and cajoled. A pleasant subject.

Layla bent over the request and where she was to stipulate her first choice she wrote 'Port Said.' Under second choice she wrote 'Port Said.' She folded the paper and jumped up, and at the same moment Ramzi got to his feet. Layla strode over to the inspector's desk. Ramzi met her halfway, blocking her path to the desk. A tremor of fear swept through Layla, and she almost capitulated to Ramzi's outstretched hand. But she looked at the serene smile that seemed to wrap her in its warmth. She gave the request to the inspector and let out her breath.

Ramzi addressed the inspector, barely suppressing his irritation. "Allow me to see the request, to check whether it is completely filled out or not." Layla's heart dropped and she closed her eyes. When she opened them the inspector was still smiling and gazing again into the distance. She drummed her fingers on the request that sat on the desk. She turned to Layla and asked quietly, "Is the request completely filled out, Layla?"

Layla was incapable of speech; she simply nodded. The inspector pulled open a drawer and tossed the request in, closed the drawer softly, and stood up.

"Fine. That is all we need, Layla. God willing, we will try to comply with your wishes. So long. Goodbye, Doctor."

When Layla reached the door she turned, smiling, her eyes blurry with tears as she met the inspector's eyes for the last time.

———

Ramzi remained indignant at the treatment they had met from the inspector, for he could not ignore the manner in which she had deliberately overlooked him. His dissatisfaction erupted into open hostility when Layla received her letter of appointment from the Ministry of Education.

He put the letter in his pocket and tried to calm the angry father's fears. He promised to set everything right. "Before twenty-four hours pass, Layla will have been appointed to a post in Cairo. Her Excellency the Inspector will get orders from above. You know, there are people like that—like dogs, they have to be commanded from above."

"Port Said?" her father shrieked as soon as Ramzi had left to go to the ministry. "Out of the question! Port Said in particular—out of the question." His eyes narrowed as he stared at Layla. "You—it was you. You asked for Port Said."

Layla turned her palms up innocently. "I asked for Cairo. Sir, you can even ask Ramzi when he comes back."

Ramzi did not return at midday as he had promised. He came after the late-afternoon prayer time to say that he had straightened every-thing out. He had gotten a clear promise from the deputy minister that Layla would be transferred to Cairo two weeks after taking up her job in Port Said. It was just a matter of formalities, and sometimes it was not such a bad idea to bow to formalities. But her father made his unhappiness clear at this resolution. He would prefer, he said, that his daughter refuse the appointment to letting her travel on her own to Port Said.

"And then who can be sure that she'll really be transferred after two weeks there?"

Ramzi was infuriated; he tried to make the father understand the extent of his influence in the ministry. He described how upset the deputy minister had become at learning of the inspector's error, and how he had promised to teach her a lesson she would never forget; he repeated that Layla's transferral from Port Said after two weeks at work was one hundred percent guaranteed. Ramzi grew calmer as he explained how Layla's rejection of the appointment would mean she would have to wait for the next graduating class—in other words, she would lose a whole year. This deal that they had made, with which he felt entirely comfortable, did not go against their plans in the slightest. Layla would start her work on the first of September; thus, she would be in Cairo by mid-September, two weeks ahead of the date they had set for the wedding.

Ramzi insisted, too, that the issue of where Layla would live in Port Said was not a problem. Luckily, the secondary school had accommo-dations for teachers who were from outside the city. From every per-spective, then, they could feel reassured. Having run through all of the points he needed to make, Ramzi turned to the older man and asked, "What do you think?"

"I'll give it some thought." He left the situation dangling.

As the first of September drew very near, he was still giving it thought. When he summoned Layla to his room, she knew that he would open the subject. She tried to prepare herself as well as she could.

"Do you want this job?"

Layla wanted to scream from her innermost depths, "Yes! Please, please Papa!" But she kept control of herself and said, shrugging as if it really mattered very little, "As you wish, sir."

He turned his back to her. "And the . . . folks there, you'll mix with them?"

Layla was not sure how she ought to respond to this question. She said, stupidly, "As you wish, sir." He turned to face her, his face drained of color, and said with a murderous calmness, "You know what I wish. You know very well."

She said nothing. Her father began to pace the room. He stopped. "You will be staying in the school. Mahmud can visit you, it doesn't matter. The woman, no. No visits to them in their home. No going outside the school." He stared right into Layla's eyes and said sharply, "Understand?"

"Yes."

The father's grey eyes narrowed and his lips trembled with his next sentence, a clear tone of threat in his voice. "Do you know what will happen if I hear that you've been to their home, or spent time with them?"

Layla shut her eyes and nodded without a word.

"Fine. That's all."

Layla stood up but remained motionless. Irritably, her father said, "That's all. We're done. Go get ready."

Layla left the room, hardly able to believe that her father had given her permission to travel to Port Said.

———

Layla packed her suitcases, although whenever she heard her father's footsteps in the front hall she got so nervous that she would start shaking. She was so afraid that something might happen at the last minute to prevent her from making the journey. Even standing at the train window, Ramzi on the platform, the fear did not leave her. She stole quick glances at her watch. The hands were not moving; something had gone wrong. Her face tense, she gazed round as if searching for something she had lost. Raising her eyes to the station clock, she took a deep breath. Praise be to God. It was noon.

It was noon. But no bell sounded; the train did not move.

"Don't be afraid, Layla," said Ramzi. "It is only two weeks, and you'll be coming right back." The clock chimed, but still the train did not move. Maybe something was not working properly, and it would not move. It would never move.

The train moved. Layla's face glowed. She called out joyfully without looking at anyone or addressing anyone in particular, as if she were singing. "I'm not afraid! Not afraid!"

She sat down, still murmuring, "I'm not afraid. Not afraid." Then she jumped to her feet again as if she had forgotten to do something. She closed the window, and Ramzi and the platform were no longer visible. The train moved forward slowly and then picked up speed.

———

Layla's reassignment was not the easy matter Ramzi had imagined. Instead of two weeks, Layla stayed in Port Said for months. And on October 29, 1956, the Israelis attacked Sinai. On October 31, Great Britain and France joined in the aggression against Egypt, and military operations against Egyptian positions began.

Chapter
Twenty-Five

It gushes forth, a storming cataract. The bogs, though, have done their best to block its course. Intent on sucking its waters dry, they try to consume it within themselves, to transform it with their sluggishness into a stagnant pond. But the cataract's depths are recalcitrant, colossal, raging, and deep. And the bogs are ancient, sedimented over their many years of existence, crouching in quiet defiance over the land of Egypt. Confident that their stagnation speaks rather of calm strength, the dark-green surfaces glint under the sun's rays.

And beneath the glittering surface lies the swirled mud.

The cataract sweeps the bogs along in its path, and swallows up their water in its own. The cataract transforms their stagnant presence into a youthful, impatient ebullience. And in the depths of the cataract, the mud dissolves. The cataract moves forward, stubborn, impassioned, deep, to the end of its chosen course.

And at the end sits a dam, a wall of solid rock. But under the weight of the cataract's tread the dam collapses. The solid rocks shatter.

The telephone rang and rang in Mahmud's apartment all morning; no one answered. Layla was at the school, Sanaa at the nursing center, and Mahmud at a military training post. When Layla returned to the apartment, as soon as the announcement that school was cancelled came, the telephone was still ringing. Her hand shook with the key as she opened the door and the sound of the uninterrupted ringing reached her ears. It must be her father or Ramzi, she knew. She put down her suitcase near the door and walked slowly over to the telephone. She put her hand on the receiver. And she heard herself say, "All right, Papa. As you wish, Papa." She took her hand from the receiver, moved quickly away from the telephone, and practically ran into the room that Sanaa had given her, shutting the door. She sat on the edge of the bed, as the ringing of the telephone pierced the closed door.

———

No. She did not want to hear that voice ordering her to come home, dragging her back to Cairo. She did not want to leave her life in the hands of her father and Ramzi for them to do with her as they wished, as if she were a stone that one would kick away with the tip of his shoe at the slightest whim. She did not want to return to Cairo. She would not return to Cairo. She must confront her father, and Ramzi as well. She must say no.

She stood up, ready to answer the telephone. She walked to the shut door and put her hand on the knob. A cold shudder went through her body. She saw her father coming toward her with short, mechanical steps, face stiff and frame rigid, a weapon trained on her, coming nearer and nearer, slowly, to crush her. She saw Ramzi shaking his head, his face stiff and closed, saying, "It's no use." And the telephone rang and rang. Even the sound of the air raid siren was lighter and easier to bear than that ringing. For it did not go on and on, heavy, insistent, throttling her. The siren went on only for a few moments; then the response always came, decisive and stern, shaking the building, shaking your heart. The Egyptian anti-air missiles rose from every side as if the earth had exploded with lava. You could gaze out the window as far as you could see, moving your gaze across the sky, and with every shot you would hold your breath and wait. Then the blood would erupt in your veins as you heard people cheering and caught sight of an airplane suddenly transformed into a torch, falling to earth or into the sea. You would hold your breath and wait again.

The telephone rang, rang, rang; the sound grew louder minute by minute. Layla clutched the doorknob, her whole body shaking with her powerlessness, her loathing, her refusal. The ringing inflamed her nerves and pounded in her head, carving out holes there that grew bigger minute by minute, leading her to madness. She burst out screaming, pushed the door and left the apartment at a run, panting. When she reached the street and the ringing no longer resounded in her ears, she breathed a sigh of relief, covering her face in her hands.

———

Mahmud was late getting home that night. Sanaa was in the kitchen, about to cook spaghetti for supper. Layla was waiting for her brother in the front room. He sat down to take off his army boots, obviously in pain from standing on his feet for such a long stretch of time.

"What news?" asked Layla.

Mahmud's eyes flashed. He opened his mouth to speak, but said nothing. He flipped his palms upward; that was the only way he could express the feelings he held inside. He took a deep, relaxed breath and finally was able to speak.

"All's well with the world, Layla." He settled back into his chair as he went on. "A twelve-year-old boy! He came into the training center wanting to get training. I told him, 'You're too young.' He gave me a look and said, 'I've grown up in the past couple of days.'" Mahmud struck his hand against the chair. "And I realized that it wasn't just him who had grown up. We all have, in the past few days. All of us, no exceptions."

The water boiled. Sanaa dropped the spaghetti into the pot and turned up the flame. Layla turned involuntarily toward the phone. A sense of shame and embarrassment flooded over her. She had not faced her father or Ramzi, after all. Mahmud started talking again.

"The whole town has become one giant military camp, all abuzz. A train arrives every hour, full of volunteers."

Layla's face lit up. Mahmud bent over, picked up his boots, and got to his feet as he spoke. "Guess who arrived today?"

Layla blushed. "Husayn?"

"No, of course not. He's in Sinai."

"Then who?"

"Guess."

Layla laughed, to hide her confusion. Mahmud said, triumphantly, "Isam."

"You're kidding! That's unbelievable."

"What's so unbelievable?"

"And my aunt? How could his mother let him go?"

Mahmud turned his palms upward again, a boot still dangling from each, and distended his face, showing his amazement with theatrical exaggeration. Layla burst out laughing. He shook his head lightly as if something had happened that defied all explanation and belief. He went toward his room, and at the door he turned to face Layla, speaking in a soft voice.

"Didn't I tell you, Layla? We've grown up."

He was almost whispering as he said, "This is the miracle, Layla. The miracle."

And they heard the air raid siren again.

—

Day after day the time between siren warnings shrank until there were no spaces left. Then the sirens stopped altogether, for the raids were now one constant attack. The anti-aircraft guns exploded so often that they were on the point of melting, and behind them crowds of people gathered to cheer. An old man with snow-white hair stood among the throngs, behind the customs battery.

330

"Keep it up, Muhammad!" And a burning airplane fell into the sea. Another suddenly swooped down, almost touching the heads of those who stood there, and directed its fire at the gunner. Muhammad bent double, howling in pain. A soldier jumped up from behind him, wanting to take his place. But Muhammad straightened up in position and with bloody hands fired his cannon at the airplane before it could vanish. He crept back among the crowd, leaving his place to his buddy, and lay on his back, his eyes fixed on the burning plane. When that plane reached the water, Muhammad smiled weakly and closed his eyes.

———

Five days later the guns were quiet. Now the airplanes had begun to flatten the city. The populace buried their dead, dressed the wounded, and waited. When the parachute troops came down in al-Gamil, al-Raswa, and Port Fuad, they found people waiting for them. The battle had joined, that was very clear; things had taken a new turn. To evacuate the remaining women, children, and elderly folk in Port Said became urgent. Yet all the roads out of town were blocked—all but one.

Chapter
Twenty-Six

Eleven a.m. on November 5, 1956. Heavy clouds clung to the air, thick and dusty. The sun penetrated from behind the clouds, cleaving blue gaps laced with white. The clouds wrapped an ash-gray, dusty sash around Manzala Lake, and on the lake's surface black shadows trembled: boats, little and big, boats fuller than they should be and others not yet filled; and people, crossing the dock toward the boats, burdened with their belongings. Other shadows threw themselves down on shore and buried their faces in the water, quenching a thirst that could not be satisfied; and there were the unmoving shadows of those who waited. On the surface of the water was imprinted the shadow of a tall, slender young woman, crossing the quay slowly, her steps dragging, going toward the lake, her hands wrapped with delicate care around a bundle that she had packed and smoothed down painstakingly. The young woman stopped suddenly, turned, and ran back in the direction from where she had come, away from the water, shouting, "Adil! A-a-dil!"

From the boat, her mother called, "Fayza! Fayza!" But Fayza did not respond. With difficulty she cleared a path for herself amidst the hundreds of children, women, and elderly people lined along the shore. She almost collided with a child whose eyes were opened to their widest, as if he felt a burning pain there. The child looked at her almost knowingly, disapprovingly, as if to say, "What are you in such a hurry about? What is there to make anyone hurry so?" The child's gaze was more that of an elderly man, suddenly decrepit; as if he had instantly grown into adulthood and beyond, nourished on the terror he had witnessed day and night for five full days. Fayza patted his shoulder clumsily and went on pushing her way as rapidly as she could through the crowd, trying to summon enough breath to go on shouting. "A-a-adil!"

A youth in the uniform of the popular resistance turned. He had given his back to the crowd of reluctant passengers but now he came running toward Fayza. He put his hands on her shoulders and stood facing her, looking into her eyes without speaking. She regained her breath and then began running her tongue around her lips, unable to express what she felt. She bit on her lower lip and spoke in a whisper. "You'll come—won't you, Adil? You'll be coming?" Her eyes reflected depths of anguish, as if the collective grieving of those women crossing the quay to the lake, having left on land sons and husbands, and the bodies of sons and husbands, had coalesced in the eyes of this young woman who could not have been more than seventeen years of age.

Adil smiled. "It isn't me who will be coming. It's you—you'll come back, Fayza. We'll get married here in Port Said—in our city." Fayza gazed at him fearfully, and her eyes met his in a long look. Her pretty face brightened with a lovable smile that set dimples in her cheeks, her eyes shining with a sweet hope as if a hand had brushed away the frightening apparition she had lived for five days. Her eyes had room only for the vision of herself and Adil, happy as children on the golden shoreline of Port Said, as if she were running, Adil chasing her, catching up to kiss the back of her neck, the sun teasing her body and dancing like a scattering of diamonds on the azure surface of the water.

The water? The shore? Where were they? It seemed as though she had not seen either one for one hundred years. Had she always lived amidst fires and decaying corpses? Her eyes swam, and she clutched the bundle she carried closer, as if to protect it from an enemy lying in wait.

"When? Adil, when?"

"Right away, Fayza. Right away, love. If the enemy comes in he'll have to come in over our dead bodies, and if he stays one day, he won't stay two."

Fayza hugged the bundle to her chest and said in a choked voice, "Adil, you have to stay alive, you have to, Adil."

Concealing the strain he felt beneath a layer of nimble softness, Adil said, "Don't worry, Fayza. The troublemaker lives long." Fayza did not laugh at his proverb, though. "Promise me, Adil. Promise me," she whispered. In a half-serious tone, Adil said, "Okay, I promise you, sweetheart." Fayza's tears and her smile mingled; amidst her tears, her eyes filled with the image of her love. Adil had promised her; Adil had never lied to her. Adil would rout the enemies, Adil and the thousands of Egyptians whose courage she had seen with her own eyes. Hadn't they destroyed the parachutists in Port Fuad and al-Gamil?

She would come back. Of course she would return to her city, her home, to the sea and the shore. She would return to Adil and they would be together, and alive, both of them. This was her right and his. God could not possibly allow anyone to steal what was rightfully theirs: their right to love and their right to live.

Adil said in a whisper, "I promise you, Fayza, that you will come back to Port Said and that all of those folks down there will come back, too." His eyes swept the shore. The boats that were already filled with passengers were unfurling their sails, and the launches were firing their engines in preparation to leave. In front of the quay a small white launch sat, empty except for a woman in braids, dressed in black, carrying in her arms a sleeping child, fearful eyes glued to him as if she were drawing her capacity to stay alive from his presence there, sleeping on her breast, as if she did not sense her own existence except through his.

Sadness hung over the scene, a gentle melancholy, gentle and soft like the glistening water, its sting lightened by the hope of rescue and of meeting again. Quickly and soundlessly but for the kisses and heartfelt words of farewell, the rest of the boats and launches filled. On the quay a mother roughly pulled away a boy who clung to his father's neck; a son carried his elderly mother to a waiting boat; a wounded man with his leg bound leaned heavily on a woman's shoulder.

On shore were left only a few people, standing in scattered groups, and an old man sprawled on the ground, his hand on his cheek, waiting patiently, submissively, while the submissive tears dribbled from the eyes of a full, comely young woman standing with a thinner young woman whose lips were pressed together tightly, next to two young men in the uniforms of the popular resistance. Silence had come over all four.

Layla could not keep back her tears. She felt a profound sense of defeat, as if someone had hit her very hard, so hard that she could not even scream in protest. Her tears pooling at the corners of her mouth, Layla said, "Do we really have to leave, Mahmud? Isn't there anything we can do here? Can't we help?"

Mahmud leant down, pushing the suitcases closer together, then straightened up and said in a stifled voice, "Are we going to get into this again? I told you—you would just slow us down. You'll get in our way. The woman who truly wants to serve leaves the place to the men."

Layla's eyes widened as they met Isam's gaze. Isam saw the insistent, silent plea in those eyes and averted his gaze. Sanaa pressed her lips tighter in anger. The sound of a woman's voice came, calling, "Fayza! Fay-ay-za!"

"Mama's calling." Adil pulled her closer, took her in his arms, and kissed her on one eye after the other. He brushed quavering lips against her cheeks and let her go. "Goodbye. Goodbye, love."

She clung to him madly. He repeated with an insistence that seemed forced, "Goodbye." She whispered, "I don't want to leave you, Adil. I don't want to leave you here alone."

Her voice shaking, Sanaa said, "And why you? Why should you stay here by yourself?"

Mahmud answered roughly, more roughly than the situation called for. "I'm a man." Then he added in a softer tone, "I think we've already discussed this, Sanaa."

She looked at him accusingly, tears glistening in her eyes. Since their marriage she had shared every moment of his life, every emotion, every experience. Why did he want to banish her now? Why must he set her aside? She opened her mouth and raised one hand to give her words emphasis, but then seemed to think better of speaking; the words froze on her lips and her hand hung in the air.

A woman's voice rose, moaning in terror and fright. "Fayza! My daughter, my girl." From above dove a flock of airplanes, the terrible screech growing as they neared the lake. Layla whispered, as if in prayer, "No, impossible. Impossible, Lord. No." The answer to her entreaty came in Mahmud's anxious stare upward. Adil's hands shook on Fayza's body as he said, no longer able to keep the anxiety out of his voice, "Run—run, Fayza!"

Fayza smiled securely in his embrace. "Don't worry. All day long they've been barking like maddened dogs." Her mother's voice floated to them again, louder than ever, in frenzied despair. Fayza kissed Adil again. "Wait for me, Adil. Wait for me." She turned and began to run toward the lake, Adil's eyes on her. From time to time she whirled halfway round, her face shining with a lovely smile, her left hand waving, her right folded carefully around the bundle she carried. She began to cross the quay. This time she turned completely around, to give Adil a final wave.

She fell on her face; the bundle flew from her arms. The woman in the braids raised frightened eyes from the child she clutched and stared skyward. She screamed, and the crazed, pained echo of it reverberated as she waved both hands wildly. The surface of the lake was suddenly roiled with big round circles interspersed with explosions and yells. Scream after scream, scream upon scream, a mountain of screams leaping from earth to sky. A short scream lasted only seconds, but a whole life weighted it, a terror, a torrential desire to go on living, a painful despair of life. Revolution, love, hatred, submission, all the specters of the past and the glimmer of what might have been in the future were in those screams.

No one could see anything. The earth exploded, and from it whirled a thick storm of dust that veiled one's eyes. The airplane withdrew, lighter now, having dropped its burden onto the people there—shadows in the lake, shadows on the shore. The dust cloud was breaking up, its place filled by a sticky black smoke mingled with the odor of roasting flesh. Smoke rose from a fire that leapt across the lake surface, covering distances occupied by boats full of people as well as empty ones. The screams grew quieter; the air cleared; the scene was visible. Little by little the circles carved by drowning bodies dwindled, until the lake was completely smooth and even again. The water once again washed to shore gently, quietly; on the surface floated bits of burning wood and a rubber doll, its eyes closed, smiling, bobbing, up and down, up and down.

—

Layla had felt nothing, except that the earth had given a violent shake as if a volcano had exploded directly beneath her feet. Something had thrown her to the ground. Buried under a heap of dust, she lost consciousness. When she began to come out of it, and before she was fully alert, the thought formed in her head that she had died and here she was, buried. The dirt filling her nostrils and weighing down her body was her grave. She wanted so much to let her body go, to lose herself, and to submit quietly. But something kept her from letting go. A broken moan, coming from here, from there, rising on all sides, as if the world itself was moaning, the world and the heavens, shaking her, again and again, keeping her from slipping into nothingness.

Now it was not just the moaning that vibrated through her. She could make out voices, frightened voices, calling out names. And one of the names was hers. Among dozens and dozens of others, hers.

And now it was not just one voice calling her name. They were all shaking her, all keeping her from going. She opened her mouth to scream, but the dust fell in and almost choked her. She closed her mouth and realized that she must shake off the dirt that had piled over her, she must do it herself, she must scrabble out her own path back to life. She supported herself on her hands and began to shimmy and crawl, slowly, as if bearing massive weights of iron, the dust still in her mouth and nose, her breathing constricted, her chest burning, her limbs wooden. A weight seemed to drag her earthward. It was not just the weight of the dirt; something else, soft, gluey, was summoning her to collapse, to rest, just one moment, and everything would be over. A single moment and she'd feel nothing. She would sleep.

But now the voices were calling her again, more and more insistently. All the voices, all calling her, all trying to get her to stand up, all preventing her from giving in. Something inside her was responding, too, something vast springing from deep within, something new and powerful that would not leave her be, something stronger than the fire that burned in her chest, than the iciness that shuddered in her limbs, stronger than that overwhelming desire to let go, than the dirt, than death.

She scrambled to her feet. The light blinded her and she closed her eyes. Her hands groped for surfaces, for her body. Gradually she realized that she had come out of a massacre, whole. She opened her eyes to the light, now more bearable and familiar, but closed them again immediately and ran, staggering, as if someone had stabbed her from behind. She paused, hesitating, then turned. Her eyes swept across the scene, and then began to focus on one detail after another, slowly, as if she feared that she might miss something. She saw figures stumbling and swaying in confusion, wading through blood, colliding with scattered body parts—arms, legs, ripped-out bits of intestine, exploded skulls. The living trampled them and ran on, overturning the corpses, gazing into the faces of the wounded. No one was calling out any more. The dead would not answer; the wounded were too weak to respond with anything other than moans. Some of those still alive had stopped searching, for the answers to their calls had come. The man bending over the bodies of his wife and two children had been answered. The elderly gentleman crouching on the shore mounding the dirt, his face grim, his hands smoothing the little mound, never pausing, as if his soul was ransomed to preserving this perfect rounded mound from collapse. Over there, the handsome youth in the uniform of the popular resistance folded carefully a white wedding dress splattered with blood and dirt. He, too, had received his answer. What had the pretty, dimpled girl called him? What had she called this young man whose eyes burned without tears, as if suddenly packed with grit? Adil. That was what she had called him, the beaming young woman with the flowing hair and dimples who had danced with the joy of life as death circled over her head. The idea of death had never entered her mind; her imagination had had room only for love—of Adil and of life. Now nothing was left to Adil but a white wedding dress spattered with blood and dirt. Adil smoothed the gown with care, as if he were patting his beloved's hair, as if he were whispering promises into her ear. He straightened up abruptly.

And the mother over there, the one in braids, the figure wrapped in black, water dripping from her clothes. Where was her son? He had been lying on her chest; she had shielded him with her arms; what could have happened? Why wasn't she calling out to her son? A man held her firmly by the arm to keep her from running—why? The answer lay in the depths. There was no fear in her eyes, no expectation; she no longer feared or hoped for anything. She had died, standing there, next to this man, the man who restrained her from rushing into the lake.

A shout of joy came from Mahmud as he felt Layla's body. Sanaa murmured something, her tears pouring out. Isam was saying, "Praise be to God, praise be to God, praise be to—" Layla's face went stiff as she realized that she had made no effort to see if they were all there, safe and sound, as if she had forgotten their existence in the deluge of pain around her, the anguish of all.

She joined the rest of those who were still alive in helping the emergency workers to move the wounded. Silently, from stretchers into ambulances they were moved. No one was wailing any longer, even the old woman with the white hair. Her tears ran but she made no sound, as if what had happened had drained her of voice. No one searched among the corpses and the body parts now, or looked into the faces of the wounded, except a little brown child of about seven who darted from place to place, a desperate hope holding her tears captive.

Layla passed Mahmud as he dressed the wounds of a little boy whose chest gushed blood. Watching him, she tried to feel some kind of solace in the fact that her brother had escaped death. "Mahmud is alive, alive, alive," she whispered. She wiped the beads of sweat from her forehead and bent to put her arms around a young woman who had lost her legs. She raised the woman to the stretcher with the help of an ambulance driver and leaned down to cover her with a white sheet. Their eyes met for a moment.

Layla straightened, her body and soul a mass of pain for which there was no consolation, not even in Mahmud's safety; nor would his death have made it hurt more. It was the pain of the young woman who had lost her legs, the mother who burned to know the waters of the lake, the old man building his sandcastle on the beach. Carrying one end of the stretcher she walked toward the ambulance. She passed Adil, his head thrown back as he strained his arms to dig a grave for his beloved. She stopped, overcome. The light that had been caged in the hole was reflected in his eyes, and in those eyes Layla saw a look that sent a shiver into her body, a look she would never forget even if she lived to be one hundred years old.

She moved forward. The ambulance driver shut the door behind the wounded woman. The van moved off, leaving a space. Layla turned to plunge again into the blood, to stumble over the corpses and pick up the wounded. Suddenly she realized that she had passed the stage of pain. She no longer hurt. She no longer lived in the immediate present, except with her body that bent, straightened, walked, bent again. Yet that moment she was physically living seemed to go on forever, a lifetime or more. She wanted it to end, she wanted to be free of this moment, she wanted to act.

The ambulances went on their way, one load after another. Only one remained. Adil leaned down and laid his beloved in the grave. He remained bowed for a moment, then straightened and began slowly to mound the dirt upon her. The old man hastened to finish his careful sculpting of the sand pile he had made. The woman in the braids was stumbling but a woman companion steadied her, whispering into her ear. And on the surface of the lake a doll bobbed, up and down, eyes closed, smiling.

The dark-skinned little girl panted, running among the corpses and torn limbs, looking at the faces of the wounded already on stretchers. Her anxious gaze shifted between the wounded and the sole remaining ambulance, as if she knew that her hopes depended on it staying in this place. Another wounded figure was slipped into the ambulance, and the little girl stood still, her eyes on the van.

———

Layla joined Sanaa and Isam. "I'm going to the hospital," said Mahmud. "You take them to the apartment, Isam. Later we'll figure out some other way. They can go with the wounded."

Layla's steps were firm as she walked over to face her brother. "I am not leaving, Mahmud." Her brother looked at her in astonishment, wondering why her voice seemed so strange, someone else's voice. The tone seemed different, too; where was the strain of conciliation, or even of threat or anger or refusal? This tone of absolute decision he had never heard from Layla. She met his gaze for a moment then turned her face away, in a gesture of indifference, and looked into the distance. This was painful: she had looked at him as if she did not know him, did not belong to him—as if he were not her brother. She had looked at him as if nothing bound them any longer, no ties of sibling loyalty or love, no family bond, nothing. Nothing at all. Aching, he shifted his gaze to Sanaa. She turned her face away. From her voice he could tell that she dreaded angering him. "Anyway, right now I'm coming to the hospital. Later we can see about it." She added, with bitter sarcasm, "I think you are going to need some nurses."

Mahmud's eyes swept the quay and came back to settle on Layla with the sudden understanding that what had happened to him during the guerilla campaign in the Canal Zone had now happened to her. She had left the circle of the family, the sphere of the self, for the orbit of all, and no one could keep her back. In her remoteness, he thought she looked taller and stronger. About to turn to climb into the ambulance, he put out his hand to pat her shoulder. But instead, he found himself shaking her hand, one comrade to another.

When Sanaa tried to follow him, he stopped and made way for her. She closed the ambulance door gently behind them and it went on its way. A ringing scream rent the silence. The little girl began to run, running in no particular direction, calling, "Mama! My mother! My mother!" The despairing cry echoed as if all of creation were repeating it. The woman in the braids shook herself as if emerging from a nightmare, freed herself from the grip of the woman charged with guarding her, and began to run. At the shoreline two men caught up. She fought desperately to free herself. When she reached the edge of the lake she began calling her child's name. She plunged into the water, her voice echoing. When the water reached her neck she was still calling, her voice soft, thin, singsong, as if she were singing a lullaby to her son, as if he lay asleep on her chest. And then there was only the echo of the little girl, calling her mother, and the mother calling her son. The little girl collapsed onto the ground. The mother disappeared into the lake, screaming, trilling, a shout of joy now, victorious. The old man collapsed onto the heap of sand, sobbing, the tears gathering in his white beard. The surface of the water was still again, and a doll bobbed there, eyes closed, smiling. When Layla turned to give a last look, Adil had smoothed the dirt over his beloved's grave.

Chapter
Twenty-Seven

From behind the tombs heads rose, and hands settled in wary readiness onto rifles and machine guns. But the signal had not yet come. The airplanes released more parachutists behind the wall of the airport, and the parachutes ballooned, one after another, white, like abscesses full of pus.

In their defense positions at al-Gabbana the forces fidgeted, hands shaking with impatient rage on the guns. But still the signal did not come. Hundreds of anxious eyes moved between the commander and the opening parachutes spread across the air. The commander sensed the heavy anxiety around him; he could almost hear the mute question that choked the air—the question asked over and over by the individuals of the popular resistance, and even by the trained army personnel who were accustomed to obeying orders without question.

What are we waiting for?

The commander went on waiting. Not a muscle in his face moved. Layla wiped the sweat off her brow and whispered to Isam, "What are we waiting for?" Isam put out a shaking hand and patted hers, smiling at her in his shy, half-smiling way. They felt close, as if the waiting that trembled in each one's depths had erased the chasm between them, when Layla had insisted on following Isam to his post and, in front of his commander, had embarrassed him into acquiescing. She fidgeted anxiously now, fear creeping through her. It was not death that frightened her, no longer. What was she? A drop in an ocean, and the ocean would surge whether or not she was there. If she were to die, she would be one of thousands who had died; if she lived, she would still be one of millions whose right to live had been plundered. No, it was not death that frightened her, nor the enemy who was hidden there behind the airport wall. Her major enemy crouched here, deep inside, waiting to attack. She closed her eyes against that weakness and pressed her lips together tightly so that no tremble could penetrate. Once again she was experiencing that overpowering desire to look out for those around her and to feel that she was one with them, part of a larger whole. She straightened a bit behind the grave that shielded her and raised her head cautiously. Before her eyes stretched rows of heads, some covered by helmets, others bare, some where black mingled with white, others very young. Her body grew slack again as she watched this huge mass of heads. When she turned to look behind, again she saw face after face, some tense, others calm, row after row of massed faces. When her eyes came to one face she sucked in her breath and held it, seeing in her mind's eye Adil digging the grave of his beloved, throwing his head back, in his eyes that look she would never forget. For it was the same expression—the same blend of love, fierce loathing, challenge, determination, and assured readiness—she now saw in the eyes of this man. Adil? She took a deep breath and swept her eyes across the faces. Every face was different but now she saw something that had escaped her notice before, the same look she had seen in Adil's eyes. She turned to gaze forward again, exhilarated. She felt strong. She was no longer alone. She was with them now. With them, and the love that pounded in their hearts was in hers, too, and so was the loathing, and something of the calm, assured preparedness. Before Layla appeared her own image, bending to snatch the oar as it sank into the Nile. Yes, at the right moment that stronger person hidden inside would push open the door, would go out calmly and coolly, would act wisely, exactly as she must. Yes, when the moment came the miracle would happen. Her eyes swam with a vision too lovely to bear.

Noticing her tears, Isam attributed them to fear. "Go back, Layla. The door, the gate—it's just over there. Crawl over to the gate." His voice became softer. "You're a woman, no one will blame you, this isn't your place, after all."

Layla felt dizzy, as if she were looking down from a high tower. Deep inside she felt that trembling helplessness again. Could she? Could she do it? Could she stay, could she keep going? When she was a woman? A woman, and that was all. Where would the strength come from? Where?

The enemy airplanes were releasing a new wave of parachutists into the airport grounds, within range of the fire of the armed defense forces in al-Gabbana. At the same time, the wind began to howl. Strong, angry gusts hurled into the air a yellow curtain of sand, as the airplanes dropped load after load inside the airport. The wind carried some of them far, in the direction of the neighboring area, toward civilian homes.

The commander gave the signal.

"Hit him! Give it to him!" It was the quavering voice of an old woman, hunched on the ground, staring straight ahead; the child she held in her arms wailed. A heavy rock in the hand of a young woman sailed at the head of a parachutist as he tried to get his balance. He fell to the ground, his skull shattered. The young woman stood straight, putting up her left hand to wipe away the sweat. But before her hand could touch her forehead she dashed forward, screaming. She had noticed more parachutists falling, a swarm of bats. Her shout reached other women, inside their huts preparing food for their children, for husbands and sons who would return—or would not. The scream told them that the danger their sons and husbands had gone to meet was knocking at their doors. The wooden slats were flung wide open and women came out armed with the weapons they had ready. Necks of broken bottles, kitchen knives, heavier blades, pestles. The high-pitched screaming reached the children standing in awe and curiosity before a hut that sat alone far to the right. They scattered, terrified. Inside the hut a woman tried to get up, fear on her face. She bent double as the pain that had gnawed at her since the morning came again. The hands of the midwife, gripping the rim of a pan of boiling water that she had been trying to lift from the burner, stopped. She straightened, ran to the door, paused to glance round. The woman inside moaned, sweat pouring from her forehead onto her eyes.

"What is it?" her voice was choked. The midwife went back inside, her face grim, snatched two rags from the floor, and raised the boiling water. She strode to the door as the young woman screamed in despair and pain. She crawled after the midwife, the sweat almost blinding her, her body convulsing in rapid contractions. At the threshold she clutched the midwife's ankle, muttering, "Don't leave me, don't leave me alone." But she could not go on, for the pain attacked her again, sharper this time, unbearable. She felt something round and hard almost pulling from her body and muttered, "I can't, I'm done for." Still at the threshold, the midwife turned to look at the young woman flat on the dirt floor behind her. Their eyes met. In the midwife's eyes the young woman saw reflected what was happening outside, she saw the death that threatened her, that endangered the life pulsing in her belly. Her grip on the midwife's leg relaxed; she curled up and broke out in sobs. The midwife left the hut, steam rising from the boiling water. The woman raised her head, tears standing in her eyes, and began to slither across the floor to her mattress. Carefully she lay down, pulled up a white sheet, and covered her body.

It was her first baby. She had never done this before, but she would do it. She would give birth, by herself, no matter what was happening around her. The child was there inside of her and wanted to come out. All she had to do was to help. She must relax, but that seemed impossible. A scream of fear from outside jolted her body; the wail of a child, a whispered "there is no god but God," a wait. Steps thrusting forward, calls, a clattering on tin rooftops as if horses galloped there, the voice of the bent old woman trembling in the air. "Hit him! Give it to him!" A moan, the howl of a dog, black smoke curling into the hut. Drops of water hissing on the fire, screams of pain, a silence harsher than the noise. A group pushing, colliding with the wooden walls, shots, the voice of the old woman ringing out, a huge explosion that shook the hut until she thought it would collapse over her. And then a wait, harsher than the explosion.

The face of the young woman, lying on the bed, her body convulsing. She bit on the hem of the white sheet, balled up in her mouth. She must . . . she must . . . relax . . . or the child would die in her belly. She ripped the sheet from her mouth and wiped the sweat off her face. She tried, with the endurance only a birthing mother knows, to concentrate all her attention on the child threatened with death inside her body.

Little by little the wailing, the fire, all of the moaning and smoke and frightened steps and long groans and suppressed sounds of victory disappeared. The outside world disappeared. There was no longer anything in her consciousness but this child, this child who wanted to come out, into life. As the children slipped from their hiding places, as the older ones gathered the butcher's knives, the kitchen knives, and the ropes used to hunt down the parachuting soldiers, as the women dried their sweat, their heads still dizzy, as if they had awakened suddenly after a frightening dream, before counting their losses and gains, before realizing exactly what they had just done, the air carried a thin, broken wail that soon became an unbroken cry, stronger, clear, a ululation of joy, the scream of life.

———

Layla screamed, a ululation of joy. The human masses pushed her forward toward the airport. The second wave of parachutists had been mowed down on the airport grounds and the remnants of the first wave were in retreat before the Egyptian forces. British airplanes hovered over the spot where the two forces engaged but could get no nearer and withdrew, powerless. A battery of explosions in quick succession erupted in scattered parts of the city, and fires broke out in the petrol depots, in homes, along the city streets. The English forces tried to slip the encirclement, tried to return to their hiding places behind the walls of the airport. The Egyptian forces pressed on to block their escape. The ground was exploding—storms of sand, fire flaming from the guns, a flood of shots leaving big circles in the sand, white smoke, green spots gleaming, reflected in peoples eyes. Bodies falling, the dead, the wounded crawling behind the lines, people pushing forward to take their places.

Among the dead lay Isam; among the wounded, Layla. The circle tightened around the English soldiers and the circle of fire tightened on the city. The sun was setting, and darkness settled on the scene. A flame, a flickering light, kept the darkness at bay, and revealed from afar the enemy in bedraggled retreat.

Chapter
Twenty-Eight

Layla's wound was not serious. It was just a surface wound, and as soon as the shards that had gone into her right shoulder were removed she began to get better. At first the pain seemed to submerge all of her senses. It was a pain that had no harshness, no violence in it, but it was constant and hard, imposing itself so that she felt nothing else and thought about nothing else. The physician at the hospital tried to inject a painkiller but she refused, as if she had to get through this stage of pain on her own.

When the wound began to close the pain lessened quickly. And like a torrent long restrained, Layla's thoughts flooded over her, thoughts and images, one after another, one on top of another. A moment in the battle when a bullet had whistled by her left ear as another had struck the ground; a stream of bullets raining down, marking out a wide circle in the sand; the circle narrowing around her as if an unseen hand were fixing it around her neck. And now she was stepping back, facing her father, protecting her neck with her hands, as Ramzi blocked her path and said, "It's no use." Now she was on the roof of their building, staring at the masses of bitter smoke on the day Cairo burned. And

Husayn was saying, "This is not the end, Layla." Walking on the seashore at Ras al-Barr, Husayn moving his finger down her arm and whispering into her ear, "I'm just waiting for you, waiting for you, darling." In her room in Ras al-Barr, her fist contracting on the knob, the closed door, Mahmud shouting, "Goodbye, Husayn!" Hanging from the wall, the elevator cord dragging her downward. Down, dragged by the weight of dirt, buried at the quayside. Under the dirt, crawling. On the cold floor tiles after her father had beat her. Jumping to her feet, shaking the dirt off. Husayn saying, "Do you know what you'll find? You'll find yourself, the real Layla." Bending to load her rifle with trembling hands, raising her head cautiously, seeing the soldier aiming at her, his face full of pockmarks, his awful yellow mustache, and jumping up, and aiming, and the enemy falling on his gun, and the circle being broken.

How many of the enemy had she killed?

At the start, when the second wave was landing at the airport, it was hard to tell whether her aim had hit its mark. The soldier would collapse onto the ground, holes filling his body as if everyone had killed him. But then . . .

Layla sat up suddenly in her bed as she saw the enemy retreat in front of her, in front of *her*. She stretched her hands around her shoulders, hugging herself, quieting the surge of love and pride and confidence that swept over her body. Everything had happened just as it was supposed to. She had made no mistakes; nothing had gotten by her; she had done exactly what she had had to do. She lay down on the bed again; the wound had begun to hurt. She would live to see the enemy make a final retreat from Port Said. She would dedicate her life—if that was necessary—to see that enemy retreat before her, before *her*.

She sighed, feeling the tension abate. Her mouth curved into a smile when she caught sight of Mahmud, just coming into the room. He swept back the curtains from the window. "Hey? How are you doing today?" The light poured into the room and Layla stretched out in her bed. "Great."

"The pain?"

"Gone."

He sat down on the end of the bed. Layla took his hand and held it. "Mahmud, I want to leave the hospital."

"Why are you in such a hurry?"

Layla gazed straight ahead, her eyes flashing. "I have to, Mahmud. I must."

"Are you sure you are in good enough shape to leave?"

She leaned over to him and spoke in a tremulous voice. "I've never been better, Mahmud. Never."

Mahmud overcame his astonishment as he spoke. "Anyway, we'll get the opinion of the presiding physician."

After Mahmud had left the room, Layla tried to recover the image of her father marching toward her, a weapon aimed at her, ready to mow her down. She tried to hear his cracked voice: "What do *you* need?" In her ears his voice echoed as he wept like a frightened child on the day she had become a woman. In her mind his image rose, leaning across the table, tears shining in his eyes, his face relaxed into a tender smile. She tried to get back Ramzi's image, staring at Gamila's breasts, that grimace playing across his mouth. She saw his face redden under Gamila's gaze, like the face of an adolescent boy. She tried to imagine him as he had always appeared in class—tyrannical, powerful—and she saw him putting out his hand to dry his sweat in the depths of winter. Now here she was standing before his desk, facing him challengingly, his hand trembling as it gripped the desk edge, his lips trembling as she leaned toward him in the sitting room and said, "Would you like to know what it is I didn't have?" And the military training suit swinging on her arm as she stood across from him on the threshold of the college building, smiling into his face, the smile of one humoring a little

353

child. The veins flared on her forehead, she was concentrating so hard, but still she could not summon the image of Ramzi shutting the door and saying, "It's no use."

Later, she tried to bring any image of him into her mind but she failed completely. Somehow his image had been blotted out of her mind, as if it had never been there. She shook her head in wonder. Of what had she been so afraid? Of her father? Of Ramzi? She smiled, hardly able to believe that all of that had happened to her. To *her*?

Before her eyes flashed the image of herself pushing forward onto the battlefield, the enemy retreating in front of her. She must, she must see the enemy retreat from Port Said. And she could. She could do anything. Nothing seemed impossible now. She jumped up from her bed excitedly, her eyes blazing. She began to dart every which way, grabbing her belongings, as if she did not know where to start. Her hand knocked into her clothes, hanging on a hanger; she had not noticed them. She flailed around again, trying to make sure that she had everything. She stopped, right in the middle of the room, her eyes gazing forward, shining as if she had just seen the most beautiful of visions and had heard a voice calling. She turned, her arms out, and called, "Husayn." But when she realized that no one was in the room, she came to her senses and closed her mouth firmly. With steady hands she packed. But Husayn was with her, as he had never before been, as if he had suddenly become a reality, a tangible presence to which she could extend her grasp, a presence she could embrace. His eyes were there, melting into a tender gaze as he brought his face close to hers, his breath stirring the tendrils of hair on her right cheek so that she must pat them into place again. Then she returned to her packing, hands steady, lips set.

Chapter
Twenty-Nine

With the English and French occupation of Port Said the resistance
had become very active. Every day it broadened, as more and more
women and men joined. Under organized leadership the units scattered, concealing themselves in homes and clinics, in shops, in every
corner of Port Said. In an old house in Abbadi Street, inside the apartment of an Egyptian resident, stood five youths studying enemy con-
centrations and the roads leading to their deployments on an immense
map of Port Said. They belonged to the engineers' unit of the Fourth
Squadron, the ground troops that had protected the withdrawal of the
armed forces on the Abu Ugayla—Ismailiya Road, then had advanced
to Port Said to reinforce the defense of the city. Among those five was
Husayn Amir, who had lived through every stage of the struggle, from
the first skirmishes in Sinai until the attempt to rout the enemy from
Port Said.

———

A week after the resistance began, Husayn came upon Mahmud.
Husayn was in charge of communicating instructions to one of the
resistance units. When he entered the room where the members were

congregated he discovered Mahmud among them. His hands shook as they embraced; with difficulty he regained control of himself, and the work he had come to do began. Mahmud briefed him on the unit's activities, and Husayn began informing those present of how successful other units had been. Everyone felt a hard joy; the future was opening before their eyes. Husayn felt a pleading hope.

Finally able to take Mahmud aside, Husayn asked about Layla. When he learned of the role she had played in the fight, he asked if he could see her. Mahmud set an appointment with him, and just before, Sanaa left the apartment.

———

On the threshold of the open door Layla stood facing Husayn. She raised her head to meet his gaze and they stood for a moment without speaking. The affection she had buried for so long sailed from her eyes. She could show the proud delight she felt in those feelings now, and her joy burst from her eyes and showed on her lips, her cheeks, to the tips of her fingers, every atom of her body, as if those feelings composed a translucent light running with the blood in her veins. In Husayn's eyes astonishment quickly gave way to unbelieving joy. He had come to see her, perhaps for the last time, and suddenly now he discovered that he *would* wake up every morning to see her face. He had come to visit assuming that she was bound to another man, was the beloved of another man, and now he discovered, standing on the threshold of the open door, that she was his beloved, his, all for him. From his eyes poured the tenderness of years, the longing of years, the deprivation of years, and a happiness so strong that it nearly caused him, sturdy as he was, to lose his balance. In a trembling voice he called her, with trembling hands he brought her closer. And on his broad chest she rested her head and wished time could stop and she could stay there, her head on his chest, her heart beating on his, with his. His hands brushed over her hair, went to her shoulders, feeling them, joy pressing on his heart. The dream was no longer a dream; the lovely mirage had become a real presence in his embrace. He felt an overwhelming desire to gaze at her face, and gently he pressed his fingers against her chin to raise her head. She said his name with a brightness that enveloped them both. He slowly brought his face to hers, slowly his lips searched out hers, as if he wanted to take the moment in completely, but withheld it, fearing that it might end. Their lips trembled, and a trancelike bliss enveloped them. Then they heard footsteps out in the street, a heavy, regular tramp. The trance vanished. Layla's face stiffened, her eyes fierce with hatred. Husayn straightened, shook his head as if awakening from a dream to a dismal reality. Layla turned and went to the window, while Husayn shut the door to the apartment and followed her.

———

Carefully, Layla pushed aside a bit of curtain. She saw an English patrol in the empty street; she felt a void in her heart, a hole, as if a blade had suddenly pierced her. Her hand knocked against the window as she dropped the curtain into place. The glinting gold ring had struck the glass with a clink. Layla spread her fingers, staring astonished at her engagement ring, as if she had forgotten that it occupied her hand. She pulled the curtain back again, again the blade stabbed her heart, and she whispered, following the patrol with her eyes as it almost vanished, "This isn't the end, Husayn, is it."

His voice held a note of disbelief. "This isn't the first time you've asked me that question, Layla." She smiled lightly and turned to face him. "It isn't a question, Husayn. I'm just confirming a fact." Calmly she sat down. His gaze focused on her face, his attention drawn by something he had never seen in her eyes, even when she had been at her most fiery. He thought he saw an assured and peaceful confidence there, that rare and amazing blend reflected only in the eyes of a person who has found the way—a person who knows, through experience, that the way is only found in the strength that allows one to stand by what one believes is right.

He spoke gently, coming nearer. "You've changed, Layla."

She shrugged lightly. "Who doesn't change, Husayn?" Her gaze settled on him a moment and her voice shook slightly as she said, "Now what do we do?"

The words were about to rush from his mouth; he thought at first that she was referring to their future together, then the words stopped on his tongue as he realized with his wonderful capacity to understand her that she meant something else, something bigger. After a pause he said, "The leadership is taking everything into account, and the resistance has really begun its work."

"What about you? Are you part of it?"

He nodded without speaking. She leaned her head forward and said, "And me? Can I help with anything?"

His gaze settled on the gold ring on her finger. And he said, provokingly, "Can you?"

"Do you have any doubts about it?"

His features relaxed into a smile, and he shook his head. In a whisper pulsing with feeling, he said, "All my life I have believed in you."

Her eyes shone with tears. "Even when I didn't believe in myself, Husayn?"

But something kept pulling Husayn's gaze to the ring. He could not keep the displeasure from his voice. "And what will you do right now?"

She stood up. "I'm coming with you." When she saw the astonishment in his face she smiled. "I want to join the resistance. Can't you suggest my name?"

He smiled and shook his head in wonder. "Enough surprises today. My nerves can't take any more." She laughed, and said in childish stubbornness, "Are you going to put my name up for it or not?"

Husayn said, testing the extent of her mettle, "It isn't that easy, Layla. It isn't a question of a day or two. The resistance might go on for a long time. You might have to be in hiding for a few months."

She turned. "I'll get my coat."

He put his hand on her shoulder to stop her, turned her gently to him, and said, focusing his gaze on hers, "And your family, Layla?"

"Mahmud can tell them I'm fine."

Husayn sighed with relief. Layla turned again and went into her room. Gloom spread across his face, as if an obstacle lay in his path. She came out of her room, a white overcoat over her white wool dress. His face lit up when he saw her, as if his fears had vanished and his dreams were to be realized.

"C'mon, let's go," Layla said. She walked before him to the open door.

Chapter Thirty

The streets of Port Said were packed with people, colliding waves, as if all its homes had emptied themselves, tossing the inhabitants into the street, wave after wave, to blend into a turbulent human sea. People laughed, or wept without knowing what sort of tears these were. Were they tears of joy at their rescue? Or tears of the painful memories that suddenly came to the surface on evacuation day? Or tears that gazed into a better future?

People carried victory banners, some were calling out, others danced alone. People clapped, hearts full of the exhilaration of victory, eyes full of tomorrow. They knew that all that had happened had been necessary: it was the price of victory. People ventured out bearing flowers to their dead but the flowers never arrived; on the way they were scattered on the victory parade, the parade of tomorrow. For those they mourned had died for the sake of tomorrow.

Where the Canal met the sea, and just slightly apart from the statue of De Lesseps, a group of people stood waiting silently. A young man in the uniform of the popular resistance stood on the highest step, plying a hand drill to carve a hole in the body of the statue. At this moment, for this young man as he stuffed the hole with explosives, the figure could no longer be a statue. Nor was it so for the crowd awaiting the explosion in agitation. It was a symbol of the ages of slavery and colonialism that they had inherited, a symbol that pulled them back into a loathsome past, that put a barrier between them and a finer future. That symbol must be shattered. The youth bent down to the base of the statue, lit the wick, and moved back to join the onlookers. The explosion shook the ground and a wave of smoke and dirt rose, veiling the scene. Then a buzz of displeasure rose. Agitated, Layla shouted, "The head! Only the head is gone!" Indeed, it was only the head and the paint that had gone; the body remained crouched in place as if its roots extended deep into the ground. Husayn grasped Layla's hand. Mahmud fidgeted. He saw himself burying his face in his palms and saying after the Cairo fire, "All that blood—it went in vain." Sanaa's eyes clouded as she thought suddenly of her mother and father, who had cut off communication with her on the day she had married Mahmud. And Layla's hand shook in Husayn's, as she saw Gamila lying on the chaise longue, Sidqi at her side, and heard Ramzi saying, "These are the laws of nature. Nature wants it like this." Layla yelled, "Rules! We must follow the fundamentals!" Then she corrected herself. "The foundation—that is what is important." The crowds pushed forward determinedly toward the statue, and the space around it narrowed again. The youth mounted the steps and began making another hole. The operation took longer this time, for he had to go deeply, as deeply as one could go. When he had finished and lit the wick, the sound of a far larger explosion rent the air. The statue and its base scattered, torn limbs and body parts. And Layla sighed in relief.

In her ears echoed the sound of another explosion in the battle, the explosion that had announced the death of Isam and of his enemies. She could see him, leaping monkey-like from above the wall, blood pouring from his wound, his right hand fisted around a bomb, his pale face shining with an ethereal transparency, his eyes gleaming, flashing, as if he saw the most beautiful of visions.

The sound of the people rose like a roaring wave, as they rushed forward to occupy whatever empty spaces remained in the lanes leading from the place.

———

Husayn seized Layla's hand so he would not lose her in the crowd that had swallowed up Mahmud and Sanaa. The masses pushed them forward, and they exploded into laughter as they moved, as if a huge wave carried them forward. The pressure lightened but Layla kept running, her hand in Husayn's, laughing her short, breathless laughs like the peals of musical bells. It was as if she could not do otherwise; she had to push forward, to run, to laugh, to do something with this eruption of happiness that fluttered like a bird's wings, in her chest and on her lips and under her skin and to the tips of her fingers and toes. Husayn looked at her hair, flying around her forehead, to the gleam shining in her eyes, the glow that had returned, the radiance that had almost made him shout out when he saw her in the elevator, that very first time. His heart pounded and he squeezed the hand that lay softly in his. She gave a shout. "Husayn!" But she had no need to shout, for he was right there, his shoulder almost against hers. Yet she shouted again, her voice trembling. "Husayn!" Then, "I want to show you something."

She stopped and took her hand from his. She spread it out before him triumphantly. He realized that she had cast away her engagement ring. He grabbed her shoulder and shouted, his voice shaking, "You're free! You're free, love!"

Layla dropped her arms and felt a lovely peacefulness creeping into her body, a tranquillity more lovely and deeper than the bubbly happiness that had filled her. She looked at Husayn and smiled. She took a step, Husayn's eyes never leaving her. No, it was not the same glow as before. It was new. There had been that flash of light that had gone out, the sun on an overcast day. This was quiet and warm and steady, a light that emanated from within. Husayn sighed happily. "Finally . . . we're there." Layla's face shone as she gazed straight ahead.

"How many years have we been waiting for this day?" said Husayn. Layla's eyes swept over the people, loudly victorious, and said, "All our lives." Husayn gazed into her eyes, ran his finger along her arm, and softened his voice to almost a whisper. "You and I, Layla." Tears shone in her eyes. "Still ahead, all our lives, Husayn." Their steps slowed; they were too full of feeling to speak. Layla felt overwhelmed, and she leaned her head against Husayn's shoulder. Her eyes sparkled with a mischievous look and she said, as if playing an amusing game, "Is this the end, Husayn?"

Husayn's face lit up and he held back his laughter as he joined in the game. "This is not the first time you have asked me that question, Layla." They both burst into laughter, like two children playing. They were silent again, gazing at the crowds pushing in front of them and behind them, too, a huge, victorious wave sweeping all before it. Eyes awash with the depth of his feelings, Husayn said, "This is just the beginning, my love."

Modern Arabic Writing
from The American University in Cairo Press